BOOKS BY PATRI

NECTAR FOR THE GOD

A MENNIK THORN NOVEL (BOOK 2)

PATRICK SAMPHIRE

FIVE FATHOMS PRESS

For my mother, Beth Samphire
For your support
And for being nothing at all like Nik's mother...

AUTHOR'S NOTE

This is the second book in the Mennik Thorn series. Despite that, I've worked hard to ensure that if this is the first book you pick up or if it's been a long time since you read the first, you should have no trouble in following the story.

However, if you really want to know everything that happened before this, you should probably start by reading SHADOW OF A DEAD GOD, the first Mennik Thorn novel – and if it's been a while since you've read it, you can remind yourself of all the details with the full recap I've posted on my website.

rat at a wet sack of grain. Despite the best – or worst – attempts of my mother to train me, I had never been able to channel significant amounts of magic. I had never been powerful. But I had accepted my limitations, learned to live with them, and made a career of sorts from what I had.

Then Lowriver and her dead god had turned up, and it hadn't been enough.

Sereh – my best friend Benny's daughter – had said something, and it had started to eat away at me with its ratty little teeth. She had said, "Do better. If you're not good enough, be better." Resting here in Benny's house, that kept echoing in my mind. Had I just given up? I couldn't be a high mage like my mother, nor have the kind of power my little sister, Mica, had. But did that mean I couldn't be better than I was?

Maybe I could do more with the power I did have, be more efficient, figure out some new tricks. Something.

So that was what I had set out to do. Day after day, I sat here, drawing in raw magic, shaping it, and releasing it as spells.

It wasn't going well.

"You know, Uncle Nik, no one will see you if you open the shutters at the back."

I started, spilling my tea. *Bannaur's battered balls!* I twisted around in my chair to find myself staring right into a pair of wide, innocent eyes. Sereh. How in all the cold, dark Depths had that girl managed to sneak up on me again? I swore she could surprise a shadow. No wonder I was on edge. How was I supposed to concentrate on practicing my magic when she kept appearing out of nowhere, trying to give me a heart attack?

"I don't know what you're talking about," I said.

"If anyone was in the courtyard, I would know." She would at that, and if they tried to get into the house, well, I wouldn't give much for their chances. Sereh wasn't a mage. Believe me, I had checked, but somehow, she still always knew. "And you've set up wards," she continued. "You don't have to hide in the dark."

"I'm not hiding."

"Of course you're not. But you're safe here with me, Uncle Nik."

I shivered and tried to hide it with a cough. How was it that an eleven-year-old girl could set me so on edge with perfectly ordinary words? She wasn't even playing with her knife right now, which really should have helped, but didn't. I loved that kid like she was my own, but that didn't mean I wasn't sometimes terrified of her.

All right, the truth was, I *was* hiding. Kind of hiding. Laying low, that was a better way of putting it. I had made a stupid choice. It had been the only choice I could make at the time, but that didn't stop it being stupid. When Benny and I had been framed for murder, I had been desperate. I had asked a favour from the Wren, the high mage who controlled Agatos's criminal underworld. Everyone who grew up in the Warrens knew better than to get into debt to the Wren. *Depths*, I knew better. But, like I said, no choice.

Long story.

By the time I had recovered from my injuries, I had already left him hanging for a week. And then, well, to be honest I had been dodging the issue. The problem was that the Wren had demanded I steal information from my mother and pass it on to him. And I couldn't do it. It wasn't loyalty. Fuck loyalty to her. It was the idea of going back into her court that filled me with the kind of panic that made me want to crawl into a corner and hide. I had been half hoping the Wren might forget about it if I didn't show my face.

Hey, I was an optimist.

The more realistic part of me had been expecting a knock on my door from the Wren's enforcers any day. It hadn't been doing my anxiety any good.

Sereh slid past me, her footsteps still not making a sound on the floorboards. If I hadn't felt her knife pressed against my delicate skin more than once, I would have wondered if she was a ghost.

She threw open the shutters, and I peeked out into the courtyard. Like she had said, there was no one out there.

"You're going to have to go out sometime."

"I was going to," I muttered, as I watched her turn and head back to the stairs. When she reached them, she stopped.

"Someone's about to knock on the door." She smiled. "I think it's for you."

Goat shit. She was just trying to freak me out. Give poor old Uncle Nik the willies. Not this time. I opened my mouth to tell her she wasn't catching me out again, when someone rapped on the door.

How in the Depths had she known that was going to happen? She must have heard them step up to the door. Or maybe they had cleared their throat. I knew her hearing was better than mine.

So why was my pulse racing like a mouse being chased by a hungry pack of street dogs?

The knock came again. I thought about pretending not to be there. That would work, right?

Bollocks.

"No point putting this off any longer," I told myself. If the Wren had come for me, what was I going to do anyway? At least he had knocked. That had to be a good sign, didn't it? I plastered a smile on my face, crossed to the door, and threw it open to the glare of the sunlit street.

The man outside wasn't what I was expecting. Mages in Agatos – most of them, anyway – wore thick, sweat-inducing black cloaks that, in my opinion, made them look like twats. I had one of my own, although I tried not to use it. Whoever this man was, he wasn't wearing one of those cloaks, and he looked … ordinary. Neat, respectable, unassuming. He could have been a successful shopkeeper or a senior clerk. If he was a mage, he was powerful enough not to have to flaunt it, and that couldn't be good news for me.

The man's skin had that olive tint of an Agatos

native, and his hair was starting to grey. He had a wide, creased face, like a rumpled bed sheet on a hot night. He was probably in his late fifties, although if he was a powerful mage, he could easily have been older. Something about the way he held himself made him seem like an old man.

He squinted up at me. "Mennik Thorn?"

All right. He knew who I was. More bad news. He wasn't just here to sell us a new broom.

I glanced suspiciously down the street and checked my wards. "Why?"

"I need your help."

I ran through all the swear words that I knew under my breath, then made up a few more on the spot. A wannabe client. That was the problem with setting yourself up as a mage-for-hire; sometimes people came around and wanted to hire you, even when you were trying to lie low. How is all the sodden Depths had he found me? No one was supposed to know I was here.

I eyed my visitor, then unfocused my eyes to check for magic. There was no shortage of magic in Agatos. It permeated the ground, the air, the water. It rose insubstantially like a mist everywhere you looked. Or that was how it seemed to me. Every mage had their own way of 'seeing' magic. I had known mages who heard it like music or smelled it or, in the case of one poor sod I had met, felt it like burning fire against his skin. Me, if I unfocused my gaze, I could see it in shifting shapes and colours. It gave me eyestrain and had occasionally made me walk into the side of a building, but it could have been worse.

If my visitor were any kind of mage, he wasn't showing it. That still didn't mean I wanted him here. The Wren had plenty of ways of dealing with problems without using magic.

"Sorry," I said. "I'm not taking on clients."

"I heard that you help people."

Yeah, and look where that had got me. "For money." I stole another glance down the street. "I don't need the money."

"I do not think that is true, Mr. Thorn." He held up a hand. "I can pay you, but I do not think you do this for money."

Yeah, that was a hard sell when I was squatting in my friend's house on the edge of the Warrens. Most mages my age lived in mansions.

My visitor didn't look like he was going anywhere. He wasn't trying to force his way in, but he looked settled and unmovable, like the carcass of a whale washed up on a beach. Stubborn, that was the word for it.

I could be stubborn, too, but I was at a disadvantage. Every moment I stood exposed like this, the greater the chance one of the Wren's people would see me.

I could tell this man to fuck off and slam the door in his face, or I could let him in. What I couldn't do was stand here in the doorway. Keeping your head down didn't work if everyone could see you.

The man must have picked up on my indecision because he added, "Please. At least hear me out."

I swore. I was going to do this, wasn't I? That had always been my downfall. Show me someone really in need, someone projecting the raw vulnerability this man was, and I couldn't say no. Mica had exploited it ruthlessly when we had been kids. It looked like I still hadn't learned my lesson.

"Then come on in, for Pity's sake, before anyone sees us."

I gave him a temporary pass through my wards, took a final glance up and down the street, then closed the door behind us.

When he was seated, my visitor lowered his head into his hands, his shoulders slumping. People didn't come to me unless they had no other choice. Your average citizen viewed mages with a mixture of apprehension and awe, in much the same way they would if they discovered an eight-foot snake crawling out of their toilet. It was true that most of my clients were after something mundane – a curse needing to be broken, a cheating spouse to be spied on, a lost ring to be found, that kind of thing. But they would only come to me if they had exhausted every other option.

I still didn't know how I felt about that.

Benny had said I should try being friendlier. This coming from a man who spent his nights breaking into wealthy people's homes and making off with their valuables.

My visitor was still sitting there, silent and unmoving. I was used to clients being nervous or coy, but I wasn't used to this. If he had died on me, I wasn't going to be happy. I tried clearing my throat.

Nothing. Brilliant. Was he even here to hire me or was he just looking for somewhere out of the sun?

Was he waiting for me to offer him tea?

"Look," I said, "I don't mean to be rude, but what do you want?"

The old man lifted his head slowly. "This is not easy."

"Tell me about it," I muttered. Yeah, I was being an arsehole, but in my defence, the stress of these last few weeks had been getting to me, and I still didn't know why this guy was here.

He met my gaze with heavy grey eyes that looked so worn down that I felt immediately guilty. "My wife is dead."

"Shit." Now I felt like a double arsehole. "I'm sorry. But what do you want me to do about it?"

Pity! I couldn't be any worse at this if I leant over and smacked him in the teeth. *Try to be a decent fucking human, Nik.*

I just hoped he wasn't here to ask me to bring her back to life, because that wasn't happening. I could do it – I had done it once before, when I had been training to be a mage – but the dead always came back wrong. No matter how much he might think he wanted that, he didn't.

"I want you to tell me why she is dead, Mr. Thorn," my visitor said. Then, never raising his voice or

me feel guilty at the idea that he wanted to hire me. How much of his wife's funeral had he sacrificed on a quest to find out a truth that probably wasn't there?

You tried to tell him no. You tried to put him off. And there might – just might – be a truth to be found. It still made me feel like a fraud.

The main burial shafts for the city occupied a large, stony field on the western edge of the Erastes Valley. Originally, the field had stood outside the city. Over the centuries, though, the city had expanded up the valley, like a belligerent drunk sprawling across a table, until it had engulfed the burial shafts. By then, the field had been riddled with corpse-stuffed holes, and no one fancied digging them out, so the burial shafts had remained, and people just kept on filling them.

I didn't hold out much hope of discovering whether Etta Mirian had been influenced by magic. The aftermath of powerful magic could linger, although not for long, and Etta Mirian had been dead for five days now. But you never knew. If there was one thing I was good at, it was working with weak magic. Without much power, I had been forced to rely on fine control of my meagre resources. If there was a trace to be found, I would find it. I just didn't think it would be there.

The Fields of the Dead might have started out as shafts driven deep into the rocky earth and sealed by field stones, but over the centuries, monuments had been built above the shafts, so when I came over the low rise at the edge of the city, they were laid out before me like a miniature city of palaces, grand boulevards, and plazas. Only the presence of a large, whitewashed building near the entrance and several burial parties preparing to drop their loved ones – or ones they hoped had left them money – into the ground showed the true miniature scale of the metropolis of the dead.

The building by the entrance was draped in red mourning banners and topped with flags, supposedly representing the various gods who were worshipped, feared, cursed, or just vaguely remembered from a drunken story told in a bar. There were a lot of them, and at best I recognised a quarter – but, hey, why risk pissing off a god who might be watching for the price of a bit of cloth?

The burial grounds pressed close to the sheer valley wall, and it was only there, where rockfalls were a regular occurrence, that the monuments faded out. This part of the Fields of the Dead was where executed criminals were buried, the assumption apparently being that rocks falling on them was no more than they deserved.

Executed criminals were buried decapitated with their heads beneath their feet. Something to do with preventing them reaching some long-forgotten afterlife. As up to half a dozen bodies could be buried vertically in a single shaft, this led to the macabrely farcical situation of each criminal sporting the head of the next one to be buried on his or her neck stump. I could have ended up here, my head balancing on

Benny's scrawny neck, if we hadn't cleared ourselves of murder. It had been a close thing. What a way to enter the afterlife that would have been. Not that I believed in any afterlife. The gods weren't that generous.

The Fields of the Dead wasn't the official name of the burial ground, of course. The Senate, in all its stuffy, quelling glory, insisted on referring to it as the Fields of Rest, but there was no telling the citizens of Agatos what to do or say, so the Fields of the Dead, or just the shafts, it was.

Mr. Mirian was waiting for me on the steps of the red-draped building. He was dressed in the traditional, long mourning robes, which hung shapelessly from his narrow shoulders. He wasn't alone. A dozen mostly older people had gathered a few paces away, shaded from the afternoon sun by the building. Not many mourners for a whole life. But Etta Mirian had – apparently – murdered a man. How many of her former friends and acquaintances had decided to distance themselves from the Mirians? No wonder Mr. Mirian wanted to clear his wife's name. I checked over the people who had come. No one I recognised, but I hadn't expected to. It was a big city.

Mr. Mirian crossed to meet me as I climbed the steps. A few of the other mourners glanced over, but no one tried to join us.

"I have to warn you," I said. "The chances of me finding any proof of magic are very low. Magic dissipates. If I had been there within a couple of hours of ...

what happened, I could have told you for sure, but it's been a long time." Too long.

His head dipped. "I understand. But you'll try?"

"Of course." It just wouldn't do much good. I still wasn't sure I was getting through to him, though. The last thing I wanted was to raise expectations. "You know, there are a lot of ways of getting someone to do something they don't want to. Threats. Blackmail. Drugs." But the smile. That smile he had told me about. It wasn't right. If it was true. Witnesses were unreliable, particularly when something traumatic happened. Finding two people who agreed on anything at all was hard enough, and if you did, they would be wrong more often than not.

"I am aware of that, Mr. Thorn, but you did not know Etta. She was a strong, principled woman. She would not kill another person, no matter what threat might be made against either of us. I have consulted with a physician and talked to everyone Etta spoke to that morning. There were no signs of drugs in her body, nor was she acting strangely."

He was thorough, I would give him that. That still didn't mean he was right. It wasn't my problem, though. My job was to find out if magic had been involved, then go home. That was all. I wasn't on a crusade for justice. It was just a job.

Mr. Mirian checked his pocket watch. "You have about ten minutes until the undertaker must bring Etta up."

"It's enough time," I said. "I'll know quickly if I can get anything."

He had managed to keep his face neutral during our conversation, but now it twitched, like he had been stung by a wasp. "Then I wish you luck. I will ask that you do not share what you learn until after the funeral. I wish now to think only of her life. I will come to you tomorrow, at ten o'clock, if that suits?"

I nodded and left him there on the top of the steps, staring out over the Fields of the Dead.

The bodies awaiting burial were stored in a vault beneath the building. I made my way past the small groups of mourners, then through wide doors at the back. Beyond, marble stairs led down, and I followed them, my eyes unfocused to look for magic. Yeah, it wasn't the cleverest way to go down stairs, but I had been doing this for a long time, and at least there was no one around to see if I made a tit of myself by falling down the steps.

Any mage who was hoping to keep their friends didn't talk about magic to ordinary people. Mages operated by sucking in the raw magic from all around us and forming it into coherent spells. What we tried not to tell people was where raw magic came from in the first place.

There were a shit load of gods around, particularly in a city like Agatos, which sat on the crossroads of most of the continent's trade routes. Gods, in this realm, at least, weren't immortal. If they died here, they left their physical bodies behind, as well as traces of their influence. Over time, those bodies rotted. The decaying effluent from the bodies was what we called raw magic, and it was everywhere. It permeated the air and the water and the ground. It penetrated buildings and furniture and your food. To me, it looked like a faint green mist. I tried really hard not to think about what it really was. Who wanted to think they were surrounded at all times by the putrefying remains of dead gods? But with my eyes unfocused, if there was magic here, raw or formed into a spell, I would be able to see it.

Somewhere in this underground vault, the bodies of the dead would be stacked like sacks of grain on shelves, but Etta Mirian had been laid out on a marble slab in a small room just off the bottom of the stairs, greenery placed around her white-robed figure, like the table-setting at an Ebbtide feast. I wondered if Mr. Mirian had been down here to see her. In his place, I didn't know if I would have been able to.

Ironically, there were no morgue-lamps in this morgue. Instead, candles had been set around the walls, as though in a futile attempt to lend life to the corpse lying here with their warm glow. The sickly green of a morgue-lamp would have been too on the money, I guessed.

Someone had done a pretty good job of repairing and disguising the cut across Etta Mirian's throat, but there was no hiding it completely. She had started on the left of her neck, slicing through the tendons and the arteries, and kept going, through the windpipe, all the way around the right side of her neck. How in the Depths she had found the strength to keep cutting, I didn't know. And there was still the faintest hint of a smile on her lips.

I couldn't deny it. This was some strange shit. No wonder Mr. Mirian hadn't been willing to let it go.

Etta Mirian looked younger than her husband, although whether that was because death had lifted the stresses of life from her face, I didn't know. It was always hard to tell the age of a dead body.

There was another door at the back of the room – this one shut, fortunately, because that must be where the bodies were stored. I wasn't squeamish exactly, and I wasn't scared of bodies, but that didn't mean I wanted a room full of dead people peering over my shoulder.

The vault down here was cold. It raised hairs on my arms. *To keep the bodies from rotting before they're buried.* I could see the spell sunk into the walls as a shivering, faintly purple crystalline pattern.

Every living person — Depths, every living thing — held a trace of magic within themselves, whether they were a mage or not, but Etta Mirian didn't. She was as dead as the stone she lay on. There was no magic there at all.

I hadn't expected anything else.

I leaned closer, straining my magical vision, looking for any hint that she might have been magically interfered with.

Nothing. Although whether that meant magic

hadn't been used or that it had faded long ago, I couldn't say.

That was that. I had warned Mr. Mirian I couldn't help him. There was only the disturbing hint of a smile to suggest anything at all was unusual, and I couldn't make a case from a smile. I didn't want to give Mr. Mirian false comfort, however tempting it might be.

I had heard that the Ash Guard could detect magical influence for longer by opening up the body, stripping back the nerves and veins, and cutting through the skull, but even they wouldn't have found anything after all this time, and I wasn't about to start dissecting my client's wife minutes before her funeral.

The other door swung open.

I jerked up, excuses cascading through my mind, expecting to see one of the priests come to wrap Etta Mirian and take her away for burial. But the man in the doorway wasn't a priest, that much I could tell, and if he was a mourner, he wasn't any better at that shit than I was. He was short – he wouldn't have come up to my shoulder if we had pressed back-to-back – and his light brown skin and straight black hair cut ragged just above his eyes marked him out as a native of one of the northern cities. He wasn't wearing mourning robes. Instead, he wore thin layers of cloth, wrapped like bandages around his limbs, and a loose shirt and trousers over them.

There were two ways you could react when you got yourself into a situation like this, when you knew you weren't supposed to be there and had just been caught

and followed the long-gone intruder out of the morgue.

At least I had managed to avoid violating Etta Mirian's body, which was the absolute minimum you could aim for if you wanted to get paid by your client.

The early afternoon sun was blinding and harsh as I stumbled out the back entrance of the morgue. Sweat sprang immediately from my skin, dampening my palms, after the magical coolness of the vault.

Fuck. Fuck, fuck, fuck!

There was no sign of the man I had been chasing. In the maze of monuments to the dead, I had no chance of finding him.

I was going to be in so much shit over this. At least a dozen people had seen me head down to the viewing room. What exactly was the penalty for tossing about a bunch of corpses and leaving them on the floor? In Agatos's long history, I couldn't imagine someone hadn't made a law about exactly this. I considered going back, trying to repair the shelves and restack the bodies, but it would be hopeless.

Maybe they would think it was an accident.

No. Screw it. I was going to have to admit what had happened and hope none of the relatives ever had to know.

I didn't even know if the intruder had anything to do with Etta Mirian or her unusual death. Perhaps he had just been a thief come to steal from the bodies. Not every thief in the city had the same sense of right and wrong as Benny.

Or maybe he did have something to do with it. It would confirm Mr. Mirian's theory that there was something very peculiar with the way his wife had died, and much as I wanted to, I couldn't deny that it was all fucked up. The cut on her neck had been too smooth and neat. You couldn't do that to yourself. Your hand would have to shake or jerk when you made the cut. Etta Mirian's clearly hadn't. *And she smiled.*

This was a terrible idea. I was supposed to be in hiding, not fucking around with more dangerous, weird shit. I was supposed to have learned my lesson. "Mara's piss!"

I couldn't let this go, not until I knew the truth.

I wondered if Mr. Mirian had known I would react like this.

I straightened with a sigh, and that was when I realised I wasn't alone anymore. Two black-cloaked mages stood only a couple of yards from me, watching. They must have come up while I was distracted, blinded by the sunlight, or under cover of a spell I had been too shaken to notice. And I had thought today was already a disaster. I recognised both of these mages. They were the Wren's people.

At least he had sent two of them. That was flattering, right? I put on my most friendly, confident smile. "I don't suppose there's any point in saying I'll come quietly?"

Magic erupted from them. I didn't even try to resist.

Blackness enveloped me.

CHAPTER THREE

I WOKE WITH MY HEAD THUMPING.

Whatever magic the Wren's mages had hit me with hadn't been gentle. My dry mouth had the familiar taste of chalk and garlic that magic left when turned on you, like a hangover without the upsides.

I swore under my breath. They hadn't needed to do that. I wasn't stupid enough to resist. It was a reminder – not that I'd needed one – that I wasn't in the Wren's good books.

I shifted uncomfortably. I had been dumped in a hard chair, but I wasn't tied. There was something over my head, covering my face. A hood. Again, not tied. What was I supposed to do? Passively leave it on to prove my compliance? The Wren knew me well enough not to believe that. I reached up and pulled it off. I didn't know why my kidnappers had bothered with the hood anyway. I, and everyone else from the

Warrens and Dockside, knew exactly where the Wren kept his headquarters. He wasn't trying to hide.

I was in his office. The man himself was seated behind his desk, writing, and he didn't look up as I pulled off the hood.

The Wren looked like he was in his sixties, but I knew damned well he was far older than that. Stories of the Wren went back generations, and, yeah, it probably wasn't all the same man, but he was a high mage, and controlling that much magic meant he aged more slowly than the rest of us. He looked the same as he had when I'd been a kid. His hair was grey, and his skin was pale. There must have been some Brythanii blood in him a generation or two back. His eyes were washed out, only a hint of muddy green in them. He wasn't as tall as me, but then most people in Agatos weren't.

I watched him scratching away with his pen for a while, then shifted upright in the chair.

To my left, a tall window looked out over the docks and the wharfs that stuck out into the harbour like a dozen jabbing fingers. Most of the warehouses that ran along the centre of the wharfs weren't directly under the Wren's control, but his influence hung heavily over them. The high mage Carnelian Silkstar had once controlled most of the trade through Agatos, until Lowriver's beast god had killed him. I supposed the warehouses must have passed to his heirs, whoever they were, but those heirs weren't high mages, and I doubted they would be able to hold onto his empire.

On the opposite side of the office, wide warehouse

doors opened onto an enormous, enclosed courtyard. From the outside, the Wren's headquarters looked much like any of the other gigantic, whitewashed warehouses that lined the docks, but it had been hollowed out so that an outer layer of rooms and offices surrounded a courtyard. The courtyard was filled with a lush tangle of trees and plants from the jungles of Tor and Secellia to the west. Even from here, I could smell the lush, damp soil and living plants. Maintaining that jungle garden in the dry heat of Agatos's summer and its icy winter must have taken an enormous outlay of money and magic.

I wasn't an idiot. I had been to the theatre – once or twice, although never voluntarily – and I recognised this whole setup. The pet jungle, the Wren ignoring me, and the wards that waited like the jaws of a mantrap all around us were a show designed to intimidate. But the Wren was missing one important factor if he was trying to overwhelm me. I already knew I was small, insignificant, and powerless, so, you know, how do you like that, Mr. High Mage?

Eventually, the Wren put down his quill and looked at me. "I remember you, Mennik Thorn. Your mother had great hopes for you." He shrugged. "I did not share her optimism, but she was useful to me, and it suited me to encourage that belief. It kept her tied to me for far longer than she should have allowed."

Yeah. I bet it had. My mother had been one of the Wren's acolytes, working as a mage for him long after she had obtained enough power to be a high mage herself. Her support must have given the Wren a great deal of leverage in the unending power games between the high mages of Agatos. Not that I hadn't been grateful. There had been times when both Benny and I might have suffered much more painful consequences for transgressing the Wren's rules as kids without his need to keep my mother on side.

Now, of course, that had changed. My mother was never going to stay an acolyte forever. When another of the high mages died, Mother had taken her spot, restyling herself as the Countess and renaming herself Anatase Coldrock. With the death of Carnelian Silkstar, she and the Wren were the only high mages remaining in Agatos, and they did not like each other.

Which was how we had ended up exactly where we were.

I had left my mother's court five years ago, disgusted by the power games of the high mages and traumatised by my mother's brutal attempts to train me to be her successor. But the Wren wanted a mole, someone to ferret out the Countess's secrets and plans, and I had been foolish enough to get myself in his debt.

Don't get me wrong. I would happily pass over my mother's secrets. After what she had put me through, I didn't have any loyalty left. But to do that, I would have to go back to her and become part of her court again, and I just hadn't been able to force myself to do it. Now, it seemed, the Wren's patience had finally run out. Even if I could have put my magical abilities up against his – which was so much of a joke it wasn't even funny – the Wren had plenty of other ways of dealing with his enemies, and I didn't want to be a body dragged out of the harbour one morning.

A door opened behind the Wren, and a tall, dark-skinned man walked in. He came up close, bent to whisper something in the Wren's ear, then stepped to one side, quietly watching.

I knew this man, too. His name was Melecho Kael, and as far as I could tell, he was a combination of the Wren's second-in-command, bodyguard, and gardener. The few times I had been here before, I had seen him pruning and raking the mini jungle. I assumed he must be a mage to hold such a trusted position with the Wren, but I had never seen him use magic. I unfocused my eyes to assess the power in the room. I could see the raw magic, the heavy, threatening wards, and the reservoir the Wren was holding within him, ready to cast in the blink of an eye. It was pretty impressive. Only the most powerful mages could hold that much magic without leaking like a cheap boat. His second-in-command wasn't holding any magic, but then why would he when he was with a high mage?

I shifted in my seat. "So. Are we done?"

It probably wasn't sensible to antagonise the most dangerous high mage in the city, but I got mouthy when I got nervous. It was the secret of my success.

His magic lashed out faster than I could react. It wrapped around me like rose briars and constricted. A thousand thorns of magic stabbed into my skin. I let out a groan through clenched teeth.

For fuck's sake, Nik!

I hadn't even seen him form the spell. The only person I knew who could cast magic faster was my mother, but there wouldn't have been much in it.

Blood seeped into my mouth. I had bitten my tongue, but I scarcely felt it above the burning pain as the thorns tightened on me. I couldn't breathe.

This is it. He's going to kill you, and no one will ever know. You stupid, fucking idiot!

I had always known my mouth would be the end of me. I just hadn't realised it would be so soon.

The Wren rose from his chair. Through tears I saw him round his desk and crouch in front of me.

"You requested a favour from my broker. You agreed a price, and you agreed conditions. It was a deal freely entered into. I understand why you have been reluctant to hold up your end, but that reluctance is at an end." The thorns tightened again. "Your mother continues to work against my interests. I will not allow the Countess to become the pre-eminent high mage in Agatos. I will know her plans."

"It's not that easy." Forcing each word out was like spitting up broken glass, but my mouth had got me into this, and it was all I had to get me out again. I could taste the blood on my lips. "She's got no reason to trust me." Yeah, I was partly to blame for that. I had made no attempt to repair our relationship after I left. I'd wanted nothing more to do with her or her fanatical acolytes. The twisted games, the corruption, the abuse of power, no thanks. I would rather be poor, and I had told her that. "I need longer. A week. Two."

My time in the Countess's court had broken me. Even thinking about going back sent waves of dizziness sweeping through me that had nothing to do with the pain. I couldn't do it.

"You will find a way. By tonight, I expect to hear that you have re-joined your mother's household. Then you will discover her plans, report them to me, and we will be done." He leaned closer. "That is now your only option. I do not know if you value your life, but I know you value the lives of your friends, so I will tell you now. You will do what I ask, or Benyon Field and his daughter will pay the price."

Fuck you! Rage welled up in me. I pulled in raw magic and threw it against the thorns binding me.

It didn't work. The Wren's power was too great. I couldn't even shift it.

The Wren reached out and tapped a finger on top of my head.

Darkness swallowed me again.

THE FUN THING ABOUT BEING KNOCKED UNCONSCIOUS BY magic twice in one day was that it left you with a shit of a headache.

I lay there, my skull thumping like neighbours having inconsiderate sex through a thin wall. It wasn't only my skull, either. My whole body was thumping like I was … like I was being…

I forced my eyes open. I was staring up at the bright blue sky between faded, white-washed buildings, and the sky wasn't staying still. It was sliding along between the buildings.

And the *smell*. Everything stank like rotting food, dead animals, and urine. What in all the Depths had the Wren done to me? He must have scrambled my brain. *Pity!* I had known messing with him would get me a beating. I had been prepared for some broken bones. I had even been prepared for him to have me knifed. But my mind? I didn't have much going for me, but I couldn't do without my mind. A brief eddy of terror swirled through me. My stomach tightened, and for a moment I couldn't breathe.

My body thumped again. The buildings around me seemed to bounce.

"What the fuck?" I muttered. This wasn't my brain. This was…

I sat up, abruptly, sending pain stabbing through my head. I was in the back of a cart. It was piled high with waste, all the crap tossed out by the citizens of Agatos and left to fester in the heat of the day. Now I knew why it stank.

"You absolute bastard." The Wren had dumped me in a waste cart. As messages went, it wasn't exactly subtle.

I twisted around to see the cart driver. "Hey!"

He glanced back, shrugged, and turned away again. Right. So that was the way it was.

We were in the Grey City, my former home. The grandeur of this part of Agatos had long since faded and flaked, rather like me, but with the state I was in, I wouldn't even be welcome here.

The cart hit another pothole, jolting me and doing my aching head no favours.

It was getting late in the day. In a couple of hours, the sun would dip behind the mountains that framed the Erastes Valley, and the cart was full. It would be at the end of its rounds, now, and I knew exactly where it was heading.

Beggars' Wharf was an old stone dock on the bank of the Erastes River, roughly half way between the Sour Bridge and the Tide Bridge, in the heart of the Grey City. It dated back to when ships had docked on the riverbanks, rather than at the extensive wharfs that now jutted into the harbour. Most of the old riverside wharfs had long since been built over, but Beggars' Wharf had remained. There, the carts that gathered the city's waste would stop, turn around, and dump the whole steaming pile of shit into the river, where it would – theoretically – be washed out to sea. It was why Agatos Harbour offered such a welcoming sight and smell to visitors.

At low tide, beggars waited on the muddy river-bank below the wharf to snatch up any useful scraps before they were lost to the waters – and, yes, I was sticking with 'muddy' for the riverbanks, even though there was next to no mud in the water before the river entered Agatos, and the sewage from the Upper City had to empty somewhere.

We tried not to talk about that.

The Wren might have been content for me to end up floating in the shit, but I had no intention of going through with it. With a piteous groan, I levered myself over the side of the cart and fell to the cobbles.

Bannaur's balls!

I crouched there, waiting for my balance to come back to me. The Wren couldn't have been any more clear if he had tattooed the message on my head. He wasn't waiting any longer. I ran a hand over my forehead, just to make sure he really hadn't tattooed it there. I wouldn't have put it past the bastard.

This was it. I was going to have to go back to the Countess. Every part of me screamed in protest. I couldn't do this. I had to. *Fuck!*

When my mother had declared herself high mage, she had got it into her head that I would be her eventual successor, and she had thrown all her efforts and resources into training me. It had been brutal and painful, and I had failed. It had broken me, that was the truth. Then my mother had abandoned me and turned all her efforts towards my little half-sister, Mica, whose own powers had surpassed mine by the time she was twelve. I had stuck it out in my mother's court for as long as I could, working as a minor acolyte, but it had been killing me, and eventually I left, just picked up one day and walked out. That had been five years ago, and when I was honest with myself, I had to admit that I still hadn't really recovered from it. I had sworn I would never go back. I didn't know if I could without breaking completely.

And if I didn't, I would be letting Benny and Sereh down. We had been friends for too long, relied on each other too much, to ever do that.

Some things weren't a choice after all.

Screw it, Mother. I'm coming home.

I WASN'T PUTTING IT OFF. I REALLY WASN'T. I JUST HAD one more obligation I had to fulfil before I did. And if that delayed things by an hour or two, that wasn't my fault, was it?

I hadn't been able to tell if magic had been used on Etta Mirian. But either Mr. Mirian's naivety had been contagious, or I was right and there was something off, because I couldn't reconcile the cut throat and her smile with the actions of a sane woman. Not unless a compulsion had been driven into her brain. I didn't have the power to do something like that, but there were mages – and other entities – who could. It itched me wrong. I owed it to Mr. Mirian to satisfy that itch. And if magic had been used in the murder, that brought me to my other obligation: I had to tell the Ash Guard, in the person of Captain Meroi Gale.

My relationship with the Ash Guard was ... complicated. On the one hand, if it hadn't been for me, the

39

rogue mage Enne Lowriver and her pet god would have killed a lot more people, and the Ash Guard would have been none the wiser. On the other hand, they thought I should have shared more information earlier, and they blamed me for many of the deaths that had occurred. As though I was supposed to do their jobs for them. What complicated it was that I kind of fancied Captain Gale, in a terrified way, and she thought I had betrayed her. Which I had.

If I turned up filthy and stinking of trash, what was she going to think?

You daft sod, Nik, I scolded myself. *Trust you to develop a crush on a fucking Ash Guard captain.*

The Ash Guard were, as Captain Gale had put it, the sledgehammer. They were there to smash the shit out of any mage or magical entity that stepped out of line. The Ash they carried or wore smeared on their skin destroyed magic, leaving even the most potent mage as helpless as a fish on an open fire.

And, yeah, I realised that was part of the reason I fancied her. I realised it was twisted, and yet I still fancied her.

I pushed myself off the cobbles, then trudged through the still-hot streets of the Grey City, until I reached Long Step Avenue and made my way to Benny's house. I tried very hard not to notice people stepping around me to avoid the smell.

Benny was up and awake when I got back. To be honest, I would have preferred it if he had still been sleeping off whatever dubious activity he had been up to last night – I tried not to ask. Benny hadn't been a fan of my approach to the whole Wren situation, and he hadn't been slow to let me know. The last thing I wanted was to prove him right.

He took a step back as I tiptoed into the house. "Fuck me, mate. What happened to you?" He raised a hand. "No. Don't tell me. But go and, I don't know, burn your clothes or something. Jump in the well."

"It's not that bad," I said, sniffing my sleeve and immediately regretting it.

"I need to have a word," he said. "Outside, though. And you can stand downwind."

Whatever was on Benny's mind, I didn't want to know it. I had enough problems. But when Benny got that expression on his dead-ferret face, I knew better than to argue.

"Where's Sereh?" I asked as we stepped out of the house and descended to the paving that ran around the edge of the courtyard. Anything to distract him.

The courtyard was empty, except for the pair of young boys playing under the lemon tree. They were out here most days while their parents were off doing whatever it was they did. I had never asked, and I didn't know the kids' names either. *Keep my head down*, that had been the plan. Look how well that had turned out.

"Out with her friends, I expect," Benny said, stopping a good few steps from me and screwing up his nose. "That's not why I want to talk to you."

I frowned. "You're letting her out on her own?"

The Wren had threatened her. The idea that she was wandering around unaware sent a shiver across my back.

"Mate, we were out on the streets when you weren't more than six, and that was right in the heart of the Warrens. Sereh's almost twelve, and she can look after herself."

Yeah, she could. Sereh was the deadliest person I knew, the Wren and my mother notwithstanding. If she knew what was coming, I would put my money on her emerging from the shadows, knife in hand. But she wasn't a mage, and a powerful mage could strike from a distance. *You're being irrational.* The Wren had threatened her and Benny, but only if I didn't do what he wanted, and I was going to do it. Soon. She was safe. There was no need to worry, nor to worry Benny.

"The thing is, mate," Benny said, "we had a deal, right?"

A deal? What deal? My brain was still half scrambled from whatever the Wren had done to me. What had I forgotten? Benny might have had a dubious relationship with the concepts of property and money, but he was deadly serious about his system of debts, favours, and obligations. If I had dropped my side of a deal, this wasn't going to be a pleasant conversation.

"About what?" I said cautiously.

"You get to stay here, but you don't use my house to see clients. Remember? That's not up for negotiation."

Ah. Mr. Mirian. "I didn't invite him," I said. "He just turned up. I don't even know how he found me."

Benny snorted. "It was hardly a secret." I must have looked surprised because he added, "Fuck's sake."

I had known, when I wasn't trying to fool myself, that I couldn't hide from the Wren if he wanted to find me, but I hadn't realised my hiding place was common knowledge. Pity! I must have looked like a right twat. Not that it mattered now.

"I'm not getting back into the business," I promised. "I'm just helping out this once. It won't happen again."

"It had better fucking not. It's not safe for Sereh." He looked me up and down. "And you're not coming back in like that. Get a bucket out of the well and dump it over yourself. I'll toss you out some clean clothes. You going to be here for supper?"

"No." I gestured at my clothes. "The Wren has run out of patience. I'm going to see the Countess." Just saying the words tightened my stomach into a fist and made my voice catch.

Benny grimaced. "Rather you than me. Good luck, mate."

I didn't trust myself to speak, so I just nodded. I was going to need all the good luck I could get, and it had been in short supply lately.

CHAPTER FOUR

As THE HOTTEST PART OF THE DAY HAD FADED, THE CITY had come back to life again, and the streets were choked with people, carts, animals, and the inevitable, impromptu punch-ups over who had bumped into whom. The air was thick with shouts, calls, and the stink of sweaty bodies. I navigated my way around them with the instinct cut into the bones of every Agatos native.

The Ash Guard fortress sat heavy and oppressive against an axe-blade of cliff that protruded deep into the western part of the city. Most people avoided the place. The Ash Guard might not have jurisdiction over the ordinary citizens of Agatos, but anyone who could take down a high mage without breaking a sweat was worth avoiding, and there was a whole fortress of the bastards just across the square. Stepping out of the chaos of the streets onto the open cobbles made me feel like a fish separating itself from its shoal and heading straight towards the sharks.

Not that I had done anything wrong. Not this time. Apart from the disaster in the morgue, anyway, and that wasn't Ash Guard business. But I had ended up on the wrong side of Captain Gale, and I didn't want to stay there. She could unseam me like a cheap shirt, magic or no magic, and I wasn't her favourite person. Maybe I could start to repair that if I could pass on some really useful information. Dealing with the magical shit this city could throw at you was her job, and maybe this stuff with Etta Mirian would make sense to her. She had more experience than I did. Depths, maybe she would be able to offer some help.

I couldn't prevent a shiver running down my spine and into my bowels as I knocked on the heavy wooden doors and asked the Guardswoman on duty if I could see Captain Meroi Gale.

The captain was shorter than me, but she had the body of a woman who fought for a living. She was tough, solid, and she intimidated the shit out of me. A long scar cut diagonally across her face, close to her left eye. The expression on her face when she saw me waiting wasn't exactly welcoming. Let's just say that I had seen people look at a dead seagull washed up on the shore with more enthusiasm. Well, what had I expected? The first time we met, she had been arresting me, and things had gone downhill from there. I took a step back into the square in case I had to run for it.

Ninety percent of my dubious success came down to goat shit, so I plastered a smile on my face and tried to look confident.

"What in the Depths is wrong with you?" she said. "You look constipated."

It took more than a gratuitous insult to knock me back. "I have some information. You told me to look out for trouble."

Captain Gale sighed. "Because more trouble is exactly what I need right now."

"Anything I can help with?" Maybe I could get on her good side. Sucking up couldn't do any harm, right?

She snorted. "I don't have the energy for that kind of help." She raised a hand before I could reply, which was probably a good thing. "What do you want, Nik? And make it quick. I've got a dozen urgent cases that aren't solving themselves."

Typical bad timing. Still, I was here now. As quickly as I could, I told her about Etta Mirian, Peyt Jyston Cord – the man she had murdered – and Mr. Mirian's suspicions. She didn't look convinced.

"You reckon there's something to it?"

"There might be. It didn't sit right."

She scratched at her scar. "Do you have any proof? Evidence? Anything other than a paying client?"

Ouch. That wasn't fair. I hadn't wanted to take Mr. Mirian on, and I certainly hadn't wanted his money. "You told me to come to you if I came across anything unusual. 'Trouble finds you like flies find shit.' Those were your words." I was hardly going to forget. "You told me to report it."

"And this is the one time you actually listened? Just my luck." She glanced around, as though expecting to see someone else. Someone more interesting, maybe. "I also told you to find me a new high mage. How's that going?"

"You were serious about that?"

Her eyes came back to me. I rubbed my face to avoid her stare. It was unsettling. Maybe I just felt guilty, although over what, I wasn't sure.

"You really think all the other mages in the city are just lining up to discuss things with me?" I said.

Captain Gale closed her eyes for a moment. "That is exactly why I asked you, not someone else. I don't want advice from someone who is part of one of the factions. I want someone no one else likes."

"Thanks." She had a great way of puncturing my confidence. It was probably perverse, but it only made me fancy her more. *For Pity's sake, Nik.*

"I'm not here to massage your ego."

Some hope of that.

She blew out her cheeks. "Look, Nik. Right now, there's a power vacuum in the city. That's what happens when you kill one of the high mages." She gave me a meaningful look. I resisted the temptation to point out that *I* hadn't been the one who had murdered Carnelian Silkstar. "With your mother and the Wren so evenly balanced, there's an opportunity for another power to tip things one way or another,

47

and every arsehole mage thinks they're the one to fill the hole. We're rushing our tits off trying to put a stop to it all before we have to start killing people."

"I thought that was what you liked doing."

"Believe me, if we killed every mage who pissed us off, there would be a lot fewer of you around. I don't have the time or the resources to chase up on suspicions or to save you doing your own legwork. Bring me something solid, and I might be able to help you out." She must have taken pity on how disconsolate I looked because she said, "I'll give you a tip. When you want to investigate a murder, there are two people you want to look at: the perpetrator and the victim. The answer is with one of them."

"I can hardly ask Etta Mirian," I said. "She killed herself, and her husband doesn't know anything." I was sure of that, at least.

"Then look into the victim. Why did she kill *him* instead of someone else?"

Which was easier said than done. "I don't know anything about him."

She sighed again. "We'll have a file. We do on all unexplained deaths. I'll fetch it for you. But that's the only favour you're getting until you prove magic was involved. And find me a high mage, Nik. I'm not joking." She gestured at the fortress behind her. "Want to come in and wait?"

I eyed the solid, looming structure. I had been in there exactly twice, both times when she had arrested me. The walls were soaked in Ash that not only stole all my magical powers but which took away that low level of raw magic that all mages used to supplement their energy.

"Nah," I said. "You're all right."

With a shake of her head, she turned and disappeared back behind the heavy doors.

THE FILE THAT CAPTAIN GALE GAVE ME WAS THIN, JUST A couple of pages in an embossed leather wallet. I settled myself in a small coffee house beneath an awning, just a block from the Ash Guard fortress, ordered a sweetened coffee spiced with cardamom, and pulled out the papers. I was high enough here to feel a faint breeze off the Erastes Bay and to see the water glittering through the gaps between buildings. A forest of masts jutted over the warehouses that lined the wharfs. High above, seagulls drifted hopefully, looking for discarded catch from fishing boats or bodies washed out to sea.

The file didn't contain much information on Etta Mirian that I didn't already know. She and her husband were reasonably successful drapers with a shop not far from here in the good part of the Middle City. She was a follower of the sea god Yttra – not uncommon in Agatos – but her devotion was more dutiful than passionate. No known enemies, no feuds that anyone reported. An ordinary woman leading an ordinary life. Not that anyone was entirely ordinary, but the City Watch hadn't found anything notable. I wasn't going to get any answers there.

I turned to the information about her victim, Peyt Jyston Cord. A Dockside boy from the tenements, pressed right up against the warehouses. A couple of steps up from the Warrens, and more of a sideways shuffle from the Grey City. His parents were still alive, but apparently they claimed not to have seen him for several years. I was hardly one to judge.

The file didn't say anything about a job but gave an address on Sester Avenue. It was in the Middle City, but only a resentful stone's throw from the beginning of the Upper City. The borderlands, some called it. He had moved up in the world, then. He wasn't married, the file said, no wife, no husband. No kids. Some mercy, at least. Fewer people to mourn him, fewer lives ruined by Etta Mirian's knife. And that was all there was. It was too flimsy a memorial to a whole life. I guessed there hadn't been anyone obvious to ask, and the Watch hadn't put in much effort. There was certainly nothing in there that hinted at a reason for Etta Mirian to stick a knife in his neck and then kill herself.

Fuck it. I was procrastinating. It was getting late. The Wren had given me a deadline, and I was pissing away what little time I had with this file. Etta Mirian and her victim weren't getting any more dead, but I might if I ignored my instructions and so might Benny and Sereh. The thought sent rage burning through me again, making my fingers tingle like frostbite. Benny and Sereh had nothing to do with any of this. They hadn't made a deal with the Wren. They hadn't failed to keep up their end. How *dare* he threaten them?

That's good. Keep that going. Stay angry.

I had been putting this off, there was no denying it. Depths, I'd been avoiding even thinking about it, because every time I did, I felt that familiar old panic start to breed inside me, swelling and churning and sucking my breath away.

I had put it off too long, and I had endangered my friends.

The whole thing was absurd. I had faced down a god! Well, what was left of one, and not so much faced down as fled. But the point was, I had walked into far more dangerous places than my mother's house, and I hadn't expected to walk out again.

Have you? a treacherous voice in my head whispered. *Really? Did they break you, too?*

Shut up!

My mother wouldn't try to kill me ... I didn't think. The worst that would happen was – what? – contempt? Disinterest? It had been a long time since I'd needed her approval and a lot longer since I'd had it.

No more delays.

I tossed back the last of the coffee, choked on the over-sweet flavour, and thumped my hand on the table in response.

This isn't so hard.

All I had to do was gain my mother's trust long enough to steal a secret and give it to the Wren. I didn't need anything big, just something relevant. The information I had bought from his broker, Squint, hadn't exactly been earth-breaking, even though it had put me in his debt. I didn't expect a fair exchange of value, but there were limits.

Go. Just go!

I lunged out of my seat.

"Hey!" a voice called from behind. "You forgot your change!"

I jerked a hand in response. If I turned back now, even to get the change, I would lose my courage.

I didn't have a plan. Coming up with a plan would mean thinking about what I was doing, and I couldn't afford that.

Get in, find something, get out. That was all. How hard could it really be?

It hadn't taken my mother long to reinvent herself once she left the Wren's service. Mages with the kind of power she had were rare, even in Agatos, where raw magic saturated the streets, a legacy of thousands of years of dead gods. She had changed her name to Anatase Coldrock, given herself the title of the Countess, and arranged election to the Senate. Within months of her rebirth, she had purchased an enormous palace two thirds of the way up Horn Hill and become one of the city's three high mages. No one – other than the Ash Guard – had asked about the sudden death of the previous high mage only weeks before, and no one had given them answers. Some questions were better left unasked.

I had spent the last five years avoiding her palace. The only time I had been here since was when she kidnapped me, and I had been unconscious then, so I hadn't had a chance to stare at it in horror. In the intervening years, my mother had turned what had once been simply a grandiose, belligerent palace into a temple to her own power and influence. The approach was lined with statues of the great and the good of Agatos's history, the kings, the high mages, and even the gods of the city. As the line of statues approached the grand entrance of the palace, they diminished in size, so that the palace loomed over them.

My mother had never been subtle with her symbolism, and she had never been notable for her taste, which meant she fitted right in on Horn Hill, where the chance to rub people's faces in your wealth trumped architectural elegance or practicality. Enormous, coloured glass windows seemed to radiate light, even in the full brightness of day. Double doors large enough to ride an elephant through were inevitably flanked by columns made of unnaturally white marble.

Honestly, it was taking the piss.

Anger had given me the drive to come striding up here and to surge past my gnawing anxiety, but I couldn't keep up that level of fury forever, and it was a long walk. No matter how hard I tried to keep my rage burning, my progress through the streets tamped it, and I found myself slowing as the palace loomed in front of me. Shivers ran along my arms. All those memories of the pain, humiliation, and abuse I had suffered from the Countess and her mages, all my failures, and how quickly my mother had dropped me the moment she decided Mica would be the one to succeed her pressed in around me until I could hardly breathe.

Come on. Benny and Sereh were relying on me, whether they knew it or not.

I realised I had stopped moving. I was standing there in the middle of Agate Way while people flowed around me.

I slammed my fist into my thigh. The pain opened a second of clarity. Once before, when I had frozen in panic, Sereh had poked me with her knife, and it had shocked me out of my paralysis. I beat my fist onto my thigh again, feeling the bruise blossom on my leg, until the pain broke through my suffocating anxiety like a hammer through ice.

Bannaur's balls, that hurt!

I was sweating, cursing, bent over. Slowly, I straightened. A small crowd had stopped to watch me. I glared at them until they broke away.

I took another slow, calming breath, then forced myself towards the palace.

I had promised myself that, no matter what, I would never come back here. I would rather starve on the streets. And yet here I was.

No choice.

I leaned on the big doors, pushing them open.

The entrance hall had been given a makeover since I'd last been here, too. The wide, marble staircase that led up to private areas of the palace was now flanked by two statues of my blessed mother in the now famous Mycedan-tat style staring disapprovingly down. A small fountain burbled pointlessly in the centre of the hall, and a couple of parlour palms wilted in the artificial light.

I had grown up in a single-room house in the Warrens. My mother had grown up in the same place. In some ways, I had never left. I wondered, briefly, if this whole façade was a sign my mother hadn't either.

No. I wasn't going to humanise her like that. This was arrogance, pure and simple, a fist stuck in the face of every person, mage or not, in Agatos. The room was unnaturally cool after the hot streets. Some poor sod would be wasting magic on this, all to daunt visitors with the puissance of my mother and her court. The whole room was a shrine to power and poor taste.

"May I help you?"

It was the voice more than anything that hit me like a sock full of stones.

You useless, pathetic pissant. You don't deserve this. You don't deserve any of it. Standing over me while I lay broken on the training floor, bleeding from my ears. That voice. The contempt. The *hate*.

Lady of the Grove! I shoved the memory aside with an effort that left me weak.

The mage sitting at a desk at the back of the hall

looked older than I remembered. He was middle aged, with the kind of squeezed face that made him look like he'd got his head shut in a door. I had pushed the memory of him away, along with so many of my other memories of the time. He hadn't been the only one of my mother's mages set the task of training me or breaking me, but he had been one of those who had leaned into the 'breaking'. *Forge*. That had been his name. *Cerrean Forge*. Even just thinking it made my skin tighten.

Behind him and to his right were heavy, polished cedar doors, inlaid with ivory. I unfocused my eyes and saw the wards saturating the walls, ceiling, and floor. They were attached to the mage by what looked to me like a thin, red strand of magic. All he would have to do was to send a little burst of power along that strand and the wards would trigger, turning me into a smear of former mage. *You would love to use it, wouldn't you, you bastard?* I wondered whether I could cut the thread before he could react, or whether that would trigger the wards, too.

"I want to see the Countess."

A patronising smile touched the mage's face. He adjusted the stupid fucking black cloak he was wearing and pursed his lips. "Do you have an appointment?"

"Tell her it's me."

His eyebrows raised quizzically.

You know who I am. You recognise me. You have to. How could he have forgotten after all he had done to me? I had to force down the surge of rage and fear.

"Mennik Thorn. Tell her it's Mennik Thorn. She'll see me." I hoped. It depended how pissed off she was with me right now. The last time I had seen her, I hadn't been polite. But then she had been telling me to leave Benny to die in gaol. I had been restrained, all things considered.

The mage eyed me with a sneer. I had to admit I didn't make an impressive sight. I didn't look as beaten up as I sometimes did, and my clothes were relatively clean, but I certainly didn't fit in up here on Horn Hill, in the Countess's palace, and I was still carrying a slight whiff of the waste cart.

Whatever the guy thought of me, and whether he really didn't remember me, he wasn't confident enough to turn me away. My mother's sycophants knew better than to anger her. Getting on her wrong side wasn't healthy. With a last sneer, he waved me to a long, green bench, and I sat with a barely suppressed groan of relief. It was all I could do not to shake.

My leg was throbbing where I had pounded it. I focused on the sensation and tried not to think of what I was doing. I didn't want to be here. That was the thought that kept hammering at the back of my head like a hangover. Anywhere but here.

"Pull it together," I whispered to myself. This was just a place, a building made from the same stone, wood, and glass as any other building. The memories that sometimes woke me screaming and which scraped like a flint knife at the back of my skull weren't held in the fabric of the building. They were in my head. Logically, being here shouldn't be any harder than being anywhere else. My mother couldn't do anything to me. I wasn't her acolyte anymore, and I had no intention of becoming so again. I was here to find something to satisfy the Wren then fuck back off. That was all.

I pushed my knuckle into my bruised leg, sending a shot of pain through the muscle.

Breathe. Focus on the pain. Don't run. This isn't rational. You're not helpless.

I wished I believed it.

CHAPTER FIVE

I DIDN'T KNOW HOW LONG I HAD BEEN SITTING THERE – I had sunk into a kind of panicked fugue – but it must have been at least an hour when someone settled onto the bench beside me. I had seen several mages and clerks pass by, but I hadn't paid them any attention.

"What are you doing here, Nik?"

I twisted and saw my little sister Mica perched neatly on the green cushions. I forced myself to draw in several slow, deep breaths and hoped she wouldn't see the dread still stiffening my body. It didn't work.

"Are you in trouble?" she asked.

Well, wasn't that typical? "Why would you assume that?"

At least the instinctive irritation pushed my panic down.

"You're here to see Mother. I can't imagine you'd do that by choice."

I didn't want to lie to Mica. All things considered,

she tolerated me far more than I deserved. But I could hardly tell her the truth. She wouldn't let me steal Mother's secrets and pass them on to the Wren without saying anything, and it wouldn't be fair to ask her to. I had been hoping to put off this encounter.

"After what happened," I said, waving vaguely, hoping to suggest all the excitement of me being framed for murder and almost being disembowelled by a dead beast god, "I missed you. I don't want to spend another five years hardly seeing you." I realised as I said it that it was true. When I had left, I had pushed so hard away from my mother that I had cut off Mica, too. But she was still my little sister. "If I'm going to see you, I have to make it up with Mother. Somehow."

She studied me. I couldn't blame her for the naked suspicion on her face. I was pulling a con here, even if I wasn't being given a choice.

"You'd better not be fucking me about, Nik."

"I'm not."

She looked sceptical, but I could see her deciding to accept my explanation. That made me feel worse. She stood and beckoned me to follow, leading me to and up the wide stairs with only a nod to the mage at the desk.

"He's friendly," I said, as we climbed.

"Who? Cerrean Forge?"

Yeah. I wasn't going to acknowledge that I remembered him. Why give him that power? "The guy who looks like his face was squeezed out of someone's arse."

"Be nice." She glanced down to him. Was I imagining it, or did she have to suppress a grin? "Mother's acolytes can be … enthusiastic. But he means well. He's loyal."

Did she not remember what Forge had put me through? She must have known. Mustn't she? "A fanatic, you mean."

This time there was definitely no grin. "You wouldn't understand."

"I don't. You're right." I leaned over the bannister and blew a kiss at Forge. He glared back at me.

"Don't be a wanker, Nik."

I held up my hands in surrender. It must have worked, because she continued, "I'm giving you a permanent pass through the wards. Don't do anything stupid, because Mother will take it away in a blink."

"That's Mother," I said. "Just overflowing with the love."

Mica shook her head. "She does look out for you, you know. She just—"

"Wishes I was someone else?"

Mica gave an awkward shrug, then strode off down a hallway. I followed.

Mother's palace was vast. It wasn't just to show off her wealth, power, and status, although she would be lying if she didn't say that was part of it. It also housed her junior mages and staff. As well as the wing of suites for the mages, there were laboratories, a large, open training ground, and practice rooms. Having a lot of space when mages were throwing power around like sweetmeats at Charo was pretty much necessary. The entire basement, hollowed out from the bedrock of Horn Hill, was lined with planks of apple tree wood and a layer of volcanic glass to impede magic, but even so, the occasional stray spell spilled out, and if you didn't want to find your legs suddenly vaporised, you tended to stay as far away as possible. I knew my mother was frustrated that she couldn't get Ash to kill any escaping spells, but possession of Ash was an immediate death sentence, and even a high mage couldn't dodge that.

"Mother's in a meeting with the Yellow Faction of the Senate," Mica said as she showed me through a side door at the end of the hallway. It opened onto another corridor that led to Mother's offices and personal quarters. "She'll be out in an hour or so if she gets what she wants." Mica could leave it unsaid that Mother would get what she wanted.

I didn't follow the politics of the Senate, and I didn't know much about the Yellow Faction, other than that they were another pro-business grouping, like most of the rest. Which particular businesses, I had no idea, and I didn't really care. I did know they weren't looking out for the interests of the ordinary citizens of Agatos. The Senate was corrupt. It was a seething mass of men and women all out for whatever they could get. Allegiances changed constantly, washing in and out like the tide, shifting, mutating, undercutting, betraying, and allying again. One faction would hold promi-nence for a while, then suddenly, for no reason I could tell, half its members would switch to some other faction, and the Senate would swing the other way. Throughout it all, though, my mother had managed to remain in the ascendancy for the simple reason that she had something no one else could offer: the power of a high mage and the favours that came along with it. I didn't even know what my mother wanted from her manoeuvrings, other than to remain in control of the Senate. What she hoped to achieve with that control had never been clear to me. Perhaps the power itself was enough. I didn't really get it.

"You know, Nik," Mica said, "I'm having a hard time believing you've suddenly decided you want to get tight with the family after all this time. You went out of your way to avoid us. What's happened? We can help, you know. Whatever you've got into, we can help."

"Why do you assume I'm in trouble?" The fact that Mica was right only irritated me more.

"I'm just saying. If something's wrong, I want to help. You're still my brother."

Pity. Why did she have to be so damned nice about it? The temptation to let it all out, to dump the whole pile of rancid shit onto her shoulders, was almost overwhelming. It bubbled up inside me, pushing its way up my throat, over my tongue, like a bad stew from the back streets of the Warrens.

But that wouldn't be fair. None of this was Mica's fault. *I* had gone to the Wren's broker for information. *I* had made the deal. I couldn't expect Mica to sort it out. My sister was powerful, but this wasn't something that was going to be fixed through raw magical force. And, to be painfully honest, I didn't want to lean on my little sister for help. This was my problem, not hers.

"It's not that," I said. The lie was easier than the truth, particularly when leavened with a measure of honesty. "I've been thinking about your dad." And I had been. It just wasn't the reason I was here. "About how—"

"Don't," she interrupted.

"Yeah." His death had been a wound to me, but it had been worse for her. She had been younger, and he had been her dad. Not that he had ever treated me any different, just that... Well, I didn't blame her for not wanting to talk about it.

"So, tell me about this boyfriend of yours," I said, to change the subject. I had seen his clothes in my sister's private rooms in her house when I had visited her a few weeks back. "Is he a mage? A senator? A merchant?"

The idea of my little sister having a lover still rubbed me up the wrong way. It shouldn't have, but I still thought of her as a kid.

"We're not talking about that, either."

Shit. This was not going to be easy. I had no right to expect it to be, and it was a good warmup for Mother. The Countess was a granite wall in comparison to Mica.

"Fine. We'll talk about me, then. I've been making friends in the Ash Guard."

"Being arrested isn't making friends, Nik."

"Ouch."

We reached the door at the far end of the corridor. Mica drew to a halt. "Just ... don't do anything stupid. Everyone is stressed right now. Too much is on the line."

I shook my head. Power games. I was sick of them. "Trust me. I'm not here to cause trouble." I was here to get out again as soon as possible, preferably with no one taking any particular notice.

"Fine." Mica pushed the door open, and I passed through the wards.

Mother's private quarters were on the eastern side of the palace. Here, the building perched hard on the edge of Horn Hill, where the slope dropped away in a terraced garden. Olive, lemon, and orange trees shaded a stream that fell in a series of miniature waterfalls to disappear beneath the packed city below. When Mother had bought this palace, much of the garden had been houses, but Mother had bought those, too, and torn them down. In such an expensive part of the city, it was a calculated display. I happened to know that it had left her nearly broke, but high mages could always get their hands on more money. Of course, the garden wasn't just about impressing the wealthy and powerful of Agatos. Nothing my mother did had only one motivation. It hadn't made her easy to live with, even before she became the Countess. Alarm wards were woven into the terraces and the trees themselves. Nobody could approach from below without Mother knowing.

You're paranoid, Mother. But then, you didn't last long as a high mage if you weren't.

The room we were in was surprisingly modest. Tapestries hung from the walls, of course, and a thick rug covered most of the floor. Couches and a single chair surrounded a low table. Wide windows looked out over the Royal Highway, past the Grey City, the Erastes River, and the Stacks, to the mountains beyond. I didn't have to unfocus my vision to know that the walls and windows were reinforced by powerful spells. No one was getting in here without Mother's permission.

"Why don't we sit?" Mica said. "Talk."

But not about anything concerned with her. She still wasn't willing to trust me with her personal life, and, Depths, why would she? I had abandoned her here. She'd had to build a life of her own without her brother in it.

She could have come to find you if she'd wanted to.

Goat shit. That was just a way to make me feel better. I had walked out on her without any explanation. She had still been not much more than a kid.

I was an arsehole.

I dismissed the offer of a seat with a shake of my head that was more of a jerk. I couldn't just sit here and wait. Despite the wide windows, this room felt like a prison cell. The door to Mother's private office stood ajar, and beyond it, a closed door led through to her own rooms. The final door, also closed, and sealed with a privacy ward, must be where she was meeting with the representatives of the Yellow Faction.

I couldn't stand still. Abruptly, I strode across the room and pretended to peer at a tapestry hanging from the wall.

"You don't have to wait, you know," I called over my shoulder.

I could sense the uneasiness from Mica. She was no idiot, my sister. "You're not going to do anything stupid?"

"I said I wasn't. What exactly do you think I'm planning right here in middle of Mother's web?"

"I have no idea, Nik. That's what worries me."

I wasn't going to push this any further. If I outright lied, I couldn't help the feeling that she would see through me like a brick through glass. "You can stay if you want. I just thought you'd have things to do, what with you being so important and all that."

Once again, without me intending it, a touch of bitterness slipped into my tone. This whole power system in Agatos – the high mages, the bought-and-sold Senate – was just wrong, and my sister was right in the middle of it. I still couldn't square that with the girl I remembered.

She's not a kid anymore. She's told you that.

"Just don't," she said. "Just ... wait and keep your hands off everything. Mother might not show it, but she's stressed right now."

"The Countess with an emotion. First time for everything."

"Goodbye, Nik. I hope you're serious about this."
Don't fuck me over again. She left that unsaid.

I waited until I heard the door close behind me, then slumped. Depths, this was harder than I had ever imagined. What was I going to do? Ask Mother for a secret she didn't mind me handing over to her greatest rival?

Now that Mica was gone, the silence of the room seemed to close in around me. My heartbeat was too loud and too fast.

I should have asked her to stay. My throat was drying up, tightening.

Here, in this room, this had been where my mother had called me to train. The blessed Countess, too busy to come down to the practice halls, too confident in her own magic to think I could pose any danger to her quarters with my meagre powers.

The memories pressed in, closing around me. My hands clenched involuntarily. Seventeen years old. Here. Back when my mother still believed she could turn me into a high mage, and I had still been willing to believe her.

"Again." My mother. Standing immobile, her face showing no emotion. Me, pulling in power, feeling agony build, tearing at my muscles, my lungs squeezing until I couldn't breathe. Fighting to form the magic and releasing it. Trying to shatter the block of granite suspended in the middle of the room.

Falling to my knees.

"Again." Pulling in magic. Forming. Focusing. Releasing. Blood standing out from my skin like sweat.

"Again."

Pain searing my body.

"Again."

Blackness.

Awaking there, hours later, the block still hanging in the air, my mother waiting. "Again."

I had never shattered that granite block, not in weeks of trying. My mother had, with a contemptuous look.

"You don't try, Mennik. You're lazy."

I stumbled across the room. *No.* I couldn't do this. I couldn't just wait. I spun, looking for anything I could grab. The door to my mother's office was open, just a few inches, as though she had left in a hurry and not pulled it all the way closed. I couldn't see any wards on it. I might not be much of a mage—

(You'll never be anything. You don't try.)

—but if there had been magic there, I would have seen it. As far as I knew, even a high mage couldn't hide magic from another mage.

This was the private part of the palace. The number of people Mother would trust to come in here unaccompanied wouldn't number much beyond Mica and a few other senior mages. Maybe she had left something lying around. If I could grab it, I could get out of here before her meeting was even over. I would never have to face her. She would know I had been here, but her opinion of me was already low enough that she would just think I had lost my nerve. Which I was on the verge of doing anyway.

"What's the worst that can happen?" I muttered, before wishing I hadn't.

Mother's office was pristine. A single, polished, dust-free desk took up a good third of the room. Bookshelves covered most of two walls. A couple of cabinets stood behind the desk, and above them a shelf displayed a couple of old artifacts, which held reservoirs of raw magic. Beside the door I had come through was a detailed map of Agatos. I peered at it. Someone had spent a long time working on this. Every street and alley was marked with painstaking accuracy, and most buildings of any significance were shown, too. Dozens of miniature, coloured flags had been pinned on the map. About half of them were blue, and these were concentrated in the Middle City, the Grey City, and near Dockside. They probably meant something, but I was buggered if I knew what, and I didn't think a bunch of tiny flags were going to impress the Wren.

The bookcases were filled with probably the most boring set of reading materials imaginable. History books, geography texts, biographies of long-dead leaders. Treatises on magic and the gods. I wouldn't claim to be an expert on any of it, but none of them looked particularly unusual. You could find most of them in the university library, and the only ones you wouldn't were because they were too common and uninteresting. I wondered if Mother actually ever read any of them or whether this was all about the show. The only other books on the shelves were what looked like ledgers or accounts.

The cabinets were locked, and so were the desk drawers. Powerful, complex spells had been woven into the fabric of the cabinets. I might be able to break them with enough time, but if I did, Mother would know, and if there was one thing I had learned, it was that playing around with a powerful mage's spells was a recipe for a quick and painful death. Maybe there was something in the desk, but if I was honest with myself, I doubted anything important would be left unprotected.

I swore under my breath. There was still the door to my mother's private rooms. I had never been in there, not even when I had been the heir apparent to her High Magedom. The wards on that door were some of the most powerful I had ever seen, the kind of thing that could tear a legion of mages to tiny, bloody pieces. Mica said she had given me a pass, but had she given me a pass to this? I hovered by the door, fingers twitching.

The sound of another door opening broke my indecision.

I took four quick steps around the desk, into the shadow of the doorway.

Voices came from the outer room, and from where I was standing, I saw three figures emerge, followed by my mother. I shrank back further, although I could hardly hide here from her forever.

The three figures were clearly members of the Senate. Each of them wore the white sash of a senator embroidered with the phrase, *I am Agatos*. Twats. On their sashes were small, yellow circles.

The woman leading the group was older, maybe in her seventies, and was wearing elaborate, folded robes that had been fashionable fifty years ago. The two men who followed her were younger. The first was maybe thirty, with the kind of dark stubble that you could never really shave away and eyes the colour of an oil spill. He was thin and not bad looking if you liked the aesthetic type, but not flamboyant. I had met people like him at the university, the kind of student who went there because they were actually interested in learning and hadn't figured out yet that most of their classmates were only there because that was what people like them did. Maybe I was reading too much into it. Maybe I was projecting. His gaze swept restlessly – almost nervously – around the room. I recognised that look. It was the look of a man who didn't feel he belonged here. I was probably wearing it, too. I resisted the urge to shrink back further. He wouldn't see me as long as I didn't move.

The last of the three moved like a man with a bad back, taking each step as though the floor might give way in front of him. I had felt like that sometimes when Mother was finished with me. The man was probably middle-aged, but he also looked like he had put on several years in only a few hours.

My mother stopped in the doorway to the meeting

room, forcing her visitors to shuffle to a halt and turn awkwardly.

"Think on what I said. Agatos does better when control is imposed."

The woman and the older man nodded to that, and the other man copied them a moment later.

He thinks he's an interloper in the Yellow Faction, too.

Ah, who cared? I wasn't here to get myself involved in the self-centred machinations of politicians. They could keep their games.

With a final, graceful lift of the hand, the Countess dismissed her visitors. No prizes for guessing the real power in this room.

When the Yellow Faction representatives had gone and the door closed firmly behind them, my mother turned towards the office. "You may come out now, Mennik."

Bannaur's leaking balls! Of course I hadn't fooled the blessed Countess. She had probably known I was here the moment I walked in the front door, and she had left me waiting nonetheless. Classy.

I stepped out of the doorway. "Just didn't want your important guests to have to see your embarrassment of a son."

"You are being absurd, Mennik. My status is assured. Neither your presence nor your actions are capable of diminishing it."

"You say the nicest things, Mother." Shit. I wasn't here to exchange jibes. I strode across to the window and looked out.

"Mennik, I am a busy woman. The Wren presses against my interests, and the Senate is uneasy. I do not have time for your foolishness. Why are you here? Do you need money?"

I gritted my teeth. "No." This was a bad idea. It was as much as I could do to stand there when all I wanted to do was leap through the window to escape.

"Then perhaps it is because of the trouble you are in with the Wren?"

"What?" *Fuck!*

"My people saw you taken by his mages."

Had everyone been watching me? *Lying low.* That had been a joke. "And you just let it happen?" I demanded.

"You have made it quite clear that you have no interest in my protection. Unless you are here to become my acolyte once again?"

You could piss that in a bucket. "I don't want to be your fucking acolyte, Mother, and I don't want your money."

"Then what?" She sounded genuinely puzzled.

"Family, Mother. How about family, if you remember what that is? Mica asked me to come back home." That was true in its way. She had asked me to make up with my mother several times and come back into the fold. I had just told her no. "I told her I would come back, but not as your lickspittle and not because I need help. I'm doing fine." And I was, in strictly financial terms. My last job had paid well, and I had hoarded my money mainly by not leaving home.

"In Benyon Field's house." The sneer was palpable even though I wasn't looking at her.

"In my friend's house. Do you know what friends are, Mother?"

"They are weakness!" she snapped. "You have always been weak, Mennik."

I spread my hands.

My mother stifled an indrawn breath. "Very well. If that is what you want. You are still my son. I am busy this evening." I heard her cross to her office. "Return tomorrow at midday. We will talk then."

CHAPTER SIX

I MANAGED TO KEEP MY SHAKES AT BAY ALMOST ALL THE way back to Benny's house, although I was nearly running by the time I reached it. I slammed the door behind me and collapsed onto the couch, where I curled into a ball until my body stopped shaking and my breath finally steadied. When I was able to look up, I realised it was dark. I hadn't even noticed as I strode jerkily through the streets. Benny must already be out doing whatever he was doing. I couldn't hear Sereh in the house, although that was no surprise.

The panic that had closed over me had left me feeling weak and exhausted. I knew I should force myself up to get something to eat or just to drag myself to my room, but I couldn't. The effort felt too over-whelming. I was spent.

Eventually, I must have fallen asleep.

I woke to the sound of the front door opening. For a moment, my body tensed in reaction, ready to ... I didn't know what. Fight? Run? Hide? Whimper? When I saw Benny slip in, I took a breath and sat upright. The first light of morning was just beginning to tint the dark.

"You know you've got a room, right, mate?" Benny said as he eased the door closed behind him. It might be his house, but he always looked like he was robbing it when he came in. He wasn't carrying anything. If he'd stolen anything last night, he had already stashed it.

"Quiet night?" I asked.

He cocked a head. "You really want to know?"

"Fuck, no." I tried to keep out of Benny's business. I winced as I pushed off the couch. I was too long for it, and the middle sagged. My back ached.

"Fancy a bit of breakfast?" Benny said. "I'm making it. That way no one has to get food poisoning."

It was a jibe that normally got a reaction out of me, but I didn't have energy for it this morning. Benny noticed. "You're in a state, aren't you, mate? Your mother?"

I shook my head. "It's not like she tried to kill me or anything. It was just being there, seeing her, you know?"

"Keeps the Wren off your back for a bit longer, though."

"Might be better if he just killed me now."

Benny snorted. "I ain't arguing."

The smell of parsley, lemon, and olive oil as Benny prepared breakfast set my stomach rumbling. I tried to remember the last time I had eaten. Lunch, yesterday, I reckoned, before I had gone to find Mr. Mirian at the funeral. It felt longer.

Talking about Mr. Mirian, it was time I got on with the investigation. My best bet, as Captain Gale had suggested, was to look into this victim, Peyt Jyston Cord. The file she had given me hadn't exactly been forthcoming, but at least I knew where he had lived. If someone or something had used Etta Mirian as a tool to kill this man, then there had to be a reason. There were a thousand ways to kill a person that took less effort and less power than possessing or controlling another human being. You wouldn't throw down that kind of shit unless someone had really pissed you off or you had no other way.

I looked up as Benny laid a plate in front of me. "Fancy helping me break into somewhere?"

He tilted his head. "Why do you need me? I've seen you with your spells." He waved a hand vaguely in the air.

"True." Unless a door had a mage lock, I could get through it. "But it's when I get in that I'm thinking about. I need to find out what this person was trying to hide, the kind of secrets they don't want anyone else to know." If there really was a reason to kill him so violently and publicly, it wouldn't be something he would leave in plain view. "I wouldn't know where to start. You know where people hide stuff."

Benny sat and picked up a slice of flatbread. "So, this is a favour?"

I winced. I trusted Benny, but I was allergic to his favours. The last time I'd had to pay one back, we had all almost been killed. For Benny, a favour was an obligation the gods themselves would have to bow to.

"Yeah. All right."

"Fine. Then let's get on with it, because I've been up all night and I'm knackered."

PEYT JYSTON CORD HAD AN APARTMENT IN A LARGE, whitewashed house on Sester Avenue. Blue shutters opened on the daylight, and honeysuckle had been trained up the wall. The street was a wide boulevard that sloped upwards through the Middle City to the Upper City. Even early, it was busy. Shopkeepers were unfurling bright awnings and opening their shops. A constant stream of well-dressed people flowed up and down the street. Benny and I looked out of place, I was sure, but no one seemed to be paying us any attention. A line of priests from the Sycophants of Oleos, the priesthood of the eel god, snaked through the crowds, banging drums, shouting, and generally pissing everyone off. Trees peeked over the top of a tall wall beside the house.

Taking advantage of the distraction caused by the priests, I pushed open the door and let us into the lobby.

It was smaller inside than I had expected. A door stood ajar on the left, from which I could smell soap and steam. A narrow wooden staircase ran up. The file put Cord's apartment on the second floor. We made our way up.

There were two doors here, on either side of a landing. Stairs led up again.

"Which one?" Benny said.

I shrugged, then leaned across and hammered on the nearest door. A stream of creative swearing answered the knock.

"Probably not that one." I crossed to the other.

A quick inspection showed there were no wards on the door. In a way, that was a shame. Wards would have spoken to magic, and where there was magic, there was normally trouble. Trust me. I had experience with that.

I popped the lock open, leaned on the door, and slipped inside.

However Peyt Jyston Cord had made his money, he had done all right by himself. We found ourselves in a large, comfy sitting room. A window opened on the far side, but the shutters were closed leaving the room in shadow. I crossed to the window, pulled it open, and threw the shutters back to let in the light. The window looked north to the increasingly grand houses. Below, a well-maintained garden was full of lush trees and flowers.

Cord had been killed at about seven-thirty in the morning. It was almost that time of day now. Cord had been on Long Step Avenue, which was no more than ten minutes away. Why hadn't he opened his shutters before he'd left? Unless he had been on his way back home. The report hadn't said which direction he had been going. I wondered if it mattered.

A low couch sat against one wall, a desk in front of another with the chair still pulled out. Cord had liked plants, that much even I could deduce. They were everywhere. Propped on the floor, on shelves and stands, growing up to the ceiling and tumbling down to the floor. No one had watered them recently, though, and they were wilting.

Benny whistled. "This is a bit different, isn't it? What did your girlfriend from the Ash Guard have to say about this bloke?"

"She's not my girlfriend," I said, hearing the irritation in my voice. "She hates my guts." My stomach twisted unexpectedly. *Get over it, Nik! She's never going to think of you that way.*

"Mate, if you rule out everyone who hates your guts, you're going to be single for the rest of your life."

"Nice. No, she didn't have much. Just where he lived, where he came from."

"Dockside you said, right? You don't get a place like this when you're from down that way, not if you're clean."

I shrugged. "Maybe he got lucky."

"Doesn't happen to people like us, mate."

The wall above the desk was covered in large sheets of paper that had been tacked up, layer upon layer. Numbers and symbols had been neatly written in columns and rows. I flicked through the layers and saw only more of the same.

"What's that, then?" Benny said. "Looks like some kind of spell."

I shook my head. "That's not how magic works."

"If you say so. How about a bookkeeper or a clerk? This could be, you know, that kind of stuff."

The breadth of Benny's lack of knowledge always astounded me, so I let him know that. "Anyway," I said, "same as before. He would never get a place like this doing bookkeeping or clerking, not if he was doing legal stuff." But that did raise a possibility. If he had been involved in something dodgy – and this looked dodgy to my eye – then that could be a motive to kill him. "So where would he hide something valuable or secret?"

Benny turned, surveying the room. "People aren't smart. They think they are. They think they've thought of somewhere original to hide things, but they never have. If I were you, I would look in or under plant pots, in drawers, under the bed, loose floorboards, places like that." He scratched at his scraggly whiskers. "You really want to hide something, you put it in the middle of a sack of flour or bag of lentils. No one wants to go emptying that shit out everywhere when they're doing a job. Too messy, too slow."

I wrinkled my nose. "I'm not going rooting through all that."

"Exactly, mate, exactly."

Starting at one side of the room, I began to lift up

pots and poke through leaves. It didn't take me long to find something. At the bottom of a glazed, blue pot holding a fern that was beginning to go brown was a key.

I tossed it over to Benny. "What do you think about this?"

He squinted at it. "Spare door key. Bit daft to hide it, 'cos if you're in here already, you don't need a key. Guess he didn't want any visitors to nick it." He pocketed it. "Keep going."

"We're not here to steal things, Benny."

"You're not. Anyway, he's dead. He doesn't care."

There wasn't anything under or in any other of the pots. I moved to the desk and pulled open the top drawer as Benny opened one of the doors that led off the living room.

"It's nice you're out and about," Benny said as he poked his head around the door. Past him, I saw tiles and a sink. "Things getting back to normal, you know what I mean? Working and all that."

"I suppose."

There wasn't much in the drawer. Some ink and a couple of pens. Rulers. Some small books in which someone had scribbled more lists of numbers and symbols in the same hand as the paper on the wall. If this was some kind of code, there was far more of it than I wanted to look through, and I had no idea as to how to start interpreting it. Anyway, if it had been significant, the City Watch would have grabbed it when they did their half-hearted poking around.

"Wouldn't be a bad place to live," Benny said.

I looked over at him. "You're thinking of moving?"

"Me? Nah. My place is perfect for me and Sereh. It's home, and no one asks too many questions there. Know what I mean?"

"Not really."

I pushed the drawer back in then reached for the next. A hiss from Benny stopped me in place. He held up a finger for silence. A moment later, I heard a footstep outside the door, then someone scratched a key in the lock.

Follow Benny's lead, I told myself. This couldn't be the first time Benny had been walked in on when he was robbing a place.

A moment later, the key was withdrawn, the handle twisted, and the door opened.

The man who came through didn't notice me and Benny until he had closed the door behind him. He froze, shoulders hunching and head ducking. I threw a quick spell at the door, jamming the lock closed. I wasn't having another unexpected visitor run out on me.

"Who the Depths are you?" the man demanded, but he couldn't stop the shiver in his voice.

He was small, with the delicate bones of a bird, but he had clearly put on weight in recent years. His shirt was just a little bit too small around the waist.

I glanced at Benny, but he shrugged. *Your problem.*

"Thanks, Benny," I muttered. I took a step towards the man. He backed against the door. "We're from the

Ash Guard," I said. It wasn't strictly a lie. Captain Gale had told me I should look into the victim, and here I was. These not-strictly-a-lies were becoming a habit.

The man wet his lips with a darting tongue, like a lizard tasting the air.

"Where's your Ash, then?"

Fair question, but I wasn't going to be beaten by a fair question. "Right now, we're just investigating. You'd better hope we don't need our Ash." I made my voice as threatening as I could, and it seemed to work. The man had nervous written right the way through him. I pushed my advantage. "What's your name?"

He glanced at Benny, but he must have realised he wasn't going to get past us. "Porta Sarassan."

"Good," I said. "You've got the idea. That's a Folaric name, isn't it?"

He cleared his throat. "Never been there."

That figured. He had an Agatos accent. Agatos was a port city. People passed through, back and forth, and some settled here, either having run out of funds, looking to make a fortune, or maybe just trying to disappear.

"So, Mr. Sarassan," I said. "What are you doing here?"

He glanced around again, as though just realising where he was. *Nervous.* But was it the normal, healthy nervousness that everyone felt around the Ash Guard, or was he feeling guilty about something? I let my eyes unfocus. The man wasn't attempting to pull in raw magic. Of course, that didn't mean he wasn't a mage, just that if he was, he was keeping quiet.

"I was supposed to meet with Peyt yesterday. He never showed up. I came to check up on him. Where is he?"

"You're a friend?"

"We know each other." That sounded defensive.

"Well enough to have a key."

The man shook his head. "Peyt's always losing his key. I have a spare one."

That would explain the key in the plant pot.

"You didn't knock," Benny said, making the little man jump in surprise. "You just let yourself in."

He shrugged again. Somehow, it made him look more birdlike. "He doesn't mind."

I reckoned I was getting a hang of this interrogating business. As long as your subject was absolutely terrified of you, it wasn't as hard as it looked. I didn't mind leaning on the reputation of the Ash Guard, as long as Captain Gale didn't find out and kick my arse across town.

"I've got bad news for you," I said. "Mr. Cord is dead. He was killed six days ago."

"Killed?" There was no hiding the shock in Sarassan's voice. "How? Why?"

"You don't need to know the how," I said. "The *why*, we're still trying to find out."

Sarassan's breath was coming quicker and shallower. I recognised the signs of impending panic. "Are you going to arrest me?"

That was an odd question. I tilted my head to one side. "Should we?"

"I didn't *kill* him!" His eyes darted around the room again.

"Then probably not." This man was all over the place. I wondered if everyone Captain Gale interrogated was the same. I wondered if *I* had been. "We just want to ask you some questions."

He sucked in some heavy breaths, then nodded.

"How long has it been since you last saw Mr. Cord?"

"Ten days. No, eleven. We went to Dalucia's."

"Tavern on Corbret Street," Benny supplied, and the man nodded.

"We always meet there. It's supposed to be every week, but this week Peyt had something on, so we delayed it, and it was going to be yesterday, and then..." He trailed off, maybe realising he was starting to babble.

"Something?" I queried.

"He didn't say what."

I made a mental note of that. Something had put off Cord's regular meet-up, something private. Something that had got him into trouble?

"You've known him for long?"

Sarassan cleared his throat. "Yeah. Years. Maybe ten. Eleven."

The man looked about thirty. The same age as Cord, according to the file. They had been friends most of their adult lives.

"You must know most things about him. How about his other friends?"

The man's eyes darted to the side again. "No. He didn't really have many friends. He was private, you know."

Goat shit. I could tell a lie when I heard it. I let it sit for now.

"How about his job. This place," – I indicated the large apartment – "this didn't come cheap."

My victim was looking increasingly nervous. "I don't know. We didn't really talk about that kind of stuff. It was just to drink, you know? Complain about the world. That's what we did. That's all. I swear."

Another lie. I remembered Captain Gale once telling me she could ask anyone questions, but she couldn't force them to tell the truth. This guy was so nervous he was lying about everything. But why? I was certain now he wasn't a mage. He hadn't even grabbed for raw magic instinctively when he had panicked.

There was no point pushing him any further. I wasn't getting anything sensible out of him, and I could hardly arrest him.

"All right," I said. "We might want to talk to you again. Don't try to leave the city." I was pretty certain that was what you were meant to say. "Just give me your address, and you can go."

He gnawed at his lower lip. "Balascra Street. Number twenty-five. It's got a blue door."

I kept him pinned for a moment, then nodded and released the spell locking the door. "You can go."

He turned and almost bolted through doorway.

"Leave the key," I called.

Metal clinked on the floorboards, then he was gone, his feet clattering down the stairs like an angry mob was on his tail.

When we heard the front door slam, Benny looked across at me. "You know he was lying, right? About the address?"

"Not the only thing," I said. "Not to worry. He was panicking too much to make up a proper story." I knew that feeling. When everything closed around you, you couldn't be smart. Your thoughts narrowed, your mind tripped. "That address he came up with. It's something familiar. If it's more than a block from where he really lives, I'll eat my hat."

"You don't have a hat."

"I'll eat yours, then."

"Fuck off."

I scratched at one ear. "We still don't know why Cord was murdered."

"We ain't finished searching yet. Come on. I want to poke around some more. Who knows? A place like this, he might have had something worth nicking."

We finished searching the living room. Apart from more of his lists of numbers and symbols, there was nothing noteworthy. There were a couple of books, but they were buried under the everyday debris, and they didn't look well-read.

"Hey," Benny called. "Come and look at this."

He had opened a door to Cord's bedroom. He

stepped through to let me see.

There was a single bed with a chest at the foot of it. The shutters were still closed, but there was enough light to show a small bedside table with a jug of half-evaporated water and some kind of statuette.

Benny crossed to it, picked it up, and carried it to the window. He cracked the shutters, letting in a wash of ocean-tinged air.

The statuette was carved from smooth, black obsidian. It had a roughly human torso and legs, but there the resemblance ended. The head could have come straight from some cruel, deep-sea fish, with needle-sharp teeth, a wide, stretching mouth, and bulging eyes. There was a reason I had never wanted to be a fisherman when this was the kind of thing that came up in their nets. A row of spines arched from just above the eyes, back over the misshapen skull, down to the neck. In place of arms, two masses of tentacles twisted out.

"Looks like you after a bad night," I said.

Benny favoured me with a baleful look. "You're funny, you are. Bleeding side-splitting."

"We'll take it with us," I said. "You never know. It could mean something." Or it could just be something he had picked up in the market to amuse his friends. I did know one thing, though: No one was going to kill him over it.

"It's got some kind of writing on," Benny said, turning it over. Scratches had been etched into the base of the statuette. I might not have noticed them if

Benny hadn't pointed them out, but now he did, I could see they had some kind of structure to them. "Ever seen anything like this?"

"Uh-uh." I had spent a little time studying old languages during my unfortunate year at Agatos University, but I hadn't paid much attention, and I hardly counted as an expert. "I'll take it to the museum. They might recognise it. Now, come on. We've spent too long here."

I opened the lid of the chest and rooted through the folded clothes inside. Three or four spare outfits. Nothing excessive, but all well-made. I lifted out the top shirt. Too small to fit me. I must admit I felt a slight disappointment. I had been in hiding for too long, and I hadn't had much of a chance to get any new clothes. I had sent Benny out for a couple of new shirts, which he had only agreed to because, in his words, I was stinking up the house.

I really had to get out to the market.

"Shit!" Benny exclaimed behind me. The exclamation was followed a moment later by a thud.

I spun, pulling in raw magic from around me, shaping it into a spear, ready to throw at some intruder. But there was no one there. Just Benny staring down at the statuette he had dropped to the floorboards.

"Shit," he repeated.

"Careful. You don't want to break it."

He turned wide eyes towards me. "It moved, mate. It fucking moved!"

I unfocused my eyes. Raw magic drifted like green

mist through the room, but there was nothing else. Not even a trace on the statuette. If something magical had happened, it would have left a residue, and there was nothing.

I nudged it with my toe. "It's just slippery. You dropped it." I knelt down beside it. The stone felt almost slick.

"No, I bloody didn't. It moved. It squirmed in my hands. Like a fish."

I picked it up. It was hard to grip, but it was solid and there was no magic in it. It simply couldn't have moved. No point arguing, though. Benny was as stubborn as I was. I wrapped it in a scarf from the chest, then kept poking through the clothes while Benny grumbled his way to the kitchen.

I was nearly at the bottom of the chest when something slipped from the pocket of a jacket I was shaking. I pushed the remaining clothes aside and ferreted it out.

It was a coin, but not one I recognised. It wasn't old, but it wasn't an Agatos coin. A '5' was stamped into it.

"What do you reckon this is?" I called to Benny, flipping it to him when he stuck his head back through the door.

He caught it easily and held it up. "Gambling chip."

"Gambling?"

"Yeah. I reckon this one's from the games down on Nettar's Wharf. I've seen enough of them around."

Suddenly it all made sense. I slapped the wall. "That's what they are."

"Yeah. I just told you."

"No. The numbers on the wall and in his note-books. It's some kind of gambling system. Odds, predictions, those kinds of things. He was a gambler."

Benny bit his lip. "Gambling means the Wren."

Yeah. Of course it did. The Cepra-damned Wren again. I couldn't get away from him.

"You sure you want to pursue that?" he added.

"No. But it would explain everything, wouldn't it? How Cord could afford this place, for a start. He has a system. He gambles. He wins. But then maybe he goes too far in one of the Wren's games. Cheats, maybe. The Wren's not going to put up with that." And if Mr. Mirian was right that someone had used magic to force his wife to kill Cord and then herself, then the Wren was one of the very mages who could pull it off. Magic like that wasn't easy. Except...

"Doesn't sound like the Wren," Benny said. "If he wants you dealt with, he'll send a bunch of blokes with knives. This seems risky. If your mates in the Ash Guard found out, they'd have him for breakfast. They wouldn't even stop for coffee."

"They're not my mates, Benny. And maybe that's what he did. Maybe he sent Etta Mirian with a knife." It didn't square with what her husband had said, but we didn't always know people the way we thought we did.

"Bit harder to pay someone to cut their own throat afterwards. That's what you said, wasn't it? Cut her own throat. Nice, straight, clean cut."

"Yeah." It was a daft idea. But someone had forced her to do it, and right now, the Wren was the only one I knew of with enough power and a possible motive.

"We should check on the warehouse. See if people know about Cord and if anything went down."

Benny stretched. "Mate, if this has anything – anything – to do with the Wren, you need to run as far away from it as you possibly can. Hand it over to the Ash Guard, dump your client, whatever, and run, not go chasing down dark holes, because you know what's waiting at the end, and it ain't forgiving. You're in enough shit as it is."

But if the Wren *wasn't* involved, I owed Mr. Mirian a real attempt at the truth. *You're not thinking of Mr. Mirian, though, are you? You're thinking of Endir.* Mica's father, the man who had treated me as his own son, until his boat had gone down, and everything had changed for all of us. The two men weren't really alike. Mica's father had been not much more than thirty when he died – I had never known exactly how old – while Mr. Mirian was twenty or thirty years older. They had different builds, different faces. *It's the eyes. Those cool, calm, non-judging eyes.* "Anyway, I'm just going to take quick look, ask a few easy questions. I'm not starting any trouble."

Benny shook his head. "You're on your own with that one, mate. I'm not getting involved with high mages again. I learned my lesson. Time you learned yours."

Yeah. Past time. But I knew I wasn't going to.

CHAPTER SEVEN

IF I HAD BEEN THINKING STRAIGHT, I WOULD HAVE arranged to meet Mr. Mirian somewhere specific: a bar, a coffee house, Depths, even one of the public forums or plazas around the city. But thinking ahead had never been my strong point. I was more inclined to charge off and only later wonder where the fuck I was going. Hey, knowing your faults wasn't the same as fixing them. When Mr. Mirian had said he would come to me at ten o'clock, I had just nodded. My mind had been on other things. I had wanted to do the job and get out of there unnoticed. But what it meant was that he would be coming to Benny's house. And I didn't think of any of that until after Benny had sodded off home.

He was going to be mightily pissed off, particularly if he got woken.

Luckily, I had almost two hours before Mr. Mirian was due, and I had his address from Captain Gale's file.

I could intercept him before he got anywhere near Benny and save myself a painful conversation.

Which meant I had an hour to kill. I was tempted to find a coffee house and tuck up there until time, but suddenly, after weeks of skulking aimlessly, I had too much to do. It was too early to check out the docks. Any gambling operation would be shut down at this time in the morning. And there was no point in pursuing Cord's friend, Porta Sarassan, until I had enough leverage to topple him off his dockside of lies into the stinking harbour of honesty, so to speak.

The statuette we had liberated from Cord's apartment was an uncomfortable weight in my hand. I doubted it had anything to do with his death, but it might fill in some of his background, and background was what I was sorely missing. Whether it was some religious icon, a trophy he had won at the gambling table, or just a piece of art he'd found amusing, the answer would tell me something about him. At least, I assumed that was how you did this job. It probably wouldn't look great if I had to ask Captain Gale for any more hints just yet. She already thought I was an idiot, and not the endearing type.

Agatos Museum stood in the centre of Poet's Corner, a part of Agatos notable neither for the presence of poets nor for being particularly corner-shaped. It was the district where most of the city's theatres, art galleries, and its sole, domineering museum could be found. As it happened, it wasn't far from Peyt Jyston Cord's apartment. I should have plenty of time to show the statuette to one of the curators and still get over to Mr. Mirian's house before he set out.

Despite the claims of the pirate king, Agate Blackspear, to have founded Agatos some four hundred and twenty-six years ago, there had been cities in the mouth of the Erastes Valley for thousands of years, and towns before them. Successive civilisations, religions, and peoples had left their detritus in layers. There were enough forgotten temples, forts, palaces, houses, and fragments of pottery buried beneath the current city to keep museum curators occupied for generations and to fill dozens of galleries.

You would have thought that would have been enough, but this was Agatos, and not content with over two thousand years of rich history, the museum had sent out raiding parties – or expeditions, as they called them – to loot everyone else's artifacts while their backs were turned. As a result, Agatos Museum held the finest collection of cultural artifacts anywhere on the Yttradian Sea, and they weren't about to give them back, no matter how nicely anyone might ask.

If anyone had seen anything like this ugly little critter, it would be the curators.

Perhaps it was the trauma of confronting my mother again the previous evening, or perhaps the Wren's threat to gut my friends, but I felt unsettled and itchy as I made my way through the streets and the increasing crowds. Or maybe I just needed a wash.

The day was growing hot, and there was no noticeable wind. Despite that, I could smell cold ocean air and the heavy, almost-rotting saltiness of wet seaweed. Sweat stood out on my palms and the back of my neck.

"It's not that hot," I muttered, making a middle-aged woman a step ahead of me turn.

"It's not that hot," I repeated louder, then wondered why I'd bothered. She shook her head and turned away again.

It was noisy on the street – the shouts of traders, the complaints of an ox-cart driver trying to manoeuvre through the press, the hungry calls of gulls, the clatter of boxes somewhere ahead, dozens of loud conversations – but somehow I could hear someone whispering, even though I couldn't make out the words.

"You're losing it," I told myself.

I unfocused my eyes to check that I wasn't under some kind of magical attack or surveillance, but other than the raw magic everywhere, the flow of magic beneath the street to the morgue-lamps, and the spark of magic inside every living person, there was nothing.

It was the stress of seeing my mother again, that was all. Trying to ingratiate and infiltrate myself back into her court, a place I had fled for the sake of my own sanity, was sending me spinning out of control. Now I was hearing things, too. I had known this would fuck me up, but I had hoped I would last longer. The sooner I paid my debt and never had to see my mother again, the better.

I had never visited the museum as an adult – not exactly embracing culture in one of the world's greatest cities – but when you grew up in the Warrens, places like this might as well have been on another continent. It was an unspoken rule that you never turned your eyes towards the wealthier parts of the city. Why, after all, drive in the nail, why think about how much better a life others had when you had no chance of attaining it yourself?

Of course, my mother's eyes had been fixed on this part of the city all along, working her way through the Wren's service, consolidating her power and wealth until she could take everything she wanted. Me, I had been a street kid, along with Benny, and our eyes had been fixed firmly on the cobbles and dirt beneath our feet. Sometimes I thought mine still were, however much I told myself I wanted to move on.

In theory, to get into the museum, you needed a ticket for one of the regular tours, and unless you knew the right levers to tug, strings to pull, or pockets to line, getting one of those could take weeks. It was a great way of keeping out the random, unwashed plebs, who couldn't be trusted not to get their dirty fingers on the carefully arranged exhibits or run off with the artifacts. If I'd been wearing my black mage's cloak, I could have strolled right in on the back of my unearned privilege. Luckily, there was more to being a mage than having a stupid cloak.

I waited in the shade of the trees that lined the plaza in front of the museum until I saw a well-dressed couple heading for the entrance, then followed them in.

The interior of the museum was dingy after the brightness of the summer streets. The high, double doors were open, but a large portico shaded the entrance, and although morgue-lamps glowed on the walls and on a row of head-high pedestals, the space was large. I paused just inside the entrance to let my eyes adapt.

The couple in front of me had approached a desk at which an older woman in the uniform of a museum attendant was sitting. I hung back while I watched them show her a pair of tickets before being waved through.

Beyond the desk, two statues of winged lions bracketed the hall and reached almost to the ceiling. I had read about these. They were remnants of a temple that had once peered out to sea. They had been dug from the mud when new warehouses were being built on the docks, long before my time. I had no idea which god they glorified. One dead and long forgotten by most of the citizens of Agatos. There was scarcely a trace of raw magic left in the stone. At the base of one of the statues, half a dozen other visitors were waiting quietly.

This shouldn't be difficult. The spell I was going to use was a variation on the spell I had used to break Benny out of the City Watch headquarters when we had been framed for murder, but this one wouldn't need to be anywhere near as powerful. Which was a good job, because I had needed the help of my overpowered little sister to pull that off, and it had still gone horribly wrong.

I gathered raw magic, shaped it into the spell, strode to the desk, and greeted the attendant with a smile.

She didn't return it. "Ticket."

Lovely. And to think my taxes helped pay for the place. Or I thought they did. I didn't actually know how the museum was funded.

I slapped down a scrap of paper I had picked up outside and let the spell engulf it.

The attendant's gaze slipped away from the paper. She wanted to examine it, I could tell, her sense of duty pushing her towards it, but when she tried, the spell told her there was nothing more tedious and irrelevant. It was an uneven battle. With a grunt, she waved me past. I put the paper back in my pocket and let the spell dissipate. Yeah. How about that? I might not be able to split mountains with my magic, despite my recent attempts to improve it, but if you wanted an old piece of paper vaguely ignored, I was the mage for you.

I joined the other waiting visitors. Now all I had to do was hope that no one realised there were too many of us in the group.

I needed to think through my next move. Cord had been a gambler, and a serious one from the looks of things. Organised gambling was illegal in Agatos, but it wasn't hard to find a game if you went looking, and the Wren made a good chunk of his income through the proceeds. He wouldn't take kindly to it if someone tried to cheat. But Benny was right. When the Wren wanted to send a message, he had less subtle ways. Ways that left what remained of you spread out over a street or pinned to a wall so no one had any doubt as to what happened to people who crossed him. Something like this would be a risk. The Wren might be rich, he might have a small army of crooks, thugs, and mages to back him up, and he might be a high mage himself, but absolutely none of that would help him if the Ash Guard decided he had crossed a line.

But maybe the Wren hadn't been the one Cord had pissed off. Maybe he had cheated someone else. With gambling being illegal, the moment you got involved in it was the moment you started to cross some very rich, very dodgy people who wouldn't think twice about having you killed. The problem was, there weren't many mages who could pull off something like this, and most of them worked for the Wren or for my mother. There were a few who were privately contracted to the wealthiest families or businesses, but they knew the rules, too. There were gods, of course, and other entities that sometimes walked the city streets, but nothing I had seen so far suggested that Cord had encountered, let alone offended, any of them.

Cord's friend, Sarassan, had known more, but whether it was anything relevant, I had no idea. When I looked at it honestly, I didn't have a whole lot more to tell Mr. Mirian than he had brought to me.

The smile, that was what it was. *The smile*. A smile

that had only been reported by witnesses to a brutal murder, people whose reliability was ... suspect, at best. They had all mentioned it, Mr. Mirian had said, and the same thing was reported in Captain Gale's file, but, again, how reliable was that? All it would take was for the first witness to mention a smile, one they might have imagined rather than seen, and then one lazy Watchwoman or -man to ask everyone else if they had seen that smile. Experiencing something traumatic like that left people shocked and suggestible.

I was second-guessing myself already. That wasn't going to help.

Something jabbed the palm of my hand. I jerked away. I had been gripping the statuette too tight. One of the spikes had jutted through the cloth into my hand. I sucked at the drop of blood that welled up.

I could still smell the sea air and faintly hear the sigh of ocean waves on stones. The entrance to the museum must funnel the sound and the air from the bay. Oddly, I couldn't hear any sounds from the docks or the city, just the ocean. Other than that, there was a vast silence in the museum, as though the massive empty spaces and heavy stone were absorbing the sound. Either this was a genius bit of architectural design or a complete accident. Whichever, I bet the architect had charged more. We were high enough here that I could just glimpse the light glittering from the water of the bay like from shattered glass.

"All right, all right, all right," a voice called. "Is this everyone?"

I looked around to see a tall, thin, angular woman striding towards us. There was something vaguely familiar about her. I shrank back into the shadows. The last thing I wanted was to be recognised. There were a handful of people I got along with in Agatos, and a whole lot more who either disliked me, I disliked, or, more usually, both ways around. I tried to remember everyone I had worked with or offended over the years, but the latter category was big, and I couldn't place her. I certainly hadn't met her here before.

"Let's see," the woman craned up, counting heads. She froze as she spotted me. That was the problem with being a head taller than anyone else around; hiding wasn't a reliable option.

"Mennik? Mennik Thorn?"

I shook my head. "Sorry." When all else failed, flat out deny it. I had learned that from Benny.

"You don't remember me?" she said. "Thira Gods-point. We were at university together."

I kept my expression blank. I did remember her now. I wasn't sure I'd ever talked to her one-on-one, but she had been a part of an interchangeable group of privileged and wealthy students who had, in my opinion, been complete bastards, a waste cart of entitlement, condescension, and petty viciousness to anyone who couldn't defend themselves. I had been able to defend myself. Things hadn't ended well.

I had spent most of my time at the university avoiding them, back when I still thought I wanted to stay there. I had quickly discovered the one place they would never be found was the university library, and while I was there, there hadn't been much else to do except read. I had picked up far more in that library than in any of my lectures, and I was now armed with a wealth of useless information about the city and its history. It had only been when I had decided I was wasting my time that I had stopped avoiding them and things had turned bad.

I guess no one had told them not to piss off a mage. The last thing I wanted was a reunion with one of those fuckers.

"You've got the wrong guy," I said, not letting any of my anger enter my voice.

She frowned, squinting. I could see doubt warring with certainty in her eyes. *Don't know what to think, do you?* It was petty, but I enjoyed seeing her try to work out if she had made a mistake or whether I was just snubbing her.

"Shall we get on with the tour, then?" a young man called.

Godspoint shot one last confused glance at me, then gathered herself. "Very well. If you will follow me, we are going to start with our exhibition of Corithian Bronze Age artifacts. The pre-Attanasian Corithian civilisation believed in cremating their dead. The ashes of famous or renowned figures were considered to grant status to those who owned them. You can see the care lavished on the canopic jars."

I followed the group, letting Godspoint's words

drift over me. Her presence had stuck a knife in my plans. I had hoped I could pass off the statuette to whichever curator turned up for the tour, but I had experience with Godspoint and her friends, and I didn't trust her. I would have to find another curator.

Somewhere in the shadows that clung to the ancient exhibits, I heard a faint whispering. My head snapped around, and I squinted into the dark. There was no one there.

Maybe it hadn't been whispering. Maybe it had just been a faint echo of waves. It was hard to say. But surely the sounds of the ocean shouldn't penetrate so far into the building?

If someone was pissing around with me, there were going to be consequences. I unfocused my eyes, looking for magic.

In a place like this, with so many ancient relics and pieces of assorted junk from religious sites, magic was never going to be in short supply. Blessed, cursed, and just generally imbued items were the stock in trade of your average priest. If a god was still living, its influence that was soaked into stone, metal, or relic might heal, protect, or completely fuck up the mind and body of anyone who got too close. If the god was dead, the item might be a potent source of raw magic.

By my estimation, a good half of the items in the museum held traces of the influence of gods, living or dead. I couldn't see anything that looked too potent, though. I doubted the Senate would allow anything particularly dangerous to be put on display, and even if they had, someone would have nicked it by now. Probably one of the high mages, for whom laws were more of a polite suggestion than any form of obligation.

Whatever had caused the whispering wasn't there. Everything I could see was old, static, essentially inactive.

Light flickered in the corner of my eye. I whipped around again.

Nothing.

That had been magic, though. Of a type. I hadn't noticed anyone draw in raw magic, but I still recognised it when I saw it. Another glint of magic appeared in the opposite corner of my other eye, on the far side of the gallery, accompanied by that hushing-whispering. I felt my fingers tighten involuntarily into fists.

Someone or something was definitely screwing around with me. I tried a probe, looking for any mage attempting to hide themselves from detection. I had no illusions that I could pick up a sufficiently powerful magic user, but some chancer trying to intimidate me might slip up.

My probe wobbled and fizzled out.

I was tense, my mind jittery. It was like there was some shadowy presence brushing against my brain, sending shivers through my concentration.

Pull it together, Nik, I told myself. I was under a lot of stress – the Wren, the Countess, this weird murder – but I couldn't afford to let this shit, this inexplicable *dread*, distract me.

There's nothing here. Just some unpredictable old relics

failing, discharging, whatever the fuck it is. Find another curator. Get out of here. Get on with the job. Jobs.

As far as I knew, the museum was one of the few places Benny hadn't tried to rob. He had strange ideas of right and wrong, and as far as he was concerned, the museum was off-limits. Which was ironic, what with most of the contents being stolen from one place or another. We had broken in once when we were kids and Benny was practicing his skills. It was the one time I had been here before. We had snuck in during the night, back when I'd been ten and Benny eleven, trying to evade the guards and dodge the wards set on the doors and windows.

Whoever had protected the building had been lazy, and they hadn't extended the wards to the roof. I had been able to see wards by then, although I hadn't been able to do any magic myself. We hadn't got far. The statues, relics, and strangely mummified figures looming out of the dark had freaked us out, and we had fled.

It wasn't much less disturbing during the day. *A cemetery for a lost time, full of ghosts of forgotten ideas and dead dreams.*

I waited until Godspoint led the group into the next gallery, then I slipped into the shadow of a pillar and waited for them to disappear from sight.

From what I could tell, exhibitions filled most of the ground floor. I wasn't an expert, but I figured there had to be a place where the curators worked on new acquisitions, storing them, repairing them, classifying them, and whatever else they got up to when a stolen piece of someone else's history arrived at their door. It stood to reason that there must be some kind of basement, and it equally well stood to reason that they wouldn't want people like me wandering around down there.

I made my way carefully through the galleries, avoiding Godspoint and her party, until I came across a set of tall, double doors with the words 'Private. No entry.' on them, which I took to be an invitation.

Beyond the doors were a loading bay, which must open from the back of the museum, well-lit stairs leading down, and a large, moveable platform supported by chains, pulleys, and ropes, which I had no intention of trusting.

At the bottom of the stairs, a wide corridor stretched in both directions. I could hear several voices to the right, so I headed the opposite way. In a crowd, someone would feel the need to assert themselves in front of their colleagues and try to throw me out.

It smelled old down here: old air, old stone, old wood, old paper, like a tomb buried beneath the city. There was something stifling and claustrophobic about it, despite the high ceiling, wide corridor, and bright morgue-lamps every few yards.

I pushed open the nearest door, glancing at the name plaque as I stepped through.

An older woman squinted up at me through glasses. Her neatly plaited hair had been curled into a circle on top of her head so she looked like she was wearing a pie.

"May I help you, young man?" she said, laying down the parchment she had been examining on her desk.

"Professor Allantin?"

She pulled off her glasses. "Yes?"

"I found something I hoped you would be interested in." I crossed to her desk without waiting for an invitation and carefully unwrapped the statuette. The stone felt unpleasant underneath my fingers, like oil. I placed it on the desk.

The professor fixed her glasses back into place. "Well. That's an ugly sod of a thing, isn't it?"

"Do you know what it is?"

She shook her head. "I've never seen anything like it." She pulled off her glasses again. "Where did you find it, young man?"

"In the market." Somehow 'I stole it from a dead man' didn't seem like the approach to take. "I thought it looked interesting."

Her tongue clucked against the top of her mouth. "That's the problem with this city. Something like this could be a thousand years old or it could have been made yesterday. If you excavate something without recording where you found it, dating it is going to be impossible." She waved a hand in the general direction of the rest of the basement. "This place is stuffed full of potentially interesting artifacts that are impossible to place because someone thought they might get a few shields for it."

There was an edge of accusation in her voice, and I had to resist the urge to apologise. She was right, though. There were layers of civilisation in the ground, buried and built upon, most of it long forgotten, and like anything that offered a hint of profit, the citizens of Agatos had burrowed into it with an enthusiasm that most other people viewed with distaste. There was an entire industry in excavating artifacts from beneath the city. Every now and then, a deep diver, as they called themselves, would uncover an artifact still soaked in the power of a dead god and make their fortune. Mostly, it was a matter of curios to decorate the shelves of the great and the good, or at least the rich.

"There is this," I said, flipping the statuette onto its side to reveal the scratched writing. I had to quash an intense feeling of reluctance to touch the repulsive little thing again.

Professor Allantin leaned closer. "Oh, this is interesting." Her hand hovered over it, as though to turn it towards the light, but never quite touching it. "It appears to be some kind of proto-Harrakian, but not a branch I'm familiar with." She sucked her teeth. "That would be quite a discovery."

"What's proto-Harrakian?"

"A root language for Harrakian." Which was about as helpful as a smack around the head with an iron bar. At my obvious confusion, she added, "An early language from Harrak. No? Don't they teach you people anything these days?"

"Not many schools in the Warrens," I said. My mother had taught me how to read and write, I'd learned things on the streets that I doubted the professor would want to know, and I'd had that one unfortunate year at the university and in the library, but that was it, and I hadn't come across proto-Harrakian, Harrakian, or Harrak.

She snorted. "Harrak was the coastal areas of what is now Melaru. Proto-Harrakian is the first group of written languages. You can still find traces of them in most modern languages around the Yttradian Sea. I would estimate that about one in ten words you speak every day have proto-Harrakian roots."

None of which told me anything about a motive for murder, unless… "Is it old?"

Professor Allantin tilted her head to one side. "If it's authentic, it could be several thousand years old. Or it could be a copy made last year. Not really my field."

So, it might be valuable. If Cord had stolen it, that would be a motive for murder. Except no one had reclaimed it.

"Can you translate it?"

"Perhaps. Proto-Harrakian languages are closely grouped. I can see similarities just by looking at it."

"And, ah… When?" I asked awkwardly.

"I can't say it would be a priority." She peered closer again. "Although it is a puzzle."

I doubted the text would be a confession to murder

or an accusatory finger pointed at someone behind the whole bloody situation. But the thought of picking up the statuette again and walking out of here sent fingers scratching up my spine. "I'll do you a deal. If you can translate it, you can keep it for the museum. How does that sound?"

She watched it for a moment longer then shook herself. "Very well. Come back at the end of the week. If I've had time, I'll let you know what I've discovered. And now..."

She let the sentence trail away, but I took the hint, and I took a hike.

CHAPTER EIGHT

I WASN'T SUPERSTITIOUS. I *KNEW* THERE WAS A LOT OF freakish, unexplained, deadly shit out there, and from time to time I had come face to face with it. Even so, the museum somehow felt less ominous and oppressive without that weird statuette in my hands.

Too much stress, too little sleep. That was all it was.

I was still glad to leave it behind me.

I had half an hour before I was due to meet Mr. Mirian. I would have time to intercept him. I took a left from the museum, along Cutter's Way, then back down Sester Avenue, past Cord's apartment, to the Mirians' shop on Harbour View Lane.

The file Captain Gale had given me said the Mirians owned a drapers' shop, and it wasn't hard to find. A sign above the shop showed a length of cloth being cut by a pair of too-large scissors. Subtlety wasn't the point, here. The long mourning banners hanging from the apartment above gave the game away, too. The shop was shuttered, but when I peered through the gaps between them, I could see neat stacks of cloth. The Mirians must have lived above the place. Mr. Mirian had lost his wife only days ago, and what with her being a murderer, too, well, I could see why he might not be opening his business any time soon.

I hammered on the door, then stepped back and waited. There was no answer. I peered at the windows above me. There was no sign of movement. Strange. I hammered louder.

Maybe Mr. Mirian hadn't been able to sleep. He was an old man. Old men didn't sleep well. Maybe he had decided to take a slow walk before coming to meet me, a stroll through one of the plazas or along the harbour or to one of the places he and his wife had treasured, to relive memories. Maybe he had gone to visit her grave. I had left it too long to intercept him. I grimaced. Benny was not going to be pleased with me.

Or maybe – maybe – something had happened to him. Maybe, lying there, alone in an apartment he had shared for decades with his wife, it had been too much.

He was hiring me to find out why his wife had murdered someone, that was all, but I couldn't just walk away if something had happened to him, if he had done something.

Idiot.

I cast a quick glance around. No one was paying me any attention, so I approached the door, sprung the lock with a spell, and let myself in.

It was dark and stuffy in the shop, but it was cooler than outside already.

The cloth they sold here looked high quality and expensive. The Mirians would have done well for themselves. At least until Etta Mirian stuck a knife in Peyt Jyston Cord's neck and ended it for all of them.

I pushed aside the curtain at the back of the shop and found a staircase leading up.

"Hello!" I shouted. "Mr. Mirian?"

There was no response. My stomach began to churn as I made my way up the stairs, testing each step to avoid creaks. Instinctively, I checked for magic, but there was none. Why would there be?

Intellectually, I knew there was no reason for this feeling, but try telling that to my taut nerves or my itching skin.

The Mirians' apartment was small, but it was immaculate, clean, and thoughtfully – if datedly – decorated. It was also empty of Mr. Mirian.

The bedroom held a neatly made bed, a couple of wardrobes, a clothes chest, and a dressing table. I couldn't tell whether the bed had been used recently. I wondered if Mr. Mirian had been able to bring himself to sleep there.

The apartment walls were painted in elaborate murals depicting scenes from the ocean and the Erastes Valley, all picked out in strong, if fading, primary colours. It was a style that had largely fallen out of fashion, to be replaced by white walls hung with tapestries, or, in the case of my former, lamented apartment, white walls stained with mould.

There was certainly no sign of foul play nor any hint that Mr. Mirian had done anything to himself, not here, anyway. He had just left early. I might have done the same in his position, rather than hang around an apartment that must seem hollow.

If I hurried, I might still catch him outside Benny's and head off that confrontation.

Except...

Except Mr. Mirian was hiring me to find out why his wife had killed Peyt Jyston Cord. I had been investigating the victim – and that was the right thing to do, because absent insanity on Etta Mirian's part, he had been killed for a reason – but it was only half of the story. Why had *she* killed him? Maybe she had been a handy tool for someone else, but maybe she'd had a motive. I could hardly say that to Mr. Mirian without absolute proof. He wasn't paying me to accuse his wife of being a psychopath. He was convinced of her innocence.

I wasn't going to get a better chance than this to poke around her life.

I sat at the dressing table and began to sort carefully through her things. There was a small portrait of the Mirians together, painted at a happier time. By my guess, it had been done at least ten years ago. Even taking into account a flattering artist's brush, they both looked much younger. Of course, the past few days must have aged Mr. Mirian, and death had laid an ageless mask on Etta Mirian in the morgue.

There was another portrait on the desk that looked much older. The style and the clothes put it at least fifty years old, although I wouldn't have gambled my life on that. The history of art and fashion had never been my areas of study. No, I had chosen the life of a freelance mage, and look at all the wonderful places it had taken me, poking through the debris of a dead woman's life. The glamour of it almost made me feel faint.

The portrait showed a couple with two children, a girl of three or four and a boy who must have been around eight. Looking closer, I could see a resemblance between the woman in the portrait and Etta Mirian. Her mother, then, and her father. And, unless that family was weirder than I had been led to believe, the other child wasn't Mr. Mirian. A brother, then, one I hadn't been told about.

I didn't like secrets.

The rest of the room didn't hold anything of particular interest. Their clothes in the wardrobes and chest were high quality but conservative, the right image for the proprietors of a successful drapers' to project.

The living room was decorated in a similar fashion to the bedroom, neat enough that it looked like no one actually spent any time there. Maybe that was just because I lived like I had been caught in a fight between rival tribes of badgers. Or that was how Benny had put it. Benny would have felt at home in this obsessive tidiness.

I found their papers in a desk, identifying them as citizens of Agatos in good standing, as well as marriage papers dated over thirty years ago, and a stack of coins clumsily hidden in a box in the desk drawer. Benny would have uncovered and made off with them in seconds. That thought made me uncomfortable. I had always known my best friend was a thief, but I had managed not to think about it. I knew Benny didn't steal from the poorest citizens of Agatos – although whether that was out of principle or because they didn't have much worth stealing, I didn't know – but I wondered where the Mirians would have fitted into his scheme. And, yeah, I knew that whenever Benny did rob someone, I was partially complicit. Years ago, I had provided him with a lens that would let him see wards and avoid getting himself fried. It wasn't that I wanted to help him steal anything. I just didn't want him to get killed. I could count my real friends on my middle fingers. I'd been proud of the lens at the time. It was my own design, and it had been a tough challenge. Now I wondered how many people like the Mirians had lost their life savings as a result.

You were protecting your friend. What he did with it isn't your fault.

It was a shit excuse.

The rest of the apartment didn't yield anything. I eyed up the sacks of rice, flour, lentils, and chickpeas in the kitchen, remembering what Benny had said about them being ideal hiding places, but I felt bad enough poking around Mr. Mirian's apartment without trashing his kitchen. Anyway, I doubted the Mirians knew many burglars' tricks.

I headed back downstairs.

People were murdered in this city every week over money, who had it, who didn't, and who would really like to have more of it. The Mirians had run a successful business. Maybe they had pissed someone off, or maybe Cord had pissed off Etta Mirian some-how. Maybe she had snapped.

And smiled while she did it.

I searched under the counter and came up with a thick book. This was more like it. I flipped it open.

The pages were filled with columns of names and numbers. Well, I assumed that was what they were. Whoever had noted down their orders and sales had appalling handwriting. It was hard to reconcile this heart-attack scrawl with the elegant neatness of the apartment above. And the apartment was still neat, days after Etta Mirian's death. I knew very well how quickly an inherently messy person could turn a place into chaos. I knew that because Benny had pointed it out to me a day after I had moved in with him and had followed it with exciting threats as to what would happen if I didn't tidy after myself.

If Mr. Mirian was the neat one, did that mean that Etta Mirian was responsible for the massacre of spiders inside the orders book? It was a leap. Maybe they had both been neat. Maybe Mr. Mirian had a hand tremor when he wrote. It would be easy enough to get him to write something for me to compare.

I flicked through the pages, working backwards and squinting at the text, trying to make it out. There. Three weeks ago. Probably. Was that the name 'Cord'? Or was that an 'L'. 'Load'? Shit. How hard could it be to write a four-letter name? If it was Cord – and it could be – did that mean he had been a customer here? Perhaps they had met. That would change everything.

Or it's one of the several hundred people with the same family name in this city.

I would have to think carefully about approaching Mr. Mirian with this. He would be pissed off at me for poking around his home, but sometimes you had to piss people off. It was better if they weren't the ones paying you.

I glanced around the shop. If there were any more clues, I wasn't seeing them. I slipped out, locking the door behind me.

Now I really was going to be late. I hoped Benny would be understanding.

BENNY WAS NOT UNDERSTANDING.

"Your friend's here," he said as he opened the door. He must have been waiting for me just inside. "Again." I could hear the judgement in his voice.

I had no one to blame for this but myself. I had known Benny would be angry, but somehow that had been … abstract. It was hardly the first time I had done something like this. I got too involved, too obsessed with the problem I was trying to solve. It was only later, like now, that I realised I had crapped on everyone else.

Knowing how you had ballsed everything up didn't mean you were any good at changing things.

"Sorry, mate."

"You know what? Don't." He stepped back from the doorway. He had settled Mr. Mirian on the couch and given him tea, but from where Benny had been waiting, he would have had a clear view of anything Mr. Mirian did. That was the problem with being a thief; you thought everyone else was trying to steal things. Just like being a mage meant you thought some bastard was always about to fuck you up with magic. Which, to be fair, wasn't far from the truth recently.

"Look," I tried again. "I got delayed, and I didn't get a chance to rearrange."

"And you didn't think of sending a message? Like a normal person?"

I hadn't. I should have. Depths, I shouldn't have gone poking around Mr. Mirian's apartment. Yeah, I had found some things out – maybe – but still. I should have thought. Bloody hindsight.

"It won't happen again." I meant it, too. I wasn't planning on any more clients any time soon. I wasn't exactly advertising this gig, and even when I'd been trying to get work, it had hardly been clients by the netful. You would be surprised how few people wanted anything to do with a mage, no matter how serious their problems. I wondered whether my mother, the Wren, and all their acolytes knew how unpopular mages were with ordinary people. I wondered if they cared.

"You're not listening, mate." Benny turned away, towards the stairs. "He's all yours. Take him somewhere. This house is off limits."

I brought Mr. Mirian up to date as we walked to a nearby coffee house – omitting my intrusion into his apartment.

The frontage of the coffee house had been folded back to leave the whole place open to the morning air. A mosaic floor and light blue and white tiles on the walls gave the place a bright and clean feel. We settled at a small table beside a potted tree.

Mr. Mirian's grey eyes fixed on me. "The Watch came to me after the funeral. Something happened in the morgue."

Ah. Yeah. 'Something.' A nice way of describing a pile of bodies knocked from their shelves and scattered across the floor like so many fish in the bottom of a boat.

"There was someone else down there when I went to examine your wife," I said. "I don't know why he was there. He might just have been a thief. But I don't know. We ... ah. I chased him away. Things went a bit..." I let it trail off.

Mr. Mirian nodded slowly. "I told the Watch you had already left. I do not think they will pursue it."

I ... hadn't expected that. I didn't know what to say. I was saved from having to reply by the arrival of a waitress. "What can I get you gentlemen?"

"Just coffee." I glanced across at Mr. Mirian. "Sweetened, I think, and spiced." He looked like he needed it. I wondered if he had slept at all.

"Sure I can't get you anything else? Our breakfast is good."

I shook my head. "We're fine."

She didn't leave straight away. "I don't think I've seen you here before."

I glanced at Mr. Mirian again, but he didn't say anything, and she was obviously speaking to me. I felt ... awkward. I wasn't used to this kind of normal human interaction. Most of the time, someone was trying to escape from me, kidnap me, or kill me. It didn't leave a lot of time for casual chats.

"I guess. I've been staying nearby for a few weeks. Around the corner."

"Then I hope we'll see more of you here." With another smile, she headed back to the serving counter.

Mr. Mirian waited until she had gone, before saying, "She likes you."

"What?" I looked over at the waitress. She was young. No, that wasn't true. She was probably my age. She just didn't look like she got battered and beaten on a daily basis. She caught me looking and smiled again.

"I may be an old man, but I still recognise that look. You should ask her name."

I shook my head. "I don't think so."

"Why? Do you prefer men?"

"It's not that. It's just..." I shrugged. Me and relationships didn't work out too well. It wasn't like I hadn't had them before. But back in my mother's court, it had seemed like the only reason anyone wanted to get close to me was so they could get close to her. And since I had left? I wasn't sure what it was, but something about me didn't say 'relationship material'. Maybe it was the trauma I hadn't even realised I was carrying. Maybe I just didn't seem part of that ordinary world anymore. My world was monsters, magic, and death, at least recently. Either way, those who had been interested had only been interested in a quick tumble, and I had been ... empty.

"None of my business." Mr. Mirian leaned forwards, grey eyes fixed on me. "I pride myself that I am a fairly good judge of men, Mr. Thorn, and I believe I can trust you."

That was a first.

Mr. Mirian tipped his head to one side. "You are not a man accustomed to trust, are you?"

"Hazards of the job." This discussion was making me uncomfortable. I didn't feel like poking my wounds. Better they stayed closed. I changed the subject. "The report from the Watch said that your wife didn't own the knife she used."

He nodded.

"Did they show it to you?"

His eyes flicked to one side. I didn't think he was about to lie. I thought he was trying to look away from the memory. The visceral evidence of his wife's crime must have been shocking. "They did. It was not ours."

Most likely she had picked it up somewhere on the way. But that would mean she had planned the murder, and how did that fit in with her activities that morning? The visit to the bakery? The chat with the proprietor? The only other option I could think of was creation magic. The power to create a knife through magic was, well, let's say I couldn't have done it. The idea that someone out there had both taken control of her mind and conjured a knife from pure magical energy was frightening. Along with the other things that didn't fit, the one thing I could say was that I didn't have a satisfactory explanation for Mr. Mirian yet.

"I don't know for sure that anyone influenced your wife," I said, "but there's enough that's odd about this that I'm willing to keep looking into it."

He smiled. It looked strained, but genuine. "I am grateful." He passed me a pouch across the table. "I hope this will cover your fees. Please. Keep me informed. You understand that I must know the truth, one way or another."

He heaved himself up, as though his body was too heavy. I had to resist the urge to offer him a hand. *He's a client. You have a job. You're not responsible for anything else.*

And I had to treat him like any other client, too,

otherwise I would be doing him a disservice. He wanted the truth, and I would never find it if I avoided anything awkward. *So what if he ends up hating you? You're not being paid to be nice.* Which was a good thing, because nice wasn't my default state.

"I did have one more question."

He paused, hand on the back of his chair.

"Your wife had a brother, is that right?"

He frowned. "How did you know that?"

"The Ash Guard compiled a file on your wife after the murder. I managed to get hold of it."

Again, not a lie. The file just hadn't said anything about a brother. I might not want to spare Mr. Mirian's feelings, but there was no point getting myself fired.

"You're resourceful. Yes, Etta has a brother. His name is Solus Tain."

So why hadn't Mr. Mirian mentioned him? Perhaps this investigation wasn't something the brother approved of.

"Was he at the funeral?" If so, I hadn't been introduced.

Mr. Mirian lowered himself back into his chair. "Solus is the first mate on a trading ship, the *Wavebreaker*. He's not due back into Agatos for another two weeks at least."

"He doesn't know?"

Mr. Mirian shook his head.

"Shit."

"I should tell you, though, before you discover it yourself, Mr. Thorn: Etta and Solus hadn't been on the best terms over the last year. It had been a while since they talked."

I should have stopped poking there. Mr. Mirian was suffering enough. Pushing this further would be unkind. But I hadn't taken this job to be popular, and he said he wanted the truth. The truth always hurt.

"Why?"

"Solus wanted to borrow money. He saw the opportunity to captain his own ship, but he didn't have his own funds. We, ah... We declined to help. He was not pleased."

I sat back, staring across the table at him. "This might have been useful information to know."

"Solus is hundreds of miles away, and he would never hurt Etta."

He might well be hundreds of miles away, but that didn't mean he couldn't have hired someone. I might be the only freelance mage in Agatos, but there were plenty of places around the Yttradian Sea where things were less ... organised than here.

"Do not become distracted, Mr. Thorn."

Yeah. I would be the one to decide what was a distraction. If he thought he could dictate this investigation, he had hired the wrong awkward mage.

"So why did you tell him no?"

Mr. Mirian sighed again. "You are a rat with a scrap of food, are you not, Mr. Thorn?" The lines on his face hung heavy. "You're not going to let this go."

"Not if you want answers."

"It was because this was not the first time. Solus

had borrowed money before to advance himself. Somehow, it had never come to pass. He had found less productive ways to spend the money. You must understand that Etta and I are not wealthy. We would have had to borrow money and use our shop and our home as guarantees. If we had thought it would truly have bought him a ship..." He trailed off.

I found myself nodding along and forced myself to stop. Damn it. Why couldn't I be objective about this man? I didn't trust people, and I didn't expect them to trust me. This ... willingness to believe Mr. Mirian and accept what he said couldn't be healthy, and it wouldn't make this job easier. I had to keep pushing, for his sake as much as anything.

"Your brother-in-law was angry."

"Yes. But he would have got over it. Solus grew restless in port, and he became easy to anger if he was ashore too long. When he sailed, it was like his resentments blew off over the waves. He would not have hurt Etta."

That was the second time he had said that. In my experience, that was never a good sign. Mr. Mirian might dismiss Solus Tain, but I couldn't allow myself to.

When Mr. Mirian had gone, I opened up the pouch he had given me and saw silver shields glinting within.

I was committed now, one way or another.

The waitress watched me as I left. I hurried my pace.

CHAPTER NINE

THERE HAD BEEN A TIME — A LONG TIME — AFTER I HAD
walked out on my mother's court when work had been
easy. There hadn't been a lot of it, and it hadn't paid
well, but it had been easy. Break a curse, spy on a
cheating spouse, find a lost pet, that kind of thing.
Yeah, there had been times when I had hoped for more
interesting, challenging work, but I had been independent, surviving, and the major powers in Agatos either
had no idea I existed or wanted nothing to do with me.

Now look at me. One of the city's high mages had
me hooked on a line and floundering, and the other,
the blessed Countess, was expecting me around for
lunch, as though none of the misery I had endured at
her hands had ever happened.

And, yeah, I knew I was the one who had gone to
her, not the other way around, but none of it would
have happened if it hadn't been for the Countess's
absurd feud with the Wren.

Even to myself, I sounded like a child whining about bedtime, but I couldn't do this so casually. I couldn't just step back in as though the last five years had been no more than an extended tantrum. If I didn't, the Wren would take it out on Benny and Sereh. He wasn't the kind of man who made idle threats.

"Fuck them all," I muttered to myself. "Fuck every one of them."

I would have to go back – that wasn't an option – but I wouldn't do it on my mother's terms, and I wouldn't do it yet.

Childish, a part of my brain said.

Necessary, another part of me responded. When you were already drowning, you couldn't keep on swimming downwards.

Cord's friend, Porta Sarassan, had said that he and Cord met up each week at Dalucia's on Corbret Street. Sarassan had lied about a lot, but he hadn't been lying when he told us about Dalucia's. He had still been in shock – genuine shock – about his friend's death. The lies had come later.

Corbret Street was one of the narrow roads that sloped steeply down to the docks. It was a fair distance from Cord's apartment and from where Sarassan had claimed to live, but according to Captain Gale's file, not far from where Cord had grown up. Old friends returning to familiar ground? I understood that. It had been a long time since I left the Warrens, but it still felt like home. *The Warrens run deep*, they said where I came from. Maybe the same was true for Dockside.

Dalucia's was barely a long leap from the docks themselves, and even this early in the day, it was busy. The crowds of sailors, hawkers, labourers, criminals, and other assorted thugs and hangers-on who haunted the docks had overflowed into the bar like a blocked sewage pipe. At its heart, Agatos was a trading city. It sat on a crossroads between the Lidharan Highway, which carried goods inland to the northern cities, and the shipping route through the Bone Straits to the Folaric Sea. Sailors, traders, and travellers from every part of the Yttradian Sea and beyond spilled onto the docks and into the city. My father must have been one of those travellers, from Tor or Secellia. My mother had never been willing to tell me exactly where he had come from, if she even knew, and in the wealthier parts of the city, my height and my dark skin drew the odd inquisitive glance. Here, I was unremarkable, and that was the way I preferred it.

I shoved through the crowd and slid into a seat at the bar being vacated by a Kendarian sailor, her red-stained hair flopping over her eyes as she stumbled towards the door. The place stank of spilled drinks and sweat, layered with the smell of burning herbs. There were windows, but they were filthy, and the light was dim, which probably helped hide the dirt inside. The bartender – a woman whose near-white Brythanii skin stood out among the tanned and wind-burned faces – made her way over. "Well?"

"I've got some questions." One day that approach would work.

"You're in a tavern, not a library." But not today. "Get a drink or get out."

For years, my local bar had been Dumonoc's, and he liked to greet his customers with a disgusted, "Fuck off!" By contrast, this was positively welcoming.

"I'll take wine. Corithian red, if you've got it." For once, I wasn't broke, and this counted as expenses.

"I've got beer."

I turned my head and surveyed the customers at tables around the room. "They've got wine." I nodded at a group in the corner.

"You're having beer. Take it or leave it."

On second thoughts, this woman might have been taking lessons from Dumonoc after all. Maybe I just had the kind of face people wanted to punch. That would explain a lot.

I smiled. "I'll have the beer." I dropped a couple of pennies on the bar and waited while she poured it. "I still have questions."

"Questions are extra. So are answers. I'm busy."

Let it never be said the people of Agatos weren't friendly to strangers. I pulled out a silver watchman and laid it by my beer, keeping my fingers on it. The bar was crowded. I was elbow-to-elbow with the other patrons, and people were jostling me from behind as they worked their way past. Money had a habit of disappearing in places like these.

"I have a question about a couple of your regulars."

She squinted suspiciously at me. Her eyes weren't the usual pale Brythanii blue. There must be some native Agatos in her past, too. People here mixed. I could attest to that.

"Are you Watch?"

"Do I look like Watch?"

She studied me for a moment. "No."

I felt vaguely insulted. "Peyt Jyston Cord and Porta Sarassan," I said. "You know them?"

"The one who got murdered? You sure you're not Watch?"

"I reckon I would know." I tapped the coin. I had no idea if she believed me, but plausible deniability was as good a currency as the silver coin around here.

"Yeah, I know them. They're here every week with their friends, have been for as long as I can remember. Local boys, or they used to be."

Friends? Sarassan had said he didn't know any of Cord's other friends. Lying shit. "What can you tell me about them?"

She glanced down the bar at the press of customers. I tapped the coin again. She sucked her lips. "Porta sold stuff, I think. Expensive, old stuff, not the kind of thing he would try to shift here, I know that much. Peyt was a gambler. He couldn't help himself. He'd bet on anything. Kept losing when he was first here, but then he started to get good. He took a lot of money off people." She leaned forward, as though sharing a secret, but it was so noisy in here, she almost had to shout to make herself heard. "He was a pain in the fucking neck, if I have to be honest. People got pissed off, and the Watch started sniffing around. I had

134

to threaten to ban him." Organised gambling was illegal in Agatos. If the Watch had found it happening here, they could have shut down the bar. Of course, that fed right into the Wren's hands. He could afford to bribe or threaten the Watch and pull in a fortune from his illegal games. "Reckon that's what got him killed. Pissed off the wrong person. Now, Marron, he's a wrestler up at the arena, although you would never know it from looking at him. Good, I've heard, although he reckons he's the gods' gift. The other one, Calovar, is some kind of lawyer. Quiet compared to the others. None of them are short of a penny or two."

"And it was always those four?" I said.

"Yeah, mostly. I mean, sometimes one of them wouldn't come, but they never had anyone else join them. A tradition, they said."

Which gave me two more people who might know what shady shit Cord had been up to.

Someone stumbled into my back, making me jolt forward on my stool. I glanced back to see who it was, but they had already disappeared into the heaving crowd. When I turned back, my coin was gone, and the bartender was heading down the bar. *Bannaur's rotting balls!* I hadn't finished my questions, and now I was going to have to spring another silver watchman to get more. I sipped my beer as I waited for her to make her way back. The beer was tart and sharp. Even Dumonoc couldn't have done that to a pint of beer. And people paid for this shit? Not that I was going to waste it now I had it. At least it would give me some false courage to face the Countess again. And if I turned up stinking of beer, it would probably piss her off, too, which was a bonus.

My elbow slipped on the bar and my head jerked forwards. *Shit.* This stuff was stronger than I thought. My head was spinning. I pushed myself up on the edge of the bar, then slipped again.

"Hey, easy, easy," a voice said beside me.

I heard a laugh somewhere and a voice call, "This one's had too much!"

I blinked at the beer. I'd only had a few mouthfuls.

Someone took my arm. "It's all right. Let's get you some air."

I pushed myself off my stool, and my legs went from under me. I had to lean on the hands supporting me.

"This way. This way." The hands were confident and strong. Which was a good thing, because by now my vision had gone, too. Then everything spiralled away from me, and I was falling.

The first thing I felt when I awoke was relief.

I had been poisoned – drugged – that was the only explanation, but whoever had done it hadn't meant to kill me. So, what? Rob me? I tried to reach for the pouch of money tucked inside my belt, and that was when I realised the second thing: My hands were tied, and so were my feet.

136

I forced my eyes open. Wherever I was, it was bright. Painfully bright. The smell had changed, too. Now it wasn't the stink of old beer and wine and the sweat of too many people too close. It was rotting food, piss, and rats.

I was in an alley, I was tied up, and some bastard had drugged me. Just put it down to another popular day for everyone's favourite mage-for-hire. There had to be a reason I kept doing this job, but I couldn't quite remember what it was right now.

I was still near the docks. I could hear the shouts of labourers, the crash of cargo on cobbles, the squawks, bellows, and roars of animals being loaded or unloaded. Even if I shouted, no one would hear me, and if they did, no one would come. Not that I could shout. The way my mouth felt, speaking was going to be hard enough. I squeezed my eyes shut and open again, trying to get a good look at my surroundings.

Every time I tried to focus on something, it swirled away from me. I worked moisture into my mouth, but I couldn't get enough to spit the bitter taste from my tongue.

A pair of legs loomed in front of me. Slowly, trying to push down the nausea that the motion brought, I tilted my head back. The man above me was short, with light brown skin and black hair that ended only just above his eyes. I had seen him before. Where? I dragged the memory out of my brain. It felt like I was pulling a leech out of my own arsehole. It hurt, and it didn't want to come, but I wasn't letting go, and it came out anyway.

This man had been at the morgue when I had gone to examine Etta Mirian's body. He had come through the side door, he had seen me, and he had fled. I had thrown magic at him, he had dodged, and, well, the less said about the results of all that the better.

He was still wearing the cloth wrapped like bandages around his limbs under his loose shirt and trousers, but he had added a long robe.

At least he didn't seem to want me dead, which was about as good as this day was going to get.

"Why," I forced out through my dry mouth, "does everyone think they have to kidnap me to talk to me?" I was getting really fed up with that. The next person who tried it was going to get my mage's rod shoved so far up them it would stop them swallowing.

"You won't be able to use your magic," my captor said. His accent was strong, northern, I guessed, but I could understand him well enough.

In my state, I hadn't even thought of magic. What a piteous excuse for a mage. I pulled in raw power from around me and tried to form it into a spell that would cut my ropes and knock this wanker flying into the wall behind him. It spun away before I could get a grip on it. I unfocused my eyes. This wasn't like Ash. Ash killed magic, but there was plenty of raw magic all around me. I just couldn't get hold of it. My mind wouldn't focus.

"What have you done to me?" I demanded.

"It's called ulu-aru. It's a drug. It interferes with that part of your brain that allows you to use magic. Don't worry. It'll wear off."

"Fucking great." I glared up at him. "What do you want?"

He looked nervous, maybe stressed. Worried, definitely. He didn't seem to be able to stay still. Nervous wasn't good. Nervous made people did stupid things.

"What happened to the boy?" he demanded suddenly. "Where is he?"

Maybe my brain was more scrambled than I had realised, but I had no idea what he was talking about. The boy? I didn't know any kids except Sereh, and nothing had happened to her.

"What boy?"

The stranger's face twitched. He shook his head, strode off, spun, and strode back. "Don't pretend you don't know. You were at the morgue. You were at his apartment. I saw you come out."

His apartment? Some boy's apartment? I bloody well hadn't been anywhere like that. Or did he mean Mr. Mirian's? But then wouldn't he have said 'shop'? Cord's apartment? Cord wasn't a boy. He had been a year older than me. Shit. I would need more of that drug if any of this was going to make sense. "I really have no idea what you're talking about."

The man studied my face. His fists clenched and unclenched.

I forced myself to calmness, fighting against the dulling effects of the drug. "I honestly don't know what any of this is about." I forced every scrap of sincerity I could dredge up into my voice.

His eyes stayed fixed on mine. Then he swore in a language I didn't understand, turned, and ran from the alley.

"Hey!" I shouted. "Wait!"

But he was already gone. He hadn't even stopped to untie me.

THERE HAD BEEN A TIME, MAYBE TWENTY YEARS AGO, when the Senate, deciding that the popular name for Agatos – the White City – was, well, just a bit boring, had tried to rebrand it as 'The City of Reason'. They had reckoned without the city's residents, for whom the accusations of reason, rationality, and common sense were a personal affront. I could guarantee that being drugged, kidnapped, tied up, asked questions that you could barely even follow, and then abandoned in an alley, still tied up, wasn't in the top one hundred irrational and irritating things that had happened in Agatos today, and my nervous friend was just following a long tradition of goat shit crazy behaviour. The city's new name had not caught on.

It took me almost half an hour to free myself from the ropes. Stopping every couple of minutes to scare off the rat that seemed to want to eat my face didn't speed things up. By the time I was loose, I was filthy, sweaty, and pissed off to a degree that was doing my headache no favours. I was also very late for my meeting with the Countess. And, yeah, I had intended to turn up late, but I had meant to do it on my own terms, not on the terms of some random lunatic who appeared to be stalking me.

The effects of the drug had finally started to wear off, and my magical powers, such as they were, were returning.

I hoped no one had seen any of this. My reputation didn't need any more dents.

I could have gone home, back to Benny's, and changed, always assuming I could root out anything clean. An extra ten minutes wouldn't make any difference now. But the last thing I wanted was to bow to my mother's requirements. I was giving up enough of myself for this debt of the Wren's. And, yes, I was aware that by rebelling against it, I was letting my mother control me just as much. Stuck between two spears, like a murderer at his execution. In any case, if I did go back to Benny's now, I might not leave again, not until the Wren's enforcers came to drag me out. I wanted to tip my head back and scream at the too-blue sky, to pound the stone wall next to me until my knuckles bled. No. That wasn't true. I wanted to pound the Wren's fucking face, to break his magic and leave him helpless. I wanted to get away from the Countess and everything she represented, like I'd thought I had five years back. I didn't like the version of me I was becoming again, the self-pity, the bitterness, the fear.

You're a mess, Nik. A pissing, screwed up mess.

No. No more self-pity. Get this done, get my debt paid, walk away.

I straightened, brushed what might have been dried fish entrails off my shirt, and marched out of the alley.

IF MY MOTHER HAD BEEN INVITING ME FOR LUNCH, THAT opportunity was well and truly blown. It was almost mid-afternoon by now. In any case, I wasn't sure I would have been able to eat anything. I still felt queasy from the drug I had been fed.

Now that I wasn't tied up in an alley at the mercy of a madman, I could appreciate the possibilities here. Everyone knew Ash killed all nearby magic, but I had never heard of a drug that could stop a mage being able to access their own power. As my captor had proved, that would take away any advantage a mage held. If that started going around, things would change significantly in the city. For hundreds of years, high mages had maintained an approximate balance, under threat of the Ash Guard. If my mother or the Wren got hold of this drug, they could tip the balance catastrophically. I wondered if Captain Gale knew about it. I wondered if I wanted her to.

It wasn't something I had to decide immediately. Depths, would anyone even believe me, or would they just think I had got drunk? If I did tell someone, that would be letting a whole swarm of rats out of the sack, and I wouldn't be able to shove them back in. Right now, as far as I knew, the only people who were aware of this ulu-aru were my kidnapper and me. Better to keep it that way until I figured this out.

I slogged through the afternoon heat towards my mother's palace. I couldn't be more than two or three hours late. It wasn't like she would expect any more of me.

My mother wasn't waiting for me – I hadn't thought that she would be. Cerrean Forge was still on the desk, though. I didn't know what he had done to earn this demotion from a trainer of acolytes to a receptionist, but whatever it was, I had no doubt he deserved it. Right from the beginning, I had known he had wanted me to fail. He had done everything in his power to prove that I wasn't up to my mother's standards. And when I had failed, he hadn't concealed his delight.

I could feel the contempt and suspicion pouring off him like heat from an Ebbtide bonfire. At least I had possessed the dignity to leave. He was still here, a glorified manservant.

Forge led me to a small anteroom and left me there to stew in my own sweat. I noticed him put his own ward on the door. Like I couldn't break it or go through it undetected. It was clumsy work. He had power, but no skill or finesse. I had never noticed that when he had been training me. No wonder he was stuck on the desk.

The blessed Countess herself didn't turn up for another half hour. When she finally arrived, a wave of disapproval and judgement preceded her like a bow wave pushed out in front of a boat. "You are late, Mennik. I clearly instructed you to be here at midday."

Instructed. Fucking instructed. "I do have a job, you know." I managed to sound petulant.

"Grubbing around in other people's business like a sewer rat."

"Right. Because everything is so pure and honourable up here on Horn Hill."

My mother took control of herself with an effort. It was good to see I could still get under her skin. Petty, but good. My mother cultivated an image as the unshakeable Countess, but I knew her better.

"There is such a thing as commitment, Mennik. It is something you have never understood."

"I guess you shouldn't be surprised, then. Now, you wanted me for something?"

She eyed me silently for a few seconds. I met her gaze, even though the effort tightened my chest and left me short of breath.

"I have a job for you," she said eventually.

I was almost grateful. Being pissed off with her was enough to break the tension building inside me. "I don't work for you, Mother, and I have no interest in doing so."

The look of contempt she aimed my way was something I was all too familiar with. "I understand that you take jobs for money. I am hiring you."

My first instinct was to snap back that I chose my own clients, not the other way around. I had to remind myself that I needed to be here. It was easy to forget the Wren's threats when I was face-to-face with my mother, but the man himself wouldn't.

"What do you want me to do?" The sullenness of my response must have convinced her. Neither of us were under any illusions as to the other's opinion of us. I doubted my mother bought my story that I wanted to get all cosy with my family again. I suspected she thought I was desperate, broke, and trying to get protection from the Wren. I could work with that.

"There is a building in the Middle City, not far from Dockside, that I want to buy. I need you to accompany my factor there as she examines it and negotiates the sale."

Fantastic. And I had just hiked up all the way from the docks to get here. I squinted at her suspiciously. "That's it? Why don't you send one of your own mages?"

"They are busy with more important things, and it would not be wise to send one of my mages so close to the Wren's territory right now. It would be seen as a provocation, and it is not yet time to provoke the Wren."

"And sending your own son isn't going to be seen as provocative?"

She waved a dismissive hand. "Everyone expects you to be poking around the disreputable parts of town."

That managed to be both true and insulting at the

same time. "Fine. But if you want me to prioritise this over my other jobs, there's going to be a premium."

"I had no doubt there would be. Please change first. I have a reputation to protect, even if you do not. Someone will show you to your room."

My room? "I don't want a fucking room, Mother. I am not one of your acolytes, and I am not living here."

"And yet somehow I knew you would need somewhere to change. Do not be tiresome, Mennik. I am far too busy."

With that, she was gone, and I was left following one of her servants into the wing of the palace where her junior acolytes had their rooms.

The room I was led to wasn't the same one I had occupied when I had been working for my mother, but it might as well have been. It was small, no more than a bed, a chair and desk, a narrow wardrobe, and a couple of bare shelves. It didn't even have a window. It was a cell, although the cells in the Watch Headquarters were nicer. I had spent years in a room like this, watching the other acolytes move on and be promoted, and feeling my hope ebb away more each time. It didn't say a lot – or rather it said far too much – about my mother's opinion of me as a mage. Well, screw her. I had done all right for myself in these last five years.

At least this had a small washroom and toilet attached, with running water. It felt like conceding defeat to my mother to make use of it, but it beat dragging a bucket of cold water from the well in Benny's shared courtyard or lugging it from the public pipe several blocks away.

There were a couple of outfits in the wardrobe. They weren't what I would have chosen, but they fit. There was a black cloak, but I left it hanging there. Only an idiot would choose to wear a thick, woollen cloak in the midst of an Agatos summer. An idiot or a mage, which was basically the same thing, as far as I was concerned.

I had just finished fastening the shirt when there was a knock on the door.

"On my way," I shouted, just as the door swung open.

I looked up, ready to give some poor sod a piece of my mind, and saw Mica slip in.

"I heard you were back." She looked around the room. "This is nice."

"Fuck off."

"I take it you're not moving in."

"I'd rather have my balls gnawed off by rats in a dark alley."

"That's what makes us all feel so loved."

"Ah, come on." I tried to straighten my shirt. It was too tight across the shoulders. "You know what I mean."

From her expression, she didn't know any such thing, and why should she? I had never really explained it. But she waved her hand, as though brushing a cobweb away from her hair. "That's not what I'm here for. I wanted to invite you around for dinner. If you're serious." She seemed nervous.

I frowned. "What? At your place?"

"Why not?"

I shrugged. "I don't know. I don't often get invited for dinner."

"Do you ever wonder why that might be?" Her tongue flicked over her lips. Definitely nervous. Why? "You could bring a friend."

"What, like Benny?"

"No. Not like Benny. You think Benny would be happy somewhere like my house?"

Benny had probably been in more posh houses than the two of us put together, although admittedly he'd mostly been stealing stuff when he had. I decided not to mention that.

"Bring a woman," Mica continued. "Or, you know, a man, if you want."

"A date?" I stared at her. "What is this? Some kind of high-class fucking dinner party?"

"Nik..."

"Oh. Does this mean I'm going to meet your bloke?"

She winced. "You know what? This was a bad idea. He thought it would be nice. I told him it wouldn't, but he doesn't know you. Depths."

She made to turn away. I held up a hand. "Wait. No. I'll come."

She didn't speak for a moment. Then she said, "You'd better not act like an arsehole. If you kick off, I'll turn you inside out." And she could. Her magical powers were so far above mine, we weren't even looking at the same horizon.

"I won't. Really." I might only be back at Mother's because the Wren had forced me, but I did want to get to know my little sister again.

"Fine. Eight o'clock. Just try... Just try not to, all right?"

CHAPTER TEN

My mother's factor was waiting in the entrance hall as patiently as only someone who worked for my mother could. She was a small, tidy woman carrying a small, tidy set of documents in a leather folder. Her olive skin could have marked her out as an Agatos native, but from the narrowness of her nose and her long fingers, I guessed there was a good amount of Pentathian in her ancestry.

"So, what's this about, then?" I asked as I followed her to a waiting carriage. At least I wouldn't be walking all the way back to the docks.

There weren't many carriages in Agatos, nor many horses to pull them. Space was at a premium, with the city boundaries firmly enforced to stop it spilling over into the valuable farmland to the north. The Erastes Valley stretched about thirty miles inland before the mountains on either side closed in, and while Agatos relied on trade for most of its goods, the Senate, in one of the few sensible decisions it had made over the last couple of hundred years, had put a limit on the city's expansion. This, of course, had the dual benefits of allowing Agatos to supply itself with essentials in the event that it was ever besieged and, at the same time, pushing up the price of land in the city, to the benefit of the already wealthy who, by pure coincidence I was sure, happened to already own great chunks of it. And when the city grew too hot and stifling, as it did in the middle of each summer, the whole lot of them could bugger off to their isolated summer palaces in the foothills at Carn's Break and leave the seething, sweaty hole behind them. My mother, who was now both extraordinarily wealthy and in a position of unhealthy influence in the Senate, was one of the few who could afford to keep horses and carriages. Not that I minded. My ankle had started to flare up from all the hiking around the city.

The factor, who hadn't introduced herself and had only greeted me with a terse, "Come on, then," didn't bother answering.

Right. It was going to be like that. I settled into the carriage and watched through the open window as we clattered down Horn Hill, then took a couple of rights onto the Royal Highway, down towards the docks. I wasn't complaining about the ride, but if my mother wanted this to be inconspicuous, she was going about it the wrong way. Half the city must be watching us.

We finally came to a halt at the end of Syparet Street, not far from Penitent's Ear Market. We had pulled up in front of a shuttered three-storey coffee house that occupied a corner of Sungazer Plaza. I had often passed this place when it had been open, although I had never gone in. It had been one of those places that had set itself up in competition with Nuil's Coffee House, where most of the city's real business deals were made out of sight of anyone who might object on behalf of the various laws and regulations that were being skirted, broken, or simply shat upon. And, like the others, this one had eventually failed, whether because of the location, atmosphere, quality of drinks, or simply because Nuil's was Nuil's. This coffee house had stood empty for the better part of a year.

I stepped out into the small plaza, shading my eyes against the sun. The heat of the day had been building steadily, sunlight reflecting from the whitewashed walls and being absorbed by the flagstones to turn the unshaded plaza into an oven. Even this close to the docks, there was no breeze from the ocean. The high warehouses effectively blocked the cooler air. In the middle of the day, most people rested indoors, but now that it was approaching four o'clock, they were re-emerging. I caught several curious glances shot our way. We weren't in the heart of the Wren's influence, which focused on the docks and the Warrens as well as parts of the Grey City, but we were close enough that I had no doubt he would hear about our presence within minutes. Well, screw it. This was my home, too, and as long as I didn't interfere with any of his dodgy business, I could come and go as I pleased.

I stepped into the old coffee house, unfocusing my vision to look out for magic, but the place was clear. The inside of the building was spacious, with a single open floor and balconies leading to private rooms in a clear imitation of Nuil's. As I scanned the place, a large man in the robes of a merchant hurried out from behind a bar and approached the factor, arms spread wide in greeting.

"Milte! You kept me waiting again."

Milte. Definitely a Pentathian name. I wasn't losing my touch.

"Nonsense," the factor said. "You love it. You'll try to hold it over me, but it won't work, and you already know that." She glanced back at me. "You can wait here. This shouldn't take more than half an hour."

The merchant slapped a hand to his chest. "Only half an hour? You wound me, Milte!"

If she had been my client, I would have insisted on accompanying her to keep her safe against whatever threat my mother imagined, but she was one of the Countess's minions, and her attitude had been pissing me off. If she got herself fucked up, that was her problem. I leant in the doorway, out of the direct sunlight, and watched the people passing through the plaza.

What I didn't understand was why my mother would be interested in a coffee house here. The fact that it had stood empty for almost a year spoke to the fact that business opportunities in this part of town didn't match the expense of the building. And, in any case, the Countess peddled in political influence, not commerce. Unless she was taking advantage of the death of the city's third high mage, Carnelian Silkstar, who had controlled most of the trade passing through Agatos, to expand her operations. Even if she was, there would be far more sensible investments than this. She could hardly mean to run a coffee house. That wasn't my mother's style at all.

Whatever it was, I hoped she was up to something really underhand and dodgy that I could report to the Wren. If I could listen in to the factor and her contact and pick up a conveniently dropped clue, I could be finished with all of this before the day was out.

I couldn't sneak up on them in this place, and they were taking care to keep their voices down, but I was a mage, and a spell to let me eavesdrop didn't need much power. I settled myself more comfortably into the doorway. Almost all spells were constructed from what were known as the Hundred Key Forms, of which there were now a hundred and forty-seven and counting. This particular spell required the use of two key forms: a fine, extruded tendril of magic (known pretentiously as Line of Sight on a Clear Day; no, I didn't come up with the names) and a tension along that tendril (Divided Loyalty) so that it was stretched like a guitar string, ready to capture vibrations in the air. That was the way I saw it, anyway. Another mage might imagine two melodies pulling away from each other. My way made more sense to me, but each to their own.

I stretched the thread into the space behind me, questing for the two of them.

Someone was watching me from across the plaza. I had been concentrating so much on the spell I was creating that I hadn't noticed. The realisation jolted me, and I lost control of my spell. I swore quietly. Maybe I was still suffering from the aftereffects of the ulu-aru drug.

The man watching me wasn't making any secret of it. He had been pushing a barrow of vegetables across the plaza and had stopped dead to stare at me.

And he wasn't the only one. A woman in a doorway was doing the same, and a couple with a young boy sitting on a stone bench in the shade of a building had twisted awkwardly around to fix their gazes on me.

This was like one of those embarrassing dreams where you found yourself standing naked in a crowd. I couldn't stop myself looking down to check I was still wearing trousers.

A couple more people entered the plaza and stopped, eyes turned on me.

All right. This was not normal. People didn't do this. I shifted uneasily in my doorway. There was something going on, and I didn't like it. Every moment, the crowd was growing larger as more people arrived and came to a halt.

Yeah. Not normal. I didn't like being the centre of attention at the best of times.

I unfocused my eyes.

Magic swirled and twisted across the plaza, like a stormy ocean breaking on the rocks. There was no structure to it, certainly none of the Hundred Key Forms shaping it, but it had the people in its grip. The power there staggered me. There were almost no mages in Agatos who could manipulate power like that – certainly I couldn't – and none who would wield it in this way. It was inefficient, unstructured, and utterly overwhelming. And whoever – whatever – was using it had its victims focused on me.

What the Depths had I done?

I thought about gathering in raw magic to defend myself, but what would be the point? I braced myself. *Run.* That was it. Outpace the fuckers. Get to the shelter of the Ash Guard.

A cold wind blew across the plaza, carrying the smell of salt and damp seaweed. Whispers slipped through the air, just beyond my hearing, like almost-heard waves on a beach. Then something seemed to *swallow*, sucking the magic away like it had never existed. Every single person in the plaza tipped their head back and screamed, a piercing, agonised sound that drove through my head. Then they were chatting and walking and laughing like nothing had happened.

"What is all the fucking wet Depths was that?" I muttered. Whatever it was, I wasn't staying around for an encore.

"We're getting out of here," I shouted over my shoulder to my mother's factor.

"A couple of minutes."

"No." I ducked into the darkness. "Now."

She didn't argue.

I KEPT MY EYES UNFOCUSED AS THE CARRIAGE CARRIED US out of the plaza towards the Royal Highway, but the magic didn't return.

It had freaked me out, though, and I was shivering in the heat of the day. That power, so unfocused and chaotic, yet able to take control of everyone in the plaza. I had never seen anything like it before. My hands clenched and unclenched in my lap. All I wanted was to leap up and stride around.

There were powers in Agatos, of course, and not just the high mages, but for the most part they kept themselves to themselves. If they didn't, the Ash Guard soon dealt with them. Whatever – whoever – had seized control of those people wasn't just acting on a whim. Things like that didn't turn on you because they were offended by your sense of fashion. If I had attracted something's notice, it was because I had stuck my nose too far into the wrong place. That was starting to become my speciality.

Something with immense power had taken control of those people. The possibility that Etta Mirian might – *might* – have been controlled, too, by some power hadn't escaped me, but it was only a theory. This could equally well be something to do with the feud between my mother and the Wren. I wouldn't put it past either of them to draw on an unknown power to fuck over the other. Making assumptions wasn't going to help me, particularly when I still had no idea why Etta Mirian had killed Peyt Jyston Cord in the first place. Find that motive, and maybe I would find out whether there was anything supernatural involved there at all.

I rapped on the roof of the carriage. "Let me out!" The driver reined in the horses, and I pushed open the door beside me. "You'll be all right now," I told the factor. "Tell the Countess I'll give her an update tomorrow."

The carriage had only just reached the Royal Highway, but I wanted to head in the opposite direction. I climbed down to the cobbles and stretched, trying to work the tension out of my shoulders and back. I could smell spices frying in a nearby restaurant, feel the heat of the sun beating down on my uncovered head, and hear the murmurs and shouts of the crowds moving up and down the highway. A caravan must have passed this way not too long ago, because I could also smell the fresh shit on the road. It was better than that cold, damp wind that had blown across the plaza and the faint, disturbing whispering in the air. Depths, I didn't even mind being jostled by the impatient crowds.

Porta Sarassan had lied to me when he had said he didn't know any of Cord's other friends. He had lied about where he lived, too, but not well enough. It took practice to be a good liar. That was why I left it to Benny, who could lie to you about your own name and halfway convince you. Balascra Street, Sarassan had said. Number twenty-five, with a blue door. It wasn't true, but it was the kind of detail that you wouldn't know if you weren't familiar with the place, and I didn't think he had made it up.

I headed back west across the Middle City until I reached Balascra Street. It wasn't far from where Cord had lived, and like Cord's, this was a good area of town. Not Upper City-good, but certainly not where a Dockside boy would expect to end up. The houses here were spacious, with walled gardens and heavy doors. The kind of place Benny would find himself at night, redistributing the city's wealth to more worthy if slightly more weaselly-looking citizens.

Number twenty-five had a blue door, like Sarassan had said. I found a coffee house table under an awning from where I could see the door and watch the street, ordered strong coffee, and settled in to wait.

I had been sitting there for an hour and a half and had switched to mint tea after the coffee jitters started to hit when I saw Sarassan trudging up the street. *Got you.* His clothes were rough and dirty for someone who lived in this area, and I wondered if this was where he worked instead. If he was a gardener or street sweeper, that would explain his familiarity with the area.

But no. He continued on a little way, then stopped at the door of a large house, unlocked it, and let himself in. I left money on the table and made my way in pursuit.

The expression on Sarassan's face when he

answered the door was something to cheer up any second-rate mage. His jaw worked soundlessly.

"Mr. Sarassan," I said. "I think you and I have some things to discuss."

I hadn't set out in life to be an unwelcome sight at any door, but life had taken me that way, and at least I had developed a thick skin. As Sarassan's face transformed from shock to horror, I stepped forward with a smile, forcing him back into his house.

"How did you—" he tried, before snapping his mouth closed.

His house was spacious and well-appointed. Wide, flung-open doors led through to a courtyard filled with shading trees. The large foyer we had stepped into had shelves covered with artifacts – stone carvings, tablets with old script on them, idols and statuettes, stained, preserved wood, and fragments broken from ancient buildings. It was an impressive collection, but nothing looked particularly valuable, and when I checked them for magic, most were clean. Only a couple held traces of magical residue, indicating that they might once have been part of a temple to a long-forgotten god.

From further inside the house, I heard the sounds of children playing.

"If you have somewhere private, that might be best." I could be a bastard sometimes, but I wasn't here to upset anyone's kids, and other than lying to me, I had no reason to think that Porta Sarassan had done anything wrong. Until I discovered otherwise, he was just someone with information he didn't want to share, and I was a mage who had no particular right to be here.

"I have an office," Sarassan said. He was so jittery he was almost dancing from foot to foot. Either that or he was desperate for a piss. Too bad. He would have to hold it in like a big boy. "Perhaps?"

I indicated for him to lead the way.

His office was more of the same, except the artifacts on display here were of a higher quality. There were a couple of statues of the now-dead patron goddess of Agatos, Sien, the Lady of Dreams Descending. They were carved from polished obsidian. Like the statuette in Cord's apartment, I couldn't help but think, although there was nothing monstrous about these, even though one had lost an arm. Another figure appeared to be cast from – or at least painted with – gold.

"You're a collector?" I asked.

He slid in behind the desk, putting a barrier between us. He still thought I was Ash Guard, and I clearly intimidated him. It was a shitty thing to do, but I wasn't giving up the advantage.

"I'm a deep diver."

"Ah." That explained the clothes. Agatos was an old city. Even before Agate Blackspear had sailed in at the head of his pirate fleet and claimed the valley for himself, there had been towns and cities here. There were layers upon layers beneath the modern city, new buildings built on top of collapsed old ones, as time or the occasional earthquake sank the remains ever further down. Deep divers were the men and women who squirmed their way into those ruins, searching out valuables from the long-forgotten past. "You've done pretty well."

He shrugged, his hands still clasping and unclasping on the desk. He didn't seem to realise he was doing it.

"So, let's talk about lies," I said. "Because lying to the Ash Guard is never a great idea. You lied about your address. You lied about not knowing Mr. Cord's other friends. That makes me wonder what else you lied about. Maybe you lied when you said you knew nothing about Mr. Cord's murder."

"No!" He gripped the desk. "I didn't know. I really didn't."

I raised an eyebrow.

He let out a puff of breath and glanced around. "Look. I'll tell you the truth. I just... You know how Peyt made his money?"

"Gambling," I said.

He nodded. "I know it's not strictly legal. I thought he might have got into trouble. I've got a family. I didn't want anything to do with it."

I looked around deliberately. "It looks like he wasn't the only one who's done well. You're Dockside boys, right? You and Peyt and Marron and Calovar," I said, naming the other two men the bartender at Dalucia's had mentioned and hoping she had remembered them right. "A gambler who actually wins, a deep diver who makes a fortune, a top wrestler, and a lawyer. Not the usual cast you'd drag off the docks." Sarassan's face had grown increasingly pale as I'd reeled off the facts. I took it to mean I hadn't made any missteps. "You can tell me the truth right now, or we can go down to the Ash Guard fortress and you can answer my questions there." I hoped he didn't call my bluff, because I didn't think Captain Gale would appreciate me turning up with a prisoner and a hopeful expression.

"I said I would." He took a deep breath. "We grew up together, it's true. We were all friends, not really any different to anyone else in Dockside. You know. Getting jobs here and there and drinking it away again?"

I nodded.

He looked embarrassed. "The whole thing was Calovar's idea. We'd all been drinking and complaining, and Calovar said we were so unlucky we should start a club. We all thought it was funny, so we did. We called ourselves the Bad Luck Club, because it seemed like none of us ever got a break. We resented it, you know? Seeing all those wealthy merchants at the port, making their fortune and never sharing it. So, we made a deal. If any of us ever got lucky, we would share whatever we got. It was just one of those things you say when you're drunk. None of us expected anything to come from it." He looked up at me again, an appeal clear on his face. I didn't react. Sometimes silence was the best way to get someone to spill their secrets. People didn't like silence. "But then... But then Peyt got a good win at one of his games, and he shared the winnings. I'll be honest, if he hadn't, none of us would have complained, because it was just one of those things you say when you're drunk. But Peyt took it seriously. The money gave the rest of us a chance, you know? I was the next one. I found a fantastic piece deep down in a collapsed tunnel under the Middle City. It was a carving from a temple to Cepra that had been destroyed over five hundred years ago. The new temple were willing to pay well for it. Then Marron won a couple of fights, and Calovar had been studying and he got his first client. And we kept our word, you know? We shared it."

"And you just kept being lucky?" I wasn't sure I bought that.

He shook his head. "Not all of us, not all the time. But one or the other of us would usually be doing well. It kept us all going. If you're careful, you can do all right that way."

To me it looked like they had done more than all right, but it wasn't completely beyond the realms of possibility. I was going to check the story.

"There was a statuette in Cord's apartment," I said. "Weird thing. Like a person with a fish head and tentacles for arms. Did you find that?"

His hands stilled for a moment on the table. "I thought he would like it. He always thought things like that were funny."

Funny wouldn't have been the word I would have used. "Where?"

He squinted, tilting his head to one side.

"Where did you find it?" I clarified.

"That one? Ah... There's a storm drain – a sewer, really, most of the time – that enters the Erastes River just below the Sour Bridge. You know it?"

"Funnily enough, no." Even if I'd been looking for a hobby, poking around storm drains wouldn't have been my first choice.

"The grating is loose," Sarassan said. "If you're looking for a quick score, a lot of stuff gets washed down from the ruins under the Grey City and caught in a blockage where the roof has partially collapsed. You don't get anything really valuable there, usually, but there's normally something."

"You know what it was?"

He gave me a curious look. "Nothing valuable, as far as I could tell. At least, I couldn't sell it to my usual brokers." I didn't blame them. I wouldn't have bought the freaky thing, either. "There's a lot of junk under there. If Peyt hadn't liked it, I would have probably flogged it at the Penitent's Ear for a couple of hands."

"And you can't tell me what Mr. Cord was into that might have got him killed?"

Sarassan looked nervous again. "No. But when you play in the Wren's games, a lot of bad people get involved, you know? I never wanted the details."

"Fine," I said. "But I'm going to be checking, and if you've lied to me again, it won't go well for you."

I left him there, sitting head in hands at his desk, and let myself out, closing the door on the sounds of the kids.

When you play in the Wren's games, a lot of bad people get involved. Yeah. I did know it. But I was going to have to look for my answers there anyway.

It was too early in the day for illicit gambling, and the Wren's people would have removed any trace of it from the warehouse on Nettar's Wharf. That was more to show willing than because they expected the Watch to raid them. As long as the Wren kept his games private and low-key, everyone could safely pretend to ignore them. You didn't piss off a high mage if you didn't have to, and then only with backup from the Ash Guard. A lesson I should have learned a long time ago.

Talking about the Ash Guard, I reckoned Captain Gale deserved an update. I wasn't quite sure how I had ended up as an unpaid informant for the Guard, but it was worth staying on the captain's good side, not least because she might think twice about executing me next time I did something I shouldn't.

She wasn't at the Ash Guard headquarters, but I left a message for her to meet me, then retreated to Dumonoc's bar in the Grey City, where I hoped no one would think to look for me.

Dumonoc's was a pit, dark, dingy, and unfriendly, but it had been my local for five years, and it had the advantage of usually being deserted. I needed some time to sit and think without being interrupted. There were too many strands floating around right now, and I didn't know which of them were attached to the cloth of my investigation, so to speak, and which were just drifting up my nose and causing irritation.

I headed down the steps and pushed open the door to the grimy interior. There was never much light in Dumonoc's, just a lantern or two over the bar and whatever the patrons brought along themselves. Dumonoc was of the opinion that you didn't need light to drink, and that it was best not to see what you were drinking, which, considering the quality of what he served, was a fair point. I squinted into the dark.

"Oh, this is just fucking great," Dumonoc called, as I descended the last few steps to the floor of the bar. "I thought you were dead." He shook his head in disappointment.

"I missed you, too," I said.

His grunt was not welcoming.

"Just bring me some wine," I said.

"What do I look like? Your pissing servant?"

I dropped some coins on the bar as I passed, then chose a table in the gloom of the corner.

There was too much going on that I didn't understand. Why had Etta Mirian murdered Cord? That was the big question, of course. But everything else spun out from that. Had she known Cord? How much did her brother resent her? Enough to arrange for something to happen to her? Was she the victim and Cord just an unlucky distraction? Or was it the other way around, with Cord the intended target after all and Mirian just in the wrong place at the wrong time? Then there had been the man from the morgue who had drugged me and ranted about a missing boy. A random lunatic? There were plenty enough of them in

Agatos. And what about that magic that had taken control of everyone in the plaza and then made them stare at me? More random shit? I was flailing here, lost and out of my depth, and every time I tried to pull myself out, something new came along and dragged me back down by the legs.

A bottle of wine thumped on the table in front of me. I didn't look up. I could do without Dumonoc's insults right now. But the person standing there didn't move. With a sigh, I tilted my head back.

Squint, the Wren's information broker, who often worked out of Dumonoc's, was squinting down at me. His grin showed the stumps of brown, rotten teeth, the legacy, I was sure, of being the only person who actually drank Dumonoc's wine.

"What do you want?" I said. "I'm not after any more information from you." That was how I had ended up in the Wren's debt in the first place.

"Got a message for you from the Wren."

"How the fuck—? Never mind."

"He wants you to find out why the Countess is interested in that old coffee house."

Was there a free newssheet dedicated to reporting every single thing I did? I really wasn't that interesting. "You can tell him I'm already on it."

"That's nice." Squint's hand hadn't moved off the bottle of wine.

"Why don't you help yourself?" I said.

Squint grinned, and I wished he hadn't. "That's

mighty kind of you." He started to draw out the chair opposite.

"At your own table. I'm not feeling sociable."

His looked aggrieved. "That's hardly news. Give a bloke something he can sell."

I shook my head. "Get lost, Squint."

CHAPTER ELEVEN

It was almost an hour before Captain Meroi Gale arrived at Dumonoc's. She strode in, paused for a moment to survey the bar, then headed for me.

Dumonoc might be brave enough to tell a mage where to go, but even he wasn't going to say anything to Captain Gale. A wise move. I hated to think what might happen to anyone who told her to fuck off.

I watched as she crossed the bar. If I were honest, the need to pass on information wasn't the only reason I had asked to meet with her. She was way out of my class, but I couldn't deny that between the implicit threat of deadly violence, her unwillingness to put up with my goat shit, and the figure that I could see hinted at by her outfit, she did something for me that not many other people did. To put it simply, I fancied her.

There was absolutely nothing to suggest she felt the same way.

"You have something for me?" she said as she sat.

"Can I get you a drink?"

She shook her head.

"Fair enough. You're on duty."

"I've seen his drinks. I value my guts. What have you got? I've been working for fourteen hours."

"Right." So, no small talk this time. "I was doing a job for my mother." Her eyebrows rose, and I inclined my head in acknowledgement. "It was just a job. She was looking to buy a building near the docks, and I was keeping an eye on her factor in case there was, you know, trouble or something."

"Let me guess. There was trouble."

"Yeah. Magic. I don't know where it came from, but it was unbelievably powerful." Understatement. "For a minute, it took control of everyone in the plaza. I can't even comprehend the amount of power you'd need to do that. And it was chaotic. A mage wouldn't use magic like that."

She frowned. "A god, you think? Because we don't need any more gods screwing stuff up right now."

"No. Gods don't use magic. Their power is something completely different." Well, that was the theory. Gods certainly didn't *use* magic, but magic came from dead gods, so it had to be related somehow.

"You're sure? Because it's not always easy to tell."

"I know the difference."

She held up her hands. "All right. So, something else. Any ideas?"

"I wish."

"Fine. Keep an eye out. I'll ask around, see if there

are any other reports. If anything is causing trouble in my city, it's going to wish it had stayed in its cave. Anything else?"

"You don't happen to know anything about a missing boy, do you?" It was a long shot. For all I knew, the guy who had drugged me might just have been a madman. *A madman who had a drug that neutralised mages.*

"A missing boy? That's not really Ash Guard business, unless something magical took him? Otherwise, you should try the Watch. If you haven't pissed them off this week, anyway. But I've got to warn you. Kids go missing in Agatos all the time. Unless they've got someone important on their side, no one does much about it."

Yeah. I knew that. I had grown up in the Warrens. The Watch had no interest in the problems of people like us, not unless our problems were about to become someone else's problems. I considered for a moment making this someone else's problem, kicking up a fuss on Horn Hill or in the Upper City. Except I didn't even know if this was real, and the bastard had drugged me and left me tied in an alley, so I wasn't feeling charitable.

When I didn't respond, Captain Gale nodded and got to her feet. "Keep me updated."

"Wait." I had her here now, and my sister's bloody dinner party was only a couple of hours off. *When are you going to get a better chance? Just do it.*

"Well?"

I worked my mouth. It had suddenly become very dry. "What are you doing later?" It came out as a croak.

She frowned again. "I'm supposed to be off duty. It depends what comes up."

"It's, ah… My sister is having a dinner party."

"You think something is going to happen there?"

Fuck. "No."

She closed her eyes. "Nik, I don't have time for this. I've got a dozen cases that all need my attention, and some day I would like some sleep."

"Right. Yeah. Sorry." I sank down in my seat.

"But if anything happens, you know? Anything real. We'll be there."

I watched her go. *Shit*. That had been humiliating. I could feel my cheeks burning. As the door closed behind her, a laugh sounded from across the bar. "You really fucked that one up, didn't you?" Dumonoc called. "Twat."

Yeah. I really had. "Just bring me some more wine."

I reckoned Dumonoc's poison was what I needed right now.

MICA'S MANSION – AND IT WAS A MANSION, NO MATTER how often she might call it a house – was in the Upper City, on Highstar Plaza, about as far away from our mother's palace as it was possible to be while remaining in the centre of power and influence of Agatos. I had often wondered whether she was deliberately distancing herself from the Countess and what she stood for. It was the one thing that still gave me hope for my little sister.

No one would have been surprised if I had turned up late to this dinner party, or not turned up at all, but I genuinely did want to make an effort. I made sure I was there before eight. When I knocked on the door, a servant – *a servant, for fuck's sake* – let me in. Mica's wards had been lifted around the front door, but not over the rest of the house, and I could see they were poised to come crashing down again. I chose to believe that was perfectly natural mage paranoia rather than a warning to me not to piss about. Which would have been fine, because I didn't intend to. I was on my best behaviour tonight.

The last time I had been here was a few weeks back, and the house had shown the scars of a recent mage battle, as rogue mages working for the wannabe high mage Enne Lowriver had kidnapped Benny's daughter, Sereh, and paid a high price for their stupidity. Mica hadn't been here at the time or there wouldn't have been much but smeared mage across the wall. You didn't piss around with my little sister. Now, there was no sign anything had ever been amiss. Music drifted through a doorway, but the servant led me past into a small receiving room. I had never really understood the point of rooms like this, somewhere just so you could greet people before going somewhere else. You could fit a family in a room like this in the Warrens. Depths, just selling the tapestries on the walls here would feed that same family for a year. It rubbed me up the wrong way.

A lot of things rubbed me up the wrong way.

The door opened again, and Mica joined me. She was dressed elegantly in a purple and gold dress that reached just below her knees. Her hair was done up with gold thread. It was hard to believe she was the same person as the kid who had run and fought barefoot and filthy through the Warrens. I didn't know how she had left all that behind. It was still there in me, dragging on me like an anchor scraping over the seabed and fucking up the coral.

She glanced around, over my shoulder. "You didn't bring anyone."

I shrugged. "Benny was busy. Anyway, he would only have nicked your plates."

"Never mind." She took my arm in hers and guided me over to the door. "There's someone I want you to meet." She let out a heavy breath. I wasn't used to seeing Mica nervous, not when she'd been a kid and not now as a powerful, adult mage. She pushed the door open. "Nik, this is Elestior Goodroad."

The man in the next room was thin, with the hint of dark stubble under his olive skin. And I recognised him.

"You're a senator, aren't you?" I said.

He nodded, frowning. Perhaps he wasn't used to being recognised.

"I saw you up at the Countess's palace. You were part of the Yellow Faction delegation that was meeting my mother." I had been hiding in her office at the time, up to no good, and I didn't think he had spotted me.

"Right." He looked flustered. I could have that effect on some people.

"What were you meeting her about?"

"Nik," Mica said.

"All right." I held up my hands. "None of my business."

The look she shot me had warning all over it. I had promised I would behave myself, and I would, but it was difficult. This was the guy my sister had hooked up with? A senator? A man from a wealthy background, if his surname was anything to go by? Traditional Agatos privilege. I resented people like that, there was no point denying it. He was probably a nice guy, well-meaning and all that, but my sister with someone like him? It almost felt like a betrayal.

And what did you want? Her to stay poor, to stay a little kid worshipping her big brother? I was being an arse-hole, again. I forced a smile onto my face and offered him my hand. "It's good to meet you." *There. See? Not being an arsehole.*

"Why don't we go and eat?" Mica said.

She led the way through to a small dining room that had one wall folded back to open onto a small courtyard. Vines trailed up the courtyard walls, and a lemon tree shaded a pool. There were even fish sweeping slowly through the water. A table stood near the courtyard with three seats. I assumed it had been set for four before I'd arrived alone. Her staff were efficient. *Her staff.* Fuck me. People like us didn't have *staff.*

"Just us?"

Mica bit her lip. "I thought it might be for the best the first time."

Fair enough. If I was going to make a scene – and I wasn't – she'd prefer not to have her friends and colleagues there to see it. Perversely, that felt like a compliment. I mattered to her, still.

So. What the fuck were you supposed to say in situations like this? I had never had trouble talking to Mica before. But five years was like a crevasse that had opened between us. I realised I knew almost nothing about her life now. We had headed in opposite directions, and I didn't know what we had in common anymore.

I was saved from the awkward silence when a second door opened and a servant came in, carrying bowls that he set in front of us. I peered down at mine. It was some kind of soup, watery with … something floating in it. It certainly didn't look like anything I had ever eaten.

"The chef is from Urdahar," Mica's boyfriend said. Elestior; I was going to have to get used to calling him Elestior. For some reason that stuck in my throat. "It's a speciality. It's really good. Try it." He shot a glance at Mica.

I returned my gaze to the soup. The bits floating in it looked like they had once been some kind of sea creature.

"A chef, is it?" I said.

Mica's fist clenched on her spoon. "What? You expected me to cook for you myself? You do know I have a busy job, right?" Elestior raised a placating hand, but my sister ignored him. "Do you always cook for yourself? Because I've heard about your cooking, and you'd be dead if you did."

How had I managed to turn this into a fight already? Best behaviour, my arse. "Benny cooks, or I go out and eat."

"And that's different, is it? If you pay someone in a restaurant to cook for you, it's all right, but if you pay for them in your home, it's wrong?"

I didn't know how this had blown up so quickly. Maybe I wasn't the only one hanging onto resentments. The difference was, Mica had good reason to be angry with me, and what did I have? Fighting with her was the last thing I wanted to do. "I didn't mean anything by it."

"Yeah. You did. You always do. You're so smug about it, like you're somehow better because you stayed poor. Well, you're not."

I had tried. I really had. I had been ready to grit my teeth and play along, but she couldn't leave it. And now I found that neither could I. "Have you forgotten what it's like out there? You're living here in a palace. People in the Warrens don't know where their next meal is coming from, and you're eating..." I gestured at the soup. "Whatever the fuck this is. You could fit twenty or thirty families in this place if you wanted to."

Her face reddened. I hadn't seen her lose her composure since she'd been a child. "And how about the ten thousand families that wouldn't help? What good exactly would it do to sell this palace? The people who pay me are the rich, not the poor."

"It would fill some empty bellies."

"And when it was gone, the rich would still be rich, the poor would still be poor, and nothing would have changed."

"Yeah? Tell that to those who weren't hungry for a day or a week or a month. You've forgotten where you came from."

I would give this to my little sister: She showed remarkable restraint. She could use only a fraction of her power and punch me right through the wall. Instead, she kept her voice tight and controlled. "And you're not seeing the whole canvas. Gestures don't make a difference. This city needs fundamental change, and the only way that we get in a position to make that change is through taking the power we need to do it. *You're* not changing anything. Maybe we will."

I had heard that argument before. Funnily enough, by the time people accrued enough power and wealth to make those changes, they seemed to forget all about of them. It was goat shit. "Sounds like an excuse to stay in your palace."

We stared at each other across the cooling soup, neither of us willing to budge.

Elestior Goodroad cleared his throat. I had almost forgotten he was there. Shit. This was not how I had meant this evening to go. Too late to do anything about that now.

We ate the soup in silence. It was all right. Salty.

I had never been any good at Upper City small talk. I had discovered that at the University. I didn't have the same points of reference, and I had never bothered to discover them. My roots were still firmly in the Warrens and the Grey City. Those were the places and people I understood.

This had been a bad idea. I didn't fit in here. I had a job to do. The sooner I got it done, the better for all of us.

"The Countess had me escorting her factor to an old coffee house near the docks," I said. "Why is she interested in buying property down there?"

Mica and Goodroad exchanged a glance. So he knew, too? Was this something to do with his faction in the Senate? What would they want with an old building, and why would it have anything to do with the Countess? The fuckers were up to something. The Wren was right about that.

"If Mother wants you to know, she'll tell you," Mica said. "I'm sorry, Nik." She actually sounded sorry. It didn't help, though.

The rest of the meal passed in awkward silence, and I thought everyone was relieved when I excused myself and left.

Night had fallen over Agatos, and a buffeting wind had picked up off the bay. In the last horizon glow, I could see heavy, deep storm clouds gathering over the ocean. Summer storms weren't unusual over the Yttradian Sea, but this looked like a big one, and not for the first time, I was glad not to be a sailor. Mica's dad had taken me out fishing a few times, running the boat down the stony shore of Fishertown, on the eastern side of the Erastes River, and out through the harbour. Although I had loved the thrill of just him and me working together, away from everyone else, it hadn't been for me. It wasn't just the seasickness. I had never been able to get past the seething depths beneath us on which the boat seemed perched so precariously.

For once I wasn't hungry, although something in the meal hadn't agreed with my stomach. Probably whatever had been floating around in that soup. The whole event might have been a disaster, but at least I had got one thing out of it: I knew my mother was trying to keep the nature of her interest in the old coffee house secret from me, and that meant it was a secret worth stealing.

It was something that could wait, though. The Wren could hardly accuse me of not trying, and I wasn't even sure what I was looking for yet.

So far, all the evidence about Cord's death pointed to it having something to do with his gambling. For all I knew, he had gambled his life with some murderous supernatural entity and lost. People had done stupider things.

Mica's house was a fair hike from the docks where the Wren ran his games, but the city was still busy. The streets were crowded and noisy, and nothing so blatantly illegal would be running yet. It was polite to pretend that the law breaking wasn't going on by waiting until the dark had fully closed in and the streets had thinned. It was a game the city played: the Wren could ply his illegal trade as long as he kept it to the poorer parts of town and didn't make it too obvious. The city wouldn't push too hard to stop him – being a high mage had its privileges – and he would keep crime to acceptable levels, so the Ash Guard didn't feel like they had to get involved.

Sarassan had said he'd found the freakish statuette in a storm drain beneath the Sour Bridge. The tide was low, so I should be able to get to the outlet. I might not be a professional investigator like Captain Gale, but I had tracked down my fair share of missing pets and cheating spouses, and I had my instincts. They told me there was something really off about that statuette. The curator at the museum hadn't known what to make of it, either. Ancient writing, an unknown figure. Yeah. That was the kind of trouble I couldn't keep out of. It would nag at me, otherwise, and with that storm coming in, any evidence that might be trapped down there could be washed away. I wished I had asked Sarassan when he had found it. If it was years ago, this whole thing would be a waste of time. Still, other than half an hour of my evening and the potential for having to wade through several feet of 'mud' on the riverbank, I had nothing to lose. It was almost on my way.

The route to the Sour Bridge took me through the

Grey City, not far from my old apartment on Feldspar Plaza and only a well-deserved stone's throw from Dumonoc's miserable hole of a bar.

There were no morgue-lamps on the streets of the Grey City, and most houses had shuttered in anticipation of the approaching storm, so little light spilled onto the streets. The Erastes River below the Sour Bridge was black and rippled like oil. It wasn't enough to hide the crap flowing down towards the sea.

Worn steps led down to the river, and a strip of gravelly mud, exposed by the low tide, bordered the water. Further down, near Beggar's Wharf, where the Wren had tried to dump my unconscious body, a couple of ragged figures picked through the debris left behind by the river and the waste carts.

The wind, which at first had been a relief after the heavy heat of the day, now sent cold shoals of air over my skin and made me shiver. I pulled my shirt tighter and for once regretted not wearing my thick mage's cloak. Over the Erastes Bay, lightning stabbed down. Most of the time, ocean storms didn't reach land, sheltered as Agatos was between high mountain peaks, but I reckoned this one was determinedly heading for us, like a landlord chasing an overdue rent.

Time to get this over with. I picked my way down the steps and along the strip of mud. Despite my best efforts, it squelched and sank beneath my feet, and I felt the water – we were going to call it water – seep through my shoes.

The storm drain emerged beneath the shadow of

the Sour Bridge. I could hear the sounds of people crossing the bridge above me – snatches of laughter and conversation – but down here the sounds were strangely muted. The brush of the river provided a quieting undertone.

The storm drain itself was a tunnel maybe six feet high, blocked by an iron grate. Stains on the tunnel walls showed that water reached almost to the ceiling at times, but right now it was dry. Debris had been washed up against the grate, but anything interesting there would have been picked clean, and if there was to be any hint as to where Cord's weird statuette had come from, it would be deeper in.

The grate had once been closed by a lock, but the bolt was loose, and it was easy to shift free. I had to duck to fit inside.

A damp, rotting smell permeated the tunnel, like something dead washed up in a storm, even though it had been days since it had rained. Sarassan had said this was sometimes a sewer. It didn't encourage me to explore further, but I was short on clues. *No one ever promised being a freelance mage would be fun.*

What little light had illuminated the river didn't make it far into the tunnel. The blackness seemed to swallow everything just a few feet in front of me. There was no way I was going in there like that. Even if I didn't fall down some unexpected hole, I couldn't shake the idea of something reaching out of the darkness to slide its tentacles over me or tear out my eyes.

Having an imagination was a terrible thing.

I took a couple of breaths to calm myself, then conjured a mage light and sent it drifting into the dark. The tunnel continued ahead of me, sloping gently up and splitting maybe fifty yards ahead. Smaller pipes opened on the walls and ceiling.

Sarassan had said there was a place where the roof had partially collapsed that collected things washed down from the ruins under the Grey City, but I couldn't see it from here. *Further in, then.* Unless the fucker had been lying to me and he just wanted me to get lost under the city.

No. That would be stupid. You didn't mess around with the Ash Guard in that way, nor with the city's mages.

I heaved another breath, then started my way along the tunnel. I wasn't particularly scared of tight spaces, but already I could hear the first drops of rain hitting the river, and this would not be the place to get caught in a storm.

Just to the junction. The storm drain wouldn't fill so quickly. It would take time for the rain to fill the streets, rush into the gutters, and then into the pipes and hollows beneath the city.

Hunched over to protect my head from the uneven ceiling, I continued on.

Somewhere, the tunnels must lead into the layers of ruins beneath the modern city, if artifacts were washed from those ruins into the storm drain. Another collapse, deep underground.

At the junction, one tunnel split off heading

roughly north, while the other continued on, sloping upwards before reaching what looked like a dry weir. The northern branch seemed older. Only a dozen feet along, the roof had fallen in, as Sarassan had said, forming a rough barrier that almost reached the height of the tunnel. Beyond it, the tunnel had crumbled further, walls slumping in, revealing rock, stone, and cavities beyond. That statuette could have come from anywhere back there. I was never going to be able to search through all that, and if there was anything interesting or odd about it, Professor Allantin could work it out. I pushed the mage light further past the roof fall. If I wanted to keep going, I would have to drop to a crawl.

As if in response, a cold wind breathed down the tunnel, bringing with it the smell of damp and rot. The sound of the air moving over the rubble seemed to suggest whispered, incomprehensible voices. Above me, a pipe began to drip water into the tunnel. The storm had reached the city above. It was time to get out of here.

CHAPTER TWELVE

OVER THE CENTURIES, AS THE CITIES TO THE NORTH AND around the Folaric Sea had grown, so had the importance of Agatos as a port. To pass through the Bone Straits to the Folaric Sea, ships would have to wait in the Erastes Bay or Agatos Port for a favourable wind, and the Lidharan Highway leading north began as the Royal Highway in the city. Agatos had become a place to trade, to lay over, to restock, or to arrange passage. Inconveniences such as homes, fishing huts, and fish markets had been swept away to make space for deeper docks and increasingly large warehouses. Only Fishertown, where the harbour was too shallow and where the seabed was solid rock, remained, and I reckoned it might not for long. A mage like the Countess or Mica would eventually be called in to turn their powers on that seabed and scrape it away. It would be difficult and expensive, but nothing in Agatos was allowed to get in the way of the determined acquisition of wealth for the few at the expense of the many. For now, a series of wharfs had been constructed jutting out into the harbour, each long enough to dock half a dozen ships on each side and wide enough to hold further warehouses. Most of these warehouses had been under the control of Carnelian Silkstar until his unexpected and extremely bloody death. His heirs, no doubt, still clung onto them, but not for much longer. None of them were high mages, and the protections that Carnelian Silkstar had offered to shipping and caravans to maintain his near-monopoly were gone.

Nettar's Wharf was one of the shorter wharfs, and being closer to the Warrens than most, was less patrolled by the Watch. I didn't know if the Wren owned the warehouses here, but the area was certainly under his control. By the time I reached the docks, the rain was hammering down like stones thrown from a rooftop at passers-by – a popular entertainment in some parts of the city. I had resorted to a magical shield held over my head to keep off the worst of the weather, but I could see heavier curtains of rain sweeping over the bullish waves further out in the bay, and if they hit here, my shield was going to be useless. Wind blustered between the tall warehouses, sending sprays of water onto my clothes, soaking them.

Nope. The shield wasn't going to help. I let it drop and felt the rain pound onto my hair and drip down my face. On second thoughts, I should have left the shield up. The true storm hadn't come in yet, but this was more than wet enough for my liking. I shielded my face with a hand and peered around the corner of a warehouse to the wharf.

The docks themselves were often still busy at this time of night, with crews from the ships out looking for entertainment, but the rain had driven most of them into shelter. The bars and taverns would be packed, while the wharf stood empty.

Nettar's Wharf was a long, solid blade piercing the waters of the harbour. The tide was still low, and the long harbour walls blocked most of the power of the waves, but even so, the ships rocked against the quay-side and wind sent strange harmonics whistling through the lines. The whitewashed warehouses that ran the length of the wharf loomed ghostly through the rain.

At least the rain had washed away the stink of the city. If it rained hard enough, it would wash away the refuse, too, and for a few hours at least would leave Agatos as the White City it claimed to be.

I pushed away from the half-hearted shelter of the warehouse and hurried across the docks to Nettar's Wharf, ducking my head against the weather. Salt spray and rain lashed across my face. Waves pounded on the harbour wall and on the Dragon's Jaw, the rocky spit of land that jutted from the east, enclosing half the harbour. One advantage of the foul weather was that nobody would be watching too closely. Even if they were, I would just be another dark shape in the growing storm.

Maybe I should have done more research, found

out exactly what the deal was with this gambling den. Squint would have told me for a price, and Mr. Mirian had given me enough funds.

Bollocks. I was just being a coward, as usual. Put off everything and then maybe you would never have to face up to anything. If I had asked Squint, word would have got back to the Wren, and he wouldn't have let me within a hundred yards of his set-up.

I licked my lips nervously, tasting the sea water with its slight seasoning of trash and sewage. All I had to do was walk up to the door, hammer on it, and get in. They would let me place a bet. Places like this weren't fussy. If you had money to lose, you were in.

Rain ran down the side of my nose, into the corner of my mouth. All I was achieving out here was getting soaked. I straightened my shoulders.

A hand closed on my arm. I shrieked like a pig stuck in a pipe and spun around.

Sereh was standing so close she could have pick-pocketed my intestines. "Dad isn't very happy with you, Uncle Nik."

"Denna's Mercy!" My heart collapsed back inside my chest. "Where did you come from? Are you trying to kill me?"

The whites of her eyes looked like sharpened shards of metal in the dark. "If I was trying to kill you, you would be dead. I've been following you. It wasn't difficult. You didn't even look around. There was someone else following you, too, but he went away."

There was something about the way that Sereh

said even the simplest things that made my whole body shiver. "What do you mean he went away? You didn't kill him, did you?"

Her head tipped to one side. "Should I have?"

"Fuck. No! Sorry."

"He turned away when you came out onto the wharf. He probably thought it would be difficult to follow you in the open. He must not know what he's doing."

"Right. Right." The strumming along my nerves was finally starting to slow. "What are you doing here, Sereh?"

"I told you." Somehow, the whites of her eyes had become even sharper. Could you cut someone with just your eyes? "My dad isn't happy with you. I don't like it when my dad isn't happy."

Lady of the Grove. Now my heart was going again. Sereh liked me. I had known her since before she could walk. I was almost family. But there was a chasm wide enough to swallow a city in that 'almost'. If she thought I was a genuine threat to Benny, she would have me dead on the cobbles before I could explain.

"I'll make it up to him. I promise." *Please don't knife me and dump me in the harbour.*

"Good." A smile lit up her face. "I like it when you and Dad get on. So, what are we doing here?"

The sudden change left me dizzy. "Um. Well. The Wren runs a gambling den around here. I was going to take a look."

She frowned. "You're not going to gamble, are you? Dad says that people who gamble are stupid."

For someone who was about to knife me a moment ago, she was damned judgemental. Well, I might be stupid, but I wasn't that kind of stupid. No one won at the Wren's games, not for long. No one except Peyt Jyston Cord, I supposed, and he was dead. "I'm just looking for some information."

"All right." She started off along the wharf. "Don't worry. I'll keep you safe." Safe from anyone but her. "Dad would be sad if you died. I don't like it when he's sad."

The warehouse stretched almost the entire length of the wharf. There was nothing to indicate exactly where the games took place, but I reckoned no one would want to walk to the far end just to find the way in, and one door was as good as another.

There were ships tied up here, but if anyone was on watch, they were hunkered down out of the storm. The slapping of lines, the creak of timber against the dock fenders, the rain on the cobbles, and the wind around the masts of ships and eaves of the warehouse conspired to hide any sounds we might be making.

I leaned against the large warehouse doors and pounded on them. With my ear pressed against the wood, I could hear the sound boom around the warehouse, but no other noise from inside. Was there a code I was supposed to know, a sequence of knocks or words shouted through the wood? Research, see? It wouldn't have been a bad idea after all.

I unfocused my eyes. Simple wards saturated the building. Nothing that was hard to break, and no mage locks on the door. Someone breaking in would do no more than set off an alarm somewhere. But why would you have wards up on a building that was full of people anyway? It was asking for trouble, unless you had a mage giving each of them a pass, and that sounded like a waste of resources.

I glanced at Sereh. "Ready?"

She didn't react, so I took it as a yes. Gently, I extended magic, eased the wards apart, and sprang the lock. These wards weren't designed to keep a mage out, even one as underpowered as me. And why had the door been locked, anyway?

I let Sereh slip through. Her preternatural ability to disappear into the shadows would mean that no one would see her if she didn't want them to.

A moment later, her voice drifted out. "There's no one here, Uncle Nik."

Keeping my eyes unfocused to watch out for magic, I followed her in, trying not to trip over anything.

The warehouse was packed high with cargo – boxes, crates, sacks, barrels – and a large, open space had been left, only just behind a wall of crates, but Sereh was right. There was no one here.

I swore. This place had been used by large groups of people. The flagstones were scuffed and stained. I could see footprints and marks where tables had been dragged. But there was certainly no gambling going on tonight.

The game must have been moved. When Cord was murdered, maybe on his way back from such a game, the Wren must have known someone might come poking around, and he had shifted his whole operation elsewhere.

This was a metaphorical kick in the balls I didn't need.

Inside, I could still hear the rain beating on the roof and the wind chasing around the docks, but it was oddly muted in the large space. It was dry in here, too. The wettest things were me and the flagstone I was dripping onto. I could see the magic being used to keep the place dry, the better to preserve the cargo stocked here, I supposed, but I could still smell damp and a foul, rotting odour, and the sea. Did the sewers run under the wharfs? It wasn't something I had ever bothered to find out. Maybe the smell just came from the harbour and had lingered here even after the storm had blown it away from outside.

"Someone's here, Uncle Nik," Sereh whispered from beside my elbow. I clenched my fist and my jaw to stop myself cursing out loud. How in the sodden Depths did she keep doing that?

"I thought you said there was no one?"

"There wasn't. Now there is."

How? I hadn't heard a door opening, and I would have heard the storm outside if it had. "You sure?"

Her head cocked to one side. "Some*thing*."

For fuck's sake. Was she trying to creep me out?

Cold, damp, stale air washed over me, bringing

with it the smell of the deep ocean and of rot. I just had time to wonder how the wind was blowing inside the warehouse when the light I had conjured went out as easily as a candle in a hurricane and we were dropped into near darkness. Lightning stuttered fragments of light around the doors and through gaps in the eaves.

Now I could hear what Sereh had heard, too. Something shuffling, *wet*, moving towards us through the warehouse. Terror swept over me. It hit me in my stomach and like nails in my spine, in my head, driving thought away like a shack caught in a tidal wave. Before I knew it, I was scrambling back and Sereh was moving with me, almost falling in her haste to get away. That shadowed sight startled me enough for my rational mind to reassert itself. Sereh? Scared? This wasn't natural.

I grabbed at raw magic, shaped it, and pushed. My tutors had called this form *The Light of a Thousand Suns, Inside*, the pretentious bastards, but it did the job. It sent uncounted spikes of magic through my brain, shredding the spell that had settled over me.

I fell to one knee, gasping, as the adrenaline that had rushed through me drained away, leaving me shaking.

I desperately conjured a light again.

Sereh was still scrabbling away, her feet and hands scraping on the flagstones as she pushed herself back across the floor, her face distorted with a fear I had never seen on her before. I could see the magic that affected her, now. It was wispy and sea-green in my magical vision, but somehow wrong in the way it moved, like it was alive. I sent my own magic after it, melting it like mist.

For a moment, Sereh lay there, terror scratched into her face. Then her expression smoothed, and in a single movement, she was on her feet and moving forwards, her knife already in her hand.

"Wait!" I forced myself to my feet. I saw the magic reach for us again, but this time I was ready for it. I sent it scurrying away. It wasn't strong, just insidious. It was like no spell I had ever seen. If anything, it reminded me of the power of a god, but there had been none of the chanting priests and clouds of toxic incense that usually accompanied religion happening nearby.

Sereh ignored my shout. I stumbled after her, pulling in raw magic, even as my light faded again like there was a leak in the spell. In the distance, almost submerged beneath the sound of heaving waves that I shouldn't have been able to hear, was whispering. Words, but in no language I recognised. The stench of rot and sea water made me choke.

Something lunged for Sereh out of the dark. I couldn't make it out. It was large, bulky, on two legs, but its top half was a swarm of limbs – tentacles, whatever they were – seeming to coalesce from the thickness of the shadows then slip away again. Sereh dodged, and her knife flashed in return. A … limb … snatched back, but then Sereh was retreating before a storm of liquidly whipping tentacles. Needle teeth glinted for a split second as lightning flashed outside the warehouse. Big, black, glistening eyes stared from a scaly face.

I sent magic roaring across the warehouse into the thing. An inhuman shriek and the smell of burned fish met my assault. A crate exploded behind it, filling the air with a cloud of tea leaves, splinters, and dust. The thing fell back, then it was up again, coming towards us with that fluid, unnatural shuffle.

I grabbed Sereh by the arm. "Out of here! Now!"

Whatever the Wren had in this warehouse, I wanted no more of it. It had taken my most powerful magic, and it was still moving.

I wondered if it had eaten all the gamblers, too.

What, and the tables and games, as well?

I kicked the door open. Rain lashed down as we almost fell out onto the slick cobbles. Wind attacked me, knocking me to one knee again. I slammed the door behind us, then locked it with a spell. I had no idea how long either the spell or the wooden door would hold.

"Uncle Nik!"

I turned. Sereh was pointing to the edge of the wharf, near the bow of a darkened ship. Something was dragging itself onto the cobbles. Tentacles latched onto ropes and bollards, hauling the thing up. Lightning flashed again, and I saw a third creature further along the wharf, heading towards us in an undulating run.

"Shit!" I grabbed Sereh's arm again. "Let's get out of here."

She resisted my pull. "Dad's working nearby. He could be in trouble. I can't leave him here."

I swore again. "Where?"

"He took a job to steal from a ship on Caldar's Wharf." She pointed across the black water to the next wharf over. "He doesn't know I know, but..."

Of course she knew. She had probably checked it out before he had even started. Sereh's protective instincts were finely honed and deadly when it came to Benny. And he thought he was the one protecting her.

The giant fish-octopus-man was lolloping along the wharf towards us. The second one was almost up over the side. And behind us, the warehouse door shook on its hinges.

"Fine. Now, let's run!"

The storm had hit Agatos full on. Ship-swallowing waves smashed into the seawall hundreds of yards from the docks, bursting clouds of spray into the air. Wind drove spray and rain into our skin like a million tiny bee stings. I had to hold tight onto Sereh's arm so neither one or both of us would be blown suddenly across the cobbles. The weather howled about us, but even under its fury I could still hear that distant whispering. Lightning forked from the clouds, over and over again. I tried not to look around, even though I could feel those things still following, unbothered by the storm beating around them.

What the fuck were they? I was as well-informed as

most about the history of this valley and the horrors it had hosted over the centuries. I knew all about soul riders – spirits of animals that possessed men and women and twisted them, whether by choice of the host or not – and of the gods that sometimes walked the streets in human form. I had even heard the speculation, rumours, and myths about the things that supposedly lay within High Karraka, sealed in by the mage-locked façade of Ceor Ebbas, and which sometimes restlessly stalked the dead hallways, but I had never heard of monstrosities like this from the sea. It was a new development in Agatos's history, and I didn't like it.

By the time we reached the start of the wharf, I was gasping for breath, covering my mouth with my hand to stop from sucking in rain. I dared a glance back. Only one of the monstrosities was following, its shape a horrifying, twisting silhouette against the lightning-wracked clouds. The warehouse door hung from its hinges. Where were the other two creatures?

Sereh tugged my hand, almost pulling me from my feet on the slippery cobbles.

"This way!" she shouted, although the words were stolen away by the wind, and I could only tell by the movement of her lips.

We ran along the dock, the storm trying to drive us away from the water towards the city. Something whipped past us, too quick to identify, and was gone – a flag, a tarpaulin, a torn fragment of sail. I ducked instinctively, but Sereh didn't even flinch. I needed every inch of my long legs to keep up with her. I kept raw magic held tight within me, even though it strained my muscles, tendons, and bones, and set my bruises flaring with heat. If that thing got too close, I would let it have it full-blast and knock it flying back into the harbour.

And people wondered why I didn't like the ocean. Look what it hid.

We reached Caldar's Wharf, and for a moment we were sheltered from the storm in the lee of the nearest ship.

Sereh pulled me down to her. "That's the one. That's where Dad is working."

Working. A nice way to put it. Nicking something, more like.

I threw another glance at the shape following us. It was still some way back, seemingly more cautious exposed on the docks, freezing statue-like when lightning flashed.

I took a few steps away, until I could see up to the ship's deck, and cupped my hands around my mouth. "Benny!"

The wind took my words. Cepra-damned storm! The next time, I put magic behind it and sent my voice booming towards the ship. A few seconds later, Benny's bedraggled, drowned-weasel head popped up from a hatch.

"What the fuck are you doing here?" he shouted back.

"Trouble."

"What?"

"Trouble!"

"You're in trouble?"

Fuck's *sake*! The monstrosity was still coming along the docks. A few more moments and it would be on us. I waved my arms wildly in its direction. "We all need to get out of here. Now!"

Benny frowned and squinted into the dark and rain.

Then a shape rose up behind him. Before I could react, tentacle-arms whipped over and around him, pulling him back towards sharpened teeth.

Sereh screamed, almost ear-shatteringly loud even in the storm. Then she was moving inhumanly fast, leaping from the dock onto the ship's gunwale. Her dagger spun through the air and buried itself in a round, black eye with a spray of dark fluid. The monstrosity reared back, limbs jerking free.

I propelled myself from the dock to the ship with a burst of magic, then threw the rest of my power at the flailing creature. The force punched it back, smashing through the rigging and the railing. It disappeared into the black harbour water and was gone.

Sereh pulled her dad to his feet. Benny's eyes were as wide as the monstrosity's had been.

"What the bleeding fuck was that? What the bleeding, fucking fuck?"

"It wasn't alone," I said grimly. I had lost sight of the creature that had been following us.

"You lost my dagger, Uncle Nik," Sereh said, eyes

fixed on the harbour, as though considering going after it. "It was my favourite one." Her shoulders slumped. "I'll have to use one of my others."

I bent, tossed the gangplank over the side to the wharf, and staggered down, aching all over.

There were too many places on the wharfs and docks for these things to hide. Alleys, stacks of barrels, ships, over the side of the docks. Depths, they could even be waiting in the shadows, hidden by the obscuring storm.

I beckoned Sereh and Benny to follow. If we could make it off the docks and out of Dockside, I didn't think these things would follow forever. I hoped they wouldn't. In my head, I plotted the fastest way to the Ash Guard headquarters. Get there and we would be safe from anything.

My sodden clothes hung heavily from me, too close and too cold on my skin. I was shivering, although whether that was from the wet and the cold or from fear, I couldn't tell.

The alley ahead of us led through a cluster of warehouses, past the cramped apartments and tenements of the dockworkers, the kind of place where Cord and his friends would have grown up, into the Middle City. There would be people, noise, light. Things like those monstrosities, the supernatural terrors that stalked the shadowed corners of the world, avoided such exposure. I didn't think it was any coincidence that they had emerged under cover of the storm.

Above us, massive, dark clouds stretched from

valley wall to valley wall, a bellying black cloak over the city, closing us in. I shepherded Sereh and Benny towards the alley, magic again held at the ready. The monstrosities hadn't abandoned us. Their insidious magic still reached for us, trying to overwhelm our minds and forcing me to beat it back. Splitting my concentration like this was giving me a headache. At least it was a distraction from the gust-driven rain still beating down.

An inhuman shriek from the edge of the docks, like an albatross being strangled, echoed from the alley ahead. We stumbled to a halt.

"They're in front of us," I said.

Benny's look was grim. "Lady of the Grove, mate. What have you got us into this time?"

I cast around. "Honestly? I have no idea."

"Fucking great."

"Come on." I headed east along the docks, away from Nettar's Wharf where the creatures had first emerged.

"Uncle Nik!"

One of the monstrosities was loping towards us from the dockside, coming fast, unhampered by the weather or the slippery cobblestones. We couldn't outrun it.

I shaped raw magic and threw it again. My power roared across the quayside and into the creature. It tumbled back, skidding over the stone. I felt something tear inside. "Shit!" I dropped to my knees.

The creature rose again. I had overdone it, hurt

myself, and it hadn't been enough. Why couldn't I wield power like my sister? Why had I never been able to raise my game? What was the point of being a pissing mage when my power was so weak? Grimacing, I forced myself to my feet. I couldn't fully straighten. It felt like someone had stuck a knife in my stomach. On either side of me, Sereh and Benny had drawn their daggers. I prepared another spell, biting down on the gasp of pain that drove through me.

The monstrosity came for us again, picking up speed. Lightning silhouetted a mass of tentacle-arms and a row of spikes running back over a giant fish head. If we timed this just right, maybe we could hurt it enough to flee.

My magic faded, sucked away like the mage light I had conjured in the warehouse. I felt my strength drain from me and stumbled again. *Bannaur's bitter balls!* I hadn't even brought my mage's rod to hit the thing with.

Long, sharp teeth glittered. I squeezed my hands into fists.

This was going to hurt.

Then Captain Gale was there, stepping past me, sword driving in and up, through the thing's chest. Her face and hands were white with Ash. The thing's shriek cut through the storm.

A squad of Ash Guard swept around us.

"Clear the docks and wharfs," Captain Gale bellowed. "I want any more of these things dead and gone within the hour." Pairs of Guards spread out under her direction. When they were gone, she turned her gaze on me. The thick layer of Ash made her look like a statue of an avenging god come to life. "I might have known you would have something to do with this."

I tried a smile. "This absolutely isn't my fault in any way." I was shaking. I hoped she couldn't see it.

She grunted and crouched over the monstrosity. Now that it was still, dead, and not trying to rip our heads off, I realised I had seen something like this before. I met Benny's eyes and saw that he recognised it, too. The torso and legs were approximately human, although scaled and unnaturally large, but in the needle teeth, the line of spines running up and back over its fish head, and the clusters of tentacles where arms should have emerged, it resembled only one thing: the statuette we had found beside Cord's bed in his apartment.

"I'm tempted to arrest you just on principle," Captain Gale said, "but it looks like I've got a busy night, and I can't spare the time. We *are* going to talk about this tomorrow. Now piss off out of here, all three of you."

We went, and I wasn't sorry to leave the docks behind me.

CHAPTER THIRTEEN

I DIDN'T SLEEP MUCH THAT NIGHT. I WOULD LIKE TO SAY it was because of the storm, but the wind and rain had passed before the night was halfway done, leaving the air fresh and energised. In the heat of the early summer, where the air pressed unrelentingly down, nights like this felt like a miracle. I should have slept like a baby. Well, maybe not like a baby. I remembered Sereh when she had been tiny. She had never slept longer than two hours at a time, and Benny, who at his best resembled a haunted rag, had permanently looked like he was one baby-scream away from being shredded.

Instead, every time I closed my eyes, a feeling came creeping over me, of something watching, a presence drawing closer, whispers on the shivering storm, until I couldn't lie still. A dozen times before the morning, I found myself leaping out of bed and striding back and forth across my little room. I knew it was just the stress of the last few days coupled with the terror of those things on the docks, but what good did knowing do? I was teetering on the edge of trauma, and my balance was gone. How could I expect to sleep?

My body needed more than a few snatched minutes of rest. The injury I had done myself by overusing magic had scarcely begun to heal. More than once during the night, I considered asking Benny to come in and hit me over the head with a brick, just so I could sleep. Only the suspicion that he might enjoy it rather too much restrained me.

Eventually, as dawn breached the eastern mountains, I hauled myself downstairs.

Benny was already up, and he didn't look like he had slept either. Admittedly, it was hard to tell with Benny, and the night was his normal time of business.

"You too, huh?" he said, as I reached the bottom of the stairs. He hadn't opened the shutters yet, even though most mornings we had an unspoken battle, with him trying to let in sunlight and me trying to stop the Wren's spies catching a glimpse of me. A waste of time that had been.

I crossed to the little kitchen. "That kind of shit keeps you up."

Benny already had a pot of dark Secellian coffee heating on the stove. I poured myself a cup, added a pinch of spices and a spoonful of honey, and joined him again.

"You know what I was thinking?" Benny said as I

perched on the lip of a chair. I was still too edgy to sit back comfortably.

"Do I want to know?"

"I was thinking about those old stories they used to tell on Ebbtide. You know the ones I mean?"

Ebbtide was a festival held roughly every seven-and-a-half years, when the tide withdrew so far that the harbour was emptied and the seabed was exposed for almost half a mile from the shore. It was a time when the citizens of Agatos stood vigil on the docks and seawalls, lit bonfires, and enjoyed the stink of rotting sea creatures stranded by the retreating tide. Ebbtide, according to those who ought to know, or at least claimed they ought to know, was caused by the body of the dead god, Kethcal, which revolved around the world in a highly eccentric orbit. When it passed close enough to the far side of the planet, its enormous mass was enough to pull the tides away. And to think that some people said the gods never did anything. Tell that to Kethcal who, despite being long deceased, still messed up everyone's shorelines every seven-and-a-bit years.

It wouldn't be a proper celebration without gruesome stories to terrify innocent minds, and so parents and random, sadistic strangers liked to tell kids of creatures that crawled out of the sea on Ebbtide to snatch away children who weren't properly keeping the vigil. The fact that there were no recorded cases of any such thing ever having happened hadn't dampened the enthusiasm.

"I've been wondering if maybe those legends ain't so much legends."

I squinted across at Benny. He looked genuinely nervous. I didn't blame him. Part of being a mage was learning about all the supernatural entities that might try to mutilate, possess, eat, or just generally fuck up the unwary, and those monstrosities last night had still given me the willies.

"You're missing one thing," I said.

"Yeah? What's that?"

"It's not Ebbtide." I swallowed the last of my coffee. It was still too hot, and it burned my throat. "Now, I'm going to find out what those things were. I don't think it's a coincidence that we find a statuette of one and the same evening a bunch of them come crawling out of the sea and attack us." I was as much in the dark as I had been in the depths of the storm, but there was some shit going in this city. When that shit started spattering me, I wanted to find out who was doing the throwing. "I'm going to see what that curator has figured out."

Benny pushed up from the couch. "I'm coming with you."

"You are? I thought you didn't want anything to do with any of this."

"I don't. But those things..." His chin jutted towards me. "Those things could have hurt Sereh. I need to know if they're still a threat, because, mate, something you've done is causing trouble here, and I ain't having it."

That wasn't fair. Was it? It was true that if I hadn't taken this case, if I hadn't started looking into Cord, I would never have found the statuette, and I wouldn't have been on the docks. And if I hadn't been hiding out in Benny's house, Mr. Mirian would never have come looking for me there, Benny wouldn't have been pissed off, and Sereh wouldn't have tracked me down to tell me so and incidentally frighten the shit out of me at exactly the wrong time. I hadn't meant any of it to happen, and there was no way I could have guessed where it would lead. But whichever way you wove it, without me, neither Sereh nor Benny would have ended up being attacked by fish-squid monstrosities from the Depths.

I wanted to argue that I hadn't asked Sereh to come along. I wanted to say that she could handle anything this city could throw at her, stick a knife in its throat, and leave it bleeding in the street. And maybe she could. But she shouldn't have to. She was a kid, and the truth was that the life I had chosen was dangerous. Was it really fair to bring that world down around a child, no matter how good she might be with a knife?

"Come on, then." It was early, but it would take us a while to reach the museum, and the sooner I figured it out and handed the whole mess over to the Ash Guard, the better.

The usual stench of the city had been washed away with the rain, along with the filth and the crap that people left outside their houses to be collected by the waste carts. It all ended up in the harbour just the same, but at least the air still held the freshness of the night.

I brought my hooded black cloak and mage's rod this time. I hated the undeserved privilege the cloak afforded me, the access, the fearful deference even when I was clearly overstepping normal bounds. But I couldn't deny that it made everything easier. I had been using it more and more recently. How many times did I have to do that before it became a habit, and I stopped even noticing the privilege I wore? I didn't want that, but would I even notice when it happened?

Fuck it. People had died. Monstrosities were crawling out of the sea. Worrying about whether I wore a cloak or not was self-indulgent wanking.

The delivery yard at the back of the museum was empty, and the wide loading doors were closed and locked. There were no guards, but there was a ward on the doors.

"Give me a hand with this," I said to Benny.

I eased the ward aside and sprang the lock. Together we dragged the doors open in an unnecessarily dramatic manner, spilling daylight into the darkened interior.

A porter was crossing the loading bay, a pot cradled in her arms. She turned as the doors opened, her jaw gaping at the sight of us.

"You want to be careful with that," Benny said, nodding towards the pot. "You don't want to drop it. Looks old."

The woman's gaze flicked between us. I could see her eyeing up my black cloak. *Come on*, part of me thought. *Stand up to the cloak. Tell us to get the fuck out of here. Call the guards.*

Instead, the more rational part of me said, "We're here to see Professor Allantin. Is that going to be a problem?"

The porter swallowed, and her hands started to shake in a way that made me worried for the pot. This fucking city. Part of me thought the whole place would be better off if the Ash Guard handed out Ash to every citizen and wiped out the power of the mages in one quick sweep. Without that unequal privilege ... what? A paradise of fairness and flowers? Love and kindness all round? Not unless you got rid of every politician, merchant, and crook in the city as well, and even then, there would be more where they came from, all ready to start the cycle again. But at least it would end shit like this. My distaste was a physical sensation in my mouth as the porter nodded towards the steps.

"We know the way," I said.

I hadn't been sure the professor would be in this early, and when we reached the musty corridor beneath the museum, I was sure I was right. Morgue lamps still glowed along the walls, but the place was silent, almost eerily so.

"A Cepra-damned tomb," I muttered.

Benny glanced over, but I shook my head.

"We could just take a look in some of these rooms,"

Benny said. "Just to see if anyone's got anything interesting."

"I thought you'd decided the museum was off-limits."

He scratched his scraggly beard. "Be rude not to now we're here."

I stopped outside Professor Allantin's office and rapped on the solid door. After a few seconds, I tried the handle. It was locked. Well, why would she be here at such a godsforsaken hour? The only reason we were was because my dreams had been so twisted up by last night's crap at the docks.

"Wanna open it?" I asked. My nerves had been growing increasingly jittery. Whether it was my general level of stress and tension or the thought of that creepy statuette waiting for us on the other side of the door I didn't know. But I didn't want to twitch at the wrong time in the spell and blow the door of its hinges. Things like that were hard to explain. Anyway, Benny was almost as quick with his lockpicks, and a bit of practice never hurt. If you thought about it the right way, I was doing him a favour.

The lock clicked. Benny glanced up. "Ready?"

I dug my fingernails into the balls of my hands and nodded. *Stop being so fucking jumpy.* It wasn't like there would be one of those monstrosities waiting behind the door. And now I wished I hadn't thought that. *Don't be stupid. There's nothing to worry about.*

Which went to show just how little I knew.

My assumption that the room would be empty was

wrong. The professor was still there, but instead of sitting at her desk, she was sprawled out across the rug. She wasn't asleep; her angle was too awkward, and the chair had been knocked over. The same chair I had sat in just yesterday. *Pity!*

I gently turned her onto her back. There was no sign of a wound, no blood, not even a bruise that might explain this, at least not one I could see, but she was clearly dead. There was a certain stillness to a dead body that was different to someone asleep or even unconscious, and no living body moved like that when you shifted it. Professor Allantin's eyes were open, staring into the distance. I had to resist the urge to glance over my shoulder to see what she was looking at. Something – maybe the way her face had been shoved into the rug – had left her with a twisted expression of horror. Her skin was cold, and her body was stiff. *Dead a while. Since last night, maybe?* How long did it take for a body to end up like this?

"Lady of the Grove, mate," Benny said over my shoulder. "How the fuck do you get tangled up in shit like this? What killed her?"

I straightened, wiping my fingers on my cloak, even though there was nothing on them.

"Heart attack, I reckon." Not that I really knew what a heart attack looked like.

"She does look kind of old."

Older than when I had seen her yesterday. Maybe it was the expression pressed into her face by the rug. Her hair had come loose from its plait, showing more grey than I had noticed before. Her glasses were lying not far from her. I picked them up and placed them on the desk, then swore again. "Look at this."

The statuette was on the desk, but it was in shards. A small hammer had been dropped beside it, still coated in splinters and dust from the black stone. She had attacked it with a fury that had left it almost unrecognisable.

"Well, that's bleeding grateful, ain't it? We could have got a few shields for that."

The desk was piled with books and manuscripts, at least half of which were in languages and scripts I didn't even recognise.

So, she had smashed the statuette and then had a heart attack? Why? It was an ugly, creepy thing, no doubt, but she had already known that when I had given it to her. This, the smashing of the stone, wasn't something you would do *while* having a heart attack, was it? I was no doctor, and I had never seen anyone die of a heart attack, but I had always imagined it involved collapsing and clutching your chest, not picking up a hammer and trashing small souvenirs. Assuming this even had been a heart attack. In the Warrens, the most common form of heart attack was a knife through the chest. Maybe her brain had ruptured or ... well, I didn't know.

"What do you reckon all this is about?" Benny said, moving around the desk and shuffling through the professor's scribbled notes. "Reckon it's worth anything?"

"Only to people in the museum."

Benny grunted.

I took a couple of pages and peered closer. The professor hadn't believed in making comprehensible notes, and those that were readable didn't make any sense to me. Half of them were scratched out.

"Maybe she was trying to translate those marks on the bottom of the statuette, and she wasn't having much luck."

Had she just got frustrated and smashed the whole thing in a fit of fury? It didn't match the image I had gained of a disinterested academic, but I had spent a year studying at the university, and I had seen enough tantrums and strops to know that not all academics coped well with frustration.

Or maybe it had moved in her hands, like Benny had said happened when he picked it up.

It didn't move. It's stone.

"Hey. Take a look at this." Benny had crouched back down by the body. I wondered for a second if he was looting her corpse. "She's got something in her hand."

He was right. I hadn't noticed because I had been focused on the fact that she was dead, which I thought was reasonable under the circumstances. Her arm had become trapped under her body when I turned her, and now Benny had eased it awkwardly free. Her hand was closed in a fist, and I could just make out a piece of paper clutched within it.

I might not be much of an investigator, but I recognised a clue when I saw one.

"See if you can get it out," I said.

"You get it out."

I shook my head. What a coward. "You're closer."

"Hey, it's your body. I ain't never seen her before today."

Benny's face had developed a stubborn, constipated look. I sighed. It wasn't that I was afraid to touch a dead body. After all, it wasn't going to do anything, and whatever essence had made her *be* had moved on. I could call that essence back – any fully-trained mage could – and talk to her. It would make this job damned simpler. Depths, I could have called back Etta Mirian, too. But I had sworn I would never do that. Dead people returned wrong. No good ever came of it, and in the end, someone would have had to kill her again.

Carefully, I eased the paper from her fist. It was difficult. Rigor mortis held her hand clamped tight, as though she didn't want to release the paper, and I had to work and wriggle it out against the resistance. I kept expecting her to jerk upright at any moment and snatch her hand away.

The paper had been ripped from a larger sheet and crushed violently in her hand. It was slightly damp. I flattened it out. The ink had smudged and run, but I could still just about read it.

"Enabgal of the many eyes," I read. "Lord of the waters. Watcher in the dark. Cold-bringer. Dreamhaunter. Hunter of the void. Deathless. Sleeping. To awake."

"Well," Benny said after a moment. "Sounds lovely. But it's not talking about our boys, is it?" He nodded at the smashed statuette. "Those things only had two eyes each. Big, black things. No way I'm forgetting them." He shuddered.

There had been a lot wrong with the monstrosities that had attacked us, but being many-eyed hadn't been one of them. This text was describing something else. So, was it a translation of the marks on the bottom of the statuette or something else?

"I'll tell you what, though, mate. You might not want to meet that Enabgal thing in a dark alley, but reading about it ain't going to drive you crazy or give you a heart attack, either."

No arguing with that. By themselves, they were just words. But I wondered if, somehow, the statuette had projected the same magical fear the monstrosities had. Maybe at the same time they had come crawling out of the sea, trying to drive terror into our minds, this statuette had done the same thing. An echo. The timing would be right from the state of her body, and she wouldn't have had any defences. She was old. Maybe fear like that would have driven her to smash the statuette and her heart to fail.

I pocketed the paper. "We should report this to the Ash Guard before someone else does."

Benny took a step back. "You do that, mate. I'm not getting involved. Mages and magic are toxic shit. No offence."

I gave the room another once-over, with both

magical and normal vision, but there was nothing else that stood out. Leave it to Captain Gale and her Ash Guard. They were trained for this. Anything I could do would just be getting in the way, and this place still freaked me out. The dead, staring body wasn't helping. I also didn't want to be here when someone came knocking on the door to offer her a cup of coffee. Things like this were difficult to explain, as I had found out to my cost before.

We slunk away, trying and probably failing to look innocent. I headed for the Ash Guard fortress for an awkward conversation with Captain Gale, while Benny went home to check on Sereh and, if he had any sense, get some sleep. The humidity had begun to rise as the heat of the sun increased, and the aftermath of the rain that had brought cool, freshness to the night and the early morning was now becoming a curse. Sweat gathered under my cloak and on my face. The cloak was proving to be a fucking pain again already.

I had to wait for a while for Captain Gale to emerge from the Ash Guard fortress. After last night's excitement, which I had left her to clean up, she was probably off duty. If she was as tired as I was, she showed no signs of it. Clearly, I did.

"You don't look good," she said, as she came through the doorway.

"I messed myself up with magic last night. I just need some sleep."

"But you came here instead."

"I'm all about public service, me."

She snorted. "Still not coming in?" She gestured behind her to the looming entrance of the fortress. The whole building was impregnated with Ash. A couple of steps through there, and all my magical powers would disappear. And most mages who went in never came out again. I wasn't pushing my luck.

"Depths, no."

She snorted. "You mages are so ridiculous. You know if I wanted to take you, I wouldn't have to trick you inside, right?"

It was a sign of how stressed and nervous I was that I didn't try to comment on the obvious innuendo.

"So where do we do this?" she asked. "Dumonoc's?"

"Nah." I didn't want Squint listening in to my business.

"Thank fuck. That place is a hole. I don't know what you see in it."

"People leave me alone there."

"I can see why." She rubbed the scar across her face. "There's a coffee house nearby I like to go when I don't want people bothering me."

And she was telling me about it, inviting me there. Did that mean something, or was she just saying it to make me think there was and open up more?

"Before we do," I said, "there's something I should tell you." This wasn't going to go down well. "There's a body up at the museum. You might want to send someone before the Watch get called."

She eyed me expressionlessly. "Is this your fault?"

"No! I mean, I hope not." I had taken the statuette

to the professor. If that was the cause, did it mean I was to blame? I hadn't intended it. "Her name is Professor Allantin. She's a curator at the museum. I'll explain everything."

I waited outside while Captain Gale dispatched a team to the museum. Then she led me to a coffee house on a side street not far from the Ash Guard fortress. We settled at a table under a blue awning. She ordered coffee, and I ordered an apple pastry, too, on the theory that she was paying and my taxes might as well be put to good use. I told her about finding the statuette at Cord's apartment and taking it to the museum. I missed out the part about pretending to be Ash Guard, as well as my accident in the morgue at the Fields of the Dead that had left the bodies of people's loved ones scattered in mounds across the floor. In fact, I kept most of my investigation to myself – hey, why distract her with irrelevancies and make myself look like an incompetent twat?

I slid the piece of paper across the table to her. "We found this clutched in the professor's hand."

"We?"

Shit. "Benny was keeping me company."

"Of course he was."

"He's not part of the investigation, though."

"Oh, don't worry. I plan to blame you solely for everything that's gone wrong."

Hmm. I hadn't exactly been angling for that. Still, it might gain me a few points with Benny, and I could do with them.

Captain Gale read the paper then tucked it into her jacket.

"Well?" I prompted.

"No idea. I'll pass it on to Gods and Sods."

"What?"

"Section II. Its full title is Divinities and Malign, Persistent Supernatural Entities. But Gods and Sods is easier. They're the Ash Guard research division that keeps track of, well, gods and similar."

That was news to me. I wondered again if she was sharing to get me to open up more or if she really trusted me. I struggled to get a read on the captain. "I didn't know you had a research division. I thought you were all..." I waved a hand at her.

"Yep. Research. Catering. Cleaning. Clerks. The whole lot. And every one of them is trained to kick your arse." She stood up from the table. "Finish your pastry. This is now official Ash Guard business. Keep out of it."

"But..."

"You can continue your investigation, but you need to keep well away from any of those creatures, the museum, the docks, or this Enabgal, whatever the Depths that is."

"As long as they keep away from me," I muttered.

The Ash Guard had more resources and more experience to follow up on the monstrosities and the magic. It made sense to let them pursue that, as long as they shared any discoveries with me, and I figured bringing these leads to Captain Gale's attention had earned me some credit. *And she took you to her favourite coffee house.* Assuming it was her favourite and not just somewhere she dragged every nark and informant she played for information. I considered asking the waiter if Captain Gale often brought people here, but I still had the last dregs of self-respect. Just.

I had other leads and other angles I could follow for now. If they came to nothing, with my track record, I could get myself back in the middle of shit with scarcely any effort.

A good place to start would be Etta Mirian's brother, Solus Tain, who apparently resented her. Mr. Mirian had said that Tain would have forgotten the snub, but I didn't believe it. Resentments grew. They seethed and festered and turned bitter inside. I should know. One thing they didn't do was disappear. You could push them down, pretend they were gone, but they never really were. They were just waiting. In my experience, clients lied to themselves as often as they lied to me, and they did both with a self-defeating frequency that only led to higher bills and delayed results. Tain was supposedly on a trading ship, the *Wavebreaker*, at least two weeks out from Agatos. It should be easy enough to see if the ship had returned early.

I pushed my chair away and headed for the docks. Stay away from the docks? I wondered if Captain Gale had believed that any more than I had.

CHAPTER FOURTEEN

THE AGATOS CUSTOMS HOUSE HAD, IF RUMOURS WERE true, been built on the ruins of a temple to Shapray, the god of Arbitrary Decisions and Unjustifiable Demands. But anyone who believed all the rumours that circled Agatos like sharks around a dying whale wouldn't last long. The building occupied a prime position on the docks, not far from Paravar Square. Among the functional, squat warehouses, it did a good impression of being a temple itself: tall columns (always the columns in Agatos), wide, sweeping steps, carved figures, and a way of squeezing money from anyone who came through the doors. And, in a way, it was a temple to the only real god Agatos worshipped: the acquisition of wealth and power.

The docks were bustling with people and animals. Goods were being loaded, unloaded, and carted away among a cacophony of shouts, bellows, roars, and shrieks. Warehouse doors stood open. Crates and sacks were stacked on the cobbles. Pickpockets, hawkers, and Watchwomen and -men threaded the crowds.

Only twelve hours ago, monstrosities had crawled out of the sea, the storm had lashed the bare cobbles, and Benny, Sereh, and I had fought for our lives. It was hard to reconcile the scene. A few thin, white clouds scudded across a blue sky. People said Agatos could shrug anything off. If it hadn't been for the nagging pain in my abdomen from overusing my magic, I would have wondered if it had all been a nightmare.

Being here, on the side of the docks, looking out over the harbour and the glittering, still-choppy sea beyond, brought back more memories, not of the horror last night, but deeper ones that were just as traumatic. I had spent too long here as an eleven-year-old, watching the unkind sea rise and fall, waiting for Endir – Mica's dad, my stepfather – to sail back in, knowing all the while that he was already dead. I hated the ocean. I wasn't at all surprised it had birthed monstrosities. Those unseeing depths had always filled me with dread.

I had been too young when my stepfather died to think too much about it – the trauma had been too enveloping – and later I had tried to drown the memories, but here, on this dockside, I couldn't keep them out: the pain, the longing, the hopelessness of waiting for a boat that would never return. I turned quickly away from the water.

Screw it. I was here to do a job. I couldn't let the memories suck me back under. I had reached a precarious stability in these last few years, and I wasn't going to lose that. I would find my information then fuck off out of here. That was all.

The Customs House was packed when I made my way inside. All ships arriving, leaving, or sheltering from the weather were required to declare their full cargoes and undergo inspection. The main hall was full of ship captains or their representatives, as well random enquirers like me, waiting to meet with the clerks at their desks. My black cloak might have bought me privilege in the city, but captains were used to being gods on their own ships, and none of them looked impressed by my shiny cloak. I supposed that out on the ocean they had access to far more impressive cloaks, what with the spray and the wind and the occasional badly aimed flying fish. No one was letting me skip to the front of the line.

Waiting here was actually quite relaxing. There was nothing I could do but stand there, shuffle forward, stand some more, shuffle... I had spent so much time rushing about, being attacked, kidnapped, knocked unconscious, and generally existing in a state of stress and panic that the stop-shuffle felt meditative. I might have drifted into a healing half-sleep if, twenty minutes in, someone hadn't stepped up close to my shoulder and breathed fish in my face.

For just a moment, I flashed back to last night's monstrosities. I was already pulling in raw magic before the absurdity of the thought caught up with me. I turned my head slowly towards the smell.

A mage was standing right next to me. He was clearly trying to be intimidating, but he was six inches shorter than I was, so all I could see was a pair of eyes peeking over my shoulder. He would have done better to have taken a couple of steps back. I was tempted to stick an elbow in his stomach to show him the error of his ways. I was weighing the pros – (satisfaction) and cons (possibly a lot of pain and consequences I wouldn't like) when another mage appeared at my other shoulder. I recognised these two now. They were the Wren's mages who had snatched me at the Fields of the Dead. *Perfect.*

"We want to talk to you," the second mage said. Her voice was pitched at a purr.

"Well, congratulations," I said. "Full marks."

"What?"

I sighed. No sense of humour, most mages. "What do you want to talk about?"

"Not here."

I glanced around. The people ahead and behind me in the line were trying very hard to look like they hadn't seen or heard anything, but I could tell they were paying attention, and why not? It wasn't often you got to see a mage-fight close up. If I had my way, they weren't going to get much entertainment. "I'm fine where I am."

"You're a fool," the first added, still trying to peer over my shoulder. I straightened, and he had to lift up onto tiptoes.

"Probably. I've been called worse. If you just came here to insult me, you're going to have to try harder."

"You're not making this easier on yourself," the second said.

She was probably right. All this switching between them every sentence was making me dizzy. I nodded towards a large pillar in the middle of the hall. "Over there." I would still be in full view, but it would allow us not to be overheard.

When we reached the pillar, I put my back to it. "So. What is it? I'm busy."

The woman squared her shoulders. "The Wren is a patient man—"

"Bollocks is he."

She took a step back, eyes widening in fury. Her colleague laid a hand on her shoulder. "The Wren wants his answers," he said. "He is tired of waiting."

"Yeah, well, I want a nice hot bath, a good rest, and someone who hasn't just eaten raw fish breathing in my face, but life is full of disappointments."

This time it was the male mage whose face turned slack with anger. I saw him pull magic, and I matched him. I wasn't going down easily this time. "You really want to do this here? Right in the middle of an official building? Denna's mercy, I've just come from the Ash Guard. They're probably watching me right now. You think the Wren's really looking for that kind of attention?"

The mages exchanged a look. I could see the decision warring in their eyes. They had better not choose a fight, because I was outgunned and out of powder.

"I'll give you a clue," I continued, before they could make the wrong decision. "He doesn't. The Wren will get his information, and soon, but this kind of shit" – I gestured at the two of them – "this makes it harder for me to get close to the Countess. So piss off and let me do my job, or you can explain to the Wren how you fucked it all up because you couldn't hold it in long enough to reach a toilet. All right?"

It was all goat shit, of course. If they were here, it was because the Wren had sent them, but right now they were confused and not thinking straight.

"Good," I said. "Now run off back to your kennels."

They went. I managed to hold in my smirk until they had made it out the doors. This was going to cause me trouble later, but it was worth it. I hoped the future me would agree.

I turned back to the queue.

My place in the line had closed up. No one looked like they were about to open it again. The bastards. I joined the end of the queue.

By the time I was finally called forwards by one of the clerks, the meditative quality of queueing had worn off. I was tired, sore, and bad tempered. I didn't take well to being threatened, but there was nothing I could do about it, which only made me even more bad tempered. Insulting the Wren's acolytes in the safety of a crowd was one thing. Doing my job and getting the Wren off my back for good was another. Fail at that, and I wouldn't last long. So how in the Depths was I going to persuade my mother to trust me when she had no reason to do so?

I really should have kept my mouth shut when I had visited her.

I seated myself in front of the clerk. He didn't look up, just kept scribbling on a form in front of him. Why did everyone feel the need to do that? My mother, the Wren, now this petty bureaucrat. What was it with the pretending not to notice me? It was a transparent, annoying power play. He would notice a fireball up his arse, I was sure of that. I cleared my throat. "I need information about a ship. The *Wavebreaker*. I need to know if it's returned to port."

"There's a fee." He jerked a thumb over this shoulder at a board on the wall.

All right. Now this was just getting rude. I didn't expect much, but at least have the decency to look up. I wasn't in the mood for any more arseholes today. And the funds Mr. Mirian had given me were disappearing too fast. I could charge him more, of course, but then he would be disappointed, and I couldn't face that. Not for this twat.

I leaned forwards, resting my elbows on his paperwork so he couldn't miss the black cloak falling over my shoulder. A spark shot from my fingers to char the edge of the paper. "There could be a fee. Or..." I let the word drift off.

I thought for a moment the clerk was going to tell me to get lost anyway, but with a shake of his head, he pushed back his chair and headed for a large filing cabinet. A couple of minutes later, he was back with a sheaf of papers.

"The *Wavebreaker*, under Captain Illa Crown, set sail for Myceda two months ago. Then it was due to cross to Dhaja, head down to Melaru, then back via Kendar and Emered in Pentath. Expected here in the next two or three weeks." He looked up. "Wind reports haven't been favourable. Could be up to a week late."

Right. So Solus Tain wasn't back. Not that he couldn't have found a mage somewhere around the Yttradian Sea to do his bidding, but it was unlikely. Distance made things harder.

I stood. "Thanks." I paused. "The first mate, Solus Tain, was on board when it sailed, right?"

The clerk examined his papers. "Solus Tain isn't listed as first mate."

"What?" I was certain Mr. Mirian had told me he was.

"First mate is listed as Coransar Jent. From Dhaja, I would guess." He flicked through the sheaf of papers. "Ah. Here, see?" He pointed to a note on the page. "Tain was fired before the last voyage. Drunkenness on watch, it says."

Well, wasn't that fucking interesting? Solus Tain had never left Agatos. These last couple of months, he

231

had been in the city, and unless Mr. Mirian had lied to me, Tain had kept that fact hidden from his family. He hadn't even shown up at his own sister's funeral. He had been resentful. He had been angry. He had lost his job. And maybe it had consumed him until he had found a way to take revenge.

Dumonoc's bar wasn't exactly on the way to my mother's palace, but I told myself it wasn't too much of a diversion, and if I wanted to track down Solus Tain, I didn't have time to root through every boarding house, inn, and dockworkers' tenement in Agatos.

I shouldered my way into the dark, underground bar, ignored Dumonoc's friendly, "What the fuck do I have to do before you take the hint? Nail the fucking door shut?" and headed for Squint's candle-lit corner.

"I'm looking for a man."

"What? Fed up with women turning you down?" He grinned, showing the brown stumps of his teeth.

"His name is Solus Tain. He's a sailor. Used to be first mate on the *Wavebreaker*, but he got fired a few months back for drunkenness."

Squint squinted at me over a bottle of Dumonoc's foul and potentially dangerous wine. "You paying in favours again?"

"Fuck, no. I've learned my lesson."

"Two silver shields, then."

I pulled the coins out of my pouch. He turned them

in the candlelight, then pocketed them. "Good. I'll have your answer by tonight."

That I would call a success. It might be the only one I got today.

Maybe it was the dark of Dumonoc's bar, maybe my disturbed night, maybe the thought of going back to my mother, or maybe just how out-fucking-classed I was by all the crap raining down on me, but when I stepped into the sweltering heat of the Grey City, I felt a profound weariness settle over me. I didn't have the strength to do everything I needed to. I just didn't.

I should go to Mr. Mirian and tell him it was more than I had bargained for, give him what I had found, which was precious little, and point him in the direction of Captain Gale. Eventually she would get around to helping him, if she had time. But again, the thought of the understanding and disappointment I would see in his eyes just left me ... empty. Scooped out.

Because you're not worrying about disappointing Mr. Mirian, you twat. You're worrying about disappointing Mica's dad, and you can't do that because he's been dead for most of your lifetime.

Even telling myself that, even knowing it was true, didn't change anything. It was a wound I had never dealt with. Mr. Mirian had unintentionally ripped off the scab and was rubbing in salt like a chef trying to hide the flavour of rotting fish.

And then there was my mother. The blessed Countess. I had known going back to her would be difficult. From the moment she had got it into her head that I would one day succeed her as high mage, she had bent her will to that end, and her methods had not been kind. Fear, pain, and humiliation, as though, somehow, she could beat me into the form she wanted. The world had always shaped itself to her will. Why shouldn't I be the same?

The mages she had set to training me, men and women like Cerrean Forge, had plunged into the programme with enthusiasm, spurred on by my mother's fervour and determination. I had been buried beneath rock. I'd had spears of magic thrown at me over and over again, even when I had lost all ability to block them. I had been paraded in front of the other trainees while they attacked my mind, trying to plant memories that weren't my own, to dredge up secrets, to feed in fears until all I could do was scream.

My mother's mages had claimed that the abuse they had piled upon me, and on the other trainees, the mental and physical torture, had been to bring out those hoped-for powers. Me, I knew better. The cruelty had been the point. I had seen the jealousy and bitterness behind it. There were only three ways you could come out of that: you could be cowed and broken, you could become the same kind of bully as the mages training you, or you could rebel against it. No wonder so many mages who stayed around were such sycophants and thugs. I had thought I was rebelling when I had left my mother's palace. It had taken me a long time to realise that I had, in fact, been broken past full repair. The only mage I knew who got out unharmed was Mica, whose powers had every time exceeded each challenge they could throw at her.

The Wren wouldn't give a fuck about any of that. He would carry out his threat against Benny and Sereh, and he wouldn't lose a second of sleep over it.

But maybe I could find what he needed without getting anywhere near the Countess. I knew she wanted to buy a building near the docks. But why? The Wren clearly saw it as an encroachment on his territory. If I could find out what her intentions were, that would be the debt paid. And there was one place in the city where that kind of information might be found without me having to face up to my mother. Luckily for me, I had a contact there.

I hadn't been working as a freelance mage for long when Elosyn Brook had come to me. She was a chef at Nuil's coffee house, and her wife, Holera, ran a restaurant only a few streets away. I had been there a few times. It was good food. But someone must not have shared my opinion, because they had laid a curse on Holera.

Most curses were ineffective. Even if there was a trace of magic in them, it quickly crumbled with little harm. But whoever had cast this one – and I never did find out who – must have had enough anger behind it and enough natural magical talent that it had stuck. Every time Holera had smelled onions or garlic, she had bled from her eyes. Not a great look if you ran a restaurant. They had both been in despair when they had finally come to me.

The curse had been easy enough to break – curses always were – but Elosyn and Holera had been far more grateful than I deserved. I didn't have many friends. Elosyn and Holera were among them, which came in handy when I needed information. I doubted most of the merchants, brokers, and factors who made their deals in Nuil's paid much attention to the serving staff. When I wanted to know what the great and the not-at-all-good of Agatos were up to, this was the place to find out. Any deal or purchase my mother might make would pass through here eventually, and Elosyn would be able to find it out.

And what makes you think the Wren would be satisfied with information he could buy himself from Nuil's?

I pushed the thought away. *Because he doesn't know what he's looking for.*

And nor do you.

Sometimes, I thought my mind hated me.

I waited in the narrow, covered alley behind Nuil's until Elosyn emerged. Her face was red from the heat of the ovens, and the smell of baking pastries followed her out. My stomach rumbled, even though I wasn't hungry. Elosyn's pastries were the best in Agatos.

She was a short woman, but muscular. I reckoned if it came to a wrestling match, she could dislocate my shoulder. All that mixing, kneading, and lifting heavy trays in and out of ovens gave her far more strength than my chasing after the odd lost pet.

She wiped the sweat off her forehead as she stepped out. "Nik. I'm really glad to see you."

"You are?" This was not the usual response I got. For some reason, half the people I knew thought me turning up was an ill omen. Elosyn's response made me immediately suspicious.

"It's Holera's birthday."

Ah. Should I have known that? I probably should have known that. "Sorry. I've been distracted."

She waved the apology away. "I've been hoping to run into you. It's been a while. I was going to drop round to Benny's after my shift."

"You knew I was there?"

"Everyone knows you're there."

Well. Fucking great. And I had thought it was such a secret.

"Holera is having a party tonight," Elosyn continued. "She wants you to come."

"Me?"

"Yes, of course you. We are friends, aren't we?"

"Yeah. Of course." A party. Shit. I didn't do well in large groups, particularly groups of strangers. I rubbed people up the wrong way. An hour in my company, and most people ended up offended, furious, or sometimes injured. I didn't even know how I did it.

"So?"

"I'll be there."

She raised her eyebrows.

"I will."

"Good. It's at eight. Don't bring anything."

A bit insulting, but fair enough. "I was hoping you could find something out for me," I said. "My blessed mother is trying to buy a building near the docks. You know that coffee house on Sungazer Plaza that tried to set up in competition with Nuil's? I want to know what her interest is in it. It doesn't seem like her usual thing."

Elosyn rubbed her flour-covered hands on her flour-covered apron. A nervous gesture. This was more like my normal reception. It made me feel much more comfortable. There was nothing like low expectations.

"I don't want to know why you want to know, do I?" Elosyn said.

"No."

"All right. I'll let you know what I find out tonight. At the party, Nik. Don't forget. I mean it."

"I won't."

If she really could get my answers, it would make this whole Cepra-damned case of Mr. Mirian's easier. I could sell out my mother and be free of the Wren. Then I could focus on Mr. Mirian's problem without the spectre of the Wren haunting my every step. It would be a relief.

The pain in my guts twinged again. Rest, that was what I needed. Some healing sleep to fix the damage, and everything would be easier. My other problems could wait.

CHAPTER FIFTEEN

My problems did wait. What I hadn't anticipated was that one of them would be waiting right outside Benny's front door, back pressed against the wall.

The problem was wearing an encompassing, loose robe, but I could clearly see the tightly wrapped strips of cloth around his arms and legs. Straight black hair almost reached his eyes.

The last time I had seen this particular problem, he had drugged me, kidnapped me, and left me tied up in an alley with a rat trying to eat my face.

He wasn't catching me like that twice.

I pulled in magic and gathered it into a blazing light around my hands, bright even in the sunlight, ignoring the stab of pain in my guts. The light wouldn't do much on its own, unless I tossed it in his face, but I had a spear of magical force ready to drive into him. *Let's see your drug deal with that.*

He sprang to his feet as I approached, holding his hands out in front of him placatingly.

"Wait. Please."

I kept advancing. "Give me one good reason why I shouldn't spread you from here to wherever it is you fucking come from." Not that my power was up to much spreading, but he didn't need to know that.

"Khorasan. Please," he said again. "I need your help."

"You need my help." This guy had some fucking nerve. "You need my pissing help. Why in every fucking deep hole of the Depths would I want to help you?" I was struggling to put into words exactly what I was thinking right now. The sheer fucking audacity on display here put me to shame. Maybe that was his tactic: leave me so gobsmacked that I wouldn't know what to do. If so, it was working.

"I will explain," he said. "But not here. I made a mistake."

That was an understatement. "Well, we're not getting a drink together, I can tell you that much." I let my magic fall. To tell the truth, I couldn't have kept it up for much longer.

Anyone with half a brain would have told this guy to fuck off or threatened him with the Watch, but I wanted to know why he had abducted me, shouted about a missing boy, and then gone running off. He could just be insane. Lunatics were hardly unknown in Agatos. Sometimes I thought they were the majority. Living here could drive anyone over the edge. But not

240

many lunatics had a way to take down a fully-fledged mage.

"This way." I nodded back along the street. "You walk ahead. If you try and run, you'll lose your legs."

I directed him to a small plaza not far from the Leap, where several benches sat sheltered by a screen of cypress trees. The benches were occupied, but at the sight of my black cloak approaching, they were quickly vacated again. I really had to dump this thing. Not only was I as conspicuous as a pair of dropped trousers at a children's party – and just as welcome – but I was sweating through my shirt and starting to stink.

I waited for my attacker to seat himself, then took up position far enough away that I could hit him with magic before he could jump me. "Talk."

He bit his lip, looking unsure. Too late for that, now. I wouldn't say I sympathised, but I reckoned he was having a hard time coming up with a reason why I shouldn't decorate the plaza with his intestines.

"I have a sister."

"Me too. Big fucking deal."

He winced, his fingers drumming on the stone bench like his hands were trying to make a run for it. "She is from Khorasan, like me. A merchant. Three months ago, she was in Agatos with her husband and their son. Her husband had never seen Agatos." Not a great loss in my opinion. "But while they were here, their son disappeared. It was crowded, they were in the Penitent's Ear market, and he just ... disappeared. He was fourteen years old. They searched everywhere.

They went to the City Watch. They paid an investigator. But nothing. So, they sent for me."

Was he lying? I couldn't tell. I didn't have a read on this man yet. The twitchiness could just be nerves, or it could be something else. If he was lying, it was a strange lie. "Why you?"

He bit his lip again, then met my eyes. "I have a very particular set of skills."

Yeah. I had encountered one of those skills in my beer at Dalucia's tavern. He pushed on the bench, as though he was about to stand, then managed to settle. He was making me edgy with all this restlessness.

"What has any of that got to do with me?"

"I managed to track down my nephew's movements until I discovered he had last been seen in the company of a group of men."

Coldness slid over me. "Men? What do you mean men?" My imagination supplied enough answers. I had grown up on the streets of Agatos, and I knew the dangers that waited out there. Fourteen wasn't young, but for a kid not used to the city... "What happened to him?"

"I don't know. I can't even say that they harmed him. He might simply have been asking for directions."

The other alternatives didn't need spelling out. "These men. Did you find them? What did they say?"

A grimace twisted his face. His features were as restless as the rest of him. "I have followed them, but I have not been able to get close. Something watches them. I have felt it."

"Something?"

He shrugged. "Something malign. I am not a mage. I just have sensitivities."

Probably a natural magical talent, then, but a minor one. It wasn't uncommon.

"You said you followed them."

"Yes. And when I saw you first at the funeral of the woman who killed one of them, and then at his apartment..."

"Right." He had thought I was connected to them. He had thought I knew something about his nephew's disappearance. That was why he had drugged me. "Was Peyt Jyston Cord one of the men you tracked down?"

He nodded.

"The others, let me guess. Porta Sarassan, Marron, and Calovar."

"Yes. Marron Bale and Calovar Tide."

A child had gone missing after being seen with Cord and his friends. Then Etta Mirian had murdered Cord. Was that a coincidence? I didn't see how the two things could be connected. The Mirians didn't have any children of their own, so it couldn't be that. Maybe she had a grudge against Cord, but if so, I still hadn't dug it out. "Do you or your cousin have any connection to Etta Mirian?"

The Khorasani shook his head. "I knew nothing of her until she killed Cord. I wondered if she was trying to cover up what he might have done."

Dispose of a link between herself and whatever

Cord had been up to? Maybe. Except for one thing. "And then she killed herself too?" What kind of sense would that make? Unless the guilt had got to her. A terrible crime, an unbearable guilt? Killing Cord and then herself because of what they had done? It was a story I would read.

But the smile. That fucking smile.

What were you up to, Cord? And more importantly, "What do you want with me?" I asked my former kidnapper.

The Khorasani lifted his chin. "I think we can work together. You are a mage. You have power, friends, access. I have information. I have followed these men. I have got to know them."

The 'friends' and 'access' parts were optimistic, but otherwise it made sense. Assuming he wasn't lying through his teeth. The question was, was I about to trust a man who had drugged me and tied me up?

"You say you have special skills. What are they?"

"I find things out."

Great. "You're an investigator?"

"Not quite. I work for the University of Khorasan."

"Oh, for fuck's sake." A scholar would be about as much use here as ... well, about as much use as a scholar in any other situation.

I must have done a poor job of hiding my expression – or maybe the 'for fuck's sake' had given it away – because he smiled. "We are not the same as the scholars at your university. In Agatos, your scholars study only things that are already known. In

244

Khorasan, we are trained to go out and discover the unknown."

Was that supposed to impress me? A scholar was a scholar. The students at the university, like Thira Godspoint, had been wankers, and the scholars teaching them had been wankers, too. In my opinion, the only point of having a university was to keep them all locked up and away from the rest of us. Scholars who went wandering around sticking their noses into stuff were the worst of both worlds. But he either had useful information or he didn't. Where we went next would depend on that. "So, what can you tell me?"

"I know where these men live, I know where they work, I know who they talk to, and I know where they go."

All right. That would be useful if it was true. I hadn't got far looking into Cord, just some names and various lines of goat shit that Porta Sarassan had tried to feed me like a plate of pastries. If my new friend wasn't lying, I could save days. Depths, maybe I could even help him find his missing nephew.

"Right. If we're going to work together, I want your name and where you're staying, and if you try to drug me again, I'll tear off your legs and shove them so far down your throat they'll come back out your arse. Agreed?"

He raised his hands again. "Of course. I am Jettuk Kehsereen. I am staying at an inn called *The Lost Head* on Harbour Street. Do you know it?"

I nodded. "Then give me" – I thought – "four hours.

I have some things I have to do first. Meet me back here."

IN FACT, I ONLY HAD ONE THING TO DO, AND THAT WAS sleep. Even my minor show of force to intimidate Kehsereen had felt like it was ripping apart whatever wound I had done to myself. I would be lucky if I wasn't pissing or shitting blood before long. Four hours – three and a half, if I was lucky, by the time I got back – wouldn't be enough to heal me completely, but it might repair the worst of the damage and leave me functional.

Benny and Sereh weren't waiting when I got back. Benny was probably sleeping, and as for Sereh, she was no doubt out threatening a god, disembowelling someone who had looked at Benny the wrong way, or whatever it was she did for entertainment. I just hoped that Benny hadn't noticed Kehsereen waiting outside, or I was in for another awkward conversation. I was coming to realise, belatedly, as always, that my promise to keep business away from Benny's home was one I couldn't keep. Whether I wanted it or not, my work, the trouble I kept finding myself in, came looking for me. I was putting my friends – Depths, my real *family* – in danger. If I really cared about their safety, I couldn't stay here. But where was I supposed to get the time to find another place to live?

I dropped onto my bed – my borrowed bed – only

pulling off my black cloak and toeing off my shoes, and I was asleep before I could come up with an answer.

I didn't have much to thank my mage-training for, unless you counted a brain full of hang-ups, resentments, and traumas, but I had learned to set a spell that would wake me up exactly at the exact time I needed. When it jolted me awake, less than four hours later, I still felt exhausted. At least I didn't think I was likely to tear myself in half with simple magic, which was an improvement, because I reckoned I would need magic again before this was done.

I slipped out, careful not to wake Benny, only stopping to grab my black cloak and my mage's rod – I really had to come up with a better name for that – in case I needed to hit anyone.

Kehsereen was waiting in the same plaza I had left him in, but he was striding agitatedly up and down in front of the bench, muttering. I wondered if he had waited there the whole time. That would be ... weird, and I didn't know how I felt about it. Not that this guy had done much to sell 'normal' to me yet, and not that he could make the only claim to weird behaviour here.

I indicated Kehsereen to the bench and sat beside him, still keeping an arm's length between us. "I've talked to Porta Sarassan," I said, "and he was about as much use as a fart in a hurricane. I want to talk to the other two before I go back to Sarassan. So, where are we going to find them?"

Kehsereen shuddered, seemingly forcing himself to stillness. "I'm sorry. These last weeks have been hard. I

247

haven't slept. I have become desperate." I had noticed that when he had tied me up. "The wrestler, Marron Bale, will be training at the arena for another hour at least. I have not been able to get in. I don't know if you can?" I could if I had to. It might not be the best idea. Kehsereen continued, "The lawyer, Calovar Tide, though, has taken to working from his house these last few days. He has not even been to court."

"That's not at all suspicious."

"Is it not?" He met my look with a blank gaze. Either my sarcasm didn't translate, or he was better at it than I was.

I decided to ignore it. "No point in trying to talk to Bale right now. We'll find him later. Where does this Calovar Tide live?"

"Petrel Avenue. It's in the Upper City."

"Of course it is." Where else would a lawyer live? There was no money to be made slumming it with the scum in my part of town. "Off the Royal Highway, yes?"

Kehsereen nodded.

It figured. It was right in the heart of the business district up there, where merchants and bankers kept their offices and the litigious rich wouldn't have to travel far to buy justice.

I pushed myself up. My guts still twinged, but the pain was gone. "Better get started. It's going to take us a while to get there."

❧

CALOVAR TIDE'S HOUSE WAS GRAND, NO DOUBT ABOUT it. You could have fitted three or four of Benny's house inside it with room to spare. But for this district, it didn't stand out. It was still a house, not a mansion like Mica's or a palace like the Countess's. Still, I doubted many kids from Dockside ended up in places like this.

The Bad Luck Club, Sarassan had called them. It was kind of taking the piss that they hadn't changed the name to *The Good Luck Club*. I wondered if there was more than just good luck in the way the four of them had ended up. Well, not Cord, but before he had his throat opened by a smiling Etta Mirian. Good luck could pay well, but crime could pay even better. Slavery was illegal around most of the Yttradian Sea, but that didn't mean people weren't bought and sold, and half the sailors plying the ocean hadn't ended up on those ships by choice. How much would someone pay for a fit fourteen-year-old kid like Kehsereen's nephew? Not enough to pay for a place like this, that was for sure. They would have had to have been snatching and selling kids for a long time to afford their lifestyles, and why would a lawyer bother when there was so much more money to be made in his trade? Anyway, all I had was that they had been seen talking to the kid. That wasn't exactly a crime.

Maybe they really had been lucky and had shared their good fortune. Maybe the kid had been asking for directions home. Maybe they had been good citizens, lent him a couple of shields, and pointed him in the right direction. A thousand things could have happened to him after that. Coincidences happened a million times a day, and they meant nothing. The chances that Cord's date with Etta Mirian's knife was related to the kid's disappearance was stretching things beyond breaking point.

Except Cord *had* been involved in weird shit and an even weirder murder. Did coincidences happen to people like that?

I adjusted my black cloak as we approached the heavy double doors of Calovar Tide's house. Sarassan had been intimidated by my invocation of the Ash Guard, but Tide was a lawyer and he probably met powerful people every day. I might need to try another tactic.

I reached for the door knocker. As I did so, Kehsereen grabbed my arm. "Can you feel it?"

"What?" I unfocused my eyes and almost stumbled back. Magic blazed from the walls, the windows, and the door. I raised a hand to block it out and squinted. "Wards."

Not just any wards. The power in these was astonishing, and they were cleverly made. Most of the time, if an Ash Guard patrol passed too close to a ward, it would collapse, its magic eaten away, but the magic here originated deep in the house. Ash would take the wards down, but the moment it was gone, they would spring back up. The power and sophistication behind them would cost an absolute fortune. I couldn't punch through these wards. No one could. In fact, I could only think of three people who could manage to create these: the Wren, Mica, and the Countess, and as far as I knew, the Wren didn't hire out his services. I felt a bitter smile twist my face. One way or another, my mother was behind these wards. Not content to have fucked up my life, she was fucking with my job, too. Yeah, I knew it was irrational, but I didn't care.

Tide knows what's going on. The thought hit me with a power that was impossible to deny. He knew Cord had been killed. There was nothing suspicious about that. But he knew magic had been used to do it. So, he had hunkered down behind the strongest wards money could buy. *Does that mean he knows who did it, how, and why?*

If so, there was absolutely no way he would tell me.

Or was he behind the whole thing? Could he have had his own friend murdered? He had access to magic, clearly, but if it was my mother's magic, I had to believe she wouldn't hire out her services to kill people, if only because she wouldn't risk the Ash Guard's reprisals. No one could accuse my mother of being stupid, nor reckless. Still, Tide knew something, and either he was paranoid, or he hadn't shared it with his friends, because there had been no wards on Sarassan's house.

Maybe he's the only one with the wealth and connections to get this done? Maybe the whole 'share everything' of the Bad Luck Club was as much goat shit.

I stepped up, tugged on the bellpull beside the door, and waited. Half a minute later, the door swung open, and a thin, well-dressed, pale-skinned man looked out. "Yes?"

I noticed he stayed behind the wards. I glanced back at Kehsereen, and he nodded. So, this was Calovar Tide. Interesting that he had answered the door himself. Perhaps he had sent the servants away. More paranoia, or a sensible precaution against whoever had caused the murder of his friend?

"Mr. Tide. I am Mennik Thorn. I am assisting the Ash Guard with their investigation into the death of your friend, Peyt Jyston Cord." The truth had been stretched far enough already that it would fit around that.

The pretence had made Sarassan crumble, but you didn't become a successful lawyer by being easily fooled. "You're not Ash Guard."

"No. Like I said, I'm assisting. Right now, it's routine. Trust me, you don't want to see the actual Guard turn up at your door."

He still wasn't moved. "I'll need to see proof."

"You can ask the Guard. Talk to Captain Meroi Gale. She'll confirm it. I'll wait." I really hoped he wouldn't. I didn't need another arse-kicking any time soon.

Tide glanced up and down the street, still not crossing the wards. Yep. He didn't want to leave the safety of his house. *Scared of something.*

"Just ask your questions. There's not much I can tell you."

I didn't believe that for a moment. Not much he *wanted* to tell me, perhaps.

"Fine. Your friend was a gambler. He was involved in games run by the Wren down at Nettar's Wharf."

"I wouldn't know about anything illegal."

"I'm not the City Watch, Mr. Tide, and I'm sure the Wren has them well paid off. What I want to know is if Mr. Cord upset anyone."

"Peyt was good at what he did. He upset a lot of people. No one likes losing."

"Anyone in particular?"

"Maybe. We didn't really talk details of work. A lot of wealthy, powerful people go to those games, as well as people from the ships and the lower city. But Peyt was always careful not to win too much from any single person."

Even so, it didn't take much to push some people over the edge. "He didn't mention anyone who concerned him?"

"I wish I could be more help."

Of course you do. "Tell me about your other friends, Porta Sarassan and Marron Bale. Were they closer to Cord than you were?"

"You would have to ask them that." His expression was bland, helpful. I wondered if he had perfected that in court, screwing people over. If he hadn't been standing behind wards, I might have punched him in that smug mouth. Uncooperative bastard.

"So, you have no idea why your friend was killed?"

"Of course not. I would tell you if I did. He was my friend."

"And these wards?" I waved my hand at the house. "What are these for?"

He peered up at me. "Protection, Mr. Thorn. It's a dangerous city. I warned Peyt and the others many times. Maybe Peyt should have listened."

Yeah. That was goat shit. But I was starting to suspect that was all I was going to get out of him. Time to change tack. "You were seen with a boy."

"I don't have children."

That's not an answer, you fuck. I could feel Kehsereen trying not to fidget behind me and failing. I didn't know whether Tide had noticed Kehsereen following him over these last few weeks, but the less he focused on my companion, the better. I pushed on. "A Khorasani boy. Fourteen years old. This would have been about three months ago."

Tide made a helpless gesture. "It's a busy city. I meet a lot of people. He was not one of my clients. What has this got to do with Peyt's murder?"

That was the question, wasn't it? Maybe nothing. Maybe everything. "You don't remember talking to him?"

He repeated the half-shrug, palms turned up.

Maybe if I could have got to him, pulled out a bit of magic to intimidate him, he might have been more cooperative, but I doubted it. A man like this knew exactly when he had to talk and when he didn't. In principle, that was a good thing, and I was pleased to see someone stand up to the black cloak at last, but it was still a pain in the arse.

"All right, Mr. Tide. I assume we'll find you here if we need to talk to you again. You don't look like you're going anywhere."

I turned away and left him standing just behind his wards. I could feel him watching us until we were out of sight.

The whole thing had been as frustrating as I had expected. He knew far more than he admitted, but I had no idea how to get it out of him.

"What did you think of him?" I asked Kehsereen.

"He is good at not answering questions."

Yeah, he was. Maybe we would have more luck with his wrestler friend. He might beat us around our heads with our own limbs, but hopefully he would be less sleazy and evasive while he did it. But not right now. The sun was dipping towards the mountains, and it would soon be night.

"We'll have to continue tomorrow. Midday. Same place as today? I've got some things to follow up." Squint should have my information by now. "And I want to find out about Mr. Tide's wards. I don't care how dangerous the city is or how wealthy you are, you don't put up wards like that unless you know of a specific threat and you are very afraid." I eyed Kehsereen. "I'm going to talk to the Countess. I should do that alone. She's not ... friendly." Understatement. And the less my mother knew about my business and Kehsereen, the better. With my mother, it was always worth having a hidden card, because she would have three.

CHAPTER SIXTEEN

I was never quite sure how Squint got his information. As far as I could tell, he almost never left his dingy corner of Dumonoc's, where he slowly disintegrated what was left of his intestines with the supposed wine served in this godsforsaken hole. But of all the information brokers who worked, at arm's length, for the Wren, I had always found Squint the most reliable. If he said he would get you information, he would. He would also sell everything you said to or near him to anyone who would pay.

I ducked the empty wine bottle Dumonoc tossed at my head as I entered the bar and crossed to Squint.

"So, why do you want to find this bloke?" Squint said as I sat opposite him. He pulled his wine bottle closer, as though anyone in the whole Cepra-damned city would want to steal it.

I smiled, then regretted it as he displayed his own

rotted teeth. "That would be information. I'll sell it to you."

"Nah, you're all right. No one really cares. Your bloke is holed up at an inn on Dockside right now. Should be there for the rest of the evening." Why would he be anywhere else? Everything led back to the docks. It was like fate was determined to squeeze every raw corner of my mind. "*The Bloody End*, it's called. You know it?"

I shook my head.

"Shithole of a place on Coldwind Alley." This coming from a man who spent his days in Dumonoc's.

"Sounds delightful." I pushed my chair back.

"I heard the Wren's getting antsy. Thinks you might be taking the piss. I'm giving you that one for free."

That was hardly news after this morning's run-in with his acolytes. "I'm on it. I've almost got what he wants." If, by 'almost' I meant 'not even close'.

Squint tipped his wine into his cup. I leaned back to avoid the fumes. "It don't bother me. You're not exactly my best customer. Just being neighbourly."

I headed for the door, ready to duck again if Dumonoc reached for another bottle, but he had sunk back into silent brooding. He didn't even react when I waved goodbye.

It took me a while to find Coldwind Alley, and I was increasingly aware that I had promised Elosyn that

I would make it to Holera's party. Eight o'clock, she had said, and it must be that already. No one expected you to be on time for a party, though, did they? I wasn't sure. I didn't get invited to many parties. But this shouldn't take long.

The alley was squeezed between the blank wall of a warehouse and a crumbling sailors' tenement, and it lived up to its name, channelling the breeze from the harbour into a chilling wind, even in the heat of the early summer. The cold wasn't the only thing the wind carried from the alley. The acid smell of piss, rotted food, and dead things washed out and over me. If you wanted somewhere no one would come looking for you, this was exactly the place to choose. I couldn't imagine either of the Mirians would ever find themselves down here. Tain would never have had to see them. It spoke to resentment.

It wasn't full dark yet – the tops of the mountains that hemmed in the Erastes Valley still glowed with evening sunlight – but the tight alley was as dark as a sewer, and no more pleasant. I was glad I had brought along my mage's rod. In places like this, there was almost always something that needed hitting. The only light was what leaked through the gaps in shutters and from a single, open doorway three quarters of the way down the alley.

My job took me to the nicest places.

A couple of drunks pissing against the wall turned to watch me pass – and incidentally piss all over their shoes as they did so – but the sight of the black cloak kept them where they were.

Squint had been right when he described *The Bloody End* as a shithole. The inn stank almost as bad as the alley, although here the urine mingled with stale beer, tallow candles, and sweat. It was crowded, though – inexplicably so, in my opinion – and most of the clientele seemed to be sailors. Hardly surprising so close to the docks. I stopped just inside the door, scanning the room. Heads turned to watch me, hostile expressions undisguised.

A lesser – or a more popular – man might have been put off by such an unfriendly reception, but I was used to it. I pushed back my hood, making sure everyone got a good look at the cloak. "I'm looking for Solus Tain."

I didn't expect anyone to volunteer the information, but I was watching carefully, and a sudden, suppressed start from the back of the room caught my attention. *Got you, you bastard.*

"We've paid the Wren. You've got no business here." The speaker, seated at a table by the bar, was well dressed, at least compared to the rest of the patrons. Clothes that were mostly clean, reasonably new, and unpatched; jewellery around her neck and wrists. A Mycedan, I reckoned, by the look of her. I ignored her and headed for my target.

A couple of big men rose from nearby tables to block my passage.

Interesting. Most people kept out of a mage's way. Why were these guys so keen to protect Tain?

"She said you've got no business here," the one on the left said.

I pulled in magic and let a glow form around my hands. I could get in shit with the Ash Guard if I threw magic at them, but I was entitled to defend myself, and there were no rules against threats and intimidation.

I didn't have my eyes unfocused, so the only warning I got was a sudden flare of light in the corner of my eye.

Instinct saved me. I ducked, and a bolt of magic seared past where my head had been moments earlier to tear through the wall.

Bannaur's holy balls! A mage. I had been too cocky, thinking I could walk in and intimidate everyone. Now I was in the shit.

I kept moving, throwing up a shield.

One of the sailors swung a knife at me, but it skimmed off my shield.

Why the fuck hadn't Squint told me this place wasn't friendly?

Because you didn't pay him to, you idiot. A man who sold information wasn't giving it away for free.

The other mage rose from his table. He was Mycedan, too, with the characteristic blue tattoo beside his left eye, and dressed like a sailor. He pulled in raw magic for another attack.

I didn't know how powerful this guy was, so I tossed a flare of light in his eyes to distract him, then while he was swearing and preparing his repost, I used magic to pull a bottle from a shelf behind him and smack him over the back of his head. He went down with a shout. I knew plenty of mages who would think that was cheating. I just thought of it as winning.

I had just long enough to feel smug when a sailor launched himself into me. My attack had drained my shield, and I stumbled back, smashing into a table and sending it flying. The sailor landed on top of me.

If I had relied on my magic alone to get me through, I wouldn't have survived half the street brawls in the Warrens as a kid. As the sailor pushed back, ready to swing for me, I brought my mage's rod down in his face. His nose exploded under the weight of the obsidian embedded in the end.

I pulled in more magic, strengthened my shield, and pushed him away. I stood and glowered around the inn. Most of the patrons were on their feet, and most of them had drawn knives or clubs.

I was starting to wonder what kind of place I had wandered into.

I raised my mage's rod and made it glow. "Next person to try anything stupid loses an arm."

The woman who had spoken earlier pushed her way through the gathered sailors. "You walked into the wrong inn, mage."

"Yeah. I realised that when I smelled the place." It wasn't my best comeback, but I was surrounded, my heart was thumping, and I didn't know how long the other mage would stay down. If I had to fight my way out, I was going to get badly hurt.

Now, where had Solus Tain got to?

There. At the back of the inn, sliding along the wall, hoping he wouldn't be noticed. Even though the guy hadn't washed or shaved for weeks, and despite the bruises of too much alcohol and too little sleep, I recognised the family resemblance. When I had seen Etta Mirian, her throat had been cut from side to side and she had been laid out on a slab. She had still looked better than her brother. I jabbed my rod towards him. "You."

His head jerked up, then he bolted for a door beside the bar. I swore and took off after him, shaping my shield to barge people aside.

I had expected the door to lead to a side alley or a back room, so when I shoved through in pursuit, I almost sent myself flying down the narrow stone stairs. I managed to stop myself just in time to see Tain disappear into a darkened hallway at the bottom of the steps. I had the presence of mind to throw a magical lock on the door behind me. A moment later, bodies hit it and rebounded.

"Weren't expecting that, were you, you wankers?" I shouted back through the door.

The magic wouldn't hold if I got too far away, and it wouldn't hold at all against the other mage.

I set off in pursuit again.

Either Tain was too panicked or too drunk to cover his trail, because the hallway opened into a room stacked with barrels, and there he had pulled up what would have been a well-concealed trapdoor and left it gaping. I could hear running, stumbling footsteps below.

I wasn't stupid enough to leap into the dark. I created a mage light and let it drift down into the opening, then lowered myself after it.

The tunnel I found myself in might once have been a sewer, but if so, that function had long since ceased. The tunnel sloped down towards the harbour, maybe under one of the wharfs, and gently up beneath the city. Tide marks stained the walls of the passage further down. One side of the tunnel had caved in to reveal a large chamber, which itself must once have been a substantial building, even though its walls, too, were collapsed in places by the weight of the buildings above. The chamber was stacked with barrels, crates, bales, and chests.

Smugglers. No wonder I hadn't been popular when I strode into *The Bloody End*. At low tide, the tunnel must open somewhere in the harbour, allowing cargo to be secretly offloaded.

If there was smuggling here, Squint probably knew about it, and the Wren certainly did. They had let me walk right into it, the bastards. I wondered if the Wren knew the smugglers had a mage of their own who was throwing power about.

The distant sounds of hammering told me the smugglers weren't waiting for the door to open itself, and I shouldn't stand around gawking at their illegal shit.

Tain had headed up the tunnel, away from the harbour. I could still hear his cursing and stumbling in the dark. I set off after him and tried to push away the nagging thought that Tain didn't seem like a man who could arrange a supernatural suicide of his own sister. Yeah, there had been a mage up there, but someone who could do what had been done to Etta Mirian and Cord shouldn't be so easy to put down. I never got that lucky.

Behind me, I felt my connection to the magical lock begin to fray. No point wasting more power on it just to hold them for another minute. I let it drop.

It was cold down here under the city, and even though this tunnel was dry, the air felt damp. I could smell the ocean, the salt, the rotting seaweed.

The tunnel I was following had crumbled and partially collapsed, leaving rubble on the floor and gaping, black holes in the walls and ceiling, from which occasional sighs of stagnant air washed over me and into which sound disappeared as though it had been swallowed. I could never be a deep diver like Porta Sarassan. Even being in this relatively intact tunnel, close to the surface, the thought of that weight of earth and stone and brick balanced precariously above me made me start at every sound and echo. I could never bring myself to slide through cracks between crushed buildings and rocks like deep divers did, searching for long lost valuables in the forgotten wreckage of Agatos's history.

I didn't think it was Solus Tain's thing, either. I could see him ahead, now, on the edge of my mage light, swearing, scrambling, and stumbling over the debris.

I had always been fast, courtesy of my long legs, and even ducking my head to avoid smashing into the brick ceiling, I was closing the distance on Tain. He scrabbled up a pile of rubble that almost reached the ceiling, slid over, and disappeared from sight. I leapt after him, threw myself through the gap, and slid inelegantly down the other side. I was lucky he wasn't waiting there with a brick to smash my head in, because I came down out of control.

In fact, Tain wasn't waiting for me anywhere. The tunnel stretched ahead to the limit of my mage light and there was absolutely no sign of him.

"Where the fuck did you go?"

I brightened my mage light and sent a fragment of it chasing down the tunnel. Nothing.

There was no way he had outrun me. I turned, slowly.

There! If the mage light hadn't been so bright, I wouldn't have seen the slight flinch. The side of the tunnel had given way, as it had along much of its length, and what I had thought was just earth behind revealed itself to be an opening. Beyond it, Tain's dirty, tired, bearded face peered out.

I crouched down and brought the light closer. Tain scrambled backwards.

"Why don't you make this easier and come on out?" I said.

He shuffled further away. I wondered if the 'make it easier' thing ever worked. I sent the mage light into his hideaway.

It was a single room, maybe once of a house. I could see murals painted on the walls. They had flaked and crumbled away, leaving only patchwork hints at pictures. I recognised paintings of a dog, a duck, and what might have been a lion painted by someone who had only heard a story about one and really got the wrong idea about it. At the back was a doorway, but the lintel stone had fallen in, as had the doorposts, and beyond was just rubble. The ceiling should have fallen in, too. I could see where a wooden beam must once have stretched across, but it was long gone. Something must have collapsed in on top of it or been built over it, leaving the space still open after hundreds – maybe thousands – of years. The remains of a counter enclosed almost half of the room. Round openings along the top might once have held bowls or pots. One now held an old nest. Perhaps this had been some kind of taverna once. There were places not too different to this in the Warrens still. Perhaps a street had run past where the abandoned sewer now ran. It could have been bustling and busy, full of chatter and laughter and lives long forgotten. It was hard to believe in the claustrophobic dark.

Someone had been sleeping here. There was an old mattress and a couple of blankets in one corner. From the stink, the same person had used it as a toilet. Tain, I guessed, from the way he scurried back to the stained, ripped mattress.

You really think this guy has been masterminding magical murder-suicides?

He was a wreck.

I built a shield around myself again – more to protect against falling masonry than anything Tain might do – and followed him in.

"You're Solus Tain?"

He cringed away. *Shit*. I wasn't enjoying this.

"Your brother-in-law thought you were on a ship halfway around the Yttradian Sea."

That roused him. He muttered something incomprehensible.

"What's that?"

"I said I would have been if they had lent me the money. On my own ship, too." The bitterness spilled out with the words.

No. I didn't buy this man as a murderer. If he had been, he would have tried to hide the hate. And, honestly, I didn't think he could organise a slip on an icy puddle.

"What are you doing down here?" I said.

His eyes darted to the side then back. "They let me."

"Who? The smugglers?"

A quick jerk of the head that must have hurt his

neck. If he could feel anything under all that alcohol. "I watch the passage. They let me drink up there."

Fuck. This was Etta Mirian's brother, a drunk watchman for smugglers in a tunnel no one used, paid in beer? Compared to the Mirians' shop and apartment, well, there was no comparison.

"Why didn't you go to your sister for help?"

His face twisted. "She won't help. She's not my sister."

He didn't even know she was dead. Down here, in his cocoon, he was in a different world. Screw it. I wasn't going to be the one to tell him, any more than I was going to kick him in the face. I wasn't being paid to destroy innocent strangers. I turned away.

"I hear it, you know."

A shiver ran up my spine, unexpectedly. "Hear what?"

"In the tunnels, sometimes. The whispering."

Oh, for fuck's sake. As though I wasn't already freaking myself out enough down here in the dark.

"It gets in your head, like ants. Burrowing. Biting."

He had been down here too long. That was what it was. Too much drink, too little daylight, too little food, too long with his imagination.

"Find help," I said. "Go to your brother-in-law. He'll..." I didn't know what Mr. Mirian could do. Help, somehow. Anything had to be better than this. I would tell Mr. Mirian that Tain was here. They would have to work it out between them. I had my own things to worry about.

I squeezed through the opening, into the tunnel. This had been another dead end. Whatever had happened to Etta Mirian had nothing to do with her brother. I just wished I hadn't had to find myself in an abandoned sewer, pursued by a gang of angry smugglers and at least one rogue mage, to figure that out.

And talking about angry smugglers, I could hear their shouts further down the tunnel, past the cave-in. I dimmed my mage light until it only illuminated about six feet in front of me. There had to be another way out of this tunnel, or they wouldn't have set a guard, even a ruined, drunk one. I started to trudge in the opposite direction to the voices, further under the city.

Right now, Elosyn and Holera's party didn't seem such a terrible prospect. "Look at you, Nik. Becoming so sociable that a party sounds better than being trapped in an abandoned, on-the-verge-of-collapse sewer." Benny would be proud.

IF THERE WAS ONE THING THAT EMPHASISED JUST exactly how much I didn't know what I was doing, it was being lost in a forgotten sewer, deep beneath the city. How deep, I didn't know. Where in the city, I didn't know. How I was going to get out again, well, that I especially didn't know.

With Etta Mirian's brother ruled out, that brought me back to the idea that Cord had pissed off someone powerful. Still, I couldn't shake the feeling that it didn't fit. Why would Cord pissing someone off cause his lawyer friend to pay for the most powerful wards in the city? Why would Sarassan lie to me like a priest trying to solicit a donation? How did Kehsereen's nephew fit in? And why had Etta Mirian been the one to wield the knife? I was missing something. Oh yeah, and there was all the weird magical, supernatural shit swirling around this like a whirlpool of turds trying to suck me down.

Why in all the Depths had I agreed to help Mr. Mirian in the first place? His wife had knifed a man in the street.

You know why you agreed. You haven't got over your hang-ups about Mica's dad. As though this was going to help.

A voice whispered beside my ear. I jerked around, shield coming up, power coalescing around my hand. My heart tripped and leapt, stuttering wildly.

No one. There was no one there. Just the sound of the breeze in the tunnel.

Fuck! Solus Tain's drunken imaginings were getting to me.

You're not doing this, Nik. Not down here. Pull it together.

The whisper came again, tuneless and old, sliding and jarring, in a horrible imitation of words.

Bannaur's bloody, beaten balls! That wasn't just the breeze. Was it?

I unfocused my eyes. There was no one here, not even hidden by magic.

You're panicking. Calm down.

Words drifted down the tunnel, almost too soft to be heard, twisting like snakes. A discharge of magic, like a miniature dart of lightning, skittered along the walls. I felt a presence, something vast, watching.

It was too much. My mind rebelled. *Get the fuck out of here!*

I lost control. I had been clutching my tension and my anxiety and my panic so close for so long that when they saw their opening, they took it.

I ran, bouncing off walls, stumbling over uneven ground, splashing through puddles, scrambling up and over rubble, while all around me the whispering worked at my mind.

Burrowing, biting, Tain had said.

Motherfucker. There were tears stinging my eyes. A choked sound escaped my throat.

Somehow, at some point, I left the old sewer behind. I didn't know if these tunnels were natural, the ruins of some palace or temple, or dug from the ruins beneath the city. My mage light flickered wildly, fading and flaring, almost out of my control. All I could think was, *Up. Out.*

I hit a dead end. A stone wall. *Shit!* I spun about wildly. Which way had I come? I couldn't tell. Everything swam around me, a chaos of looming shadows. *It's panic. It's just panic.* I couldn't breathe.

My light went out. I clamped my teeth to cut off a scream.

The whispering closed in. A hundred voices, none I could even understand. Syllables, words, imprecations, all in a language I didn't recognise.

I stumbled into something that went crashing to the ground. I lost my footing. My knee hit a rock. Pain stabbed through me. For a second, the whispers retreated.

I crawled. I didn't know where I was going. My hand scrabbled like a spider through the rubble. Then my fingers closed on something sharp. Without thinking, I grabbed it, drove it into my opposite forearm, and kept driving. I felt skin part, then muscle. I didn't know if I screamed again. The pain crowded everything else out.

I folded up around the wound, there in the dark and the damp, clutching it, until at last control returned. Warm blood trickled down my arm and soaked my sleeve. Thank all the bitter gods I hadn't hit an artery, or I would have bled out here.

I conjured another mage light and forced myself to look at the damage. The wound was a mess, jagged, dirty, and torn. My makeshift weapon lay on the ground beside me. A fragment of pottery, old, too. Intact, that would have been worth something to a deep diver. I kicked it away.

It wasn't easy to wrap the wound with one hand, particularly when that hand was weak and shaking. I had to rip a sleeve from my shirt. "Stupid, fucking stupid," I kept muttering as I pulled it tight. Maybe if I kept talking, I wouldn't hear any whispers from the dark. Maybe I would be able to tell myself they were echoes of my own voice. I didn't think the bandage would hold up to any vigorous movement. The wound hurt like all the Depths, too, but right now that helped me focus. "There were no whispers," I told myself. It had been my imagination, stress, and exhaustion combining into panic. "That's what you do. You panic."

Who are you trying to fool?

I retrieved my rod from where it had fallen and took a proper look around. I was in some kind of ruin, but of what, I couldn't tell. Some building. It had mostly fallen in, leaving slabs and tumbled blocks of stone propped haphazardly around. There were footprints in the dust and dirt, too, which I was certain weren't mine. *Deep divers.* That mean there *was* some way out. Water dripped from above me. My mage light showed it coming from a ragged opening in the ceiling.

Up was good. Up was the living city. Up was not down here. If I kept going up, I would find my way out eventually. I reckoned I could scramble to the opening over the fallen blocks. It would be difficult, it would hurt, and I wasn't going to enjoy it, but I could manage.

It took a while, and I could feel my arm bleeding again by the time I reached the opening, but at last I hauled my sore body through and found myself once again in a sewer. I had a brief moment of terror when I thought I was back where I had started, but this sewer wasn't abandoned. A thin stream of water – definitely water! – ran along the bottom, the last legacy of the previous night's storm. It wasn't high enough to spill over the opening I had climbed through. It must be filtering between bricks to drip down to the chamber below. I wondered if the whole thing was about to crumble beneath my feet.

The sewer tunnel sloped gently down to my right and up to my left. Down to where it emptied, maybe into the harbour. Up to … wherever it drained from. I didn't want to go back to the harbour – the last thing I needed was to run into the smugglers again – but not all drains emptied there. It could equally well open onto the river. And down had to come out *somewhere*.

Yeah? A few minutes ago, you were thinking up was out.

I was lost. I didn't know how to navigate this maze beneath the city, and my earlier panic had left my brain spinning. Up? Down? Either might lead out. Either might lose me further. Despair threatened to overwhelm me. It was already leaching my strength. *Just go somewhere.*

Down. I closed my eyes and settled my breath. There would be a way out.

Unless it's blocked. Unless it's beneath the water.

Knowing I was making the wrong choice, I forced myself on.

I didn't know how long I had been walking – not long, I suspected – when the thin stream of water reached a stepped weir and dropped down. I clambered over it. Ahead, I thought the tunnel looked lighter. I dropped my mage light and let my eyes adjust. Yes! The end of the tunnel was dark, but it was a different order of darkness to the black of the deeper tunnels. As I squinted, I began to make out details sixty or seventy yards ahead. The sewer tunnel opened onto the night. Not far ahead of me, another branch cut off to the left. I recognised this place. I had been here before, and not today.

As if in response, a cold wind drifted from the side tunnel, carrying a damp, rotting smell and the distant sound of whispering.

I broke into a run.

I came out through the loose grating onto the riverbank beneath the Sour Bridge. The tide was higher than it had been last night, and I had to splash though the water, but fuck it. Even if it had been neck-deep, I would have launched myself into it rather than spend any more time under the city. From now on, I wasn't even going in a basement. I wanted the open sky, the mountains. Maybe I would go and live as a hermit on some peak.

It was full dark now, not a hint of sunset washing out the sky. I didn't know how long I had been down there under the city. Hours, maybe. I did know I had made a horrible mistake deciding to find another way out.

And – shit! – I was very, very late for Elosyn and Holera's party. I looked down at myself. I was a mess. My clothes were filthy, my shirt was ripped and bloodstained, and my shoes and the bottom of my trousers were soaked in whatever foul water I had tramped through. I probably stank, too. At least my stupid black cloak was still miraculously intact, as always. I wrapped it around me, pulled up the hood, and headed off across the city. Everything else might be going to the Depths, but I could keep my promise to my friends.

CHAPTER SEVENTEEN

THERE WERE STILL LIGHTS THROUGH THE OPEN SHUTTERS on the front of Elosyn and Holera's house when I finally limped into sight, but it was quiet. It must be later than I had realised. Too late? It had to be better to turn up too late than not at all. Right?

I hoped Elosyn and Holera would feel the same way.

I puffed out a breath, straightened my shoulders, made sure the cloak was tight around me, and knocked on the door.

Elosyn answered – unfortunately for me – and it only took a second for her expression to change from puzzled to furious.

"What the fuck is this, Nik?"

I guessed Elosyn didn't feel the same way after all. "I got held up."

"Narth's tits, Nik! You got held up?" Elosyn was a good friend, but if you got on the wrong side of her, you would regret it. It probably came from having to put up with all the entitled pricks at Nuil's. Or maybe from having to deal with me on a regular basis. "I asked one thing of you – one thing – and, what? You got distracted. I even went round to look for you when you didn't turn up. Benny said he hadn't seen you. At least he came to help celebrate."

"Benny came? Did you count your cutlery?"

"This is not a fucking joke. How many times have I bailed you out? How many times have I been there when you needed me?"

No. It wasn't a joke, and I wasn't going to get out of this by trying to make it one. I had messed up. Again. "I'm sorry."

Holera appeared in the doorway behind Elosyn. She was taller than her wife, with long, unbound hair that was brushed straight. "Nik. We missed you."

"Elosyn was just letting me know."

"I heard from the back room. So did the neighbours, probably. Why don't you come in?" She laid a hand on Elosyn's shoulder. Elosyn shot me a glance that promised she wasn't done with me, but she stepped back.

I didn't suppose telling her that I hadn't intended any of this would make a difference?

I followed them in. Their main room was still piled with the remains from the party. My eyes found their way to the food left behind. I hadn't eaten for ... well, since that morning, I supposed. I was starting to lose track, and that was never a good sign.

"Why don't you help yourself?" Holera said. "It's only going to waste."

"I'll help him with something," Elosyn muttered.

I ignored the threat and reached for a plate.

"What in the Depths?" Elosyn sputtered. I froze, then realised my cloak had slipped open as I reached. She was staring at my shirt beneath. "Take that cloak off, Mennik Thorn!"

I licked my lips. I really wanted those leftovers. "I don't know…"

"Take it off."

Wincing, I eased it from my shoulders.

"Pity, Nik. What happened to you?"

In the light of the lanterns, I looked worse than I had realised. My makeshift bandage was almost black with drying blood, and more blood was still seeping out from under it.

"I had a bit of a run-in with some smugglers." I didn't tell them the wound was self-inflicted.

"How are you even still standing?"

For a while, I hadn't been. If I had seen this wound properly, I might not have made it. "I've had worse," I said.

"You know that doesn't make it sound better, right? Come on."

She led me through to their kitchen and peeled off my bandage, then washed the injury. The bandage was stuck to the raw wound with dry blood. I suffered through the whole procedure with an absolute minimum of swearing, cursing, and threats towards the various gods. I could tell Elosyn was impressed by my fortitude. "For fuck's sake, Nik, will you just stay still?" She peered at the wound. "Actually, it's not as bad as I thought. Doesn't look like a knife wound."

I grunted. "There was a lot of stuff flying around. I didn't see it." *Liar.*

"You should get a proper physician to look at this. It needs stitching." She wrapped a bandage around it.

"I'll be fine. I just need sleep." A wound like this should mostly heal overnight. One of the advantages of being a mage.

"Maybe next time don't pick a fight with smugglers, eh?"

"Yeah, well. They didn't exactly have a sign on the door." I resented the implication that I had been the one starting the fight, even though I supposed I had been. "Anyway, I have no intention of going back there."

"Good. I've got your stuff."

"My what?" I wondered for a moment if Benny had finally kicked me out and dumped all my things with Elosyn and Holera. The mood Elosyn was in, she would probably kick me right back out again.

"The information you asked me to find out."

"Right. Of course." Thank the gods. Benny wasn't done with me just yet. I had forgotten I had asked Elosyn to look into my mother's purchase of the old coffee house. "What did you find out?"

"The Countess has been buying property around the Middle City, a couple of places in the Grey City. A dozen buildings so far and a couple she's still interested in. All big places, coffee shops, things like that. One thing they've got in common is that they've got large open spaces inside, and they're in decent but not posh parts of the city."

This didn't make any sense. My mother was hardly about to open a string of coffee shops or restaurants. The money she made from her magical services and her position on the Senate dwarfed anything she could earn like that. "Any idea why?"

"Nothing. Her factor is keeping it quiet. Purchases with no questions asked." She handed me a sheet of paper. "Here's the list of the places."

Whatever my mother was up to with these, it wouldn't stay secret for long. If I wanted this to be my ticket out of the Wren's debt, I would have to figure it out before it became public knowledge. "Thanks." I pocketed the list. "And, you know." I waved a hand towards the main room. "About all this. Sorry." I glanced across at where Holera leant against the doorway. "Um. Happy birthday?"

Holera let out a laugh, which only deepened Elosyn's scowl. She bundled the bloody remains of my sleeve and dropped it into a bucket. "Find another job, Nik, before this one kills you."

I AWOKE THE NEXT MORNING AT BENNY'S TO THE SMELL OF breakfast cooking: garlic frying in oil, and fresh bread. I still didn't feel great. I felt like I had been worked over by a horny ox. But when I pulled up my sleeve, unwrapped the bandage, and examined my wound, it had closed, leaving a raw, red scar. A couple more days and it would be gone completely. I changed my shirt – *down to one good shirt again* – and pulled the sleeve straight to hide the scar.

Benny was putting out plates of food as I came downstairs.

"What's all this about?" I asked.

"It's food, mate. Some people eat it, you know?" He cocked his head. "Did you even eat yesterday?"

"I think so." I'd had breakfast of a sort with Captain Gale. Had that been yesterday?

"Sereh worries about you."

"Sereh?" I found it hard to imagine.

"Kid. Lives here. Remember her? Course she worries about you. You're family. Like a dodgy uncle or something."

I didn't know how to respond to that. I had just been called dodgy by Benny. *Benny.* The most shameless thief in Agatos.

"Thing is, mate, I heard you got yourself into trouble with the Hawkhurst Bastards."

"Who?" Most of the people I ended up pissing off were bastards of one type or another, but I didn't remember this bunch.

"Mycedan smuggling gang operating out of *The Bloody End*."

I groaned. "Oh. Them."

"They're bad news, mate. Nail-people-to-walls kind of bad news. In that part of town, they're second only to the Wren in people you shouldn't piss off."

Now was probably not the time to remind Benny that I had pissed off the Wren, too.

I blamed this on Squint. He hadn't mentioned anything about smugglers or nailing to the wall. I could imagine him sitting there in his dark corner of Dumonoc's, sniggering into his drink.

"Guess they'll have to wait in line, won't they?" I said. All this talk of vengeful smugglers was ruining my appetite. I heaped a pile of vegetables and lentils onto a flatbread and shoved it into my mouth before I could lose it completely.

"I don't think they do that."

I chewed, swallowed too quickly, and had to flap for a glass of water as I choked. When I was done, I said, "Do they know it was me?"

"Nah. Not yet. I just heard that a tall mage came striding into their headquarters like he had no idea who they were and started making demands. I thought of you straight away. They're out there looking, though, and asking questions. They're pretty pissed off from what I heard." It was hard to imagine why. I mean, yeah, I had knocked out their mage, fucked over a couple of their thugs, and discovered their hidden smuggling lair, but it wasn't personal. "Did anyone know you were heading down there?"

"Well, Squint," I admitted.

"Lady of the Grove, mate! He'll sell you out like cheap beer on Charo eve."

"I know." And when he did, they would come here. I had already put Benny and Sereh in far too much danger. They were my family, Benny was right about that. You didn't do that to your family. The decision settled over me like a lowering winter cloud pressing down. "I need you to do me a favour, Benny. I want you to put out the word that I've moved back into the Countess's palace. I don't care how hard they think they are, they won't come for me up there."

Benny's scratching fingers stopped. He looked up at me, worry etching new lines into his mummified-corpse face. "Yeah, but you aren't really doing it, are you? I mean—"

"I think I am." I held up a hand to stop his protest. "Every day I stay here, that increases the risk to you. To Sereh." If he didn't care about himself, he would protect Sereh before anyone. "I thought if I kept my head down, people would leave me alone, but they won't. Everyone knows I'm here, and this – these jobs I've been getting – they're not what I thought they were going to be. They're way out of my league. The Countess's palace is the safest place outside an Ash Guard cell."

"Not for you it isn't." He let his food fall to his plate. "Don't think I've forgotten what it did to you last time. Pity, Nik! It's going to fuck you up big time, and you're already fucked up enough. If money's the problem, I can lend you enough to get a new place.

It's not like I do anything much with it. Come on, mate."

He knew as well as I did that I didn't have time to find a new, safe home before the smugglers found me. Maybe I should have laid down a heap more damage in their inn, put them off permanently. Ah, I was fooling myself. I didn't have that kind of power.

"I have to do this, Benny, for everyone's sake. Anyway, it's going to be different this time. I'm not going to be her acolyte again."

He watched me over his plate. We both knew it wouldn't be different, but neither of us wanted to be the one who admitted it.

Benny dropped his eyes before I did. "You better let me tell Sereh. She's not going to be happy."

"No." I got up and stretched. "I should. Is she here?"

"Your funeral. Nah. She's having her violin lesson. Up at Highstar Plaza, you know? Opposite your sister's place."

"Right." Oddly, I had never actually heard Sereh practice her violin. I had once come across the body of a mage who had attacked her lying dead with her violin bow driven into his eye socket.

Maybe he had criticised her playing.

"Green door, blue shutters," Benny said. "You can't miss it. Have fun!"

THE ASH GUARD FORTRESS WAS A BIT OF A DIVERSION

from both Highstar Plaza and the Countess's palace, but it wasn't too far out of the way, and to be honest, I wasn't looking forward to either of those encounters. At least if Sereh knifed me, it would be a good, honest knifing, rather than the slow, crushing torture from my mother, but I would happily put both off. I was already regretting my good intentions. I should have let Benny tell Sereh. She was his kid.

The Ash Guard must have been used to seeing me by now, because when I pounded on the fortress door, one of the guards disappeared back inside without waiting for me to speak. I wasn't sure that was good news. I slouched down in my cloak and tried to keep a low profile, for all the good that would do.

"Well," Captain Gale said, when she appeared. "This is getting to be a habit. I'm guessing you're still not brave enough to come in?"

Well, when she put it that way... "Um. No."

"Well, I'm not buying you breakfast this time. We do have a budget."

"I've eaten, thank you," I said with all the dignity I could muster. "I just thought I should check in. I ran into a Mycedan mage down at *The Bloody End* inn last night. He almost took my head off with magic."

"What, you think I should be giving him a reward?"

Fuck's sake. "I just thought you might want to know there's a mage running around town who's not shy about tossing magic at people."

"A mage other than you, you mean."

I threw up my hands. "I was just trying to be helpful."

"Just winding you up." She grinned. "I'll take a look down there later when I get a few minutes free. It's still bloody chaos in this city."

At least having the Ash Guard show up might slow the smugglers down a bit. When the Ash Guard came looking for you, you laid low. "You might need to take back-up," I warned. "They're not friendly."

She eyed me expressionlessly. Then she touched the sword at her belt. "I'm not going to need back-up."

Yeah, she probably wouldn't. Even seeing the Ash was enough to scare the shit out of most people, and she could fight. I had personal experience of that. The thought sent a shiver down my back.

"Anything else?" she said.

"There's still weird stuff going on. Something in the tunnels beneath the city. I don't know what."

She considered for a moment. "I don't think I can spare a patrol for down there. There's too much underground and not enough of us. If whatever it is sticks its head out, though…"

Fair enough. I could hardly argue. I wasn't bringing her anything solid. For all I knew, it was just my anxiety and panic in the dark. I wasn't going to push it. "Did you happen to find out anything about that text from the museum I gave you?"

"It's been one day, Nik. Gods and Sods are slow at the best of times. Comes from spending all your time researching ancient history. Nothing seems terribly urgent, and you should see the books they have to go through. Anyway, half of them have been seconded for patrols."

I hadn't expected any more. I didn't know why the curator had dropped dead part way through translating the inscription on the statuette. Maybe my theory that she had started to hear the same whispers I had been hearing and she'd had a weak heart was true, but more likely I was imagining the whole thing. And this ... this was just putting off the inevitable, and I knew it.

Sereh and my mother awaited.

"All right." I clenched my fists. Time to go. "I'll let you know if I find out anything else." I turned to go.

"Nik."

I looked back.

"The other day at Dumonoc's, when you asked me to come to your sister's house. Were you... You weren't asking me on a date, were you?"

Shit. For a second, I sent out a prayer that the ground would open up and swallow me. "Fuck, no!"

"Good. Because I don't do that. Certainly not with a mage."

"Yeah. Me neither. With the Ash Guard, I mean." *Bannaur's bruised balls!* What the fuck was I even saying. 'Not with the Ash Guard.' Twat.

"All right. Now, I have to go."

"Me, too." And never, ever come back.

CHAPTER EIGHTEEN

I DIDN'T BRING MUCH FROM BENNY'S HOUSE. I DIDN'T
have much. I was twenty-nine years old, and all I had
were a few clothes. I had some money, too, which
wasn't a given most of the time, and there were a
couple of bits of furniture and my optimistically large
metal safe, but there was no point in hauling those all
the way up to the Countess's palace. It would look
more pathetic than turning up with nothing.

I was aware that I had agreed to meet Kehsereen at
midday, and time was already creeping on. If I wanted
to squeeze information out of my mother and get back
to Kehsereen by then, I was going to have to break my
news to Sereh as quickly and with as few knives in the
throat as possible.

The Upper City of Agatos had been built around a
series of grand plazas, and Highstar Plaza was one of
the grandest. Mica's house dominated the plaza, but
none of the houses could exactly claim to be modest.

In any other part of the city, the house Benny had described would have stood out from its surroundings like a peacock in flock of pigeons. Here, I would have missed it if I hadn't been looking for it.

The question I had was how a violin teacher could afford such a place. Inherited wealth, I supposed, the stagnant weight that kept the poor in their place and the rich in theirs. Not that I was resentful or anything.

The door was opened by a tall, elderly woman with almost black skin and white hair. Dhajawi, I guessed. Standing on the doorstep, she was almost tall enough to be level with my eyes.

"I'm looking for Sereh. Is she here?"

Her eyes searched me. "You've missed her, I'm afraid."

Well. How about that? I shouldn't have delayed. *Don't pretend you didn't take your time in the hope she would be gone. Coward.*

Benny was better at this kind of stuff than me, anyway. It would hurt less coming from him.

Coward.

"You're Mennik Thorn, aren't you? The mage."

"How did you know that?" I hoped I wasn't getting famous. I couldn't do my job if people knew who I was.

"Sereh talks about you."

"She does?" I found that hard to imagine. Sereh wasn't exactly the sharing type.

"Would you like to come in?"

I glanced past her to her grand entrance hall. *Yes.*

Then maybe I can stay all day and not have to see my mother at all.

I pushed the temptation away. "Um. No. Thanks. I'm in a bit of a hurry. But..." All right, I had to ask. "You teach Sereh violin?"

The woman nodded.

"Is she... Is she any good?"

The woman tipped back her head and laughed. "No. It is not her intent."

"What? You mean she doesn't try?"

"Oh, she tries. It's just not her intent."

Did she mean talent? I had no idea how the Dhajawi word translated. Screw it. I wasn't here to discuss Sereh's musical abilities. "All right. I'd better get going. I'm sorry I missed her."

"Come and listen to her play sometime. She would like it."

"Yeah." Not in every dark Depth was I going to voluntarily listen to someone play the violin.

I ducked my head and hurried away. At least I could say I had tried. She would understand. I hoped.

"Mennik!" The shout came from the other side of the plaza. I glanced up. *Shit!* Mica's boyfriend – what was his name? Goodroad, or something like that? An Upper City name, anyway – was hurrying across the plaza towards me. Cepra damn the whole thing! I should have known better than to come anywhere near here. I couldn't pretend I hadn't seen him now. Reluctantly, I came to a halt and waited for him to reach me.

It probably wasn't polite to open with, 'What the fuck do you want?' so I waited for him to speak.

"Elestior Goodroad. Remember?"

Ha! At least I had got the surname. That was something, right? "Of course. What can I do for you?"

He glanced back across the plaza. "You, ah... You and your sister. Are you always like that?"

"Like what?"

"Fighting over everything."

Depths. I was not in the mood for a lecture. "Don't you have siblings?"

"A couple of brothers, but we don't fight."

Either he was feeding me a bucketload of goat shit or there was something wrong with him. "That's nice for you." This wasn't a conversation I wanted to have, particularly not with someone I had only just met. "Look, I'm supposed to—"

"You weren't very fair to Mica the other night."

I stared down at him. If it had been anyone else than Mica's boyfriend saying that, I would have to told him to ram it up his arse with a long stick, and I would have offered to lend him the stick. Instead, I said, "That's not really any of your business, is it?"

"Yes. It is. Whether you like it or not, I'm her partner."

Partner. Fuck that. "She doesn't need you to protect her."

"I am well aware of that. But she worked really hard to make it special for you. She won't admit it, but she worried about it all day."

And I had been an arsehole. Pity, I had known I was doing it even while it was happening. I hadn't been the only one to show my spikes, though. We might hardly have seen each other in the last five years, and she might move like a waft of perfumed air through high society while I slithered along in the muck, but we were still more alike than not.

"She really is trying to make the city a better place. We both are."

Not this again. What did he want? A Cepra-damned medal? "You're with the fucking Yellow Faction. I may not know much about politics, but I know they don't stand for the poor and downtrodden. You're about helping the rich stay rich. And what the fuck would you know about the way things are for ordinary people in this city, anyway? This city doesn't need another rich wanker – no offence – thinking he knows what's best for everyone."

He didn't look offended. Being a politician, he probably had people calling him worse every single day, and as he was dating my sister, one of the most powerful mages in the city, well, I probably didn't intimidate him. His mistake. Mica wouldn't shove a mage's rod down his throat and out his arsehole.

"Do you know how we met?"

"How would I know that?" And why would I even care? I wasn't in the mood for some cute little meet-up tale.

"It was in Fishertown. Mica was trying to find out

more about her dad. He was from Fishertown originally, you know."

"Of course I bloody know." This guy was pissing
me off more and more every second. I had no idea how
Mica put up with him. Endir might not have been my
father by blood, but he had still been my father.

"That was all Mica knew about him. Your mother
didn't share much."

Did he think he was giving me news? Mica's
boyfriend or not, there was only so much patronising I
would take. "Great. So Mica went looking for answers."
I couldn't help a stab of jealousy. My mother had never
even told me who my own father was. "And what were
you? A tourist? Come to gawp at the little people?"

"I was one of the ones who helped her."

"What? You're going to pretend that you're from
Fishertown? Goodroad is an Upper City name."

"Your mother isn't the only one who can reinvent
herself. Fishertown is the forgotten part of Agatos. No
one goes there unless they have to, and not many
people have to. But we are a community, and we
organise."

He was serious. Depths. I had assumed he was a
privileged kid playing at caring, and I had been a
massive arse. I still didn't like him, but... "I'm sorry. I
shouldn't have assumed."

"It doesn't matter. Just ... think about what your
sister and I are trying to do. We do want to change
things. Sometimes that means making alliances with
people you would rather tip into the harbour."

Which was all well and good, but I had seen him coming out of a meeting with the Countess. Whatever my mother's motivation might be, it wasn't making the city a better place.

"Hey." I looked around and saw Mica hurrying towards us. She was trying to hide it, but I could see the worry on her face. She probably thought I was about to swat her boyfriend, and she wasn't so wrong. "What are you two doing?"

Goodroad gave her an easy smile. "Just getting to know each other."

Mica shot me a suspicious look. "Really."

"Really," I said. "You never told me he was from Fishertown."

"I don't recall you asking."

Fair enough. I hadn't exactly wanted to know. "Look. I really do have to go. I have to talk to the Countess."

"I'll walk with you."

People really didn't want to leave me alone today. "You don't have to."

"I'm going anyway. Unless you want to walk on the other side of the street?"

I was tempted. But this whole thing was going to be hard. I could still feel the reluctance holding me back, the incipient panic pushing against my thoughts. Perhaps having Mica would distract me. "Fine."

I waited and pretended to look the other way while they said goodbye, and then Mica and I headed for Horn Hill.

"He's all right, you know," Mica said, after a minute.

I rolled my eyes. Not this again. Why did they both seem to want my approval? "Yeah. He's great."

Mica shook her head. "You know, you look like shit again. Whatever you've been up to out there, it's not doing you any favours."

"It's my job. Helping people. Not all of us have near-high mage powers to fall back on."

She eyed me. I could tell she was thinking of saying something. *Don't say it. Just don't say it.*

She said it. "Have you ever thought that maybe the reason you can't draw in much power is more psychological than physical? You never really wanted to be a mage. Depths, you don't even like most mages."

Oh, fuck me. This was just what I needed. "When your mate Lowriver and her pet god tried to kill Sereh, I pulled in a shit load of power. Not power like you or the blessed Countess, but still a lot, and it almost ripped me apart. I could *feel* my flesh starting to rupture. That wasn't *psychological*."

"It's because you've never practiced controlling it. I'm not saying you'll ever be a high mage or even a particularly senior mage, but you hold yourself back."

She had hardly seen me in five years. What the Depths did she know? "And you just want to believe your brother is more than he really is."

"Is that so bad?"

"It's a fantasy. And it doesn't help. Mother never understood that, either. It doesn't help."

I HAD BEEN RIGHT ABOUT ONE THING. WALKING WITH Mica did take my mind off my upcoming encounter with my mother. Angry, resentful, awkward silence didn't leave much room for dwelling on anything else. It was only when the Countess's vast palace-temple came into sight that the thought of what I was doing hit fully. I was moving back into my mother's home, and I was doing it voluntarily.

I was fucking crazy.

"Are you coming?" Mica asked, and I realised I had stopped walking.

I pushed the raw wound on my arm into my hip and let the dull pain break my paralysis. "Yep."

Cerrean Forge was sitting as always at his desk in the absurdly grand and tasteless foyer. He kept his face neutral in the face of my sister's presence, but I could still tell he wasn't happy to see me. I gave him a friendly wave as we made our way up the marble steps. He didn't return the gesture.

"Do you want me to ... ah ... Should I come with you?"

"What? To talk to my own mother."

"You don't always..."

I raised my eyebrows.

"Fine. Do what you want. You always do."

The irony of that was like a punch under the ribs. It left me unable to speak. Did she think I *wanted* this? If the Wren didn't have a metaphorical knife to my friends' throats, I would be nowhere near here and heading the opposite direction fast.

She means well. She's trying to help. Despite everything. I probably didn't deserve it.

"I'll be all right. I'm not going to antagonise her." Not on purpose. Not that I had a good track record on that.

The Countess was in her office, working on a sheaf of papers, but when she looked up, she didn't seem surprised to see me. She had probably felt me pass through her wards. I supposed I should count myself lucky she hadn't set them to vaporise me.

"Mennik. I had assumed you must be dead. I could think of no other reason why you would take so long to report back to me."

"Yeah. I noticed all the mourning banners."

My mother sighed and placed her papers into a drawer. *What are you working on there, Mother?* Maybe I should just grab her papers and make a run for it. Throw them at the Wren and tell him that settled our debt.

"Mennik, if you wish to work for me—"

"I don't."

Her forehead creased in puzzlement. When I had been a kid, my mother had never tried to hide her expressions and I had been able to read her, but as she had transformed into the Countess, her thoughts had become increasingly veiled beneath a blank veneer. It wouldn't have surprised me if one day her face was completely replaced with a gold mask, like the Mycedan emperors of old.

"Then what?"

"I told you, Mother. We're still a family – you, me, Mica. I'm trying to act like it."

For a moment, I thought she was going to respond. Then her back straightened. "And yet you accepted a job from me. I have been waiting for a report."

Well. No one could say I hadn't tried. I wondered if she suspected me of working for the Wren. But if she did, she would never have let me through her wards. "What do you want to know?"

"You cut off the meeting abruptly. Why?"

Yeah. That was the fucking question. "Someone was using magic to watch us at that coffee house." Me, specifically. "Whoever they were, they were powerful. I thought that if they made a move against us, I wouldn't be able to stop them, and I wouldn't be able to protect your factor." Which was an understatement.

"The Wren or one of his senior mages?"

"No. The magic wasn't structured or properly controlled. It was wasteful. Whoever was doing it wasn't formally trained."

She tilted her head, studying me. Depths, I hated that look. "You are sure it was a mage? Not a god or a similar entity?"

Why did no one have any faith in my ability to tell? "I could see the magic. I know the difference."

"Hm. Then someone has taken an interest in my business. No matter."

Easy for her to say. She was a high mage. Not many things were a threat to her. Even so, that magic had been powerful. I reckoned it could give her a shock.

"Why are you so interested in that building, Mother?" I nodded up at the map on her wall. The old coffee house was marked by one of the blue flags, and even though I hadn't memorised Elosyn's list, I thought the buildings on it matched the other flags. "Why do you want to buy up property? What are you doing with it? And what does it have to do with the Yellow Faction?"

Once again, she studied me. "It was my understanding that you did not wish to work for me."

I stretched back in my chair. I knew it annoyed her. "Just curious as to what you had me doing." Time for a change of topics. "I was at Petrel Avenue yesterday, visiting a lawyer called Calovar Tide. Do you know him?"

My mother didn't answer.

"You do know him. I couldn't help but notice he had some ridiculously powerful wards up. There aren't many people who could create wards like that. I'm curious. Why would a lawyer want wards that could keep out anything short of a god?"

My mother's expression remained neutral. "*If* I had been employed to create such wards, I would not ask why. I am not in the business of asking people why they need protection when they are paying me."

"Of course not. Why would you care what someone did with the magic you sold them?"

"They are wards, Mennik, not weapons."

Right. "And, hypothetically, if you had created these wards that you wouldn't be curious about, when might you have done them?"

"You are persistent."

"I guess you taught me something, Mother."

She moved suddenly, reaching for another pile of papers. "I am busy. The lawyer came to me two days ago. He was desperate. He wanted the strongest wards I could provide, and he wanted them straight away. He was willing to pay whatever was necessary. I undertook the job myself. Are we done?"

Two days ago. The same day I had confronted Porta Sarassan in Cord's apartment and told him of the murder. Sarassan must have passed on the information, and Tide had known, or suspected, what had happened. He had been terrified enough to immediately blow a fortune on impenetrable wards. Then he tried to imply to me that he'd had them for ages. Lying shit. What wasn't he telling me? What did he have to hide, or to hide from?

"Thank you." I tried to act as though the thought had just come to me. "You know, I think I might stay around for a few days. Get in some family time. If you don't mind?"

"Your room is always there, Mennik."

Yeah. With the novices and junior acolytes. *Know your place*. It still tasted bitter.

I stood. At the door, I paused. "I've been wondering. Back when Endir died, when he drowned out there on the ocean, you were still working for the

Wren. But you had the power of a high mage. You had the magic to see what had happened to him. Yet you never told either me or Mica."

The Countess's pen stilled on her paper. Her face remained composed as she looked up at me. For several moments, I thought she wasn't going to speak. Then she said, "There are some truths you are not yet ready to hear, Mennik, for your own good."

I DUMPED MY STUFF IN THE LITTLE ROOM THE COUNTESS had set aside for me, but I couldn't stay there. Even if I hadn't promised Kehsereen we would continue our investigations together, I couldn't be in this room. There was no space to think, and, surprise, my talk with the Countess hadn't calmed me down. *There are some truths you are not yet ready to hear.* What kind of bollocks was that? Endir's boat had gone down. That was all. I had just wanted... What had I wanted? To know where it had happened? To know he had hit a rock, or his boat had sprung a leak, or...? Was she suggesting there was more to it? Or was she just trying to mess up my head? If she was, she had done a great job of it. I was torn between storming back and demanding she explain herself or dismissing it as a stupid mind game to keep me in my place. I wouldn't give her the satisfaction.

I dropped my bag on the bed. No one would be stupid enough to steal from inside the Countess's palace. My mother would turn them inside out, and she wouldn't be fast about it. But even so, I pushed my money under the pillow, only pocketing enough for a couple of days, in case I couldn't make it back here. I had worked hard for this. I wasn't taking any chances.

My mother was talking shit. Mica's dad had been a fisherman. The sea was a dangerous, unpredictable place. He had been in a small boat. There was nothing more to it than that and my mother's own guilt that she, with all her powers, hadn't been able to save him. There hadn't even been a body, just the wreckage of a boat swept up days later.

My mother's self-appointed guard dog, Cerrean Forge, was waiting outside my door when I headed out.

"Shouldn't you be on the front desk?" I said.

He glowered at me from his squashed face. "I know who you are."

Like he hadn't known from the moment I had walked in. But two could play at that game. "Glad to see I didn't waste my time introducing myself." I made to step around him. He shifted into my path. I was tempted to punch him, but I didn't have what I needed from my mother yet, and I needed to look like I wanted to be here. "What do you want, Forge?"

"I don't trust you."

Which, you know, fair enough. It still didn't mean I liked the guy. "I guess it's a shame you're not the high mage here, then, isn't it?"

His lip twitched. "The Countess might want to

believe you, but we're not all taken in. I'm watching you."

My mother's bloody sycophants. No wonder I had wanted to get out of here. The drooling, servile loyalty stuck in my throat. "You're not my type," I said, "but you're welcome to look." I strode forward, and he leapt aside before we could collide. I saw his hands work. Some kind of spell. No wonder he was confined to the front desk most of the time. Only novices usually needed to use hand gestures to help them form magic. *You used to be afraid of him.*

It wasn't until I was out of my mother's palace and heading down Agate Way that I unfocused my eyes to see what he had done.

He had cast a tracking spell on me. A long, orange thread of magic stretched from my back to the Countess's palace. It was strong and it wouldn't break on its own, but it was clumsily made. I could cut it easily enough, but then he would know and try something else. I couldn't match Cerrean Forge's strength, but it had become obvious that I could tie him in knots when it came to skill and finesse. Why had I not realised that years ago? I unhooked the spell from my shoulders with my own magic and transferred it onto a passing priest of Chaerd the Unkind. *Figure out what I'm up to from following this guy.* I wondered how long it would take Forge to realise I wasn't actually spending most of my time in a temple to the god of missed opportunities. It would be damned poetic, if you asked me.

KEHSEREEN WAS SHIFTING AND FIDGETING ON OUR USUAL bench when I made it there, like he was sitting on an ants' nest. Just watching him made me want to start fidgeting, too. I wondered if he ever stopped moving so restlessly. It was fucking annoying, if I was honest.

"You know, if you relaxed, you might find the whole thing easier," I said.

Maybe I should take that advice myself. It was harder than it sounded.

Kehsereen looked up. "My nephew has been missing for weeks. Every day, every hour that passes makes it less likely that I will find him alive. Would you find that relaxing?"

Yeah. Fair enough. Now I felt like an arsehole again. *Bit of a theme today, Nik.*

I changed the subject. "I couldn't find out as much as I wanted about the wards on Tide's house. They are new, though. The Countess created them on the same day Porta Sarassan found out Cord was killed. Tide paid a fortune to have them done so quickly. I'm sure he knows why Cord was killed, and he's worried the same thing will happen to him, but the only way we or anyone else will get to him through those wards is with the help of the Ash Guard."

"And will they help?"

"Not without some evidence." And I didn't want to go back to Captain Gale without something to show. Just remembering the last time we had talked made me cringe. "Let's try the wrestler, then take another swing at Sarassan." He would have had days to stew over what had happened. He might even be wondering why his friend Calovar Tide was holed up so tightly. Maybe I could work on his fear and suspicions. "I doubt they know how to coordinate their lies." They certainly hadn't run with the same story last time. "One of them will let something slip, and when we catch them in a lie, we'll have them."

Kehsereen squinted up at me, shading his eyes from the sun with one hand. "You are sure?"

I considered lying. Instead, I said, "It's the best chance we've got. Come on. Let's go and threaten a professional fighter."

IF YOU WANTED TO SEE BIG MEN AND WOMEN PUNCH, kick, and choke each other, you could hang around any street corner in the lower city. If you wanted to do it without being caught up in the fight yourself and possibly arrested, and if you wanted to try to win some money at the same time, you could head up to the arena, where fights took place most days. Yes, occasionally those fights spilled out into the audience, but that was apparently part of the fun. I had enough people wanting to give me a good kicking on any given day, so I didn't see the appeal, but each to their own.

We settled outside a coffee house opposite the fighters' entrance to the arena. Kehsereen had assured me that Bale would emerge in the next hour or so to return home, only coming back to the arena for further training or a bout in the early evening. I figured we would follow him and then confront him somewhere quieter, where I could use magic to my advantage and hope not to get punched in the face.

We were still in the Middle City here, on the far side of Horn Hill to the theatre district and the museum, and not far from the Street of Gods, making it convenient to get a quick bit of worship in before cheering on people beating each other to a pulp.

The street in front of us was busy. Hawkers selling religious paraphernalia and souvenirs of famous fighters moved through the crowds. A fortune teller with absolutely no magical ability had set up a stall a little way down the street. A juggler had tried her luck but had soon given up and moved on. The coffee was bad, and I left mine to go cold.

"Here," Kehsereen said, and I brought my gaze back from the crowd.

The door to the arena had opened and a garishly dressed man emerged. He wasn't particularly tall or well-built. *You would never know he was a champion wrestler from looking at him.* That was what the bartender who had first told me about Cord's friends had said. She was right. You would never pick him out as a wrestler. He looked fit, but more like the son of a wealthy merchant determined to show off to his friends than a man who fought for a living. His face was smooth, not scarred or bruised. I disliked him immediately, and, yes, I was aware that this was my default position with most people I met, even when I didn't suspect them of involvement in a murder and the disappearance of a kid.

He turned left, joining the flow of people. We let him get a little way ahead, then followed him. If he wanted to stay inconspicuous, the bright green shirt and yellow hat weren't doing him any favours. I wondered if he knew what his lawyer friend knew. He certainly wasn't cowering behind wards. Had Tide just not told his friends his suspicions, or was there more to it? Did Tide not want them to know? Something else to ask Bale. He looked like he might be a talker.

"You told me something was watching these men," I said to Kehsereen. "You said it put you off approaching. Is it still here?"

Kehsereen nodded. "A presence. That's all. Something that is focused on them. It made me uneasy. All I knew was that I didn't want that presence to notice me."

I unfocused my eyes, but all I could see was the omnipresent green mist of raw magic. No spells. Bale wasn't being watched by a mage or any magical creature, but Kehsereen was right. On the edge of my consciousness, there was something. A pressure, an awareness. I didn't like it, and I could see why Kehsereen had been cautious. Had it been there when I had confronted Sarassan? I didn't remember it, but I hadn't been paying attention, and this thing wasn't obvious. If you didn't know you were looking for it, you wouldn't notice it. Kehsereen was a natural mage. He might not be able to manipulate magic consciously or at all, but in some ways that made him more sensitive than a mage who had been trained to control their powers and senses.

"It's stronger than it was."

"And why not?" I muttered. Just my luck. I seriously considered backing out until I knew what I was getting myself into. But I had talked to Sarassan and Tide without this ... presence ... intervening, and that was all I wanted to do here. Talk.

"Let's get this over with." I increased my pace. "Mr. Bale," I called. "Just a minute, please."

The wrestler turned, a smile forming on his face. Maybe he had a lot of fans. Maybe he got stopped in the street for autographs or handshakes all the time. But the moment he saw me, his expression dropped. "You. You're the Ash Guard mage, aren't you?"

"Well...," I started. That would be pushing the truth several streets too far.

"Fuck!" Bale spun and sprinted away, shouldering aside a couple who were bartering with a hawker. I stared after him. This was taking my unpopularity to new heights.

Kehsereen slapped my arm. "Come on!" He broke into a run. I took off after him, wondering what I was supposed to do when I caught up to Bale. I prepared an arrow of magic, but there were too many people around. I darted through the crowd, dodging outthrown arms and ignoring shouts of protest.

Bale changed direction, heading for the thicker crowds. I swore and pushed myself on. I couldn't use magic here without hurting innocent people, and without it I didn't fancy my chances against a champion wrestler.

It all happened fast. One moment, Bale was leaping over a blanket stacked with souvenirs. The next, a man jostled out of the crowd and collided with the flying wrestler. Bale tumbled, flailing, and crashed into the side of a building.

He was good at his job, I would give him that. He hit the ground, rolled, and was back on his feet almost immediately. But he had taken a blow. He staggered and reached for the wall to steady himself.

Kehsereen and I closed on him, easing our way through the curious crowd.

Then magic hammered down around us, engulfing the crowd like a landslide. It came so suddenly I had almost no warning. It was unstructured but overwhelming and burning with rage. I had never felt anything like it. If I hadn't already been holding in raw magic, I wouldn't have had a chance. Even with that, it was all I could do to throw up a shell around my mind and retreat within it, unable to act, unable to move, while the magic stormed over the crowd.

The rest of the crowd had no such luck. The magical rage swept through them and took them. I could feel it wanted me, too, battering at the shell that protected me. It would have got through, but the rage was too overpowering, and it wasn't focused on me. It was focused on one person: Marron Bale.

The crowd converged on the stunned wrestler, coming for him in a reckless wave of feverish humanity. Bale tried to back away, but there was nowhere to go. A man, a clerk in a sober black jacket, reached him and swung. The blow caught Bale on the cheek, rocking his head and drawing blood. Then the crowd was on him. Fists and feet thudded into the wrestler, and I lost sight of him. All I could hear were screams of fury and hate, and all I could see were flailing limbs. I pulled in more magic and shoved out, trying to regain control of my body, to stand, to do something. But I couldn't. The magic that seethed around me was too powerful. Even though it hardly noticed me, even though it didn't care that I was there at all, I couldn't do a thing except crouch, listening to the sound of fists impacting flesh, and try to keep the magic from taking hold of me too.

Then, as quickly as the magic had come, something seemed to *swallow*, and it was gone, snatched out of existence.

CHAPTER NINETEEN

I FELL. I HADN'T EVEN REALISED I HAD BEEN PUSHING SO hard against the magic, and when it was gone, it was like a door I had been leaning against had suddenly given way.

The screams from the crowd changed. The rage was gone, and now the screams were filled with horror.

Kehsereen's hands on my arm helped me up. Together, we pushed through the packed people. No one resisted.

There wasn't much left of Bale. If I hadn't known what I was looking at, I might have thought it was a pile of sodden rags. Flesh had been split, pummelled into a shapeless mess. Bones had been cracked and shattered. I couldn't even tell where his face had been. Blood and other fluids pooled on the cobbles, forming a little maze of rivulets between the stones, trickling away. If he had been caught in a rockfall, he couldn't have been more broken. Behind me, someone threw up violently.

I pulled Kehsereen away. "What the fuck was that?" I just couldn't bring my mind to comprehend the power I had witnessed, to overwhelm so many people so completely. My mother couldn't do it. Nor could the Wren. *Fuck!*

My thoughts rebelled at what I had seen. That ... thing on the ground. Just a couple of minutes ago, he had been a man in a green shirt, turning in the crowd, a smile forming on his face. Now ... that. Meat torn by a pack of dogs. It had happened so quickly, so absolutely. I felt my stomach turn, acid fill the back of my mouth. I forced in a breath.

Kehsereen shook his head mutely.

"You felt it, right?"

He nodded.

"But... You weren't part of the crowd that ... that did it. The magic didn't affect you. Why didn't it affect you? Was it that drug of yours? The..." What was it called? I couldn't focus. I couldn't get the sounds of fists hitting flesh out of my mind.

"The ulu-aru."

"Right. Does it make you immune to magic?"

"It does not, and I would not take it. It confuses the mind. I felt the magic, but it passed over me. I do not know how else to describe it." He looked genuinely mystified.

"Fuck." I shook my head, trying to clear my thoughts. It didn't help. It was like a scream had got stuck inside me and was battering around my skull like a moth in a lamp.

Come on!

Etta Mirian had killed Peyt Jyston Cord with a knife, and then she had killed herself. That had been a much more controlled action than this. More rational, if murder and suicide could be rational. But the power that had grabbed hold of the crowd and battered at me had certainly been strong enough to have taken control of her.

This was an escalation, an anger that had only grown and a power that had grown with it. No. Anger was too gentle a word. A burgeoning, impossible fury.

Think. Focus. Be logical. Ignore that scream. Ignore the wet sound of fists.

The lawyer, Calovar Tide, had known there was a threat, and a powerful one. He had hidden behind unbreakable wards. He hadn't gone to the Ash Guard for help. Depths, maybe he hadn't even warned his friends. He had just barricaded himself in and let everyone and everything else go to shit. He was going to talk to me. He might not think he was, but he was, before anyone else died. If he didn't, I would come back with Captain Gale, we would walk right through his wards, and I would cut the words out of him, one by one. I was tired of being pulled this way and that like a fish skewered on a hook.

A hand touched my shoulder.

I turned to see a man with a scar across his mouth and one missing ear. He was staring right at me. I blinked, trying to understand what was going on. What did this man have to do with any of it? Was he—

"The Wren says you have until tonight. Then you pay the price, you and your friends."

Then he was gone, disappearing into the scattering crowd. All I could do was stare after him.

No, my mind said. *Not now. Not with all ... this.* I couldn't cope with the Wren's shit after what I had just seen. It was too much.

My legs felt numb and shaky. I didn't know whether that was from the chase, the magic that had rolled over me like rocks tumbled in an ocean surge, or my shock at what had happened to Bale. I did know that I needed to sit. I staggered away from the body and to a nearby coffee house, where I dropped into a chair. I heard Kehsereen settle himself across from me. I had to keep pulling my mind away from reliving Bale's fate and seeing what he had been turned into.

Whoever – whatever – had taken the crowd and driven them to such brutal rage wasn't the same as the presence that had been watching Bale and his friends, and it wasn't the same as the thing that had whispered madness in the tunnels. The magic used on the crowd was the type a mage would wield, even though it was untrained and undisciplined. So, did that mean there were three powers sniffing around this case? Or were the presence in the tunnel and the one watching Bale the same? Two powers or three, they were more than I had bargained for, and they all made me look like dry grass in a summer fire. I couldn't stand up to any of them.

Just what the fuck was going on here?

"Who was that man?"

I looked up, startled. I had forgotten Kehsereen was sitting there. "What?"

"The man who just talked to you."

Ah. Yeah. That. As though a bunch of malign, hidden supernatural entities weren't enough to be getting on with. There was another one who could crush me like an eggshell on a beach. "You've heard of the Wren?"

"The criminal high mage?"

"That's him. I've … ah … got to do a job for him. It's a long story. I've just been told I have to complete it today."

Kehsereen eyed me. "What is this job?"

Did I trust him? I shouldn't. He had drugged me. But to be fair, in his circumstances, and with the information he had had, maybe I would have done the same. And it was hardly credible that he would be working for my mother to spy on me. Fuck it. It could hardly make things worse. "I need to steal some secrets from the Countess and deliver them to him."

Kehsereen's gaze remained still. "And how will you do that?"

"Yeah. That's the question, isn't it?" I had no clue. There had to be something in my mother's office, and while I could get in there, I couldn't do it without her knowing, not while she was hanging around her palace like a vulture at a slaughterhouse waiting to get at the bodies. If I could get her out of the place, well, she would probably still know, but she wouldn't be there to stop me, and I could always claim I had been looking for her. She might not believe it, but if I was smart and careful, she wouldn't be able to prove anything.

If. It was the kind of big 'if' that beat you around the head, metaphorically speaking, and left you bleeding in the dirt.

"I don't suppose you've got any great ideas." I didn't expect much from a scholar. In my experience, if it wasn't in a book, they wouldn't know it, and if it was, they would tell you to find it out yourself. Useless, patronising bastards.

"I do not know your mother." He knew she was my mother, though. Well, he had said his job was finding things out. "But have you considered just asking her? Would she not wish to do anything she could to protect her child?"

If she did, there would be a price, and I didn't think it would be one I could pay. "You really don't know my mother. She won't take a single step back in her feud with the Wren." Not unless it offered a way to take two steps forward. I had never quite understood why the feud had started between the two of them, nor why it was quite so vicious and determined. My mother had worked for the Wren for decades, and he had supported her elevation to high mage, reluctantly or not. Was it just ambition? Pride? Ego as to who was the most potent arsehole in the city? While the presence of the Ash Guard stopped them from direct conflict, they invested an absurdly high proportion of their effort and resources into attacking each other's interests, a war by proxy of wealth and influence that treated the rest of the city as tools, weapons, or something to be trampled. I knew what I was doing for the Wren was just another manoeuvre in that war, and I knew that, however minor, I would be handing an advantage over my mother to him. But I didn't care. They could both drag each other down into the Depths for all I cared. Captain Gale said she wanted a third high mage for balance. I would be happier getting rid of the whole lot of them.

Being angry at the high mages was at least enough to distract me from obsessing over Bale's fate. Anger might not be healthy, but it was useful.

The coffee shop I had stumbled into was mostly empty, but by the half-finished drinks and food, it had been busy only minutes ago. We were fifty or sixty yards away from where Bale had been beaten to death. I could see a crowd milling and gawking around his body. I doubted these people were the ones who had been caught up by the magic. I had managed to resist, courtesy of my own power. I couldn't imagine the horror of being driven to such acts of violence, unable to stop myself, not in control of my mind or body. No wonder they had fled. The gawkers were those outside of its influence, abandoning their drinks to get a closer look at what was left of Bale, a moment of excitement and vicarious horror to gossip with their friends about.

Sitting here, so close, in full view, wasn't a great idea. The Ash Guard and the Watch would arrive soon. I would rather not be here when they did. I didn't have the time or the answers to explain what had happened.

"This changes things," I said. "Sarassan and Tide can't pretend this has nothing to do with them anymore. Two out of their little group are dead." Whoever had killed Cord and Bale was after all four of them. Tide's wards surely confirmed that. *Unless one of them is trying to kill the other three.* Tide was the one hiding behind wards, so did that make Sarassan the likely candidate? But he had seemed genuinely shocked when I had told him Cord was dead, and why would he warn Tide and let him set up protective wards? And if it was Tide with all that power at his disposal, why would he need my mother to create such expensive protection? And how did that other presence – or presences – fit in to it all?

I had no idea. But one of them would talk. I had run out of patience. "Who first? Sarassan or Tide?"

"Are you not concerned about your job for the Wren?"

"The Wren can stick it up his arse." Never do now what you can put off until later, that was my motto when it came to my mother. "I'll work something out. I want to hit these two before anyone can tell them what happened. Gauge their reactions." Maybe only one would be surprised. Maybe one would be able to fake it.

"Then we should try Mr. Sarassan," Kehsereen said. "We cannot reach the lawyer, and he will not talk anyway."

We would see about that. But Kehsereen was right. Tide would try to hunker down. Sarassan was more prone to panic. He was the one who would crumble first.

It took the best part of an hour to walk through the heat of the early afternoon and the busy streets to Sarassan's house on Balascra Street. There had been no wards on his house last time I had been here, and there still weren't. Why? Complacent? Guilty? Too poor? I would be asking that, too. There was a whole shitload of questions he was going to be answering if he wanted to keep all his delicate parts intact, because I wasn't pissing around anymore.

"The presence you were talking about?" I said. "Is it here? Is it watching?"

Kehsereen stood still in the street for a minute, his eyes closed, his head tipped slightly back. The crowds had started to thin as people more sensible than me took refuge from the growing heat, but even so, he drew a few glances. Still, enough dramatic and weird crap happened in Agatos that a man standing still in the street like he was receiving a vision from a particularly chatty god didn't rate much notice.

Abruptly, he shook his head. "No. It is gone."

That was good news. Was that good news? I would take it as good news. I was hardly drowning in the stuff.

"Ready?"

He nodded.

I drew myself up, pulled in magic, and rapped loudly on the door with the lump of obsidian on the end of my mage's rod. The sound echoed satisfyingly through the house. I waited.

Nothing. I kept my magic ready and knocked again, listening to the sound fade away.

Well. What a big fucking disappointment. No one was home. Or if they were, they were hiding. I wasn't putting up with that shit. Not today.

I popped the lock, then cautiously pushed the door open.

Last time I had been here, I had heard the sound of children playing deeper in the house and looked out through doors to the shaded courtyard. Now it was all locked down.

My lips were dry. The heat of the day. That had to be it. I moistened them. The house was silent.

Deathly silent.

"Fuck off," I muttered at myself, then shook my head in response to Kehsereen's quizzical expression.

Sarassan was rich. Maybe not as rich as the lawyer, but his house was big and extravagantly built. Marble floors and columns, frescoed walls – not fashionable, but expensive – and running water from taps. The bedrooms had thick mattresses, cedar wood beds, and gold edging on the giant mirrors. I could sell one of those mirrors for the price of a home in the Warrens. What none of the rooms had was Sarassan or his family. So, had they gone out for the day, or had they fled before an overwhelming, psychotic magic power? If Sarassan knew what was happening, if he was involved in some dodgy business, if he knew what it was that threatened them, if he knew the Ash Guard were looking into him, well, he would have fled as far and as fast as he could.

But could you flee the kind of magic that had killed Cord and Bale? A competent, powerful mage – not me, sadly for my business – could track down a target almost anywhere. How would you classify the power behind these attacks? Frighteningly potent, no doubt, but there was no training there. Maybe you could hide from a power like that. Maybe you couldn't. All that mattered was what Sarassan believed. I would know he was wrong if his mutilated corpse showed up in the next few days. But fuck him for running off when I needed information.

From the look of things, Sarassan had found more than his fair share of luck as a deep diver. The artifacts and treasures he had found beneath the city had paid for all this – or so he said – and he had displayed many of his unsold items throughout the house. Just thinking of the hours I had spent lost below the ground made me shiver. Sarassan was welcome to it.

There were ledgers on his office desk. I leafed through them, trying not to be shocked at the size of some of the numbers in there. People paid that? For old junk from under the city? When they could buy new junk for a fraction of the price? All right, some artifacts could be potent sources of raw magic, but they were rare and the market for them was surely limited. Or maybe not. Sarassan had been far richer than I had given him credit for. So why no wards? Maybe he hadn't wanted to blow his fortune on them. Maybe he had spent it already on ... Well, I couldn't really imagine what anyone would spend a fortune on. A house, but he had one. Other ... stuff.

"This is wrong," Kehsereen said.

I closed the ledger and glanced back at him. He was peering at a set of shelves holding artifacts.

"What? The statuette of Sien?" Sarassan had a couple of statuettes of the now-dead goddess. The Lady of Dreams Descending, they had called her. She had been the patron goddess of Agatos before it had become Agatos and before Agate Blackspear had killed her. There were whole dramas performed about it each Charo eve. I avoided them on the assumptions that they were probably bollocks and too much culture wasn't good for me. The statuette Kehsereen appeared to be examining was fairly standard, if old.

"Not that. The wall."

I tipped my head, squinting. "Um. What's wrong with it?"

"It is in the wrong place."

If I had known we were here to discuss architecture, I would have left Kehsereen outside. "It seems to be doing its job. Holding up the ceiling. Stopping the shelves from toppling over."

"We looked in the bedroom next door. There is a space between the rooms. A large one."

I would take his word for it. I hadn't been paying much attention to the walls. I had been busy working out if I could flog one of the mirrors. Benny would be proud of me.

"Here." There was a click, then half the wall moved back and slid to the side.

Well, shit. He had been right. I conjured a light and let it drift into the opening.

The space wasn't enormous. It might have been a closet in an Upper City house or a family bedroom in the Warrens, but here it was another storeroom for Sarassan's artifacts, and I could see why he kept them out of view. The collection was mainly statuettes and fragments of slabs from what might have once been temple walls. Not all were complete, and I was glad of that. The statuettes were twisted and nightmarish, things that couldn't and shouldn't be, a collision of scales, tentacles, claws, and so very many teeth. Eyes bulged madly. Wounds gaped. The slabs of stone were no better. Tortured figures writhed and contorted. Hints of *things* seemed to slip across the stone whenever I turned my eyes away. And the writing.

Cut everywhere, as though by a person in the grip of insanity, was that same strange, scratched, angular writing that had been worked into the base of the statuette in Cord's bedroom. Sarassan had said he found the statuette washed up in a tunnel, but he had clearly lied, unless that spot in the tunnel had been stacked high with this crap.

Enabgal of the many eyes. That had been the translation of the writing on the bottom of Cord's statuette. *Lord of the waters. Watcher in the dark. Cold-bringer. Dream-haunter. Hunter of the void. Deathless. Sleeping. To awake.* So, what in the cold Depths did all the rest of this writing say? And did I really want to know?

Suddenly, the presence was here again, pressing against my senses. *Watching.* That same thing I had felt beneath the city, and with it came the whispers. Unintelligible words, working into my brain like beetles with sharp legs. The presence was close, hungry. The hairs on my arms stood painfully on end. Kehsereen's eyes were wide, too. Shocked. Scared. Fear wormed its way into my stomach and up my spine.

Run. The urge came over me so strongly I took a couple of paces before I realised.

What in all the cursed Depths have you been doing, Sarassan?

When were people in this city going to learn to leave old shit well alone? Sometimes, buried things were better off staying buried. Sarassan had dug this stuff up, and something had come with it. Now his friends were dying.

And how does that fit with the missing kid or the maybe-mage who was killing the Bad Luck Club? I didn't know yet, but I did know that this ... collection ...

325

shrine ... whatever the fuck it was should have stayed forgotten under the city.

Captain Gale needed to know about this. It was what the Ash Guard existed for. Not just to stop mages getting out of hand, but to protect Agatos from every weird, supernatural, or unnatural danger.

The whispers came again, old, corrupt words I had never heard before, words I suspected no living person had spoken, eating into me, promises, threats, madness.

There's someone behind you! I spun, pulling up magic.

No one. Fuck.

My magic drained away from me, like water from a sink. I didn't release it. It just ... went.

Kehsereen had backed up against the wall, staring. I snapped my fingers in front of his face. "We need to get out of here. Now." I grabbed his arm. He didn't resist, but he made no move to follow. I wrenched him bodily around and dragged him out of the storeroom.

Sarassan had kept this collection for how long? Years? Sitting behind a wall in his office. Had it whispered to him all that time, brought nightmares to his sleep? I wondered how long his sanity had lasted. And he had seemed so normal, so ordinary when I had talked to him. A bit skittish, to be sure, but no hint of this. I hadn't read him at all. But he had to be behind it all. There was power in these artifacts. Had he found out how to use it then turned it on his friends? And why? I would ask him that after I broke both his legs and pinned him under a fucking boulder. But first we had to deal with this ... whatever it was. The presence that lurked in the relics Sarassan had brought up from their forgotten tomb, the thing that had whispered fear and madness at me in the ruins. Or, more to the point, Captain Gale and her Ash Guard could deal with it.

The presence seemed to withdraw as we retreated from the house, and the whispering faded. I started to shake. Sweat drenched me. Kehsereen didn't look much better. His usual restless motion seemed to have drained out of him. "What was that?" he managed as we made it onto the street. It was hot and humid out here, but if felt clean.

"I don't know. Something old that should have stayed forgotten." I sucked in air. Every breath I had taken in that room felt like rot in my lungs. I needed to flush it out. "I have to report this, then you and I are going to track down Sarassan and squeeze answers out of him until he screams." I considered. "We'll have to talk to Calovar Tide again. If anyone knows where Sarassan would hide, it should be his friend. They grew up together, they helped each other..." And then Sarassan had started to kill them. Some friend.

So why did he look so shocked when you told him of Cord's death? Maybe he had done it in the confusion of madness. Maybe he hadn't remembered. But he had fled after Bale's death, so madness or not, he must know what he had done.

Speculation wasn't going to help me. Finding Sarassan and punching him in the face just might.

THE PLAZA IN FRONT OF THE ASH GUARD FORTRESS WAS empty, as always. Anyone sensible – particularly any mage – kept well away from the Guard. I had become a frequent visitor. Take from that what you will. I waited outside while one of the Guards went to look for Captain Gale, and Kehsereen examined the building far too closely for my comfort.

"I have never seen this famous Ash," Kehsereen said. "I would like to study it."

"That's not going to happen. They're not the sharing type." That was the problem with scholars. They didn't know when it was unhealthy to stick their noses into things. Yes, I did recognise the irony of me saying that.

Captain Gale didn't take long to arrive. Her eyebrows shot up when she saw me. "Look who it is. My favourite mage."

"Really?"

"What do you think?"

"Um…"

"I see you've been making friends." She nodded at Kehsereen, who looked like he was trying to lever some mortar from between the stone of the fortress. The Ash Guard weren't stupid. The Ash itself was kept well within the fortress walls, even if its influence could be felt where Kehsereen stood.

"More like a colleague, I would say." That probably

sounded better than saying he had drugged me, tied me up, and left me in an alley. How we had got from there to here was something I wasn't sure I could even explain to myself.

Captain Gale eyed him with more interest. "Should I know about him?"

"He's not a mage. He's a scholar, I guess. Look. I don't have time for ... whatever this is."

"Exchanging pleasantries?"

"Yeah. That. I've run into something bad. If I'm right, it's already been used to kill people. It might be linked to the death of Professor Allantin up at the museum, as well as to my original case. I don't know what it is, but it's more than I can deal with."

Captain Gale peered up at me for a few moments. "Well, I'm proud of you. I'm glad you learned something from last time. Is it magical?"

I ignored the barb. "It's a power. That's all I can say. Someone might be using it as a source of magic." Except I had no idea how Sarassan could. Raw magic came from dead gods, and whatever that presence was, it wasn't dead.

She turned to Kehsereen, who had finished picking at the wall and was now watching us, fidgeting with a barely suppressed impatience. "What do you know about this?"

"Mr. Thorn is correct. There is a presence. I have felt it watching this man, Sarassan, before. It is malign, but..." He trailed off with a shrug.

"Whatever it is, it's powerful," I said. "It's not something to take lightly."

The captain's scar pulled her face into a one-sided smile. "Oh, we don't take these things lightly. I would tell you to ask some of the things we've dealt with over the years, but you can't, because when we deal with them, they stay dealt with."

I couldn't tell if that turned me on or scared me more, so I just said, "There's a house on Balascra Street. Number thirty-three. The owner, Porta Sarassan, was keeping artifacts behind a false wall in his office. That's where the power is coming from. He's done a runner, but the artifacts are still there."

I was aware that neither Kehsereen nor I had mentioned Calovar Tide, nor Sarassan's other friends. I guessed we both wanted a shot at Tide before the Ash Guard scooped him up and out of reach.

Captain Gale turned to re-enter the fortress, then stopped and looked back. "You know, this is good work, Nik. It's the kind of thing I was hoping you would root out. Take a rest. You've earned it. And keep well away from this. Both of you."

I raised my hand in acknowledgement and tried not to go dizzy from the compliment. "Of course," I said. *Like fuck.* I would rest when I found Sarassan and he admitted exactly what he had done to Mr. Mirian's wife and Kehsereen's nephew. Without that presence to back him up, we would see how long he could hold out.

CHAPTER TWENTY

WHEN I HAD SET MYSELF UP AS A MAGE-FOR-HIRE, FIVE years ago, I had imagined a lot of things, most of them involving a comfortable living and generous compensation for my hard work. What I had not imagined was tramping backwards and forwards across the city in the searing summer heat like a cat chasing a toy. I wasn't built for this. My feet were sore, my knees ached, and the old injury in my ankle felt like a knife blade driven into the bone.

If I were honest, I was feeling sorry for myself. I had wanted a quiet life, beneath the notice of the real powers that hung over the city, and for most of those five years, that was exactly what I'd had. Easy, insignificant jobs, at least by the standards of most mages. Whether the people whose curses I broke, lost valuables I found, or ghosts I exorcised would agree, I didn't know. To them, I hoped, what I did mattered. Being a freelance mage hadn't paid well as a career, but

I had thought – or told myself – I had been happy. The truth was, I had been avoiding. Avoiding my problems, avoiding anything that might stretch or challenge me. It had been comfortable, safe, and ultimately it hadn't helped me.

And now? Now I had swung in exactly the opposite direction. I had got on the wrong side of the Wren, become tangled in my mother's bastard schemes, and caught the eye of ... something. And while I limped the streets of the city, the Wren's patience was growing ever thinner and the time I had ever shorter. That was the problem I should be dealing with. But I still couldn't. I couldn't do what I had to for Benny and Sereh. So, I told myself I had time, that I would get to it, that I just had one more thing to do first, and I made myself believe it, because somehow, I had to keep going.

There were a hundred mages in this city more qualified and able to handle these murders than I was. If there had been a hundred who were willing, this city would have been a better place. But there was just me, and I was tired of being fobbed off with evasions, lies, and half-truths. Calovar Tide was the only one left who could tell me and Kehsereen what in the Depths was happening. He would speak to us, whether he liked it or not.

I was fuming, and I kept that anger stoked because, yeah, I was also afraid. Whatever that presence really was, I wanted it dealt with, I wanted Mr. Mirian to find his peace, and I wanted to get the Wren off my back for good. Tide was standing in the way of all that. I wasn't going to let him stand there any longer.

The moment we turned onto Tide's street, I knew something was wrong. The unease grew with every step I took, and I could see Kehsereen felt it, too. A small crowd had gathered outside Tide's house, peering at it, but not approaching.

"What the fuck now?" I muttered. I didn't need any more complications.

I unfocused my eyes.

The wards had been shredded. They had been ripped apart like a shark might tear through a sack of meat. Remnants of the magic seethed and snapped in the air, chasing across walls, sparking against each other, and ricocheting away. Every now and then, the magic exploded against something in the house, causing it to shatter. Now I was closer, I could see where a window had been sucked in, leaving a gaping hole and wood and glass scattered across the room inside.

No. That was impossible. No one could do that to my mother's wards. No one. The Godkiller himself wouldn't have been able to.

Except someone or something had. The magic that had killed both Peyt Jyston Cord and Marron Bale had come for Tide, and the wards hadn't stopped it.

"What's happening?" Kehsereen said.

I shook my head. "You should stay back. This is dangerous." If one of those magical discharges inter-sected with a person, well... It would make what had happened to Bale look like a gentle massage at the public baths.

Tide had been in there. He had to have been. He had been hiding behind those wards, sure they would protect him.

I rubbed my hand across my face. *Pity*! I was going to have to be sure. Was he really there, dead? Or had he got away? And what evidence might he have left behind?

Stray magic erupted through the roof, sending fragments of terracotta spinning like knives through the air. The crowd responded with 'oohs' like it was a fireworks display. *Idiots*. That could equally easily have come through the wall.

I couldn't wait forever. Whatever source had powered the wards wasn't running out anytime soon, and eventually the house would collapse.

Why did I get myself into this shit?

"Stay here," I said. "I can't protect you against this."

I drew in raw magic, pulling it to me until every bruise and injury on my body flared with pain. Then I formed it into a shield around me and headed for the collapsing house.

My shield wouldn't take a direct hit from one of those big discharges. I would have to do this fast, I would have to keep my eyes unfocused to watch the magic the whole time, and I would have to hope I hadn't pissed off any of the gods more than was absolutely necessary.

Not too much to ask, then.

"You're crazy," I told myself.

The door wasn't locked. Tide had been relying on the wards to keep him safe. Look how that had turned out.

Outside, you would have had to be really looking at the house to realise something was wrong. Inside, it had been ripped apart. Furniture was splintered, walls punched through and sagging, rugs and tapestries charred and scattered into threads. The smell of burned wood filled the air, overlaid with the electric taste of lightning. Beams groaned, and in another room, something shattered explosively. Uncontrolled magic burst and fizzled.

I didn't even know why I was doing this. Mr. Mirian had hired me, but I hadn't signed on to this chaos. I hadn't promised to walk into the magical equivalent of an erupting volcano. I could tell him that he was right, his wife had been magically compelled, that it was beyond my ability to go further. I could pass it all on to Captain Gale. One way or another, Sarassan would face justice.

I pushed further into the house.

I could tell Mr. Mirian all that. He would understand. He was a reasonable, kind man. He hadn't asked me to risk my life.

And I knew he wouldn't be able to hide the disappointment in his eyes, and I knew he wouldn't blame me, and I knew that would be worse.

I'm not failing you again. I'm not a kid this time. I'm not helpless.

Magic hit me from behind. It was only a glancing blow on my shield, but it was enough to knock me from my feet.

Pay attention!

I eased myself up. *Keep moving.* I staggered on.

The ceiling above me dropped abruptly. I jumped forwards, deflecting the plaster and wood that rained down.

"What exactly are you expecting to find?" I asked the empty room. Did I think I would have time to read through Tide's papers for some clue that probably didn't exist?

The next door was jammed. The lintel had slipped, pinning the door shut. I hit it with my shoulder, but it was too solid. Fucking rich people and their fucking solid wood doors.

I had come as far as I could. I couldn't use magic to break down the door without dropping my shield, and that would leave me helpless against the stray magic bouncing around the house. It was time to get out of here.

I dropped my shield and smashed through the door.

The lintel creaked and dropped. Bricks rained down in billows of dust. I covered my face with my cloak, coughed, spluttered, and then scrambled over the rubble.

Calovar Tide had been in his study when the wards had been broken. I could tell it was his study from the ripped, charred paper, toppled shelves, and smouldering desk. Tide was there, too, but he wasn't going to be any help to me. He was impaled. A cracked timber the width of my wrist protruded three feet from the wall, where the force of the rupturing wards had smashed a hole. Tide looked like he had run at it and thrown himself onto the splintered end. It entered his body just under his sternum and had been driven up into his lungs by the force. Blood had pooled beneath him, soaking his shirt and trousers on the way down. His bowels had loosened, too, in death, and the stink cut through the ozone smell of magical discharge. Then, as his weight rested on it, the timber had bent down, and his body was slowly sliding from it. The wet, tearing sound of flesh giving way made me want to throw up. I stepped back as the wood abandoned the uneven battle with gravity. His body finally came free and dropped loosely to the floor. His head hit the floor-boards with a dull thump.

I stared down at this man who only yesterday had stood so arrogantly behind his unbreakable wards and parried away my questions. It was hard to see that man in the body now. The arrogant expression was gone, replace by a mindless terror.

The magic that had killed Cord and Bale hadn't had any handy bystanders to take control of and turn on Tide. Instead, it had gone straight for him. I wondered if it had seized his mind and forced him to throw himself onto the wood that had impaled him or whether he had been fleeing in terror. It didn't much matter either way. Tide was dead, and Sarassan was gone. If I had been quicker, maybe I could have got to Sarassan before he turned the power of those relics against Tide.

Too late now, and I didn't think Tide deserved my sympathy. He could have told me what was happening. He could have gone to the Ash Guard. Instead, he had smugly thought himself safe and fuck everyone else.

I looked around the room. I wouldn't get anything from here. The uncontrolled magic had caused too much damage. I didn't have time to look through charred scraps of paper.

The building groaned. More plaster rained down. Bricks burst. I brought my shield back up and sprinted for the street.

I was only just in time. I ran from the front door, hunched over, shield held over me, as the building finally gave up the struggle. The walls wavered, bowed, and as a new discharge vented from deep within the house, gave way. The ceiling fell. Glass, bricks, wood, and stone splintered outwards in clouds of roiling dust.

I watched it from behind my shield, then retreated to where Kehsereen had taken shelter in the lee of the building opposite.

"So much for your invincible shields, Mother," I muttered. I couldn't wait to see the expression on her face when she learned about this.

And suddenly I knew how I was going to get into my mother's office unnoticed. It would work. I knew it. I just didn't have much time to waste.

Honestly, this was a fucking terrible plan.

When it had come to me, it had been a stroke of brilliance, but as we hurried towards my mother's palace, the flaws became more and more apparent. There were so many things that could go wrong, starting with me and Kehsereen being accidentally vapourised by my mother's wards and going downhill from there.

Spying on my mother was never going to end well. When she found out – and she would, now or later – there would be consequences. Waiting for a better plan was no longer an option. *A bad plan is better than no plan.* Was that a saying? It should be. It would make me feel happier.

Screw it. This was going to work. Nothing would go wrong. I was due some luck.

I found a spot in the shadows opposite my mother's palace and waited. The heat in the city had grown throughout the day, as had the humidity. Even here, near the top of Horn Hill and out of direct sunlight, it was nearly unbearable. In a week or two, the great and the good of Agatos – or at least the obscenely wealthy and powerful – would shift to their summer palaces and mansions at Carn's Break, leaving the rest of us to swelter our way through to autumn. But I didn't think it was the heat or humidity that was sending shivers across my skin and sweat down my back or causing the growing tightness in my chest. I couldn't even blame my fear on those relics in Sarassan's hidden storeroom. I hadn't heard a hint of that crawling whisper since we had fled, and by now the Ash Guard would have dealt with them. No, this terror came entirely from within me. Standing here, gazing on the building that held so many of the traumas I had tried to forget, allowed them all to creep back, pulling themselves up into my mind on tiny, sharp claws.

This was the wrong plan. It was a fucking disaster.

I had sent Kehsereen in ahead of me, posing as a messenger from Calovar Tide, to tell the Countess that her wards were under attack and failing and pleading for help. I knew my mother. She would reach out, find her wards shattered, and head there like an avenging god to find whatever fucker thought they could go up against her so directly. And while she was distracted by the disaster at Tide's house, I would wander right into her office, find ... whatever, and be out again before she returned.

So where was she? Why hadn't she come rushing out? And where was Kehsereen?

It was a pissing stupid plan. The Countess would see right through Kehsereen. She would lean on him, and he would break, like everyone did when the blessed Countess exerted her powers. Always assuming he hadn't just gone right to her and spilled the whole plan in exchange for far more help in finding his nephew than I could ever offer. I was putting an awful lot of trust in someone I had only known for a few days. I needed to get in there and either rescue him or intervene before he told her too much.

So why was I still standing here? Why weren't my legs moving? Why couldn't I fucking *do* anything?

My vision was closing again, narrowing, blackness edging in, until I felt I was peering down a murky, enclosed alley.

Move!

I couldn't. I just couldn't.

You failure. You fucking useless piece of shit.

Sereh was relying on me, even though she didn't know it. Benny was relying on me. If I didn't do this, the Wren would kill them. He wasn't a man who backed away from his threats.

Depths, even Kehsereen might be relying on me.

And yet ... I couldn't. A scream was building up inside me with nowhere to go.

You're too weak. Too broken. Pity! Why did that sound like my mother's voice?

I should get back to Benny. Tell him to take Sereh and run.

Run where?

Somewhere. Anywhere.

From the back of the palace, my mother's carriage appeared, pulled at a gallop, swerving into the road. Pedestrians leapt aside as it headed down Horn Hill. I had no way and no time to see if my mother was inside, but I didn't believe she would send someone else to deal with this problem. My mother had grown up in the Warrens, just like me. You dealt with your own shit there. It was a lesson you never forgot.

It was twenty minutes' walk to Tide's from here. The carriage would take ten, maybe fifteen if the traffic was heavy. I would have to time this carefully. If I hit my mother's wards before she reached Tide's house, she wouldn't be distracted enough. She might guess what I was up to and turn back. But I also didn't know how long it would take for her to figure out what had happened. The abilities of a high mage were so far above my own, she might have the whole thing dismantled and Sarassan pinned down in minutes for all I knew. I didn't want her coming back before I was done.

Ten minutes. Then straight in, up to my mother's office, grab what I could, then out again. I could see the clock on the Senate building from where I stood.

Seven minutes after my mother's carriage had disappeared from sight, Kehsereen emerged and headed down the street without even glancing in my direction.

What did you tell her, Kehsereen? I could scarcely resist the urge to chase after him and demand an account. But someone might notice, and that would bring the whole plan crashing down.

Trust. Why was that so hard? It wasn't that he had drugged me and left me tied up in an alley. That had been a genuine misunderstanding, and who hadn't assaulted and tied up a stranger by mistake? I just wasn't good at trusting. The Warrens in me, again. *The Warrens run deep.*

Two minutes to go. Why were the clock hands moving so slowly?

A pair of senators, wearing their patronising sashes and accompanied by four bodyguards, made their way down Agate Way, past the palace. One of them carrying a protection charm, the kind of junk you could find on a dozen stalls in the Penitent's Ear market. Even I could break it without raising a sweat.

One minute.

I licked my lips. Why was it so fucking hot? I could hardly breathe. Was it my imagination that the sun was brighter than it had been?

Time. My mother would be approaching Tide's house. Her attention would be on the shredded wards. Like me, she would be wondering what could possibly have destroyed her work. She might even remember me asking about the wards, but she would dismiss the idea of me having done anything to them, because I couldn't. Neither could Mica or the Wren or any other mage in Agatos or around the Yttradian Sea. I didn't even know how those relics could have given Sarassan the ability to do it. You had to have the ability to control power. Having access to raw power wasn't enough.

None of which mattered now, because it was time to do this, and it was my only chance.

So why was I still not moving?

I felt disconnected. I could feel my racing pulse, the

sweat streaking my shirt, the painful tension in my muscles, my throat closing, but I couldn't do anything about it. My feet wouldn't move. It was as though the link between my brain and my body had been severed.

You're wasting time.

I knew what I had to do. I knew how to break this paralysis. Slowly, feeling like my muscles were tearing, I reached for my belt, fingers scratching towards it like crabs. My hand closed around my knife. I jerked it from my belt and drove it into my thigh.

I screamed. Blood flowed over my fingers. I dropped to my knees. People were looking, then turning hurriedly away.

Fuck. That hurt!

I pressed down on the wound, then knitted magic around it, holding it closed. Fucking gods, it hurt!

This spell wouldn't last long, and it wouldn't heal the wound, but it might stop the bleeding long enough.

I wiped the blood from my hands onto my cloak where the black wool hid it, then staggered up and across the street.

By the time I reached the palace doors, I was striding, coming close to running, using the pain of every step to hold my panic in check.

This wasn't going to be so bad. I had been here before. I had faced down my mother, and this time she wasn't even here.

Cerrean Forge wasn't at the desk, thank the spiteful gods. He was a complication I didn't need. I ignored the startled shout from the woman in his place and headed straight for the stairs. Mica had given me a pass through the wards, and as of this morning, it had still worked. I felt the wards fizz over my skin as I passed through them and kept going. I could hear the panting of my own breath, preternaturally loud in the marble hallway at the top of the stairs. My wound had started to leak blood again, despite my magic.

Anything. That was all I needed. Anything would do, as long as it was enough to stay the Wren's brutal hand. The Countess's accounts, a list of her business contacts, her alliances in the Senate. Even if it wasn't enough to pay my debt in full – and it should be; the favour I was supposedly paying off had been a minor one, just some information – at least it might count as down-payment. The Wren had said he wanted to know why my mother had been interested in the old coffee shop near the docks, and, yeah, I was curious, too, but I wasn't going to have time to be fussy. If my mother caught me, that would be the end of Benny and Sereh, and I wasn't letting that happen. I wasn't.

I reached the door to my mother's private quarters. The wards blocking the way were as powerful and as potent as the ones that had protected Tide's house. When I unfocused my eyes, they teemed black and red in shifting, jagged shapes. If she had taken away my pass, if I tried to force my way through them, someone would need a mop to clear up what was left of me.

I pushed forward.

I could hardly feel the wards beneath the shivers

that trembled up and down my body. At any moment, I might freeze or collapse, and the Countess would find me here, broken. My pulse was punching like a flurry of fists.

This had to be over. I couldn't do this again. Depths, I didn't know if I could do it this time. How did I ever think I had escaped this ... this fucking trauma? This Cepra-damned place was like one of those monstrosities that had crawled out of the ocean, claws and teeth sunk into me and slowly ripping. I had to get out, away, and never come back. For just a moment, I stood unmoving, ready to turn away, but the thought of failing Benny and Sereh kept me moving on. *You don't abandon your family.*

I remembered standing here five years ago, when I had found the courage to finally tell my mother I was leaving. The look of contempt she had turned on me had been like a knife in the chest, even when I had told myself she couldn't hurt me anymore. "You will always be a disappointment to your family, Mennik. You will always let us down." Somehow, I had let it become a self-fulfilling prophecy. Benny and Sereh had become my real family, and I had disappointed them. I had let them down, just like my mother had said.

Not again.

The waiting room outside my mother's office was empty. Through the wide windows, afternoon shadows draped the eastern side of Horn Hill, the houses below it, and the Royal Highway. The Grey City was still in full sunlight, as were the Stacks and the Ependhos mountain range beyond. Time was running out.

The door to my mother's office was open. And yet ... And yet once more I couldn't move. To go in there, to search through her papers and books and files, it was another step too much. The monstrosity had a hold of me, and I couldn't lean into that gaping mouth. I had to, but I couldn't.

Just like I couldn't walk into the palace? I kept telling myself I couldn't, that I was too weak, too scared, too damaged. It was a lie. It was cowardice.

I drove my knuckle into the wound on my leg.

I couldn't help it. I screamed again. My leg buckled, and I tumbled onto the rug. But the pain cut through. Hauling myself up, I lurched towards my mother's office. Blood trickled down my thigh, making my trousers sticky. I tightened the spell clamping the wound.

I could do this.

What secrets are you hiding, Mother?

I unfocused my eyes. There were wards on the cabinets and on the door that led to mother's personal rooms. No point trying any of those. A couple of artifacts on a shelf held reservoirs of raw magic, and there was a cursed dagger beside them, an old one. None of which would help me.

I examined the map on the wall, matching the blue flags to the addresses Elosyn had given me. *Why are you so interested in those buildings, Mother?* Maybe if they had been grand houses in the Upper City, I would understand them as an investment to stash her wealth, or as residences to keep her senior mages loyal. But these were all near Dockside and the Grey City, in the Middle City, and other than their locations in the parts of the city that verged on but never quite achieved respectability, I couldn't see a pattern to them. It didn't make sense, and that pissed me off. It itched at me. I was missing something.

There were ledgers on the shelves, too. I pulled a couple down. Accounts, business holdings... She certainly wouldn't want them shared with the Wren, but would they really be enough? They wouldn't give him any significant advantage over my mother. I couldn't shake the feeling of unease that suffused me at the thought of delivering these to the high mage of the underworld. Would this really buy the lives of Benny and Sereh? Depths, with a good accountant, most of this was probably publicly available. Nothing worth sending a spy into the Countess's lair for.

I put the ledgers back and moved to her desk. Letters. Business papers for the Senate. A half-drafted speech. A schedule of jobs for her senior mages. Pens and ink and her personal seal.

I opened the desk. More papers. A motion to adjust taxes on imports of silk. The renaming of a street. Denna's mercy, the business of the Senate was dull. I flicked through the rest of the papers. All little schemes and deals to enrich the already rich. Nothing that would help the ordinary citizens of the Warrens, Dockside, Fishertown, or the Stacks. People there knew all you could do was try to survive. There was nothing that would interest the Wren here, either.

I was about to close the drawer again when a particular sheaf of papers caught my eye. There was nothing unusual about it. It was just another motion to be presented to the Senate, but a single word stood out, and everything clicked. 'Gambling,' the word said.

If it hadn't been for Cord and his involvement in the Wren's underground games, it would have slipped past me. Instead, I pulled it out.

It was a bill proposed by my mother and the Yellow Faction of the Senate to legalise organised gambling in Agatos, and it was due to be presented to the Senate in a week's time.

Although gambling itself was legal, organising gambling was not. The games run by the Wren drew in men and women from across the city and from the stream of sailors and merchants passing through. The Wren didn't exactly submit accounts to the tax authorities, but it was well known that illegal gambling made up a significant portion of his income. If he lost that, it would take the legs out from under him. He could set up his own games, of course, but if he didn't know this was coming and if someone was ready to set up in competition... Someone, maybe, who had been buying up spacious, empty buildings in strategic locations.

That's what you've been up to, Mother.

Elation swept through me, dulling the pain in my leg and washing away the panic that had been eating at me. This would buy me free of the Wren a dozen times over. It would keep Benny and Sereh safe: My mother's plot to undercut and financially ruin the Wren.

I supposed I should feel bad for handing back advantage to the Wren, but fuck it. I would just be keeping the balance, like Captain Gale wanted. This city couldn't work with one high mage dominant. And, yeah, that was just me justifying it to myself. Honestly, I didn't care.

I couldn't take the document with me. My mother would notice. But the Wren would know I wouldn't lie to him about this when there was so much at stake. I set the papers carefully back in the drawer, making sure nothing was disturbed on or in the desk.

When I straightened, there was a figure in the doorway. I stuttered to a halt. The figure was outlined by the bright light from the windows behind, but I could make out the black cloak of a mage.

Not my mother, was my first thought, and the relief was almost enough to drop me. The Countess never wore a mage cloak. Something we had in common most of the time. Maybe I should wear mine more often. That first thought was followed by, *But one of her mages*. It wasn't much better news. I had relied on getting in and out without anyone seeing what I was up to.

As I squinted into the light and my eyes adjusted, the mage's face came into focus. *Cerrean Forge*. Who else? The bastard had hated me from the moment my mother brought him into her service. I didn't know what it was. Jealousy, maybe? The belief that I hadn't earned the position my mother had placed me in. Whatever it had been, the bitterness hadn't faded with time or my absence. He had been looking for a chance to bring me down.

"I knew you were up to no good," he said. I could almost hear the smirk in his voice.

No. This arsehole was not going to screw this up just to win some credit with my bloody mother. "Good for you. Now get the fuck out of my way."

He shook his head. "Oh, no. I've got you."

"Got me doing what? Looking for my mother? Trying to leave her a note?" The guy was pissing me off, more so because he really had caught me this time. In my books, you could get away with being an arrogant prick or you could get away with being right, but you couldn't get away with both.

"Rifling through her drawers."

"I guess you're not going to believe I was looking for paper for the note?"

He stepped into the office, drawing in raw magic. He was more powerful than me, I already knew that. Depths, I'd *felt* that a hundred times before I left this place. I hoped he wouldn't have the balls to trash the Countess's private office just to catch me.

Although I would probably get the blame if he did.

"Last chance," he said.

I tossed an arrow of magic at him. He batted it aside.

All right, then.

I came around the desk, drawing in more magic.

The pressure of it inside me made my bruises throb, and I felt the wound on my leg open up again.

He shaped his own magic and threw it at me. I saw the net coming for me before it even left his hands. I had a blade of magic ready to slice it. His face reddened as his spell collapsed. I almost laughed. Had he always been that slow and clumsy?

He was getting pissed off. Good. Pissed off people made mistakes. That was what I was telling myself, anyway. Either that or they tore out your guts and used them for Charo decorations.

He sucked in power. His face twisted in pain at the pressure of the raw magic. Oh, yeah. He was pissed off.

On second thoughts, perhaps it had been a mistake to antagonise him.

I dived to the side, throwing up my shield as Forge sent a sheet of fire at me. The fire deflected from my shield and ricocheted into the shelf holding the cursed dagger. The shelf collapsed, spilling the dagger and the other artifacts to the floor.

Forge's face drooped, his mouth falling open in realisation and shock at what he had done. Maybe he was imagining my mother's reaction. I scrambled up, took two steps towards him, and swung my mage's rod up between his legs. (Yes, that still sounded obscene; I really did have to think of something else to call it.)

Forge didn't even scream. His mouth gaped and worked silently as he slowly folded and collapsed to the floor, where he convulsed and spewed his last meal over my mother's expensive rug. I looked down at him.

I had been scared of this fucker for a big chunk of my life. I should have done this years ago.

Today, though. Today had been a fucking awful time to finally take him down. I had wanted to get in and out clean. Now my mother would know exactly what I had been up to. If I was still here when she got back, I would never make it to the Wren in time.

Fuck Forge and his suspicions. No one should have got hurt. No one should have known.

I took off for the exit, trying not to run or even limp too badly.

CHAPTER TWENTY-ONE

I STOPPED IN AN ALLEY BETWEEN TWO GRAND HOUSES TO tear a strip off my last good shirt and tie it around my bleeding leg. It left me with a gap of about an inch around my stomach. Depths, that wasn't so bad. If I pulled my cloak around me and shuffled, it was hardly noticeable.

I followed the narrow, steeply-stepped alley down the side of Horn Hill to the Middle City below. I knew I didn't have much time. The sun was plunging behind the mountains like a drunk falling off the edge of the docks. The Wren's man had said I had until tonight. He hadn't said whether that meant dusk or the dark hours.

The temptation to sprint directly for the Wren's warehouse was almost overwhelming. My head kept playing me visions of Benny and Sereh lying dead on the cobbles. But there were too many people looking to jump me, starting with Cerrean Forge and not ending until the smuggling gang had carved their vengeance in my bruised flesh. So, I took the back ways, keeping alert and trailing a web of magic to warn myself of anyone approaching. It was harder than it sounded, and it didn't do my injuries any favours. Every creeping minute made my teeth grind harder and sent tension shooting up into my head.

The Wren's base was in a warehouse on the docks. From the outside, it didn't look any different from the dozens of other warehouses that surrounded it – bulky, plain, whitewashed brick and stone, with high, mostly-shuttered windows – but anyone who had any contact with the underworld knew it for what it was. When it came to the Wren, it was the façade that mattered to the city. As long as the Wren pretended he was a legitimate businessman, the city would pretend they didn't know what he was really up to, and everyone could avoid the confrontation that would leave half the city flattened and the Wren impaled on an Ash Guard sword. No one benefitted from that, and there were a fair few who enjoyed the bribes the Wren provided. It was a fucked-up system, but it was a fucked-up city, and it had lasted longer than most other cities that had tried to un-fuck things.

The mage guarding the entrance doors, dressed unconvincingly as a dockhand, passed me into the warehouse, and another mage, this time in a black cloak, led me up to the Wren's offices.

The Wren was working at his desk, and his hulking bodyguard/advisor/gardener, Melecho Kael, was standing just behind him. I felt oddly flattered that the

Wren had felt the need for a bodyguard or advisor to deal with me. Maybe he was just there to give me some gardening tips. The smell of the Wren's miniature jungle drifted through the wide-open internal doors, and I heard the call of an exotic bird somewhere in the deep canopy.

I marched over and sat opposite the Wren. *Confidence. Project confidence.* Because that would fool him.

"I had imagined you would be here sooner," he said, not looking up from his writing. To a casual glance, he looked like a clerk nearing retirement. Thin, greying hair, pale, lined skin. But the power rolled from him. I wondered if anyone could be unaware of it, even if they weren't sensitive to magic. It was palpable in the room. I didn't even need to unfocus my eyes to notice it. "The sun has already set over the mountains."

The words sent a shudder through me. Was he saying I was too late? No. This was just a show of dominance to put me in my place, to throw me off balance.

It was working.

"The sun's still shining out there." I jerked my thumb towards the window that looked over the Erastes Bay and the ocean beyond. Evening sunlight sent silvered threads skating across the waves.

"We are not out on the ocean, Mennik Thorn. We are in Agatos, and if I say the sun has set, the sun has set. I am surprised that you would trust your friends' fate on the setting of the sun."

My mouth was dry. My heart pounded too fast.

"What have you done with them? If you've hurt them—"

The Wren's power rose above him, pressing down on me like the weight of a mountain until I could hardly breathe. "You will do what?"

Depths! I fought for air. "Where are they?"

The magic cut off abruptly, and I almost fell from my chair. I sucked in breath, while the Wren watched me from the other side of the desk. When I pushed myself up, he said, "My men are on their way to your friends."

And I hadn't warned them. I had thought I would sort it out and Benny and Sereh would never need to know.

"That's not going to end too well for your men," I said.

"Are you making threats again, Mennik Thorn?" His magic rose and dipped, like an enormous beast leaning over him.

"No. No." I was thinking of Sereh. If the Wren's men entered Benny's house, she was going to leave bodies on the floor, and even if she and Benny survived, the Wren would feel the need to get involved personally. Things would spiral out of control very quickly.

"Then speak. Your friends have very little time."

Right. Now that I was here, my information seemed so thin. I wasn't warning him of a magical attack. It was just about business, hardly a threat to the Wren's life or welfare. It was just about money.

And what else does the Wren care about?

"My..." I wet my lips. This was all I had. It was the wooden spar from a shipwreck holding Benny and Sereh above the waves. "My mother has been buying buildings in the Middle City, near Dockside and the Grey City."

"This I know."

Yeah. I struggled to keep my hands still. "Big buildings, with plenty of space within them."

"Your point? Fast, Mennik Thorn."

Breathe. "My mother has also been gathering support for a bill she intends to present to the Senate in a week's time. It is to legalise gambling in Agatos."

The Wren's expression didn't change. His pale gaze stayed steady on me.

"If she does," I said, "with the buildings—"

"I understand my business, Mennik Thorn. You may leave."

I stood. "Benny and Sereh. You'll call off your men?"

"You may leave."

Fuck! I sprinted for the exit.

WITH THE DARKNESS CLOSING IN, AGATOS HAD BECOME busy again, as the citizens emerged from the shelter of their houses to the cooling streets. It wasn't far from the docks to Benny's house, but the alleys and roads were narrow and crowded. I kept running, shouting for people to make way and using magic to shove aside those who didn't clear a path at the sight of my mage's cloak. There were no morgue-lamps lighting the streets in this part of town, but the last glow of the evening and the light from windows was enough to stop me falling as I ran. My ankle speared pain all the way to my knee, and the wound on the other leg leaked under the bandage.

The Wren couldn't have gone through with it. He had to have called his men off.

Didn't he?

The Wren liked his lessons, and his lessons were bloody. If he thought I had stood up to him too publicly... Why in all the cursed Depths had I humiliated his mages where everyone could see? Why couldn't I just keep my mouth shut?

I burst out of a side street across from Benny's house and came to a halt. I couldn't see anything out of place. The shutters and doors were still closed, and my wards were still up. There were no large groups of thugs sizing the place up. Maybe I was in time. I hurried across and hammered on the door.

Benny's expression when he opened it was a mixture of surprise and amusement. "Back already, mate? I told you—"

I pushed past. "Close the door."

His weaselly face creased. "All right, mate."

I crossed to the back and peered out into the courtyard. Nothing.

Benny followed me. "What's up?"

"Has anyone been here? Anyone..." How the fuck was I supposed to explain all this?

"Nah. There's been no one. It's fine. Have a sit down."

Bannaur's balls! I had almost given myself a heart attack. I slumped onto his couch.

"They were here," Sereh's voice drifted out of the shadows. I hadn't seen her there, of course. I couldn't even summon up the energy to be startled. "There were four of them, and they had a mage with them. I was watching them. They were going to come in through the side window. That would have been a mistake."

I was familiar with most of the booby traps Sereh had set around the house, and the one on that window was particularly vicious. Sereh's voice was coming from beside the window, too. Anyone trying to enter that way would have encountered a very short, bloody surprise.

"What happened?"

Sereh emerged from the shadows. "After a while, they left." So, the Wren had called them off after all. There was still a warning in it. "They scared off the smugglers who had been watching the house, though. You need to be better at making friends, Uncle Nik."

Fair point. I pushed myself upright. "I think it's all right now. I think I've given the Wren what he needs. He'll leave us alone. Probably kind of ballsed things up with my mother, though."

"Hold on, mate," Benny said. "Are you saying those were the Wren's people?"

"Um. Yeah. They won't be back, though."

"Why the fuck were they here at all? Didn't he know you had moved out?"

Ah. Yeah. I had really hoped Benny would never need to know about any of this. "He knew. It was just —" I cleared my throat. "He said that if I didn't do what he said, he would have you both killed."

Benny stared.

"It's all right," I said again. "I dealt with it."

Hardness flattened Benny's eyes. He took a step towards me. "No. It's not fucking all right. He threatened Sereh, and you – what? – you were fucking around with your stupid case instead of throwing every pissing bit of effort into getting him what he wanted. You didn't even tell me."

"I didn't want to..." Worry them? Goat shit. I hadn't wanted to make it harder for myself. I hadn't wanted the pressure. If I had told Benny, I wouldn't have been able to procrastinate and avoid, to put everything off at every opportunity. I had done it for me. I kept telling myself that Benny and Sereh, even Elosyn and Holera, were my true family. But I had let them all down every time it came to a choice between looking after myself or helping them. Kehsereen had uprooted himself and come all the way to Agatos when his nephew had gone missing. He had put his family above everything else. What had I done?

"Yeah. That's what I thought." Benny took another

step forward. "You know what, Nik? Fuck you both ways and upside fucking down. Get out of my house!"

⟞⟞

I HAD RUINED EVERYTHING. I HAD BEEN EVERY BIT AS unreliable as my mother had always said I was. I had told myself my friends were everything, but I had let them down when it had been easier to do so.

Maybe I was just an arsehole.

I didn't know if I could make it up to Benny and Sereh. I wouldn't blame them if they never talked to me again. Depths, I was lucky to make it out of there without one of them knifing me. I did know that Mr. Mirian still needed his answers. I could do that, at least. Sarassan had used Etta Mirian to kill Cord, but I still didn't know why. Until I did, it would be like a hanging nail, catching unexpectedly on cloth.

I had agreed to find Kehsereen in our usual spot, under the cypress trees in the small plaza close to the Leap, so I headed that way. When I reached it, tables had been set out, lit by lanterns strung across the plaza, and a nearby taverna was serving food. My stomach rumbled painfully at the smell. Again, it had been too long since I had eaten. The buoying effect of magic could only carry me so far.

"Your plan worked?" Kehsereen asked as I hurried over to meet him. He was as fidgety as ever. Who could blame him? I might be getting closer to my answers –

might – but we still didn't have a single lead as to what had happened to his nephew.

I nodded. No point in sharing all the fuckups along the way. The consequences would be mine, not his. "We need to find Sarassan. He's the last of them, and he's behind all of this. He's the only one left who can answer questions about your nephew."

"I have done some research. Mr. Sarassan's family owned an apartment in Dockside. It was where he grew up. His parents are dead, but Mr. Sarassan still owns it." I was reluctantly impressed. I doubted the scholars at the university would have found this out so quickly, if at all. Practical information wasn't their strength.

It was good information, but Sarassan wouldn't be stupid enough to flee to somewhere so obvious, would he? Maybe. He wasn't a career criminal. He wouldn't know how to properly disappear. If he had tucked himself into an apartment he assumed no one else knew of, we could corner him.

I just hoped Captain Gale had dealt with those artifacts of his. If they were still active... I shuddered.

Of course she's dealt with them. She was Ash Guard. They fucked over high mages on their tea breaks. She wouldn't let me down.

THE AREA CALLED DOCKSIDE CONSISTED OF A STRIP OF warehouses, tenements, shops, bars, and inns that stretched most of the width of the Erastes Valley, from the river in the east to the dry docks and the Warrens in the west. Every few years, someone would come up with the idea of tearing the whole thing down and replacing it with grander buildings – preferably adorned with statues of senators and wealthy merchants – to provide a more fitting approach to the great city. Having met more than a few senators and merchants, the sight of them peering down at me as I sailed in would have been enough to make me turn my ship around and sail right back out again. These proposals always foundered on the same problem: Dockside might be a decaying shithole, plagued by thugs, thieves, and sailors, but the warehouses were the source of most of Agatos's wealth, and the dock-workers had to live somewhere. No one in the Upper City wanted them up *there*, and without warehouses, trade wouldn't come. It was, everyone would eventually agree each time, highly undesirable, but what could you do? (Obviously the thought of just doing up the place so that it was more pleasant for both the residents and the incoming visitors never entered their heads, because there was no profit or aggrandising statues in it.) When the whole place became too much for their delicate sensibilities, the senators could console themselves by looking at their piles of money, and nothing else really mattered.

I wasn't much of a fan of Dockside myself, although that was more to do with my own hang-ups and the presence of the ocean beyond. I *really* wasn't a fan of the ocean. The fact that Dockside was also home to a smuggling gang who apparently wanted to use my skin as a rug didn't make me feel any warmer towards the place.

The tenement building Sarassan had grown up in was a four-storey, rectangular block, built to the same design as the warehouses, and it wasn't in a good state. The roof sagged. Windows were broken, and whitewashed plaster flaked from the walls. The alley leading to the entrance stank, despite the breeze. Rotting food and urine combined with the smell of salt air and dead sea creatures. The air was close and clammy. Gulls argued raucously somewhere out over the bay. Waves broke on the sea wall, and ships creaked at dock. For a moment, I thought I heard whispering, too, but when I focused, it was just the water pulling over pebbles somewhere beyond the sea wall and air hustling through the lines on the ships. It was full dark now, and figures hurried like frightened or strutting shadows through the streets.

I studied the building, looking for magic, but if Sarassan was in there and if he had brought any of those magic-infused relics with him when he'd fled, he wasn't using them. If anyone was watching us, they were too good for me to spot.

"Let me go first," I told Kehsereen. "I'll take him down, and you grab him. If you've got any of that drug you used on me—"

"Ulu-aru."

"Whatever. Dose him."

"It will make it harder to get answers."

"Better than him ripping us apart."

I took a look around, then hustled over to the entrance. In the dark, and with the alley surprisingly busy, I didn't think we would stand out. I held in as much raw magic as I could. I would have to hit Sarassan hard and fast. This would be our one chance to get answers, and I didn't want to screw it up.

Stairs led up inside the tenement, lit by a single gas lamp halfway up. It guttered unhealthily, and the glass around it had been shattered. Soot stained the wooden wall above it. If I started throwing fire around in this building, the whole thing could go up. I wanted answers, but I wasn't here to burn down anyone's home.

This was no place to bring up children. No wonder Sarassan and his friends had wanted out. It was only one step up from the Warrens. I could hear muted conversations behind thin doors, the crying of a baby, children shouting. The stairs sagged under my feet.

Sarassan's family apartment was on the third floor, halfway along a hallway. I kept my eyes unfocused and my raw magic held tight as I approached. There were voices inside, whispering quietly. A woman and children.

Not just Sarassan, then, but his family. I wondered what they thought about being dragged here so suddenly. It must have been terrifying and shocking after their grand, luxurious home. Surely Sarassan hadn't told them he had been murdering his best friends and was now hiding from the Ash Guard? That wasn't the kind of conversation that went down well.

I checked Kehsereen was ready, then I blew the door off its hinges.

I went in fast, another spell ready to let loose and my mage's rod raised to smack someone around the head.

Screams came from my left. I spun towards them. A woman in a long, gold-trimmed robe was flattened against the wall, kids pulled to her.

I checked the other side. The room was small, and there was no one there. There were two doors opposite. I ran to them and threw them open.

No sign of Sarassan.

I spun again, magic still raised. Kehsereen blocked the doorway. Sarassan wasn't here.

I turned and approached the woman and children. One of the children, a little boy, no older than five, screamed over and over again, terror turning his face red and wet.

Fuck! What was I doing? I dropped into a crouch and lowered the rod to the floor, then lifted my empty hands.

"It's all right. I'm not going to hurt you." It probably wasn't very convincing with the remains of their door spread across the room.

Why hadn't I just knocked? I had heard children in here. I pushed my hood back and sat, cross-legged, on the floor. "I'm not going to hurt you," I repeated.

"What do you want?"

"Are you Mrs. Sarassan?"

Her eyes flicked around the room, as though searching for the right answer. She was trying to figure out whether it would be safer to confirm or deny it. She didn't need to. I could see the echoes of Sarassan's features in the children.

"We just want to talk to your husband." No. That wasn't going to help. If I was a thug looking to beat her husband senseless, I would say just the same. And hadn't I planned to give him a good kicking, anyway? Maybe she wasn't wrong. But seeing her and her children crouching here, terrified, my anger disappeared. I just wanted answers. "I'm assisting the Ash Guard. You know your husband's friends have been murdered? We're trying to find out why and how." Almost all of that was true. "Do you know where he is?"

She shook her head, an abrupt, jerking movement, like a toy with worn cogs. "He said we would be safer if we were nowhere near him."

Safer? He was the one doing all this. Had he lost control of the power? Or did he mean safer from me and the Ash Guard? That didn't make sense. Neither I nor Captain Gale would come after his family, even if the shattered door told a different story.

"Is there somewhere he might have gone? We really do need to talk to him. Whatever he's caught up in, it's not safe for anyone. He might be in danger." I almost gagged saying that last part, but she needed to think we were on his side.

She just stared mutely at me, pulling her kids in

closer. She wasn't going to tell me anything. I wouldn't, either, in her situation. I glanced across at Kehsereen. He shrugged.

"Take my advice," I said, standing again. "Take your kids and go to the Ash Guard headquarters. Tell them everything that's happened. Whatever it is that your husband is scared of, it won't be able to touch you in there. The sooner you tell them, the sooner your husband will be safe, too." Or executed by the Guard, but that wasn't my call, one way or another.

This had been a bust. Sarassan was still out there, whether hiding or planning his next move. I had no idea what his endgame was. He had killed his friends. Maybe he had killed Kehsereen's nephew, although I wasn't saying that to Kehsereen. If the man was any kind of investigator or scholar, he already knew it. But what had Sarassan hoped to gain? And did he still hope to gain it, or had it all turned to shit in his hands?

It was late. I was exhausted and injured. I was also homeless and close to broke. I needed rest, I needed time to think, and I needed no one else trying to kill me, at least for a few hours.

"Where was it you said you were staying?" I asked Kehsereen.

"*The Lost Head.*"

"Good. Then I'm going to see if they have a spare room. There's nothing more we can do tonight."

CHAPTER TWENTY-TWO

I would say this for Kehsereen. He knew how to find a nice inn.

He knew how to find an expensive one, too. *The Lost Head* was clean, spacious, and despite being near the docks, managed to avoid the stench that pervaded so much of the area. It also took almost half of the money I had just to book a room for a single night. The university in Khorasan must have paid better than I had realised, but then I didn't know how much the University of Agatos paid, either. Maybe I should have been more conscientious in my studies.

I could have gone looking for somewhere cheaper, but the idea was just too much. I wanted to collapse, and it made sense to be in the same place as Kehsereen while we planned our next move.

Not that I got to do any of that planning. I pulled off my shoes, sat on the bed, and was asleep before I could douse my candle.

It shouldn't have come as a surprise that my sleep would be restless. After the strain and gut-churning terror of the last few days and the unease I felt about Sarassan still being out there, my dreams were ominous and ill-formed, as though something slunk through the dark, just out of sight, watching me, following me, whispering in a forgotten language that unravelled my mind in unknown directions, and nothing I could do would shake it. I would have woken if I could, despite my exhaustion and my injuries, but my dreams had a hold of me in the way nightmares sometimes did, and the dreams kept stalking me.

When I finally did awake, it wasn't my nightmares or my willpower that did it. I lay there, panting and sweating in the dark while something twitched urgently at my mind. It took me far too long to figure out what it was. I had set wards around the room, not deadly ones – that was frowned upon in public places like inns – but wards to warn me of any intrusion. Someone had crossed those wards. I heard a faint breath beside the bed.

I threw myself away, tumbled to the floor, tangled in my sheet, and came up, throwing a magical light at the intruder's face. They staggered back, and in the burning light I saw who had come for me.

Sarassan. Here. In my room. Standing over me.

I hauled in raw magic and crashed it into him in a barrage of pure force. He flew back, hitting the wall behind with an impact that rained plaster from the ceiling and dropped a picture to the floor.

I followed him, leaping over the bed, kicking my feet free of my sheet. I summoned a spear of magic, lighting it up so he couldn't miss it, and pushed it against his throat. Blood trickled from his broken skin and evaporated in the heat of the magic.

"No," he managed. "Stop. Please."

I pushed the spear a fraction further in.

Someone hammered on the door, followed by a voice shouting, "Is everything all right?" Kehsereen.

"Yeah. Come on in."

The door opened, and Kehsereen slipped through. His eyes widened at the sight. Honestly, my reaction wouldn't have been so calm.

"Got the drug?" I asked.

He reached inside his shirt and pulled out a small vial of clear liquid. "Just a couple of drops, or he won't be able to speak."

"How much did you use on me?"

"More than a couple of drops. I needed you unconscious."

I bit back a comment. Not the time, and I had already decided to let it go. The bastard. I uncorked the vial and held it above Sarassan's face. "Drink this, or I'm going to stick my spear right through your throat." He looked scared, but I already knew he was a good actor. He had fooled me when I had told him Cord was dead. I had been convinced it had come as a surprise to him. At his reluctance, I added, "It's not poison. If I wanted to kill you, there are easier ways."

He hadn't tried any magic. Perhaps he really was

helpless without those relics. He didn't seem to be carrying a weapon, either. What exactly had been his plan here?

Sarassan opened his mouth, and I let a couple of drops fall in, then a third, just to be sure. He swallowed. I glanced over at Kehsereen, who nodded. Relief released the tension from my shoulders. I let the spear dissolve. Sleep had helped heal my wounds. I was no longer bleeding, and my bruises had receded, but it would take more than the few hours I'd had to restore me fully, and using magic *hurt*.

"Time to talk."

Sarassan stayed where he was, hunched between the wall and the floor. His hand reached for his neck and came away with streaks of blood. He started shaking. I didn't have any sympathy. I had cut myself worse shaving, and he had killed a lot of people.

"I need your help," he said.

"My help." Was that supposed to be a joke? "Peyt Jyston Cord. Marron Bale. Calovar Tide. Etta Mirian. All dead, and who the fuck knows how many others?" I jerked a thumb over my shoulder towards Kehsereen. "His nephew, missing. And you want my help?"

"I didn't kill them." I could see the yearning to be believed in his eyes. But was that because he was telling the truth or because he wanted me to believe another lie?

"Then talk. Fast. Or I'm going to turn you over to the Ash Guard, and fuck me, you do not want that."

He looked broken. *An act. Another shitting act.* He wasn't catching me out that way again.

"It was my fault," he started.

"I'm not arguing with that one."

His head jerked side to side, although I didn't know what he thought he was denying. "I found it when I was deep diving. You know when..." He made a vague gesture with his hands. "There had been a new collapse under the Grey City. You look out for those. It's hard to find anything worthwhile in the usual tunnels and ruins down there, but collapses open up new buildings and new areas. I found a way through. It was tough. Dangerous. Not everyone tries those, but I was desperate. We had no money, nothing."

"If you're looking for sympathy," I said, "you broke into the wrong room."

He grimaced. "That was when I found it. There was a ruined temple far beyond the collapse, and it was untouched. You probably don't know how unusual something like that is. It's what every deep diver dreams of, a find to make your fortune." He wasn't looking at me anymore. His eyes were focused on what he was remembering.

"And what? You didn't fancy sharing with your friends? The whole Bad Luck Club thing wasn't looking so great when you got greedy?"

"No! I'm talking about how it all started, eight years ago. That was when our luck changed, you know? That's what I thought, anyway. We all did, for a long time, because it wasn't just a temple. There was a pit."

His eyes tightened. Was that fear? Disgust? Something else? "And down in the pit..." He shook his head again. "There's always a price. Always."

"What do you mean?" I couldn't have forced sympathy into my voice if I had wanted to, and I didn't want to.

"Enhuin. That's what I found in the pit. The dream haunter. The watcher in the dark. The god. And it was so, so hungry."

I didn't like where this was going. "What did you do?"

His eyes closed. "We fed it, and it gave us everything we wanted. With me, it was my finds. It showed me where the most valuable artifacts were beneath the city. With Peyt, it was winning his blasted games. It gave him luck. With Marron, the wrestling, and Calovar got to be the successful lawyer he had always said he would be, never losing his cases. If we dreamed it, Enhuin gave it to us, as long as we kept feeding it. But this last time, something went wrong."

Fucking understatement. "And what, exactly, did you feed it?"

Sarassan still wouldn't look at me. "It was weak. It needed magic. It *ate* magic. But it couldn't eat, you know..." He waved his hand at the air.

"Raw magic?"

"Yes. It couldn't eat raw magic. It needed help. It needed the raw magic transformed."

And there was only one way magic got transformed. "You fed it a person. A mage." But not a trained mage, not if they didn't want their intestines smeared around their precious temple. "Someone helpless. A natural mage." Natural mages weren't uncommon. Most didn't even know what they were. They might realise that curses they laid had more effect than those of other people. They might notice they were less susceptible to illness or hunger. But very few would understand that they were using raw magic to do it and, in the process, converting it.

"And it worked! Enhuin could take magic from him. But then—"

"How many?"

"What?"

"How many natural mages did you feed to this thing?"

"I don't know. Ten. Twelve, maybe."

"You don't fucking know?" My hands were tingling. I wanted to let go of my control and blast this wanker into a million tiny, wet pieces. "You fed people to your god, and you don't even remember how many? How about their names? Did you know those? Their lives, their families?"

"We needed more help," he protested, suddenly looking up at me. "It could only help us if we fed it magic. And they couldn't—"

"They died. Your god drained them dry. And now it's killing you." Was he expecting me to care? "You deserve it. Etta Mirian didn't. Those natural mages didn't."

"No."

"No?" The self-righteous bastard.

"It's not Enhuin."

What the Depths was he on about? "Explain."

"It's not Enhuin that's killing us. It's him. The new natural mage. We made a mistake. He was far, far too strong. Enhuin is feeding, but... I don't know how he's doing it, but he is. You have to protect me."

I didn't even feel angry anymore. Just cold. "No," I said. "I don't."

This time they hadn't just fed a natural mage to their god. They had found a natural high mage. He was hurt, confused, angry, lashing out with uncontrollable powers at his tormenters. It was almost unheard of. High mages needed training, but in the terror and the pain of whatever was happening to him, the natural high mage's powers had emerged, unformed and untrained, but no less deadly. I turned back to Kehsereen. "Did you ever suspect your nephew might be a natural mage?" Kehsereen himself had magical sensitivities, which were a sign of natural talents.

"Maybe. I sensed something about him, but his parents never wanted that for him."

They were kinder than my mother had been. If it hadn't been for Sarassan and his friends, Kehsereen's nephew might never have been anything but an unusually healthy man going about his life. They had taken that from him. They had known the god would kill him eventually, and they hadn't cared.

The boy's family might have been kinder than my mother, but it had ended the same, with him trapped, tortured, broken in the name of a brutal hunger for power. But, unlike him, I'd had a way out, even if it had taken me years to realise it. This kid didn't have years. He might not even days or hours. He was being drained. Everything in me rebelled at the thought. But this time it didn't manifest itself in panic. It was anger. Rage that sent fire burning up my nerves and into my brain. *Not again. Not this time.*

"We found your hidden stash of invested objects," I told Sarassan. "The Ash Guard has them now. Your god is finished."

"No." A smile flickered briefly on Sarassan's lips. "Those were nothing. Enhuin is still there, in the pit, and he has drawn on so much power. The lord of dark dreams is ready to rise once more."

I shook my head. "Then we'll stop him, too. And as for you, hand yourself into the Ash Guard, because I'm not even going to try to protect you." I gestured to Kehsereen. "Come on. Let's finish this."

Kehsereen's brow furrowed. "But where?"

"Down," I said.

Into the tunnels beneath the city, where the god of dark dreams whispered his madness and fear into the minds of men.

CHAPTER TWENTY-THREE

MAYBE I SHOULD HAVE DONE SOMETHING ABOUT Sarassan. Maybe I should have arrested him and marched him over to the Ash Guard. Maybe I should have tied him up, or broken his legs, or ripped off his arms and beat him around the head with them.

In the event, I did none of that. I had only two jobs. Firstly, to find Mr. Mirian his answers, and secondly, to help Kehsereen rescue his nephew. The first I had done. I knew what had happened to Etta Mirian, and I knew why. She hadn't been a murderer, or at least not voluntarily. She had been a victim of Sarassan and his friends in their greed for success, a weapon seized upon by the tortured boy-mage in his anger and madness to lash out at one of his tormentors. I wasn't looking forward to explaining it to Mr. Mirian. It was such a meaningless death. It could have been anyone else on that street at that time when Kehsereen's nephew had fought free from the consuming god for long enough to reach out and take revenge. I wondered if it was worse to lose someone for no reason or out of directed malice. Maybe it didn't make a difference.

My second job, helping Kehsereen rescue his nephew, wouldn't be made any easier by having the Ash Guard rushing in, skin smeared white with Ash and weapons swinging. The truth was, Kehsereen's nephew had murdered people using magic, and the sentence for that was death. Every mage knew it. But this was different. The boy might not even know he was a mage. And he was being tortured, literally eaten by a god. When you were in pain and fear, you didn't always act rationally. I could attest to that. I wouldn't be able to hide this from Captain Gale forever, but I could make sure I explained it very clearly, that she understood it had been self-defence, and that she believed he was no longer a threat. I had to give him the same chance I had had, because without people like Benny on my side, I would never have made it either.

And look how you repaid that.

We left Sarassan pushed up against the wall, blood still trickling from the wound on his neck. It didn't seem enough, but the Ash Guard would get him, and he would pay for what he had done. I had no doubt about that. It was the one promise you could rely on in Agatos: when the Ash Guard came for you, you wouldn't escape.

~

THE STREETS OF AGATOS WERE NEVER EMPTY, EVEN IN the depths of the night. There was always someone about. At the beginning of the night, the city bustled with revellers out enjoying the city's pleasures and shoppers who had put off their chores during the heat of the day. The Penitent's Ear market was never busier than in the hours leading up to midnight.

As the night progressed, those pursuing legitimate interests started to fade away and others emerged from the shadows and dark alleys, hunting for anyone foolish enough to straggle or wander into the wrong area. Eventually, only those up to no good would be found on the streets. If you met someone out at that time, you had better be ready to run or fight. Then, eventually, the predators would return to their lairs, and the workers would emerge into the pre-dawn: servants and stallholders heading for the markets, dock workers readying ships to depart or unload for a morning caravan.

I didn't have time to wait for the thugs to clear the streets, and I wasn't in the mood. I was ready to fight, and any daft fucker who stepped out of the shadows would regret it. I had been up against too many too powerful people recently. I wanted some bonehead with a blackjack or knife to try his luck. But whether it was because of my black cloak, because there were two of us, or because of the restrained fury in my every step, there weren't any takers. It was almost disappointing.

The air was cool and clear in the night, and I would

hear the lap of waves on the distant sea wall. The occasional faint shout or cry from the docks sounded like ghosts of birds. My footsteps were sharp on the cobbles. Beneath it all, the stench of rotting seaweed and dead ocean creatures permeated the air.

"Do you hear it?" Kehsereen asked.

"What?"

"Listen."

I didn't need to. I had been hearing it all along. I had just been telling myself I hadn't. Whispering on the sea air. A voice made of a thousand discordant, unintelligible words, dark, disturbing, crawling over my skin like miniature tentacles or delicate crab claws. The god. Enhuin. Enabgal. Whatever the fuck it was called. Sarassan hadn't been lying about it. The relics I had turned over to Captain Gale hadn't contained the god's power. Instead, I was walking towards it, towards the madness, the terror, the doubt that ate hungrily inside me.

What the fuck was I doing?

We turned off the Royal Highway, into the Grey City.

Something was watching us, too. A presence. Was it the god or the kid? I didn't know which I wanted least.

When the kid had lashed out at Marron Bale, seizing hold of the crowd and sending them into a violent, murderous fury, he had left Kehsereen alone. Somehow, through the madness, he must have recognised his uncle. That was a good sign, right? But if he had, he hadn't seen us as allies. His rage certainly hadn't passed me by.

I heard and smelled the river before I saw it. I didn't know how many sewers opened upstream, and I didn't want to, but the stench was unavoidable. The water was higher than it had been when I had stumbled out of the tunnels the previous night, driven almost to insanity by the whispers of the god in there. I couldn't believe I was going back in there voluntarily. At least I knew what I was facing now. That had to help, didn't it?

The rusted grate was partially submerged now. It must be almost high tide, and we were going to have to wade through ... whatever.

The Sour Bridge was empty above us as we descended the steps into the cold water. There were *things* bobbing in it. I made a point of not looking too closely. Benny would have moaned the shit out of this – literally – but Kehsereen didn't complain. Emotions still chased over his face like rats in torchlight, but he kept his mouth tightly closed – probably wise with the water we were wading through.

At least I wasn't putting Benny or Sereh in danger for once. It was hardly going to make everything all right with them again, but it was something. Right?

Sarassan said he had found the statuette of the monstrosity washed up inside these tunnels. That wasn't true. It had come from Enhuin's temple. But, as with the lie about where he lived, I was certain he had given more away than he had intended. The temple was down here somewhere, through that partially collapsed tunnel. If I followed far enough, I would find the source of those harsh, cruel voices, tuneless and old, sliding and jarring, that I felt twist and snake inside me, like some disgusting sea creature.

I conjured a light in the tunnel and let it drift ahead. There was nothing here to dry ourselves on. My trousers, shirt, and shoes were all soaked. If I looked half as bad as Kehsereen, I didn't want to see myself. People died from diseases from this kind of water. At least I wasn't likely to live long enough for that to be a problem, and at least my Cepra-damned mage cloak seemed to be mainly waterproof. I shivered in the sudden chill.

"I don't suppose you brought a towel?" I nodded at the small backpack Kehsereen carried with him.

He didn't dignify that with an answer. "Where do we go?"

I nodded ahead. "We take that junction to the right. It's down there somewhere."

Not anywhere easy to find, though, or someone else would have found it.

Maybe they did. Maybe they never came back. Deep divers often didn't return. It was dangerous in the ruins and crevasses under the city. How many had actually found the temple and the hungry, forgotten god?

A collapse, Sarassan had said, a way through, a temple. A pit.

I had stopped the first time I had reached this junction. I had told myself it was because the rain had begun to fall, and I didn't want to be caught in here during a storm. It had been a convenient excuse so I didn't have to acknowledge my unease, that almost unheard voice, the cold air with its hint of damp and rot.

The second time I had come past here, I had been fleeing.

This time, the layered whispers were louder. The god had eaten and grown strong. It could be feeding right now, draining the kid as he struggled hopelessly to free himself.

I wasn't all right with that.

"This way," I said.

A dozen feet in, the northern branch had collapsed leaving a barrier across the tunnel. I dropped to my hands and knees to crawl over it. Sarassan had claimed the statuette had washed up on the far side. There was nothing there now, but as I crossed the barrier and straightened, the stink of rotting, dead things intensified, and the whispers grew.

I couldn't understand the words, but they were unsettling and cruel. They twisted inside me like leeches in my belly, picking like fingers in my head, feeding fear into those old parts of my brain.

"Stop listening!" I bellowed into the darkness.

From the look on Kehsereen's face, he was hearing those whispers, too. We weren't even close to Sarassan's god yet. If it found a way into our heads, we wouldn't make it there at all, let alone save the kid.

And how do you think you're going to get him out if he can't free himself? He's a fucking high mage.

Because I'm trained. I'm not a helpless kid. Because I know what I'm facing.

Do you?

"Fuck you."

This tunnel was older than the one we had been in. It might have been repurposed as a sewer or storm drain, but the brick and stonework had fallen away in patches, revealing the living rock behind. It was damp here, too, and cold, and I could smell hints of the ocean, even though we were far from the docks. My magical light flickered, and I had to feed in more power to keep it alight.

We were still within shouting distance of the grate and the river beyond. Every deep diver in the city must have passed through here dozens of times over the years. We needed to go deeper. Much deeper.

We made our way through and over the rubble and into the dark.

It was impossible to tell where the insidious whispers were coming from. They echoed from walls and openings, piling upon themselves until they seemed to surround us on every side. But the presence watching us was like a gigantic hand pressed against us, and I could follow that pressure, stopping at each junction or opening and feeling the disquiet push upon me. It would have been very easy to get lost down here – Depths, I had got lost before, and we were going further in now. If Kehsereen hadn't pulled out a sheet of paper and a pencil and started to map our path, I would never have remembered the route. I suspected we were going to get lost anyway. I doubted we could follow any map back through this maze. I doubted we would have to. You could only push luck so far before she turned around and kicked you in the balls.

I didn't know where we were anymore. We were deep beneath the city, of course, but whether we were under Horn Hill or the Grey City or even the Warrens, I couldn't have told you. Perhaps we had become so turned around we were under the ocean now. The cracks and tunnels we were crawling, squeezing, and climbing through were a mixture of ancient, crumbled stonework and uncut rock. The ruins down here must be thousands of years old. The weight above us made me want to cringe. Even a small earthquake or subsidence might shift all of this and seal us in forever. I found my pace slowing, reluctance piling on like the weight of the city above.

You walked into your mother's palace. If you can do that, what's an old, forgotten god?

At least the god hadn't broken me. It might overwhelm my mind or disintegrate my body, but it hadn't broken me.

You think you know what fear is, you bastard? You haven't got a clue.

My mother had always said she was teaching me to be strong. She hadn't done that, but perhaps I had learned how to survive being weak and afraid.

I pushed on the pace.

The whispers were growing louder, almost resolving into words, but not in a language I could understand. It didn't sound like a language any human could speak. It plucked at my thoughts and my reason, sending them spinning away, until all I could focus on was that one clear determination to keep going.

We squeezed through a final crack in the bedrock, and the space opened in front of us.

It was a temple, like Sarassan had said, but it looked like it had dropped into a crevasse at some point in the distant past. Either that or it had been carved from the deep rock and then the ground around it had shifted in. Great pillars lay tumbled across the tilted floor. Archways opened onto rubble or bare rock. In my weak mage light, the stone seemed to glow faintly.

Statues had fallen and shattered in whatever upheaval had broken the temple, but I could still make out tentacles reaching from strange, misshapen bodies of deep-sea creatures, too many teeth, staring eyes, and claws. I doubted anything like these monstrosities had ever been dragged up in a net. If they had been, they would have been tossed back in a hurry, accompanied by desperate oaths never to mention them again. If the fishermen hadn't been dragged down first.

The whispering disappeared the moment we entered the temple. My sudden clarity of thought made me stumble forward. All I could hear was our breathing coming back to us, layered in echoes that were far louder than they should have been, and the distant drip of water. The place smelled of the decaying detritus washed up by the waves. It made me gag. My heart sped up.

More to fill the silence than because I thought he would have an answer, I asked Kehsereen, "You recognise any of this?"

His restless gaze roamed across the temple. "The world holds the remains of many forgotten gods."

"Yeah." That was far less reassuring than he probably intended. This god might have been forgotten, but it wasn't dead. It had just grown weak, until Sarassan had found it and fed it. I wondered how many others like it there were. The thought sent a shudder through my body.

Why can't people just leave shit alone?

Cracked steps led to the slanted floor. We picked our way carefully down. Cold air brushed across me.

Like breath.

Shut the fuck up.

"This way." I pointed in the direction the air had come from.

The pit lay behind a tumble of pillars. It wasn't a natural opening. It was circular, twice as wide as I was tall, and cut from the rock. From it came a low, distant heaving sound, a susurration of something brushing and subsiding against stone far away.

The ocean. Maybe this opens to the ocean.

The darkness down there was complete. I wasn't the kind of person who was scared of heights. I had plenty of hang-ups, phobias, and scars. A fear of heights wasn't one of them. But as I peered down at that liquid blackness, I realised that I did have a fear of depths, not just a fear of the deep ocean.

I pulled over my mage light and drifted it down into the pit. Light played over writhing figures carved into the stone walls. Some were human, but some were most distinctly not. Age had worn away features, grinding down and smoothing out stone, and turned the faces blank, but somehow that made them more disturbing. The figures were twisted into poses of agony, backs bent, arms or tentacles or fins thrown out, wounds hacked into flesh. I imagined the person who had carved these, all those hundreds or thousands of years ago, down here in the dark, mind filled with those scuttling whispers, cutting madness from rock.

My light guttered and went out, and for a second, we were in complete darkness. I conjured a new light. It took more power than it should have.

You're scared. You're not focussing.

Kehsereen's hand closed on my shoulder. I looked down. In that second of darkness, I had stepped forward without realising it and my toes jutted out over the pit. I shuffled back quickly.

The pit seemed to call me, urging me to step forward again.

It'll be a relief. A kindness. Just one step. No more worries or fears. A mindless, formless, ecstatic agony, for eternity.

"Fuck you!"

I wrenched my mind free. *You're not getting me that easily, you Cepra-damned bastard.*

Kehsereen must have been hearing the voice, too, because this time he was the one who took a step forward. I placed an arm across his chest and snapped my fingers in front of his face until he blinked. "Don't listen to it."

I might have hated every single second of my mage training, but my mother had made sure I could withstand magical assaults on my mind. That she had done this by encouraging her acolytes to violate my mind repeatedly was only one of the many reasons I'd had to leave. This assault wasn't magical. It was a god pouring its malice and temptation into us. But I still knew how to protect my thoughts now that I realised what was happening.

I brought my mage light down again, sinking it into the pit, and once again it went out before it had descended more than ten feet.

This time I was ready for the insidious call of the pit, and I kept my arm as a bar across Kehsereen's chest.

Conjuring a third light was harder again.

It eats magic.

"I'm not going to be able to produce light down there," I told Kehsereen. "Do you have anything?"

He nodded, reached into his pack, and produced a hand lamp. When he had it lit, I released the mage light with a sigh of relief. Maintaining it here had been difficult and painful.

In the flickering light of the lamp, the figures carved into the wall of the pit seemed to move unnaturally.

"There are steps in the side, see?" Kehsereen said.

I peered down, resisting the urge to step forward. They were hardly steps. Just jutting stones that had been worn smooth and become sloped over hundreds of years. Some had cracked and broken away.

You can do it. Sarassan and his friends did it. They even brought prisoners.

Or they used ropes. If they had, they hadn't left them lying around, and I wasn't going back to find out. If we did, I might never find the courage to return. *And Enhuin is still feeding, growing strong, while the kid weakens.*

I led the way. I didn't want to. My feet were too large for the steps and my shoes too loose. The voice still tugged at the barriers of my mind, urging me to take an extra stride over the edge, away from the steps. My hand ran over the corrupted figures on the wall as I steadied my descent, and every moment, I expected them to move beneath my touch, like the statuette had when Benny had held it. But I couldn't ask Kehsereen to go first. We didn't know what was down there, and I was the one with the magic. Failing that, I had my mage's rod, and I was in the mood to hit something. Letting Kehsereen lead the way would have been cowardice.

I didn't know how long we descended. There was no light above or below to give meaning to our progress. All I knew was that the muscles in my legs were burning with the tension of keeping my precarious footing, and my jaw hurt where I was clenching my teeth. I had tucked my mage's rod into my belt, and it banged uncomfortably against my leg with each tentative step. Sweat ran down my back and face and neck. The air was fetid and stale, but cold, like a fish rotting on the floor of an ocean trench.

Then, the steps ended. We hadn't reached the floor. The pit continued down until the light was eaten by blackness. The steps weren't broken away. They just ended.

Sarassan came this way.

With a rope.

But why build steps that didn't let you reach the bottom?

Perhaps... Perhaps they came this far and dropped sacrifices to their god.

No. That didn't make any sense.

If I could rely on my magic, I could leap and cushion my fall. But I had seen the way my mage light had died. I didn't want to imitate that.

Carefully, I reached into my pouch, wobbling on the last step as I did so, and pulled out a coin. I eyed it. That was a full meal, that was.

Which was a fucking absurd thing to think right now. Going hungry was the least of my worries.

The sound of the coin hitting the bottom was dull, but it came quickly. I looked back at Kehsereen. "How far do you reckon?"

He shrugged. "Ten feet. Maybe fifteen."

Or maybe twenty. The difference might be between knocking the breath out of my body and shattering both my legs.

Screw it.

All right, voice. Let's see what you've got.

I lowered myself into a crouch, wobbling. This was so fucking stupid. Benny would have told me I was an idiot and I was going to kill myself. Kehsereen just watched. I missed having someone telling me not to kill myself. I would have done it anyway, but it still felt like a lack.

I wrapped my hands around the last jutting stone, swung over the edge, and dropped before I could think better of it.

My feet hit rock. I had no time to brace. I felt something snap in my foot. I let out a yell even as I rolled. When I tried to stand, it felt like a spear stabbing up through my leg. I stumbled, then caught myself and staggered to the side.

Bannaur's broken balls!

"Is everything all right?" Kehsereen called down. His voice was muffled.

I looked up and saw the glow of his lamp in the dark above. It was dulled, as though there was a layer of smoke or water between us.

"Yeah." Apart from my fucking foot. When I put weight upon it, the pain made me gasp. "It's about fifteen feet. Lower the lamp, and I'll try to catch it."

I hobbled across so I was underneath him and

reached up. If I moved carefully and didn't lean too heavily on my right foot, the pain was manageable. A good night's sleep would probably heal it. I wasn't getting a night's sleep down here, so I would have to cope until then.

I saw Kehsereen carefully kneel and lower the lamp.

"Drop it."

I caught the lamp, juggled the hot metal and glass, and eased it to the ground. Yellow light played over bare rock and carved walls.

"You can see?" I called up to Kehsereen. He had disappeared once more in the thick darkness, but he wasn't far above.

"Yes."

I shuffled to one side, and a moment later, Kehsereen landed on the rock floor and rose smoothly. He tilted his head. "You hurt yourself?"

Was it the shriek of agony or my lopsided, hunched posture that gave it away? "I'll be fine."

He bent to retrieve the lamp. "This place is old. Older than the temple, I think." He lifted the light high to examine the walls. Down here, the carvings in the rock were rougher, more jagged and frenzied. I imagined Sarassan climbing down here that first time, and rather than fear, his mind being full of greed, seeing only wealth and success in the horrors of the temple and the pit. And then, the god.

A breath of cold air and a deep ocean stink were the only warning we had. From the darkness, a monstrosity loomed suddenly behind Kehsereen. Tentacles whipped around him, and jagged teeth closed around his shoulder. He screamed.

I wrenched in raw magic, formed it into a spear, and ... it was gone, sucked away, like a wave retreating down a beach.

Blood flowed from Kehsereen's shoulder. I heard something crunch and tear. He screamed again, and his free arm flailed at the monstrosity behind him.

The god eats magic. I couldn't use my power down here. I wrenched out my mage's rod. The solid wood felt good in my hand. I swung it up and over, onto the monstrosity's head. The chunk of obsidian split the creature's scaly skin. A thick, stinking liquid leaked out. Its tentacles jerked. I brought the rod down again and again, hammering blows on its skull. Its jaws opened as it let out an inhuman shriek, and I heard flesh tear once more.

The monstrosity tried to back away. The scales and the spines running back over its head were tattered and split. Foul liquid ran freely down its body. I must have hit one of those bulging, black eyes, because it had burst. I kept moving, feeding all my fear and anger into my blows. My hands and arms were numb from the repeated impacts.

Then something inside the creature's head cracked, wetly. It crumpled. Tentacles shuddered spasmodically and then stilled.

I was sweating, spattered with the creature's foul-smelling, cloying liquid, and my shoulders burned with pain. I wiped my cloak across my face, smearing my eyes clear.

Kehsereen had dropped the lamp. It lay on its side, glass cracked, but still burning fitfully. I righted it, then crouched next to Kehsereen. He was conscious, but his shoulder was a bloody, torn mess. I wouldn't even know where to start with this. He needed a surgeon, but all he had down here was me.

"We need to stop the bleeding," I said. *Yeah, that's fucking helpful, Nik. No one would have guessed that.* A few strips from my shirt weren't going to do the job this time.

"My sleeve," he gasped. That wasn't going to do much good, either. "Beneath," he added.

I pushed up his sleeve. His arm was still wrapped with the bandages I'd noticed the first time I had met him. "This?"

He nodded, and the movement made him wince in pain.

I unwound the bandage. The skin underneath was red and raw, like it had been burned. As a kid, I had seen a man who had fallen into the wrong pit in one of the remaining tanneries. It had taken too long for them to find him and fish him out, and his skin had looked like this. But at least Kehsereen's skin wasn't leaking, and the bandage was reasonably clean. Carefully, I wrapped it around the wounds on his shoulder.

"Tighter."

I did as he asked. Blood began to seep through

almost immediately, but I reckoned it would hold long enough.

Long enough for what?

"Don't ask stupid questions," I muttered.

I helped Kehsereen up. If there were any more of those things down here, we were in trouble. Depths, we were in trouble anyway. Kehsereen was bloodied and torn. I had a broken foot and no magic. What exactly were we good for?

Above us, the pit stretched up, out of reach. A single passage led out of this small chamber. Without a word, we started along it, looking like a pair of drunks kicked out of a tavern at dawn.

CHAPTER TWENTY-FOUR

THE AIR IN THE TUNNEL FELT SOILED. SICKNESS ROILED through it, slipping like poison between my lips, up my nose, into my eyes and ears. Terror clutched at my throat with hard fingers, squeezing. My skin was cold, my hairs standing on end. My legs felt like dead meat.

Images flashed into my brain of people burning and screaming. I wanted to throw up and drop to the floor, curl into a foetal ball, never to get up again. I wanted to sink into the stone.

"I know what you're fucking doing!" I shouted into the blackness. It was eating into me, eroding my barriers, burning that madness and terror into the deep parts of my mind.

But this was just a tunnel, a passage sloping down through the rock, and none of the things Enhuin was trying to show me were real. The air was just air. This thing, this forgotten god was just a nightmare. *Dream haunter*, they had called it. *The watcher in the dark.* Just fucking watch this.

I staggered on down the tunnel, holding on to Kehsereen for support, just as he was holding on to me. All around, the dream haunter bombarded me with images of pain and torture and fear. I ignored them. This thing had no idea what really scared me.

Then, suddenly, we were there.

The tunnel widened and flattened and finally opened. Ahead of us was only a deep, purple darkness, like a sickly night sky, a space of unimaginable size, dropping away from a stone ledge. The space seemed to bend and shear, as though the world itself were being warped, dimensions as fluid as the heaving sea. It tugged and squeezed my perceptions.

We had found the god.

Enhuin wasn't the only god to walk the world. There were gods of almost everything, some powerful, some weak, some dead, others forgotten. But few people ever encountered them in their full power. If they were lucky – or unlucky – enough, they might feel the presence of a god in a temple, although more likely they would be experiencing a priest's carefully-crafted magic or were under the influence of the drugs burned in the temples. Alternatively, they might encounter an avatar of the god or see traces of its influence in relics or the stones of its holy places. But this god was still trapped down here, and we had found it. The weight of its power, even weakened, distorted reality around it.

"Isn't it magnificent?"

My head whipped around. Porta Sarassan was standing to the side of the tunnel, on the edge of the flickering light, balanced on the ledge.

"How the fuck did you get here?" We had left him slumped and scared in my room at *The Lost Head*.

"You are not a deep diver, Mr. Thorn. There are a thousand ways through the undercity, and I know them all."

What a pile of shit.

The Sarassan standing here wasn't the same person I had met in the city above. I mean, it was him. I could still see the blood on his neck. But that Sarassan had been scared, shocked by the deaths of his friends, afraid for his family. Here, in front of his god, he seemed entranced, yearning towards the darkness. The god had seeped into his mind, too, I realised, but it wasn't offering him nightmares. It was offering him something else.

"When I found it," he said, "it was nothing like this. It was small and weak and slumbering, but I knew, I just knew that it was what we had been looking for. The Bad Luck Club wasn't a joke. We wanted more than Dockside, but every time the coin tossed, it came down the wrong way. We never had any luck."

"What? You want me to feel bad for you? Fuck me." I had heard some shit self-justifications in my time. Depths, I had engaged in a fair amount of it myself. But this was world-beating crap.

I eyed Sarassan. He wasn't looking at us. He was watching the folding, stretching darkness as though hypnotised, his toes thrusting out over the ledge. He was still bird-boned and becoming overweight, but he spent his time crawling and clambering through the spaces beneath the city, and you couldn't do that if you weren't tough. It would be a mistake to underestimate him. I didn't have any magic down here, but you didn't grow up in the Warrens without learning to fight. I guessed you didn't grow up in Dockside without learning to fight, either, and I was injured. I wouldn't be able to reach him before he could react.

"He is almost ready to arise, you know," Sarassan said, sounding almost hypnotised. "To take his place above the other gods." And I bet every god told their worshippers they were the number one, totally up above all the others. It was surprising how many people believed that shit. "When he does, the stars will shiver at his presence."

"Yeah, I'm shaking already. Cut the crap. What have you done with the kid?"

Sarassan waved a hand at the purple darkness. "He is in there."

Where else had I expected? "So let him go, or by every Cepra-damned god out there, I will shove this through your mouth and into your brain." I lifted my rod.

His gaze flicked to me, considering. "I will let him go, but first you have to do something. First you have to look."

For Pity's sake. I should have broken this bastard's legs when I'd had the chance. "Look at what, exactly?"

He spread his arms to encompass the tangible darkness beyond the ledge. "At what awaits you. At what awaits you all."

"You know what? I already looked. I wasn't impressed."

"Open your eyes."

Fuck this. Dealing with fanatics was a major pain in my arse. I turned back to the great space with its shifting, bunching, stretching dimensions.

And then I saw it. There was something in the dark. Something vast and incomprehensible, like a cliff about to fall into the sea. A shadowy, chthonic weight, crushing in its immensity. It pressed down on me. The god, weakened, forgotten, still trapped, turned its many eyes upon me. Voices shrieked in my head. Terror battered at my mind.

None of it is real.

I wrenched my head away. "I looked. I'm still not impressed." I had to force the words past the nausea in my throat. I advanced on Sarassan, leaving Kehsereen leaning against the wall. I probably didn't look like much, limping, battered, and dirty, but I reckoned he could see my intent in my posture and the way I swung my mage's rod. He pulled out a knife and took a step back.

"The boy was a mistake. We had no idea how powerful he would be. But he fed Enhuin well. It is almost ready to rise. Except..." His face twitched. "The boy shouldn't be able to break free of Enhuin, not even for a moment. I can't risk him doing it again." Yeah. He might be all right with his friends being murdered, but he didn't want the same thing for himself. "I will release the boy," he continued, "but Enhuin still needs to feed."

I didn't like the sound of that. The god fed on magic. On mages. But Kehsereen's nephew was too dangerous. Which just left one second-rate mage who had wandered down here thinking he would be the great hero. Sarassan had wanted me down here the whole time. That was why he had come to find me at the inn. To let slip just enough information to have me come running down to this lost temple. And I had fallen for it.

"Just step forward," Sarassan said. "Embrace it."

That was the deal I was being offered. Give myself to this god of madness and terror to save a kid I had never met. Sarassan was crazy. I could get out of here, fetch Captain Gale and a squad of her Guard, all smeared with Ash. How would fucking Enhuin like that, huh?

And if I did, I might be too late. I would never forgive myself if I let the kid die down here. Denna's mercy. I had no choice, did I? I was really going to do this. What a fucking miserable end to my life. I turned my gaze on Sarassan. If I was doing this, I wasn't doing it alone.

"Lady of the Grove help me," I muttered, and threw myself into Sarassan.

His knife came round and up, but too slow. I batted

it aside and crashed into him. My momentum threw him back.

Together we tumbled over the edge, into the abyss, where the forgotten god awaited.

Madness rained down upon us like molten rocks from a volcano. Distantly, I heard Sarassan screaming. My mind was tossed and pummelled like a rowing boat in a maelstrom.

The god's presence towered above us, immense and unstoppable. It unfolded again and again, like a venomous flower opening in a thousand dimensions. Scenes of destruction and pain seared through me.

My mind fled, a tiny, fearful thing, an ant fleeing from an avalanche. The god's presence followed, expanding to fill every crevice my mind took refuge in, its hunger hammering me. The urge to pull in raw magic became overwhelming. *Do it. Sate the hunger. It's the only way to stop the torment.* I raged, fought, but nothing could be enough to resist this assault.

Nothing?

Fuck you, Nik Thorn. I had been broken before by my mother, by her mages, by my own mind, and I had survived. This? This came from outside me. It could never match the terrors my own mind conjured. Enhuin was the god of dark dreams, but dreams were just dreams.

I was a trained mage, not some helpless victim.

Waves of pain and madness pounded me. I saw my body torn and eviscerated. I felt fire raging in my chest and pouring up through my mouth. I saw Benny and Sereh and Mica dancing like string puppets while monstrosities ripped at their bodies. I saw oceans boil and mountains rupture. I saw fields of ice roll down, crushing everything before them. One by one, far above, I saw the stars go out.

"You can't do any of that!" I bellowed, not knowing if anyone or anything could hear me. "It's just dreams."

And I saw the god unveil itself at last.

It was shapeless, ever forming and reforming. An abomination. An atrocity. Thousands of eyes stared down. Mouths ripped at its own flesh with dagger-like teeth. Pus-yellow scales, slick like raw oil, glistened in unnatural light. Tentacles whipped and lashed. Behind it, a cyclopean fastness opened and opened and opened, dripping with seawater and slime, great mountains of dark green stone, giant pillars, a drowned city that went on forever, emerging from the depths.

The power and the magnitude of it were supposed to overwhelm me and make me lose hope, but strangely, it was this vision that gave me the strength I needed. The full force of the god's insane mind raged down on me, demanding that I give up what few shreds of myself I still held, that I share its insanity and be overwhelmed. But amid that madness, I looked at Enhuin unveiled, and I saw that it was just a thing.

Vast, unimaginable, terrifying, but a thing, nonetheless.

Nothing in the flesh could ever be as frightening as the terrors of the mind. It was a lesson that had taken me too long to learn. But I had walked into my mother's palace. Against everything, I had walked in. However loathsome the dream haunter might be, it was nothing compared to what was in my head.

And if Enhuin was a thing, no matter how dreadful, I could stand against it. Win or lose, I could stand.

So I did.

IN THE GRIP OF ENHUIN'S MADNESS, IT HAD SEEMED AS though we were falling forever into an unending abyss. In truth, we were lying on a sloping, stony floor maybe ten feet below the ledge. I had cracked my knee when I'd fallen, but I hadn't felt it. Above, and further into the cavern, the chaos that was the god folded and unfolded, deforming, bulging, and slipping, scarcely seen in the thick, purple murk. Its madness spilled around it, but it couldn't touch me. Its rage lashed impotently.

On the ground next to me, Porta Sarassan writhed, screaming noiselessly, his mind lost. He might have been a disciple of Enhuin, but that hadn't been enough to protect him here in the heart of its madness.

We weren't alone, either. The floor of the cavern was littered with human bones. A skull, still bearing dried skin and the remnants of hair, stared eyelessly up at me. Other bodies were less damaged, and one, the corpse of a woman, still stank of death.

On his side, curled up, was a boy in his teens, emaciated, with straight, ragged black hair, dressed in filthy rags, and with his eyes screwed shut. He was still breathing. Sarassan's nephew, the high mage.

It wasn't easy to get him out of there. Kehsereen and I were both a mess of injuries, but the boy hardly weighed anything. I wondered if Sarassan and his friends had fed him at all or just left him to survive on the restorative effects of natural magic.

After some searching, we found a ladder stashed at the back of the small chamber beneath the pit. It must have been what they had used to climb in and out. Despite the discovery, getting the boy up the ladder and the narrow steps and through the tunnels, ruins, and caves almost killed us several times. We got lost twice, but Kehsereen had a better sense of direction than I did, and we found our way back.

The sun had risen when we emerged, burning hot and too bright in the sky. We didn't have to walk too far before we found a cart that agreed to carry us to the Ash Guard fortress. It cost too much, and it stank of animal shit, but we smelled worse and Kehsereen paid, so I didn't complain.

The cart driver dropped us on the far side of the

square to the Ash Guard fortress. Like most natives of Agatos, she seemed to have a superstitious fear of getting too close to the place. It did mean that we ended up limping, swaying, and tripping our way across to the building like a trio of seabirds caught in a fishing net.

By the time we reached the heavy front doors, a whole crowd of Guard had gathered to watch us approach. We were just reaching them when Captain Meroi Gale emerged and sent them scurrying back inside with a furious glare.

"I know I'm going to regret asking what happened to you," she said as we finally staggered up. "But I'm going to guess that it started with you ignoring my instruction to keep well away from it all."

Kehsereen's nephew had fallen into a deep unconsciousness soon after we had rescued him, but he started to show signs of waking as we hauled him across the plaza. I didn't like the idea of him coming to, confused and still scared, with his powers ready to hand. The choice was to bash him over the head right here or, "Can we talk inside?"

Captain Gale's eyebrows rose. "You sure about that?"

No. I really wasn't. But I was making a habit of going places I didn't want to go. "Please."

The exhaustion in my voice must have convinced her, because she stepped aside and waved us in. "Your friends look in a bad way. I'll send for a doctor. We always have one on hand. Hazards of the job." She looked at me critically. "You should probably get one of your own. You need them often enough."

The effect of the Ash that was mixed into the mortar of the fortress was apparent a step inside the doors. A wave of weakness washed over me. In some ways, this was worse than being down in Enhuin's pit. There, I had still had access to the raw magic that helped sustain me. Here, it was gone, and I felt every bruise, broken bone, and half-healed injury in my body, and the exhaustion of these last few days. Bringing the kid in here had been a gamble. If he truly had been surviving on raw magic for a long time, this might finish him. He went limp as we carried him in.

"The kid's going to need water and food quickly."

"You know we're not a hotel, right?" Captain Gale said. But she waved one of the Guards off to the chore, then led us to a small room with a couple of couches and a pair of chairs facing each other across a low table. It wasn't the room she had interrogated me in a few weeks back. It was more homely and comfortable. I didn't let that fool me. This place was designed to put mages at their ease so they would be more inclined to spill their secrets. All three of us were in danger here if Captain Gale decided we had broken their inviolable laws. But at least I knew she would listen.

We laid Kehsereen's nephew on one of the couches, then I helped Kehsereen himself to the other. Within moments, the scholar had closed his eyes and slipped into either sleep or unconsciousness. I wished I could join him, but I didn't fancy being kicked back awake by

Captain Gale. Not long after, a doctor in the uniform of the Ash Guard entered. I could tell he was a doctor because he didn't look like he wanted to kill me immediately, unlike most of the Ash Guard. He was followed in by a Guardsman carrying a tray of food and water.

"Now." Captain Gale indicated the chairs. "Talk."

I told her everything I could that didn't obviously implicate me in a crime or make me look too stupid. So, it wasn't as long a story as it could have been. When I was done, Captain Gale sat back and ran a hand through her hair.

"Why the Depths didn't you come to me, Nik? Look at you."

I glanced across at the unconscious form of Kehsereen's nephew being tended by the doctor. "None of this is the kid's fault."

She seemed to understand. "You should still have come to me. You're not equipped for stuff like this."

I winced. She didn't need to remind me that I wasn't up to much. "I survived."

"This time."

I reckoned it might be a good idea to divert the conversation away from my failures and inadequacies. "What's going to happen to the kid?" I said.

She looked thoughtful for a moment. "We'll be keeping him here, I think."

"But it wasn't his fault," I repeated. "He was a victim." I had really thought I could convince her to let him be. He had been through enough.

"And if what you say is true," she ground out, "he's

411

a traumatised high mage with no control of his powers, and he's already killed at least one innocent person." Yeah. Etta Mirian. His first weapon. I wondered if he had known what he was doing or if he had been too drowned in Enhuin's madness. "I can't let him out on the city. It would be irresponsible, and it wouldn't be fair to him."

She didn't have to elaborate on that. If he used his magic on someone again, if he killed again, even if he didn't mean to, she would have to come for him and she would have to kill him.

"So, he's a prisoner forever? That doesn't seem right." He hadn't asked for any of it.

"Until he learns to control his powers and he recovers from this ordeal. It won't be soon. What happened to him would be enough to break anyone. Who knows? Maybe one day he'll join the Ash Guard."

I blinked. "But... He's a mage."

She sighed. "Everyone in the Guard is a natural mage, Nik. I thought you knew that. We need the sensitivities to magic."

No, I hadn't known that. It was a fucking big revelation. I wondered if my mother and the Wren knew. I wondered if it mattered.

"I would offer you a job," Captain Gale said, "but let's be honest, you would be absolutely shit at it."

As good as it was to get back to being insulted by her (and, honestly, she was right; I would be shit at it) this wasn't over.

"What about the god? It's still down there."

Her face hardened. I shivered involuntarily at the sight.

"We will go down there," she said, "in Ash. We will destroy every part of its temple and its pit. We will find every object and stone that bears its trace, and we will bury them here, deep in Ash. We can't kill it, but we will remove every bit of its power. It broke the rules. It's finished."

"But it's a god," I said.

She smiled. "This isn't the first god we've dealt with."

CHAPTER TWENTY-FIVE

I SLEPT ALL THE REST OF THE DAY AND ALL THE following night, and I would have slept the day after, too, if the innkeeper at *The Lost Head* hadn't hammered on my door demanding that I pay for another night and threatening to call the Watch.

I was coming to terms with the idea that saving Agatos from madness and destruction wasn't going to buy me any gratitude. I wondered if Captain Gale felt the same way.

I was out of money, and while I couldn't say I felt fresh or revived, or clean, my injuries were mostly healed. I was starving, though, so I went to find Mr. Mirian and share the conclusions of my investigation with him. I was sure he would want to talk over coffee and food, and he wasn't the kind of person to let his guest pay. I wasn't wrong. I found him at his shop, and I didn't even have to suggest heading out.

He led me through the streets, passing several

nearby coffee shops. I guessed he was avoiding anywhere he might meet people he knew. I understood that. The weight of well-meaning sympathy could be too much to bear.

Eventually, we settled at the coffee shop near Benny's house that we had visited together before. Maybe he thought I was still staying nearby and was trying to be considerate.

I had no idea where I would be staying tonight or any other night.

I watched Mr. Mirian as he ordered coffee. He looked older still than he had when he had first come to me, and he didn't look much like Mica's father, if truth be told. Even if Mica's father had lived, he would have been years younger than Mr. Mirian. They didn't have the same build, either, nor the same hair. But he reminded me of him, nonetheless. It was the eyes, and the slow, deliberate, understanding manner. How Endir had ever ended up with my mother was a mystery.

"Are you all right, Mr. Thorn?"

I blinked. The waitress had brought our orders, placed them on the table, and retreated, all without me noticing. The same waitress who had served us before, the one Mr. Mirian had said I should ask out.

He had better not be trying to set me up with a date.

"Yeah." I rubbed my face. "Sorry. It's been a tough few days."

He nodded sympathetically, and that immediately

made me feel worse. *I* was complaining about these last few days? He had lost his wife just over a week ago. "The case was difficult?"

"Not just that. There have been other things going on." I had to bite my tongue to stop from telling him about them. I didn't ever tell anyone about my issues, except maybe Benny, and I doubted Benny would be in the mood for listening. All of this had left me vulnerable, but that wasn't his problem. "You were right. Your wife wasn't to blame." How did I explain all this? "She was—" Fuck it. This was such an empty cliché. "She was in the wrong place at the wrong time. Peyt Jyston Cord and his friends had discovered an old, forgotten god and were using it to bring themselves unnatural luck. But they lost control of it, and it lashed out." That wasn't the truth, but it was close enough. Kinder than telling him that Kehsereen's nephew had been the one who had used her, that I had rescued the boy, and that he was under the protection of the Ash Guard. Mr. Mirian might understand. But it wasn't a clean answer, and it might still eat at him in his low moments. Better to blame Enhuin, and in truth, the god was to blame. "They're all dead now. The god killed them, and the Ash Guard have dealt with the god. It's over."

Mr. Mirian nodded, then sat there in silence for several minutes. I didn't interrupt him.

Then he straightened his shoulders. "Thank you, Mr. Thorn. It is a relief. I could not bear to have Etta's memory so sullied." He reached to his belt and pulled out a pouch of coins, which he slid over the table to me. "The rest of your payment."

"You don't have to—"

"I do. I think you have earned far more than this, but it is what I can afford. I will forever be in your debt. You may call on me for help if you ever need it."

I nodded. For some reason, I couldn't speak.

"I will tell all my friends how helpful you have been."

That was enough to return my voice. "Please don't!" I didn't want any more cases like this. I wanted to go back to breaking curses, finding lost pets, and magically spying on cheating spouses. I would rather be poor than have every monster, mage, and god in Agatos try to eat me, fry me, or turn my vital organs into soup.

"As you will." He made to stand, then lowered himself. "I did have some bad news. It is not your problem, but I thought you should know."

I tilted my head.

"You remember that Etta had a brother? Solus Tain? You were right about him. It turns out that he did not leave the city on his ship after all. He was fired for drunkenness. The harbour guard found his body floating in the water just yesterday. I do not know what happened to him, but it seems his demons must have got the better of him. I cannot help but wonder whether, if we had lent him the funds to buy the captaincy of his own ship, things might have been different, but I suspect they would not have been."

With a last nod, he left me there.

Pity! In the chaos, I had forgotten to tell Mr. Mirian that his brother-in-law was in the tunnels under Dockside. I didn't know whether Enhuin's madness had taken Solus Tain or whether the smuggling gang had turned on him when they couldn't reach me. Either way, I hadn't helped, and I should have.

There was a city full of people like Solus Tain who needed help, and I was only one freelance mage. What in the Depths could I hope to do?

Mica had been right when we had argued. The city needed big changes. I was a pebble thrown against a mountain when Agatos needed an earthquake to bring it down. Maybe Mica and her boyfriend could achieve what I couldn't, with their power and their influence.

I knew what I had to do.

The waitress was eyeing me from across the coffee shop again. I downed my coffee, grabbed the remains of my pastry, and fled before she could come over.

I HAD TO WAIT A COUPLE OF HOURS OUTSIDE THE ASH Guard fortress for Captain Gale to return from patrol. I found another coffee shop on the far side of the square with a view of the fortress and sat under the awning, near to a group of men playing a noisy game of High Ground, and eked out another coffee and pastry. Mr. Mirian had paid me generously, but I didn't know

418

when I would be paid again, and I needed somewhere to live.

I amused myself by trying to guess which pedestrians would cross the square and which would divert around it. By my estimation, about half made a complete detour, not setting a single foot in the square. Another third curved away from the building, but didn't avoid the square altogether. The remainder hurried nervously across, heads down. Every now and then, someone would stride calmly and confidently straight through the square, not even glancing at the Ash Guard fortress. These latter I put in a group I labelled 'narcissists, fools, psychopaths, and visitors from out of the city.'

Eventually, Captain Gale emerged at the head of a patrol, smeared in Ash and looking weary. I hurried after her, calling. She waved her patrol on and stopped until I caught up.

"You're looking better," she said.

I raised my eyebrows. "Is that a compliment, Captain Gale?"

"I didn't say you looked good."

Depths. She could puncture me like an old sack. I tried not to let the hurt show. "You found the god?"

"And dealt with it." She glanced around, then beckoned me to follow. Dutifully, I let her lead me into the fortress. "Gods and Sods found it in their archives at last. The names Enhuin and Enabgal threw us off. They're translations of an older name of the god. In Agatos, it was known as Niarret."

Niarret? That sounded familiar. "Where have I heard that name before?"

"You've heard of Sien?"

"Of course. The city's patron goddess before Agate Blackspear killer her. They have plays about it and all."

"I wouldn't rely on those for your information. Niarret was her opposing twin. She was known as the Lady of Dreams Descending, and Niarret was known as the Lord of Nightmares. Before that, it was a minor ocean god. The fucking things are always evolving. When Blackspear killed Sien, everyone thought Niarret had died, too, because it disappeared. The two gods opposed and sustained each other, and without Sien, the theory was that Niarret couldn't survive. But it seems the thing was only weakened." She shrugged. "Nothing stays buried forever in this city, unless you bury it in Ash."

And Sarassan had dug it up.

"I've been thinking about that other problem of yours," I said

She lifted a weary eyebrow. "Care to narrow it down?"

"A new high mage, to restore the balance of power. I think you need my sister, Mica."

Captain Gale wiped a hand across her forehead, smearing the Ash. "How is that balanced? I'm not handing your family an advantage, Nik, and I'm surprised you would. Are you telling me your mother has won you over?"

"Fuck, no." What a horrible thought. "Mica has her own agenda, and I think it's one worth pursuing for the sake of the city. She's not going to take our mother's side, and she's no fan of the Wren, either. She's not as powerful as either of them yet, but I think she's strong enough to provide the balance. Other mages will side with her. You'll have your third, independent faction."

She considered for a few seconds, then nodded. "The Ash Guard don't choose high mages, but we can nudge things along. I'll put your suggestion forward."

"Thanks." It was the right thing. I didn't know if Mica would feel the same way, and I was sure as the Depths my mother wouldn't. I couldn't deny that gave me a twinge of satisfaction.

I was turning away when Captain Gale said, "It was a good thing you did, Nik. It's made the city safer."

"Which bit?"

"All of it, in your own way." I must have started grinning, because she added, "Don't let it go to your head. You got lucky. Next time you might not."

Well, I hadn't expected her to let me go with a compliment. I raised a hand, then headed away from the Ash Guard fortress, hopefully for the last time. After this, my life was going to be much more boring. With luck, I would never have to come back here.

The thought left me feeling oddly hollow.

I FOUND A SMALL APARTMENT A COUPLE OF STREETS FROM the Penitent's Ear market and about as far from the smuggling gang's hideout as I could afford to get. I didn't know if they were still looking for me, but there was no point dangling temptation in their way. Mr. Mirian had paid me enough to cover a couple of weeks' rent, and it seemed the Wren had lifted his prohibition on dealing with me. I tried calling on Benny – to apologise, to explain, to make up, I didn't know which – but either he wasn't in or he wasn't answering. But the next day, a cart arrived with my things. There wasn't much. Just a few pieces of furniture, my mattress and bedding, and my empty iron safe. That had to be a good sign, right?

Kehsereen came to see me the day after I moved in. He seemed less jittery and restless than before, although he still didn't seem like someone who would ever sit still for long.

"I wanted to thank you," he said. He still moved awkwardly, but someone had done a good job on his shoulder. "I promised my sister I would find my nephew, but I had come to think I would not be able to."

"Have you heard anything?" I asked.

"I was able to visit him in the Ash Guard fortress. He is recovering physically. I do not know if his mind ever will."

"Captain Gale is a good person." For someone who had threatened to kill me multiple times. "She'll make sure he's looked after. What are you going to do?"

"I will stay in Agatos. He should have family close, and there's much work I can do here. I think the scholars at your university have been negligent in their acquisition of knowledge."

Talk about a fucking understatement. A more useless bunch of tossers it would be hard to imagine. Kehsereen had turned out different.

There was work for me to do, too. It was time to start advertising my services again: Curses broken, ghosts hunted, pets found, spouses followed. Strictly no gods, monsters, or mages.

For the first time in ages, I reckoned I finally had some balance back in my life. I was going to be all right.

And I truly believed that, all the way until reality showed up and stabbed me right in the eye.

THIS PARTICULAR KNIFE IN THE EYE CAME ON MY FOURTH day in my new home.

I had been doing well. I had already broken two upsetting curses and tracked down one lost tortoise, and at this rate, I reckoned I would be able to afford my next rent on time. The novelty of that made me feel all warm inside.

When the knock sounded on my door, I was feeling confident, positive, and hopeful, a feeling that lasted all the way until I pulled open the door and found my mother standing outside.

I had known I couldn't hide from the Countess if she wanted to find me. I just hadn't expected her here in person. The blessed Countess didn't come to places like this, even if she had grown up in the dirt and despair of the Warrens.

I stood there, gaping.

"Come, Mennik," she commanded, and turned on her heel.

Which was my mother all over. No 'good morning'. No asking how I was. Depths, not even the controlled fury I had imagined over me being caught in her office and then nearly crippling one of her mages. Just a summons she expected to be obeyed without question. Was I supposed to follow for my execution or for a morning coffee, or did she just have another job for me? How the fuck was I supposed to know when she just didn't ever explain?

I stood there for a couple of seconds, watching her go, wondering if I should just ignore her, before my defiance crumbled. I grabbed my mage's cloak and hurried after.

Her carriage was drawn up outside, blocking the narrow street completely. Small crowds had gathered to gawp at the sight, but no one had come too close. The Countess's reputation was well known. But it was my reputation I was worried about here. The last thing I needed when I was trying to set up my new business and settle in was to be associated with the Countess. I pulled my hood tight over my head and scurried in after her.

My mother didn't speak for the entire journey, instead giving her attention to a pile of papers. I reckoned she knew how jittery I was and was taking advantage of it to ratchet up the tension.

Within fifteen minutes, the carriage had turned onto Agate Way and begun the long ascent of Horn Hill. But we didn't stop at her palace. The carriage continued on until we came into sight of the Senate building.

In a city full of tasteless monuments to ego and wealth, the Senate building lorded it over all the rest. Columns, statues, friezes, gigantic windows, sweeping steps, fountains, pools, the Senate building had the lot, added to and modified by each new generation with no plan or style. It was the perfect embodiment of Agatos.

My mother's carriage pulled up outside the widest set of steps, which led to a colonnade and grand marble doors, which were big enough to swallow most of the buildings in the lower parts of the city. My mother beckoned me to follow again, and I trailed behind her like seaweed caught on the rudder of a ship.

At least I didn't think she was going to execute me here. But it didn't look like I was getting coffee, either.

"Now, Mennik," she said, as she led me onto a balcony that looked down onto the stepped seating of the Senate. "I have business to attend to. You will wait here, watch, and try to learn something."

I was too jumpy and off-balance to argue. What in the Depths was she up to? Why wasn't she ripping strips off my skin and using them for bookmarks? Had her mage, Cerrean Forge, not told her he had caught me rooting through her desk? Had he been too embarrassed? I couldn't think of any way of asking that wouldn't drop me in twenty feet of crap. So, I lowered myself into a seat and watched the senators gather in the chamber below.

After a few minutes, a bell sounded, and my mother walked out into the centre of the chamber.

"I present to the Senate a bill to legalise organised gambling in Agatos," she called.

Oh. Oh fuck. This. Her precious law to get one over on the Wren, which I had sabotaged by warning him. Why the Depths had she brought me along? What exactly did she know? Not only were the seagulls coming home to roost, but they were spraying me with shit as they flew past.

I listened, frozen, as one-by-one, the senators came forward, gave their little, self-serving speeches, and cast their votes.

My mother watched them, too, her expression unreadable. Only when the last vote had been cast and it was clear that my mother had been defeated did she finally turn her head to stare up at me.

Lady of the Grove! The Wren had done it. He had used the information I had given him to defeat my mother's plan. And she knew I was to blame.

The urge to flee was almost overwhelming. But where could I run to escape her power and influence? I waited.

Eventually, my mother appeared on the balcony, and she was smiling.

I eyed her warily. "Why are you smiling?" I demanded. "Your bill failed. I betrayed you. You lost."

She raised an eyebrow. "Did I?"

"But... You were defeated. You spent all that money on property, and now it's wasted, worthless."

My mother sighed and seated herself so that I had to twist around to see her. "This bill would have ruined the Wren, you are right. He had no choice but to use his wealth and influence to block it. He was forced to call in favours and debts built up over years to do so. And now, when I make my true move against him, he will find he no longer has those favours and debts to call upon."

Finally, it hit me. Far too late, it hit me. The map and flags on her wall. The errand with her factor to the empty coffee house. The bill just sitting there so conveniently in an un-warded drawer of her desk. "You knew all along. You planned this. You used me."

Her face twitched. I couldn't tell if it was contempt or sympathy. "And it is when I am no longer able to use you that you will be truly useful to me." She stood and smoothed down her dress. "You should thank me, Mennik. I have not told your sister what you did. She would not understand." She headed for the steps, then paused and looked back at me. "You will, of course, be walking home."

- End –

Mennik Thorn will return in *Strange Cargo*.

KEEP IN TOUCH

Subscribe to my newsletter to get a free short story in the world of SHADOW OF A DEAD GOD and NECTAR FOR THE GOD, and to be the first to find out about future books:
patricksamphire.com/newsletter/

You can find out about all my other books and stories at my website: patricksamphire.com

You can often find me on Twitter (twitter.com/patricksamphire) as well as on my Facebook page (facebook.com/patricksamphireauthor/).

A REQUEST

PLEASE REVIEW THIS BOOK!

Reviews help authors more than you probably imagine, and for independent authors, they are everything. It would mean an awful lot to me if you could leave a brief review - a sentence or two is perfect! - on Amazon.

I love finding out what readers thought of my books - good or bad - and I make sure I read all the reviews.

READ MORE

THE CASEBOOK OF HARRIET GEORGE

Mystery, murder, and adventure on Mars...

Mars in 1815 is a world of wonders, from the hanging ballrooms of Tharsis City to the air forests of Patagonian Mars, and from the depths of the Valles Marineris to the Great Wall of Cyclopia, beyond which dinosaurs still roam.

Join Harriet George and her hapless brother-in-law, Bertrand, as they solve mysteries and try to save their family from ruin.

Volume 1: The Dinosaur Hunters.

Volume 2: A Spy in the Deep.

Available in paperback and ebook.

ABOUT PATRICK SAMPHIRE

Patrick Samphire started writing when he was fourteen years old and thought it would be a good way of getting out of English lessons. It didn't work, but he kept on writing anyway.

He has lived in Zambia, Guyana, Austria, and England. He has been charged at by a buffalo and, once, when he sat on a camel, he cried. He was only a kid. Don't make this weird.

Patrick has worked as a teacher, an editor and publisher of physics journals, a marketing minion, and a pen pusher (real job!). Now, when he's not writing, he designs websites and book covers. He has a PhD in theoretical physics and never uses it, so that was a good use of four years.

Patrick now lives in Wales, U.K. with his wife, the awesome writer Stephanie Burgis, their two sons, and their cat, Pebbles. Right now, in Wales, it is almost certainly raining.

He has published almost twenty short stories and novellas in magazines and anthologies, including *Realms of Fantasy*, *Interzone*, *Strange Horizons*, and *The Year's Best Fantasy*, as well as two novels for children,

SECRETS OF THE DRAGON TOMB and THE EMPEROR OF MARS.

NECTAR FOR THE GOD is his second novel for adults. It is the sequel to SHADOW OF A DEAD GOD.

facebook.com/patricksamphireauthor

twitter.com/patricksamphire

instagram.com/patricksamphire

ACKNOWLEDGEMENTS

As always, this book would be far less if it was not the for the encouragement and feedback from my wife, Stephanie Burgis, who reads my books more times than anyone should ever have to.

I also want to give enormous thanks to Emily Mah, Martin Owton, and Jarla Tangh for reading and providing their invaluable comments on the novel. You guys are heroes!

I wish I could individually thank everyone who has provided me advice, feedback, and critique over the years on my stories. Your help, encouragement, and insight made me a better writer.

I would also like to thank my proofreader, Taya Latham (www.editingbytaya.com), for saving me from plenty of embarrassment, and to Jim C. Hines and Richard A.A. Larraga for picking up some last remaining typos that the rest of us missed.

Thank you all.

Printed in Great Britain
by Amazon